JAMES P. BLAYLOCK

# Night Relics

HarperCollins*Publishers*

HarperCollins Science Fiction & Fantasy
An Imprint of HarperCollins*Publishers*
77–85 Fulham Palace Road,
Hammersmith, London W6 8JB

A Paperback Original 1994
1  3  5  7  9  8  6  4  2

A catalogue record for this book
is available from the British Library

ISBN 0 586 21780 0

Set in Times

Printed in Great Britain by
HarperCollinsManufacturing Glasgow

# NIGHT RELICS

James P. Blaylock was born in Long Beach, California in 1950. Winner of the World Fantasy and the Philip K. Dick Awards, he is the author of *The Digging Leviathan*, the highly acclaimed *The Last Coin* and *The Paper Grail* amongst others. A professor of English at the Fullerton University of California he lives in Orange, California.

For Viki, John and Daniel

And this time,
For the Duncan Family,
Syndee, Kelsi, Hope, Mark, Pam, and Scott
(and Jake)

10,000 video tapes
900 ducks
8 bottles of Bachelor Bitter
4 pounds of bratwurst
2 canoes
1 barbecue
a carpet of snow on Thanksgiving morning
no earthquakes

# ACKNOWLEDGMENTS

A number of people spent heaps of time, energy, and patience helping me with this book, and I'd like to thank all of them right here: Tim Powers, for his endless invention and friendship; Lew Shiner, for his insight and his relentless standards; Merrilee Heifetz, who tirelessly read and edited fledgling chapters; and Art Stone, one of the world's most generous humans, for all of his cheerful help in ways both literary and non-literary. I'd especially like to thank John Accursi, who has an almost eerie talent for sensing what a book ought to be and how it might arrive there, and Craig Yamasaki, who did more than he knows to help me push this vehicle in the right direction back when it was still just a creaking collection of oddball parts. And finally I'm grateful to my friend Chris Arena, whose far-flung talents and his knowledge of both practical and arcane things make him the best kind of reference source.

# **S**ATURDAY

. . . we no longer see the devil in the bedcurtains nor lie awake to listen to the wind.

—Robert Louis Stevenson
"Child's Play"

□ □ □ □ □ □ □ □ □

**1**

ANOTHER WINDY NIGHT, WARM FOR LATE NOVEMBER AND SMELL-
ing of sagebrush and dust. Restless autumn dreams. The night
haunted by a slow and deliberate creaking in the bones of the old
house, by the rattle of doors shaken in their frames, by the sighing
of the wind beneath the eaves, murmuring past the stones of the
chimney. Tree branches tossed and rustled out in the night, and
dry leaves skittered across the screens and scraped along the brick
path.

The full moon hung above the ridge like a lantern on a dark
wall, and leafy moon shadows swayed across the kitchen floor.
Peter Travers put a match to the mantle of a propane wall lamp,
and the lamp hissed alive, turning the shadows into pale, flitting
spirits. He measured coffee grounds and water into the shell of a
stove-top percolator and lit the burner beneath it.

Leaning against the counter, he looked out through the window,
waiting for the coffee to boil. Beyond the oaks and sycamores,
the hillside glowed under the ivory moon. Dust devils rose off
the dry earth, whirling up out of the sage and sumac like uneasy
spirits. The first smells of percolating coffee leaked out into the
air of the kitchen, masking the desert smell of the wind. Ghosts.
Even coffee had begun to smell like the ghost of mornings past.

A gust of wind shook the house, moaning past doorjambs and
windows and through the crawl-space cellar under the floor.
How Beth could sleep through such a racket was a mystery, especially in a nearly strange bed. He felt a quick pang of guilt for
not being there himself. It was almost like leaving a good-bye
note on the bureau, except he wasn't going anywhere and this
was his house.

The wind simply made him restless. For the past couple of days
it had whispered across the back of his mind even when he slept,
and he had awakened a dozen times in the night to the sound of
the casements rattling and the walls creaking, sleepily certain that

the wind would pull the old house apart piece by piece and shingle the canyon with it.

Another gust shook the house now, and an unlatched shutter banged open against the clapboards, hard and flat like someone beating on the wall with a wooden mallet. He walked into the living room and pulled open one of the casements in the bank of windows on the back wall. The loose shutter swung out on its hinges, leafy moonlight reflecting off the chipped white paint. He pushed it all the way open and locked it in place with its iron hook. The night air smelled of oak and sycamore and just the faintest scent of jasmine. He leaned out the unscreened, open window and watched the dark woods and the high shadow of the ridge beyond. After a moment the wind fell, leaving behind it an uncanny silence, as if the night had abruptly quit breathing.

And then very faintly, from somewhere in the trees behind the house, there arose on the still night air the desolate sound of someone weeping. . . .

The house was a quarter of a mile from the nearest neighbor. There was no phone or electricity anywhere in the canyon. The refrigerator, the lights, the stove and water heater, all of it ran off propane. Although it was only five miles to the highway and civilization, it took half an hour to drive there on the badly maintained dirt road that followed Trabuco Creek on its winding course out of the mountains.

The canyon widened out at the Trabuco Arroyo, where the dirt road dead-ended at highway pavement. On the ridges east of the Arroyo, hundreds of nearly identical stucco houses crowded the edge of the wilderness, the far-flung fringe of neighborhoods that sprawled for eighty miles across what used to be cattle ranches and farmland and orchards. When the Santa Ana winds cleared the air, much of Orange County was visible from the Holy Jim Trail that climbed toward Santiago Peak, a couple of rough miles north of Peter's house, although often the coastal plain was obscured by a yellow-brown layer of smog.

Six months ago, when he and Amanda separated, he had said good-bye to all that, to the smog and the suburbs, and bought a piece of solitude in the wild back country of upper Trabuco Canyon.

"Peter?"

He shut the window and latched it. "In here," he said. He was relieved that Beth was awake, even though he'd done his best to let her sleep.

He walked back into the bedroom, where she was sitting up in bed, clutching a pillow. She looked rumpled and sleepy. Her blonde hair was a mess, falling across one eye. "Prowling around the house in the dark again?" she asked.

"Yeah. I heard the weirdest damned noise just now." He sat down on the bed. "I didn't mean to run out on you. I was making coffee."

"A woman like me can't compete with a good cup of coffee," she said. "What time is it?"

"At least four."

"Four," she said flatly. "Maybe I'll go ahead and sleep late, at least until five or five-thirty. After this morning I'm a parent again." She collapsed back onto the bed and pulled the covers up to her neck. Bobby, her son, had been visiting his father in the east somewhere; Peter couldn't remember the place and didn't want to. The less he heard about Beth's ex these days, the better.

"Listen," Peter whispered, sitting at the edge of the bed.

After a moment she said, "I don't hear anything but the wind."

"*Ssh*. Wait." Peter held his hand up.

For a moment there was nothing, just trees rustling outside the window. Then, very clearly, the sound of crying again.

"Did you hear it?" Peter asked.

"Yes," Beth said, turning over and plumping up the pillow. "I heard it. You can come back to bed now if that's what's got you up. That's not a psycho killer. Wrong kind of noise for that. Psycho killers laugh; they don't cry. Horrible rasping laughter."

"What is it then? Sounds almost like a lost child, doesn't it?"

"Sounds like a fox," Beth said. "They cry like that, especially if they've lost a mate. Foxes mate for life."

"People should study their habits," he said.

"Come back to bed and we can study them now." She turned to face him, smiling sleepily and propping herself up on her elbow.

"I guess I'm a little edgy," Peter said.

"The coffee will help that."

Peter sat there silently.

"Sorry. Didn't mean to be snotty." She squeezed his forearm and then lay back down on the bed.

"That's all right," Peter said. "It's this wind. Get some more sleep."

Beth shut her eyes and shifted around, as if trying to make herself comfortable. She pulled one of her hands out from under the cover and patted his knee, then put it back again, turning over onto her other side. "This mattress feels like a sack full of rope," she said, and then was silent.

After a time Peter heard the crying sound again—the fox that had lost its mate, if that's what it was. The sound came from a long way off now, and shortly dwindled away to nothing.

The week before, he had spent four days in Santa Barbara, staying with his brother near the harbor. They had sailed his brother's catamaran every morning. Next month, maybe, if they got a few days of good weather, he would do it again. He would bring his son David along this time. Right now David was in Hawaii with his mother. If Amanda could take David vacationing in Hawaii, then Peter could take him sailing in Santa Barbara. It had gotten to be something like a contest between them since their separation six months back.

Beth lay sleeping, or pretending to. He kissed her lightly on the cheek before getting up, thinking that the last few months had changed everything and nothing. His marriage had dissolved, but his past still held on to him, more tenacious ghosts. . . .

Closing the bedroom door, he walked out into the living room again. The moonlit curtains moved in the draft, and behind them the silhouettes of leaves tumbled past on the wind. Peter walked slowly toward the windows again, listening to the wind's whisper, imagining that he heard laughter on it now, buried under the moaning and whispering and rattling like a counterpoint to the crying he had heard just minutes ago. The floorboards creaked beneath him. A branch scraped against a window screen.

Then, from somewhere far beneath these other sounds, like the echo of something whispered into a deep and narrow canyon, he heard his own name murmured, breathed like a sigh in the air of the old house.

A shadow flicked across the parlor doorway just then. And slowly, as if someone were turning up the flame in the propane lanterns, a pale light illuminated the open parlor door, casting a silver glow out onto the living room carpet.

**2**

"*PETER* . . ." HE HEARD HIS NAME AGAIN, JUST THE FAINTEST murmur. It wasn't Beth. It wasn't coming from the bedroom.

Shadows moved across the carpet at his feet—the dark shapes of slender tree branches waving in a soft wind, like a willow tree hung with green leaves.

"*Peter* . . ."

He stepped into the faint light, the shadows seeming to entwine him.

There was suddenly the heavy smell of orange blossoms on the air. Then, as distinct and clear as a memory, there arose the smell of new-mown grass and of hamburgers sizzling on a barbecue, and, drifting lazily over all of it, the warm, hazy smell of a summer evening.

His breath came in gasps, and he felt suddenly numb and dislocated. Like a sleepwalker, he stepped slowly across to look into the parlor, full of nostalgic longing as if he were stepping through a doorway into a fragment of some past time carefully manufactured from his memory.

His tools lay scattered on the floor, the rug turned back, shadowy furniture piled in the corner beyond the stone fireplace. The light that suffused the room seemed to be drifting like smoke from out of the littered hearth. A ghostly willow tree stood rooted in the middle of the floor, its tangle of branches drooping at shoulder height and obscuring the ceiling overhead. Peter anchored himself against the doorjamb, holding on with both hands, watching the room shimmer like a desert mirage. A summery breeze ruffled the leaves of the willow, and pale sunlight shone through the branches, turning the leaves nearly gold. The dilapidated furniture beyond the tree was merely a lumber of dark shapes.

As if from far away he could hear the hissing of lawn sprinklers and what sounded like laughter. There was the clanking of pots and pans in a kitchen. From somewhere beneath these sounds

came the whisper of his name again, "Peter . . ." like the sound
of a letter slid under a door.

He stepped in among the lacy, glowing branches of the tree.
"Yes," he said, and instantly, as if in answer, the wind rose
outside with a howling that shook the house. The ghostly light in
the hearth vanished as abruptly as a blown-out candle flame. The
old furniture rematerialized in the darkness, and the willow tree,
the summer smells, all of it was gone like an interrupted dream.

Peter held his hands in front of him, closing his fists to try to stop
their shaking. He was aware suddenly that the air was full of the ac-
rid smell of overcooked coffee. Mechanically, he went into the
kitchen, moved the coffeepot to a cold burner, and turned off the
stove, then slumped back heavily against the counter. He pressed
his eyes shut, trying to recall the details of the dream. That's what
it must have been, some kind of waking dream, a hallucination.

He picked the mug up off the counter and tried to pour himself
a cup of coffee. His hand still shook, and he slopped the coffee
across the stove top. Suddenly light-headed, he clanked the pot
back down onto the burner and forced himself to breathe evenly,
holding on to the edge of the stove. The wind, the moonlight, the
weird crying outside—all of it must have been rocking like a pry
bar in some mental crack. . . .

He managed to pour the oily coffee into the cup now, along
with plenty of grounds. Out the window the moon was just going
down beyond the ridge, and the sky was gray in the east. A flurry
of dry leaves blew past. Shivering suddenly, he went into the
living room, opened a drawer in the hutch, and pulled out an
envelope of photographs, then sat down at the kitchen table and
sorted through them—pictures of David on a skateboard, and
playing baseball, another of Amanda and David and himself in
front of the Christmas tree.

He searched through them for his most recent photo of
Amanda, taken last Christmas, not a particularly happy time of
the year for her. They had been dressed to go out, and she had
looked like a model in her black evening dress. He had looked
at the photo just last week and had thought without any hesitation,
"Of *course* you married her."

Surprisingly, that Christmas had been a good one, maybe because neither one of them had expected it to be. There was no
hurry, no fighting, no forced holiday cheer. He and Amanda had
even taken turns reading out loud in the evenings from Jack Lon-

don's *South Sea Tales*. Even then they were planning the trip to Hawaii—the trip that eventually hadn't included him.

He shuffled through the photos again.

"Are we drinking coffee or turpentine?"

At the sound of Beth's voice, Peter jerked in surprise, his hand knocking his coffee cup, the coffee spilling out across the photographs and off the edge of the table.

Beth grabbed the towel off the hook, snatched the photographs up, and dried them off one by one. She was dressed, as if ready to leave.

"Sorry," she said, wiping the table clean. She looked at the photos then, laying them out on the table to dry more thoroughly. "I didn't mean to set you off."

"It's nothing," Peter said. "I'm a little gun shy. I've been . . ." He took the towel from her and sopped up the coffee on the floor.

"Thinking about your family," Beth said, finishing his sentence. She picked up a picture of Amanda and him, looked at it for a moment, then laid the photograph back down. "I've always thought she was pretty."

Peter waited.

"Walter and I ended up hating each other. You and Amanda didn't?"

"Not really. Not like you two."

"You don't hate her?"

"No," Peter said. "I guess I don't." He sipped gritty coffee from the half-full cup and then set it aside on the table.

"You know," Beth said after a moment, "Bobby's coming home this afternoon. It's a week early. His father's too . . . busy to keep him the full month."

"Walter's a jerk," Peter said. "I knew he was a jerk when you married him." He felt suddenly bitter, as if in some vague way he shared Walter's weaknesses. Maybe all men did.

"Yeah," Beth said. "I've always known how you felt about him. You were right. If I had known more about the way things worked, about how men are, I might have protected Bobby from some of it. I didn't know enough."

"I don't buy that part about 'how men are.' Some of us just aren't like that." For a minute they listened to the sound of the wind.

"Yeah," she said finally, "that wasn't fair." She thought for a moment, as if choosing her words. "Let's just say I know more now. I won't let it happen to Bobby a second time.'' She looked away, studying the photograph of Amanda again. "Can I ask you something?"

"Go ahead," Peter said.

"When you found out about Amanda, about what had been going on between her and the other guy, was it already over by then?"

"What do you mean 'over'? For who? Between us, you mean?"

"No, I mean her affair. Was it still going on?"

Peter shook his head. "Dead and buried."

"But you chose not to live with it? Not to let bygones be bygones?"

"*Chose?*" Peter said. "I guess it was a choice. Some things, though . . . I worked at it, but—what? It spoiled things. Maybe if I hadn't known him . . ."

"And you weren't ever guilty of the same thing?"

"Not once," Peter said. "I'm a confirmed monogamist."

"Like foxes," Beth said. "I guess if you're a confirmed monogamist you won't stand for anything less in a mate."

Peter shrugged. "Since we're telling the truth," he said, "tell me what you meant about Bobby, about how you wouldn't let that happen to him a second time."

"I don't know," Beth said. "What did I mean? I guess it's just that in the last three months he's become pretty attached to you."

"I guess he has," Peter said.

"His life is all full of Peter this and Peter that. I bet his father is sick of hearing your name. I *hope* he is."

"Remember that we're not all alike," Peter said.

"I know you're not. Why do you think I'm here? If you were like that you wouldn't be sitting in an empty room at dawn staring at photographs of the woman you broke up with after fifteen years of marriage. I guess what I wish is that you'd . . . figure out what you want right now, and settle down to it. Find a way to let the rest of it go."

She stepped across and picked up the coffeepot, wrinkling up her face, trying to act cheerful. "And you complain about *my* coffee." She set the pot down.

"You going?" Peter asked. "Stay for breakfast."

"Can't. I've got lots to do today before Bobby's plane lands. He's flying into John Wayne at noon."

She put her arms around him and kissed him, long enough to take some of the fear out of him. "Cheer the hell up," she said. "This isn't the end of life as we know it. It's just time that we got to know it a little better, that's all. It's time we got serious."

After she left, Peter sat in the kitchen chair staring into his empty cup. He could still feel the pressure of her lips against his. His hands remembered the shape of her body from last night, and he recalled the lilac smell of the scented powder she put in her bathwater and how, with her skin still damp from the bath, she had slipped into bed. . . . Each part of him seemed to have its own singular memory of their lovemaking.

The woods outside were gray-green now in the dawn light. He got up and made a fresh pot of coffee, thinking now about the ghosts of summer afternoons. He went out into the living room and rummaged through the hutch again, pulling out more envelopes of photographs, sorting through them as he stood there, barely conscious of the wind sighing in the trees.

There was something in the photographs, in their captured memories, that reminded him again of what he had seen before dawn that morning. He set them back into the drawer, then walked to the parlor door and looked in. Early-morning sunlight slanted through the shutters, dimly illuminating the room.

On the carpet directly in front of the cold hearth lay a small flute, delicately carved out of wood, lying in plain sight like another hallucination. It was tipped across the edge of the tiles as if it had just that morning rolled out of the open fireplace.

OLD, OUT OF DATE—THAT WAS THE ONLY WAY POMEROY COULD describe Mr. Ackroyd's place. It was the nicest in the canyon, because it had always been maintained, but the interior was like some kind of time-warp place, all wood and wool and books and old pottery. There were doilies sitting around on things, too, which was weird in a bachelor's house, but the whole place was clean, and that was something to admire. Most men couldn't keep a clean house. There was even a little closet near the front door with a broom and dustpan in it.

When Pomeroy had arrived that morning, Ackroyd was sweeping up the leaves and rose petals on the front porch, and had picked up the debris with the dustpan and put it into the bin instead of just sweeping it under the railing. Pomeroy had committed the scene to memory, playing it through in his mind to get the phrasing just right so he could tell the story to customers. That kind of attention to cleanliness and detail was why the place was in the shape it was in. That would be a selling point.

"I'd miss a television if I lived out here," he said, watching Ackroyd prepare sandwiches in the kitchen. The old man moved slowly and methodically. Surprisingly, he had offered Pomeroy something to eat, for no reason at all—a sandwich, even though it was only eight-thirty, more like time for breakfast. Still, that was real hospitality, and Pomeroy made a mental note to that effect. Recalling it later in conversation could be impressive. He was a man who appreciated a good deed, regardless of the time of day. . . .

"Don't you miss television sometimes? On a rainy afternoon with nothing to do, say?"

"Never had a television," Ackroyd said. "I don't have anything against them, I just never got the habit, living out here."

"It's the old movies I'd miss—Judy Garland, Maureen O'Sullivan, Laurel and Hardy. I saw a great one just last night—*Going My Way*, with Bing Crosby. Have you seen it?"

"At the old Gem Theatre in Garden Grove. That must have been upwards of forty years ago now."

"How about when the old lady comes in at the end? If that didn't bring tears to your eyes . . ."

"Shameless," Ackroyd said, "but effective."

"Der Bingle," Pomeroy said, sighing.

"Yes indeed."

"That's what they called Bing, people who knew him."

"Ah," Ackroyd said.

"Der Bingle. It's German, I guess."

"Sounds distinctly German, doesn't it? Lettuce?"

"You don't mind washing it pretty well, do you? I'm not tolerant of insecticides."

Pomeroy looked around the living room, calculating the square footage. "Ever think of moving the hot-water heater out of the kitchen?" he asked. "That would be a selling point, moving it outside."

"Is that right?" Ackroyd said, running the lettuce under the tap. "You wouldn't think something that simple . . ."

"No, I'm serious. Just a couple of changes would make all the difference in the world. I'm talking a few hundred bucks. Wall-to-wall carpeting, maybe, and white paint on the woodwork. This place wouldn't last on the market a week with upgrades like that."

A coughing noise came from the faucet, as if there were air in the lines. Pomeroy grimaced. "Where do you get your water?" he asked.

"Spring up the hill, mostly. Late in the season or in drought years I draft it from the creek."

"From the *creek*?" Pomeroy could see through the window that the property behind the house rose steeply up the hillside. It was green with undergrowth, most of it shaded by live oak and sycamore and maple. A water tank, maybe a thousand gallons, sat at the end of a dirt path a hundred feet up the hill. "Must be tough out here—pretty primitive for year-round living."

"It's all I know."

"I'd like a place like this for a weekend getaway. Bottled water all the way. What do you think you'd need out of it?"

"I've always gotten what I need out of it."

"I mean seriously. What kind of offer would I have to make?"

"I wouldn't sell it." Ackroyd laid the sandwiches on plates along with two variety-pack bags of potato chips. He poured iced tea out of a big jar into glasses and carried all of it out to the dining room table.

"Well, like I said out on the porch before we got to talking," Pomeroy said, "I'd like to make you an offer."

"I'm afraid it's a waste of time. Napkin?"

"Thanks." Pomeroy took a paper napkin from a holder and unfolded it on his lap. "I mean a *serious* offer. What I'd give you on this place would make a healthy down payment on one of those new condos out in Tustin Ranch. All the amenities right there—stores, jacuzzi, pool. You wouldn't have to drink water that's had fish swimming in it. Or worse." He opened the sandwich and looked at the lettuce inside. "A condo's a sound investment."

"I've never been able to think of my home as an investment," Ackroyd said. "That's probably a personal failing of mine."

"Hey," Pomeroy said, shrugging. "Some people have no head for business. But then the right kind of money comes along and they learn fast. Crash course. That's the best kind of education a man can get. You won't find it in any of these books." He gestured at the rows of books, dismissing them all. Then he waited a moment, giving the old man a chance to chew the idea over along with his sandwich. "What do you say?"

"Pardon me?" He was staring at the photos that hung on the wall above the bookshelves. "I'm afraid my mind wandered."

"Name your price."

"My *price*? Somehow what you're suggesting sounds so exotic that I think we're speaking different languages."

He sounded almost testy. Pomeroy nearly laughed out loud. The old man was shrewd as hell; you had to give him that. Pomeroy winked at him, one salesman to another. Clearly he'd underestimated the old man, sold him short. "Money's the universal language," he said. "But I don't have to tell *you* that. You're good." He shook his head in admiration. "Scotchman in the woodpile somewhere, eh?"

"In the *wood*pile?"

"Look, I'm serious. Quote me a figure. See if you can make me laugh out loud. What? Fifty K? Sixty?"

Ackroyd stood up without saying another word and walked into the kitchen. He was probably thinking about the money now, putting together a counter offer. Pomeroy would pretend to be shocked at the figure when the old man finally spit it out. The thing was that old boys like Ackroyd had been out of things for so long that they didn't know what a dollar was worth when it came to real estate. You flatter them with the idea that they're driving a hell of a hard bargain, and when you knuckle under and pay them off, they think they took you to the cleaners. Car sales was like that: *well, there goes my commission. . . .* Pomeroy pulled that old chestnut out of the fire every night of the year.

Ackroyd returned, carrying a paper lunch sack.

"All right," Pomeroy said, "what would it take?"

Ackroyd picked up Pomeroy's uneaten sandwich and put it into the sack along with the bag of chips. "I'm awfully tired all of a sudden," he said, gesturing at the front door.

"What?"

"I'm afraid I need fairly regular naps. I've got to leave in a half hour, and I'd like to lie down for a moment first. If you'd like to take the iced tea with you, I can put it into a jar."

"No, thanks." Pomeroy was momentarily confused. The old man ushered him toward the door, showing him out. "Go ahead and sleep on it, then. . . ."

"Please, Mr. Adams," Ackroyd said, calling Pomeroy by his current business alias, "I'm not interested in selling my house. I've lived here for upwards of fifty years, and I mean to die here. There are things connecting me to this canyon that would bore you utterly if I tried to explain them to you, but I'll guarantee that they're sufficient to keep me here despite the lack of amenities, as you put it."

He smiled briefly as the door swung shut. Pomeroy found himself standing alone on the porch. The old man was serious! He was apparently a nut. Pomeroy hadn't pegged him for a nut. He got into his rented Thunderbird and turned out onto the road, pitching the lunch bag out the window when he was out of sight of the house. Nut or no nut, it was cat-skinning time. If he couldn't take out an old fool like Ackroyd, then it was past time to retire.

THE WIND WAS STILL BLOWING AS PETER DROVE ALONG CHAPman Avenue, over Orange Hill and down into the suburbs. He turned on the radio, punched through the buttons without listening to anything, and then turned the radio off again. There was something familiar and comforting this morning about the billboards and telephone poles and housing tracts, something safe and predictable.

From the top of the dashboard, he picked up the flute he had found on the parlor floor. It belonged to his son David. Peter had bought it for him in Louisiana a year or so ago. Last Sunday David had brought the flute out to the canyon and had spent half the afternoon messing around with it, getting down the first few phrases of "The Merry Old Land of Oz."

So, what had happened? David had dropped it and then gone off without it? But then it would have been lying on the floor throughout the week, in plain sight.

There must be some easy answer. Perhaps David had laid it down on the fireplace mantel and forgotten about it. Maybe the wind, or a rat, had knocked it off onto the floor. That was probably it—rats. Rats were to blame for everything—the appearance of the flute, the hallucination, the crying in the woods, the coffee burning. No doubt rats had also stolen the pocket watch that Peter had left lying on the front porch railing the night before last. The mayor of the rats was wearing it now, tucked into a vest pocket.

A car horn honked behind him, and he realized that he was driving far too slowly, paying no attention. He sped up, thinking suddenly about Beth and about their talk that morning. The words "confirmed monogamist" rang in his ears again, as jarringly off-key as the flute on the parlor floor. In a way he had meant the phrase to be funny, but instead he had sounded a little too much like someone striking a holier-than-thou pose, *choosing*, as Beth had put it, to be offended by something. He hadn't looked at it that way before. It was almost always easier just to blame your wife.

He and Amanda had agreed to share custody of David, who was ten now. Peter's move to the canyon was the one thing in the business that bothered Amanda. She could understand Peter's wanting to live like a hermit, but David, she said, needed more. David wasn't always easy. He could be moody, and in the last year or so, what with the breakup and Peter's moving out, he had gone through a sullen phase. Peter's attempts to fix things with him too often brought silence and shrugs.

On impulse he pulled into the parking lot of a Sprouse Reitz dime store. There were eucalyptus trees and fall flowers growing in newly built concrete planters, and the stores had a recently tacked-on pastel facade. Peter was surprised to find that he couldn't remember when the place had got a face-lift.

Inside the dime store, things were the same as ever. The air smelled of yardage and popcorn. Near the door there were bins of Halloween candy and racks of plastic masks and wigs and skeleton suits. He looked the stuff over, tempted to buy one of the skinny rubber chickens that hung by its feet from a clothespin. A woman about seventy years old, very neatly dressed and with purple-gray hair, stood at the only open register a few feet away.

She smiled at him when he inspected the chickens, as if she thought they were funny, too.

It seemed to him that a dime store wouldn't be a half bad place to work, wandering around with a feather duster among knick-knacks and bolts of brightly colored cloth, sticking price tags onto glass tumblers and pincushions and putting in a few hours at the register, shooting the breeze with the occasional customer. It was a sort of haven built of trinkets, a. never-never land where you watched the world slip past beyond plate glass windows. You could live back in the stockroom among the cardboard cartons, resting your feet on an old desk covered with invoices and with pens advertising wholesale dry goods.

He caught sight of himself in the mirrored backdrop of a jew-elry display, and with his fingers he smoothed out his wind-mussed hair. Yesterday evening Beth had told him that shaving his mustache had made him resemble Gene Kelly and then had tried to get him to dance with her to a tape of old Motown songs on the portable cassette player. It turned out that shaving his mus-tache didn't make any difference at all. He still could dance only a sort of two-step that Beth finally began to refer to as the "Clod." Gene Kelly, though . . . He was built about right, al-though he was a little tall. He tried smiling at himself in the mirror. Well, maybe with a hat and umbrella, kicking through a puddle . . .

He gave up and walked toward the rear of the store where there were two long counters full of toys, most of them tossed together, some of the packages ripped open. Peter picked through them, flipping a Nerf football in his hand. The football wasn't enough; there probably wasn't a kid alive who didn't already have one. He found a rubber stack of pancakes wearing a hat and carrying a submachine gun, plenty weird enough to impress the modern child, but he decided he didn't want that, either.

Then, sorting through a row of plastic revolvers, by accident he found just the thing—something called a Spud Gun, a pistol that shot pieces of raw potato. There were two of them, dusty and lonely, misplaced behind the six-shooters as if they had been for-gotten there in some more innocent age. Raised plastic letters spelled out the word "Spuderrific" on the barrel, and there were instructions on the back for loading the things with potato plugs. Feeling lucky now, he took them up to the counter and handed them to the checker, who pretended to be surprised.

"Robbing the bank?" she asked.

"Brink's truck," Peter said.

"I got one of these for my grandson," she said. "When he was six or seven."

"Did he like it?"

"He loved it," she said. "His mother wasn't crazy about it, though."

Peter hadn't thought about that—hundreds of little potato globs stuck to the kitchen wall. It was too late now, though. The deal was done. She counted out his change and put the guns in a bag, stapling the top shut through the receipt.

"How old is your son?" she asked, as if she wanted to chat, to hold him there a moment longer.

"One's ten and the other's six," Peter said, which was only a small lie, since Bobby wasn't his son at all yet. Suddenly full of unanswered questions, he thanked the woman and walked out into the wind.

SOMEBODY HAD GOTTEN OVER THE FENCE DURING THE NIGHT AND glued a bumper sticker to the front door. "Save a lion," it said, "shoot a developer." It wasn't meant to be a death threat. Klein knew that. It was put there by a local backwoods no-growth hippie who couldn't think of anything better to do with his time than screw up another man's property with petty acts of malice. Since when had it been a crime to be a building contractor?

People said that Orange County was one big suburb, but the truth was that there were thousands of acres of wilderness left in the county. You could draw in another half million people and not even crowd them—not any more than they were already crowded. What the guy with the bumper sticker needed was a dose of reality therapy. Progress actually *was* manifest destiny. There was no stopping it.

You could define it any way you wanted to. You could hate the very idea of it. You could go to community meetings and make speeches from a plywood podium. Your opinion wasn't worth a steel slug. The stone-cold fact was that smart people were going to make a dollar by putting their money on growth. The thing was to figure out how to do it right, without screwing things up.

Klein looked out through the french doors into the backyard, where the wind ruffled the surface of the pool. He had built this house on spec a few years ago, at the end of the road in Trabuco Oaks, where the old Parker ranch had been. When he couldn't sell it, he and Lorna had moved into it. Now it was worth upwards of half a million dollars.

Most of that was a result of the last couple of years of heavy real estate inflation, and all of it was leveraged, most of the equity sunk into the deal he had going out in Trabuco Canyon. When it paid off, though, he'd walk away with double what he owed.

That's when he'd tell Lorna about it. He had found over the past few years that you kept most of your dreams and schemes concealed. Your wife wasn't your business partner. He unbanded the newspaper that lay on the coffee table and took a look at the headlines, then dropped it again. Later he'd read the baseball. Somehow he didn't give a damn about the rest of it.

He heard the rattle of a Volkswagen engine out on the street—his only neighbor, waking up the local dog population. She was one of the community's assets, although sometimes she was too smart for her own good. Her kid was okay, too—all boy. Klein had shown him how to catch a baseball the right way, holding his glove up instead of upside down, like most kids wanted to do. The kid would get right out in front of a ground ball, too, and stop it, instead of stepping aside and reaching for it. Klein would have coached Little League if he'd had a son.

For a moment he daydreamed, picturing a son of his own. Somehow he knew just what the boy would look like. It was strange how you could miss something that had never existed. Klein was a practical man, and he knew that dreams were just so much air. And yet when it came to the son he wanted but couldn't have, the air that filled the empty space was just as solid as flesh and blood and bone. It was probably crazy, thinking like that, but as long as he knew it was crazy, then he could go ahead and dream.

He walked into the kitchen and spread low-fat cream cheese across a puffed rice cake. He was up to two hundred sit-ups a day and eighty laps in the pool. In two weeks he'd be fifty-five

years old, but he had never been as fit as he was now. After
checking his watch he looked at the portable phone on the
counter, wondering whether the call this morning would be good
news, bad news, or just the usual games.

Klein had a man making inquiries out in Trabuco Canyon, but
he was pretty much a dough-head, or pretended to be; you
couldn't always tell. His name was Bernard Pomeroy—"Just call
me Barney." Although that wasn't the name he was using at the
moment. He shook hands too much and he wanted to call you by
your first name, a lot. There was nothing that sounded more like
a car salesman than first-naming people you didn't know, and in
fact Barney Pomeroy hustled cars at a Mercedes dealership down
at the beach during the week. He worked for Klein on the side.
There were other partners, but all of them were silent. Barney
Pomeroy should have been. He was worthless, or worse, in about
eighteen ways.

Klein's business angle out in the canyon wasn't illegal, strictly
speaking, but aspects of it were edgy, and the whole thing was
strictly under the table. There were other reasons, too, that Klein
couldn't just tell Pomeroy to go to hell. Getting rid of him would
be a complicated thing, and Klein didn't need that kind of com-
plication right now. He had enough without it. His marriage, his
bank account, his nerves, everything was strung tight as a wire.

"¡Imelda! ¡Escuche!" he said suddenly, looking back out into
the living room. The young Mexican maid rubbed at the furniture
with a dustrag. "¿Donde está la señora?"

"Está durmiendo."

Asleep. Lorna was still asleep. Sometimes it disgusted him how
she could spend so much of her life unconscious. And when she
woke up, long about ten, she'd spend two hours putting on her
face. Why bother getting up at all? On the other hand, once she
had her face on she was what a man in his business needed—a
wife that *looked* right, who knew what to wear and how to wear
it. It took Lorna a while to get the engines up to full rev, but then
she was showroom quality.

Last night she had looked dynamite. There wasn't a man at the
party that hadn't been cadging looks at her. What had Klein said
at the party that had been so funny? He tried to remember exactly
how it went; otherwise it didn't make any sense. A television had
been on, out by the pool. A highbrow historical program on
PBS—some sort of documentary about Israel. A little man with
a crazy person's idea of a haircut had been speaking. "Who the

hell's that?'' Klein had asked out loud. "He's Begin," Winters had said, and Klein had nodded seriously, and then said, "Hell, if you looked like that, you'd be beggin', too."

The joke had torn everyone up, especially Winters. People couldn't repeat it enough times to satisfy themselves. It had gone from room to room like a laugh virus. He had roped in something like six potential front men just on the strength of having said something that funny. Thinking about it now, he nearly laughed all over again, and he pictured Winters, a big man with a face like a boiled ham, laughing so hard that it had left him gasping for breath. Winters was one of his silent partners. He represented a firm called Sloane Investment Services, which would pretty much own the deed to Klein's house if his business dealings out in the canyon failed.

He pushed the thought out of his mind, then abruptly remembered Lorna trying to tell her own joke right afterward. She had been out in the kitchen for an hour or so with Uncle Gin and Aunt Tonic, and that hadn't helped matters. When everyone was laughing at Klein's joke, she had come into the room, and then when someone told her what Klein had said, she had smiled, but pretty clearly hadn't understood it. Almost at once she had announced that she had a better one.

Somehow, she had thought it would be a good idea to work through the naked man and the elephant joke, of all the damned stupid things: "What did the elephant say to the naked man?" the joke went. Then the punch line: "How do you breathe through that little trunk?" Hah, hah, hah. That's what it was worth, about three hahs, and that was when you told it right.

Anyway, while everyone except Lorna was still laughing about the Begin joke, she had stood up straight, as if reciting, and started out: "What did the elephant say to the naked man?" There had been a silence in the room, partly out of embarrassment. Klein had wanted to kill her. Then, with a loopy grin, she had delivered the punch line, or what she remembered as the punch line: "How do you breathe through that dick?" she had said.

The silence lasted another five seconds, and then the room just came apart. People were laughing so hard that drinks got sloshed onto the carpet. One man got chest pains, and they had to lay him out on the couch until he could take his nitro tablet and boost his heart back up to full power. Klein's Begin joke was forgotten, although when he had reminded people of it later, they still thought it was pretty funny.

On the way home, Lorna had wanted to talk about her joke,
how successful it had been. "Wasn't I funny?" she had asked.

"A scream," he had said, and then he realized that she had no
clue that she had screwed up the punch line, that people were
laughing because she had gotten it so stupidly and inconceivably
wrong. She had never figured that out. So he had told her, very
patiently, right there in the car. . . .

He elbowed the unpleasant memory into the back of his mind
and watched Imelda's legs as she dusted her way across the room.
She was just about to leave when he signaled her again. She
smiled, and he wondered what her smile meant. There was a lot
in a smile, if you knew how to look. Sometimes he wondered if
her smile was meant to ridicule him.

"*Quita usted el papel de la puerta,*" he said, gesturing toward
the front of the house where the offensive bumper sticker was
still glued to the door.

"*Sí, señor, ¿cuál puerta?*"

"*En . . . el frente. De la entrada.*"

Feeling lousy, he broke up the rest of his rice cake with the
point of the knife. Lorna drank too much. Unless it was a social
occasion, she didn't get started until evening, but then she got
toasted fast. By seven-thirty she was gone. You might as well
talk to the television set. It had gotten to the point where she'd
sleep all night sitting in her chair, oblivious, but that had scared
her badly enough that she'd cut back a little.

He stared out the window toward the tree-shaded hills, suddenly recalling the dream that had awakened him again early that
morning. There was something in the windy morning, in the sagebrush smell of the air, that suggested the dream, and he sat forward, his heart racing, watching the tree shadows on the grassy
hillside. He could almost swear that one of them hadn't been a
shadow at all, that a woman in a black dress had been walking
beneath the trees along the trail that descended from the ridge.
Now there was nothing.

His heart fluttered, and unconsciously he rubbed his chest. The
first moments of the dream replayed in his mind—the anticipation, the windy moonlight, the sudden appearance of the
woman—and he watched uneasily as the wind stirred the trees
now, their shadows shifting like the surface of a dark sea.

# 6

PETER CLIMBED INTO THE SUBURBAN, TOSSED THE BAG WITH THE spud guns onto the backseat, and drove out onto Chapman Avenue again. Just before Amanda and David went off to Hawaii last week, David promised to send postcards. It was his first plane trip, complete with a ride in the airport limo, and so he was going to send the first card from the airport. Peter had given him a little packet of stamps. No postcards had come, from the airport or anywhere else.

It wasn't like David to neglect to send the card. Like Amanda, he was organized and responsible to a fault, especially for a ten-year-old. It shouldn't have taken two days for the card to make it across town.

Regardless of what his marriage had come to, fifteen years of it had made Peter feel necessary, and the feeling was something he couldn't lose overnight. He had told Amanda that he would look at the front brakes on her Honda while she was gone. He couldn't have her paying a hundred fifty bucks for a brake job, not for something that took thirty minutes and a twelve-dollar trip to the Pep Boys.

The banners at Selman Chevrolet whipped on their lines, blowing straight out toward the ocean, and a big tumbleweed, freed at last from whatever lot it had grown up in, rolled across the Tustin Avenue intersection, only to be knocked to pieces by a pickup truck gunning away east, toward the foothills.

Instead of stopping at the Pep Boys for brake linings, Peter crossed the intersection and turned right on Monterey, pulling up to the curb outside the house. *The* house now rather than his house. Each day brought new revelations. Just out of habit he was tempted to haul out the lawn rake and clean up the windblown leaves and papers that choked the flower beds.

Through the open window of the Suburban he could hear the distant growl of a lawnmower, and he could see that the girl down

at the corner house on Maple was washing her car in the driveway. Weekend mornings in the suburb—the smell of bacon and
coffee through an open kitchen window, kids playing on the sidewalk, the hissing of lawn sprinklers. Maybe you had to get away
from it to see it all clearly again.

He climbed out of the car and walked up onto the porch. The
blinds were drawn across the front windows. He knocked but he
could tell straight off that the house was empty. They were in
Hawaii. They wouldn't be home for a week. He had known that
but had knocked anyway. It wasn't his house anymore and he
couldn't just walk in uninvited, even when he knew the house
was empty.

He headed up the driveway into the backyard, found the back
door key inside a hollow plastic rock in the flower bed, then
stepped up onto the back porch to let himself in. Amanda's cat,
Tully, appeared out of nowhere and darted up onto the porch,
brushing against his leg and purring loudly. A neighbor was feeding it, but it was used to having the run of the house. Peter stooped
to pet it, then blocked the door with his leg and slipped inside.
If he let Tully in he'd be chasing the cat around the house all
morning.

"Relax," Peter said to it. "You've only got a week to go and
you're back in. For me there's no end in sight."

He closed the door behind him. The house smelled and sounded
empty, nothing but dusty echoes. With no idea what he was looking for, he wandered from the service porch into the kitchen. A
glass pitcher half-full of lime Kool-Aid sat on the kitchen table
alongside two nearly empty glasses, a plate speckled with cookie
crumbs and a single broken Oreo, and a dealt-out deck of playing
cards.

Crazy Eights. It was David's favorite game, and the three of
them had played countless hands of it, drinking green Kool-Aid
and eating Oreos, arguing off and on about the wisdom of dunk-
ing the Oreos in the Kool-Aid and whether you ought to unscrew
them first and eat the center and then dunk either half separately,
so that you seemed to have two cookies instead of one. Suddenly
hungry, he opened the cupboard and searched for the open pack-
age of Oreos, but he couldn't find it.

How could it still be going on without him? Peter was a part
of it, part of the ritual. It was Peter who had always made the
Kool-Aid.

Well, now somebody else was making it. He carried the glasses

and pitcher to the sink and rinsed them out. He could play out
that part of the ritual anyway. It wasn't like Amanda to leave
dirty dishes on the table—an open invitation to ants.

He went out into the dining room and then into David's room,
which was almost appallingly neat. Books and toys were carefully
arranged on the shelves that Peter had built when David was—
what? Two? He sat at the foot of the bed, looking around at the
posters on the wall and at the airplane models and sets of high-
tech building blocks. Over one of the headboard bedposts hung
a wooden heart on a string. Peter and David had cut it out on the
band saw five years ago, when David was on his Oz kick. The
only sign of disorder in the room was that the closet door stood
open, blocking some of the sunlight that shone through the window.

Peter gave the wooden heart a shove, so that it swung back
and forth like a pendulum. It dawned on him that he was chasing
ghosts, driving like crazy out of the hills in order to wander
around the empty house. What did he expect to find? A clue to
what? Outside, the wind blew past the lonesome willow tree in
the yard, making the branches sway. He sat daydreaming for a
moment, nearly hypnotized by the easy dance of the slender willow branches.

Then, in a rush, he was struck with the uncanny notion that he
had seen this very same thing before—early this morning. Except
that his predawn hallucination had been even more real, if that
were possible, with its kitchen sounds and smell of charcoal
smoke. Now, except for the swishing of branches beyond the
window, all was quiet, and the only smell in the air was the faintly
dusty odor of a closed-up house.

He was looking at the tree from the same angle, from underneath, looking up at the silver-white undersides of the leaves. It
was a different season and a different wind, and the shadows were
wrong, but what he had seen that morning had clearly been a
view of the backyard willow tree as seen through David's bedroom window, through David's eyes. It had been something almost telepathic, like a borrowed memory—David's memory.

The wind picked up outside now, and the sunlit willow
branches flailed away, showering the air with leaves. He stood
up. It was time to go. There was no use drowning himself in
memories and regrets.

He stepped across and swung the closet door shut. Sitting behind it, where it had been hidden by the open door, was a piece of canvas luggage. It was David's overnighter, the zipper open, the bag full of the clothes that he should have taken to Hawaii.

BERNARD POMEROY LOOKED HIMSELF OVER IN THE REARVIEW mirror. His skin was dry and itchy along the side of his nose and flaking where he had shaved that morning. He dabbed on moisturizing cream and rubbed it in carefully, then worked a little drop of cream over each eye. He took out his pocket comb and smoothed his eyebrows. Hard to believe it was only an hour ago that he'd parted company with Mr. Ackroyd. He had made a quick decision, but if you hesitated you were lost in this business. And there'd been no question that the old man's mind was made up. He wasn't going to move unless he was pushed.

Pomeroy's face was blemish free, the flesh almost translucent, his nose small and straight. Overall his appearance was perfectly bland. A woman had told him that once. She had said that he looked like someone out of a composite drawing by a police artist, facial features copied from a book of common noses and eyebrows and ears.

Actually, it had been a fairly clever thing to say, under the distressing circumstances. Since then he had realized that a bland man is very nearly an invisible man, and the idea didn't bother him at all. Through the windshield he could just see the creek through the trees. Bushes on the hillsides jerked and shuddered in the wind. That was what screwed up his skin—this damned wind dried everything out. He put the vial away and began fastidiously to brush his hair back. Then he opened the leeward window of the car, took a travel-sized bottle of hair spray out of his toiletries kit, and sprayed his hair until it was stiff. He checked his smile in the mirror, hauled a container of mint-flavored string out of the kit and flossed his teeth, then threw the used floss out the open window.

One thing he had learned selling cars was that people naturally liked a well-groomed man. It sounded superficial, but that didn't make a bit of difference. Grooming was essential to success. People understood it to be sign of quality. He had business cards that read, "Quality, an American way of life." One of his other cards displayed a fish symbol along with chapter and verse numbers from the Bible. He could scope a customer out in half a second and give them the right card nearly every time.

Another thing he knew from selling cars is that you don't let up on people. You don't take no for an answer. If there's any hesitation, you've got to *tell* them what they want. He had miscalculated with old Ackroyd, though, when he talked to him this morning. He knew the man was a Christian—he had learned that much from Klein—but the fish card hadn't worked on him. It had only seemed to irritate him. Pomeroy had read him for a tough nut right then and there. Nothing that couldn't be cracked, though, if you knew where to squeeze.

He opened the door, stepped out into the weeds of the little turnout, and locked up the rented Thunderbird. Then he opened the trunk and pulled out a white plastic garbage bag. Carrying the bag, he set out up the road, dressed in a pair of Jordache jeans and Reebok tennis shoes and with a cashmere sweater draped casually over his shoulders. He cocked his head as he walked so that the wind kept his hair pressed flat.

Ten feet from the car, the wind abruptly yanked the sweater off his shoulders and threw it onto the dirt road. Pomeroy grabbed at it with his free hand, but the wind was quicker, and the sweater cartwheeled backward into the side of the Thunderbird, crucifying itself momentarily against the red paint of the fender. Dropping his trash bag onto the side of the road, he lunged after the sweater just as the wind snatched it up again and dragged it under the chassis, trapping a sleeve beneath a tire.

He tried to yank the sweater loose, but the sleeve wedged itself tighter, and he had to get down onto his hands and knees to wiggle it out. He stood up, shaking dirt out of the sweater and dusting off the knees of his jeans. There was a dirty oil smear across the chest of the sweater. He'd have to get the damned thing cleaned now. Trying to pull himself together again, he reopened the trunk, dropped the sweater in, and then checked his hair in the window reflection. Not a strand had moved. He looked professional.

A partly decomposed rat had fallen out of the open trash bag on the road. Pomeroy found a piece of stick and shoved the thing back inside, where there were two other rats, more recently dead. They stank like hell in the hot plastic bag. Pomeroy hated to touch it, but the morning was wearing on. There would be people around soon.

The old man wasn't home—Pomeroy had seen him leave, driving into town for his weekend grocery run. He glanced around quickly, making double sure that there was no car beside the house, nobody walking along the road, and then he walked to the rear door, where he wouldn't be easily seen. For safety's sake he knocked before he tried the knob. There was no answer, and the door was dead-bolted tight. The windows were latched, too. It would be easy enough to break one, climb in, and just tear the place up, but then Ackroyd would know that someone had been screwing around there, and that might blow the whole deal. Pomeroy would save that for later, if it was necessary. Breaking and entering wasn't in the cards today. And anyway, Klein would have a coronary over it.

Pomeroy laughed out loud. Klein was a high-blood-pressure type. His face got red like a sunburn when he was mad. Telling him about this morning might just be the last straw for him. His circuits would fry and he'd drop dead.

The water tank was up on the hill behind the house, mostly hidden from below. He hiked up toward it, carrying the bag of dead rats along a little overgrown trail slippery with loose rock. The rats stank to high heaven, and the smell nearly made him sick. He looked behind him down the steep hillside, and right then a Siamese cat darted across the yard below. It stopped outside the back door of the house and sat staring into the trees, then started to wipe its face with a paw.

Pomeroy hesitated, struck with his second brilliant idea that morning.

**8**

PETER PICKED UP DAVID'S BAG AND LAID IT ON THE BED. INSTINC-
tively he knew what it meant, even before his mind had come to
the obvious conclusion. He sorted through it carefully, tilting the
open bag toward the window to catch the sunlight. There were
two pairs of swimming trunks on top. Underneath were comic
books, a pair of zorries, a T-shirt wrapped around a Sony Walk-
man, headphones, and the little packet of postcard stamps.

Peter dropped the bag and went out, up the hall and into Amanda's bedroom. Her luggage was spread out over the bed, opened
up, only half-packed. Bathing suits, beach towels, sandals—all
the vacation stuff was there. It was clean and neatly stacked and
organized, by a person systematic about packing, someone going
away, not someone returning. A few pieces of folded clothing
were piled on the bed and chair. There was nothing on the floor—
no dirty clothes, no souvenirs.

Peter ran out into the living room, looking for something to
explain what was obvious. He found the week's mail scattered
on the floor under the mail slot. Frantically he sorted through it,
checking return addresses, searching for anything at all. Nothing.
Just bills, junk, magazines, some of it addressed to him. He let it
lie and headed back into the kitchen.

Leaning with both hands against the edge of the counter, he
closed his eyes and forced himself to think. Amanda and David
hadn't been home for a week. That much was clear. And wherever
they'd gone—if in fact they'd gone anywhere—they hadn't taken
anything with them.

Possible answers to the riddle filtered into his mind, and the
atmosphere of the house was suddenly threatening. He found that
he was listening hard, like someone awakened by a noise in the
night.

But aside from the mail strewn on the floor, there was no sign
of anything out of place in the kitchen or living room, no evidence

of trouble, of an intruder. Carefully, not knowing what to expect, Peter pushed open the door of the den, letting it swing wide before looking in, half expecting something that he couldn't picture or put into words.

It was just another empty room. Both bathrooms were clean except for the windblown dust on the countertops and windowsills.

The fourth bedroom, Amanda's study, was as tidy as the rest of the house. For a moment he hoped he would find an explanatory note there, but the only thing on the desktop was a check register and last month's canceled checks, sorted and stacked.

Seeing them there propelled him back into Amanda's bedroom. He pulled open her carry-on bag and hauled out a sweater, a paperback novel, a hairbrush, and a crossword puzzle magazine. He unzipped the inside pocket. Three stacks of traveler's checks lay inside, tucked into plastic cases along with three hundred dollars in twenties. Two sets of airline tickets were slid in alongside, enclosed in a heavy paper envelope advertising Slotsy Tours and Travel. His hands shook as he set the tickets down on the dresser.

*Move*, he told himself, and he sprinted to the back door, pulled it open, and ran to the garage, going in through the side door. He flipped on the light switch, half expecting to see Amanda and David slumped in the parked car. But the Honda Accord sat there as ever, empty, bad brakes and all.

He shut the light off and went back out into the sunlight, knowing that he wouldn't find any answers in the house. Amanda and David hadn't come home since their trip out to the canyon to visit him last Sunday afternoon. There was no use quizzing the neighbors. He would make one phone call and then go to the police. He found Amanda's telephone book in the kitchen, scanned a couple of pages, then punched a number into the phone.

It rang once, twice, three times; he closed his eyes, listening to the fourth and fifth rings. "Answer it!" he said out loud, straight into the mouthpiece, and a voice on the other end, sounding puzzled, said, "What?"

"Peggy!"

"Peter?" she asked.

"Yeah," he said. "It's Peter."

"I nearly hung up on you. What were you yelling about?"

"I thought you weren't going to answer."

"Oh," she said. "How's it going? What's up? Hear from Mandy?"

"No," Peter said. "Not yet. I'm over at the house, though. I came over to work on her car." He watched through the window as he talked. The wind was tearing across the backyard now, blowing the limbs of the willow tree nearly horizontal. Leaves whirled away up the driveway. He forced himself to sound calm and reasonable.

"She told me you were going to fix the brakes. I think she thought it was a little funny. Don't be too nice, Peter."

"I've never been accused of that before, actually, but thanks. What I want to know," he said, choosing his words carefully, "is how upset she seemed a week ago when you drove her home from my place."

"You mean when I drove her up there. I didn't drive her home."

Peter sat down hard on a kitchen chair. "That's what I meant," he said.

That was it. He could hang up now. He knew what he had to know.

"Well, she was kind of upset," Peggy said, "because I didn't have time to stop at the store so she could get the stuff you wanted. Frankly, she said you'd be a pain in the ass about it."

"I was," Peter said. "That's just what I was."

"It was my fault, really. I left something at home and then had to go back for it. It was a real mess. I was late for work, so she said to pass on the groceries. Did you yell at her?"

"No," Peter said. But actually he had. Both of them had done some yelling—very quietly so that David wouldn't know about it. Over the years they had got used to yelling quietly. Peter had wanted to make an early dinner for Amanda and David that afternoon, in celebration of their leaving for Hawaii. He had asked Amanda for a bottle of olive oil and a bunch of garlic and some slipper lobster tails along with a few other odds and ends—stuff that he couldn't buy at local stores. She was going to be passing a gourmet sort of market on the way out with Peggy, so he had left it up to her. She hadn't brought any of it.

After all the yelling, Peter had gone after it himself, driving all the way out to east Orange when he would have saved time just driving down into El Toro or across the canyon into Coto de Caza. He could have made spaghetti, for God's sake, hamburgers. Somehow, though, he had wanted to *show* her. He didn't know exactly what that meant now.

When he had gotten back, something like an hour and a half

later, Amanda and David were gone. Amanda had threatened that before he left. She had told him that Peggy would gladly give them a ride home. Peggy was only working a four-hour shift at the Trabuco Oaks Steak House. Amanda and David could walk across the ridge and down into the Oaks in about forty minutes, not much longer than the time that it took to drive there on the dirt road. Peter had taken off for the more distant market anyway, despite Amanda's warning. *Because* of Amanda's warning. When he got back they were gone.

"So why did you call?" Peggy asked.

"What?"

"Why did you call? Just to talk?"

"No real reason," Peter said. "I'm just trying to keep on top of it all. You know. I can't give it up just like that."

"It isn't easy, is it?"

"Not much, no," Peter said.

"It's not easy on Amanda, either, you know. I'm sorry about screwing up your dinner, though."

"I screwed it up," Peter said. "Just another mistake."

"Keep in touch," she said.

"Sure." He hung up and sat for a moment thinking, his throat and stomach hollow. He had no real way of knowing that Amanda and David had ever left the canyon on that windy Sunday afternoon a week ago. He had taken it for granted that they had, and the next day he had driven cheerfully off to Santa Barbara. If he set out right now to make a list of the things he had taken for granted in his life, he'd go broke buying paper.

RATS IN THE WELL WOULD MAKE ACKROYD A SICK MAN, BUT A dead cat in the well would make him something worse, especially when he found out it was his own cat.

Upending the bag, Pomeroy dropped the three rats beside the trail, then shoved the empty bag into his back pocket and started to climb back down, anxious not to move too fast and scare the cat. Then he stopped, thought again, and went back up after one of the two freshly dead rats, which he picked up by the tail, nearly gagging at the rubbery feel of the rat tail pressed between his fingers.

He went back down, smiling in the cat's direction, holding the rat visible. The cat watched him, its tail flicking back and forth now. Pomeroy took the bag out of his back pocket with his free hand, although he wasn't quite sure what to do with it. He had killed small animals before by putting them into a plastic bag, then shoving the mouth of the bag over the exhaust pipe of a car. The carbon monoxide put them right out. It was very humane.

A live cat would tear the bag to shreds, though. He looked around for something to hit it with. He didn't like the idea of the animal suffering. There was nothing close by, and he didn't want to go looking for something. The cat would get away.

He decided just to grab it by the tail and slam it into the wall of the house. That would stun it long enough for him to get it up the hill and drown it in the water tank. The cat wouldn't suffer at all that way.

Pomeroy spoke to it, dropping the bag and flexing the fingers of his right hand. He laid the rat carefully on the wooden porch, and the cat batted at it with its paw, as if it wanted the rat to get up and run.

"That's right," Pomeroy said softly. And then, quick as a snake, he grabbed the cat's tail and spun around toward the house, snatching the cat up off the porch. Surprisingly, the cat retracted, balling itself up, latching on to his forearm with its claws. Then there was the sharp, hot pain of teeth fixed into his bicep as the cat scrabbled up his shirt, clawing the sleeve to ribbons.

Pomeroy trod backward across the porch, stepping on the rat, trying to yank the frenzied cat away from his neck and face. The creature sank its teeth into his hand, lacerating the soft skin of his palm, and when he tried to fling it away, it held on long enough to tear out a piece of flesh. Then it let go and dropped, somersaulted forward, and raced away into the underbrush.

He held his fist closed. His whole hand throbbed. The rat's head was crushed where he'd stepped on it, but he forced himself to pick it up anyway, by the tail again. He grabbed the bag off the ground with the same hand and walked stiffly back toward the trail to the water tank. Blood trickled down his forearm from the scratches, but it was the bite that ached, and he could feel blood leaking out of his closed fist onto the edge of his hand.

Next time he'd be ready for the cat.

After climbing back up the hillside, he located the other two rats, forced himself to pick them up, and then had to put them down again to push back the little trapdoor in the lid of the steel tank. He put his lacerated hand into the icy water, flexed it, and gasped when the cold pain lanced up his arm. He pulled his hand out, closed his fist again, and dropped the rats into the tank one by one before pushing the door shut.

He tucked the bag into his pocket and started down, holding on to roots and branches with his free hand to steady himself. There was no sign of the cat anywhere, but he bent over to pick up a grapefruit-sized rock just in case it showed its face. When he straightened up, there was a woman not twenty feet in front of him, walking on the road.

"Linda!" Pomeroy gasped. His throat constricted and for a moment he was afraid he would pass out. Then he saw that he was wrong. It wasn't Linda. Same blond hair, tall. Jesus, same build. It was her mouth, too, the full lips . . .

For a moment he allowed himself to imagine that it *was* Linda, and he pictured her alone in her bedroom, unhurriedly sorting through the things in an open dresser drawer. Now she had come to him alone like this, out of the forest, having finally noticed him, understood him. He would forgive her, and together they would go into the trees. . . .

Now that she was closer he could see a certain suspicion in the woman's eyes, and he smiled brightly at her and nodded.

"Haven't seen Mr. Ackroyd this morning, have you?" he asked. Before she could answer he said, "My name's Adams. Henry Adams." He almost shoved his hand out for her to shake, but his palm was slick with blood again. He dropped the rock behind his back. She seemed to have visibly relaxed when he mentioned Ackroyd's name. Thank God she hadn't been standing there two minutes ago when he was dropping rats into the water tank.

Or had she?

He stopped himself from turning to look at the tank.

"Name's Beth," she said.

She looked so much like Linda that he nearly couldn't trust himself to speak. He had never had a chance to explain himself, his love for her. Beth—her name filled his mind.

Then he realized that she was looking at him uneasily, and he made himself smile again. "I was just thinking that I knew you," he said. "You remind me of . . . of a woman I knew once."

"I've got a common face," she said. "What happened to your hand? It's bleeding like crazy. My boyfriend's place is right up the road. He's got a first-aid kit. You ought to put some hydrogen peroxide on that and bandage it up."

"Naw," Pomeroy said. He was pretty sure why she had mentioned the boyfriend. She was attracted to him, but was a little too modest to be open about it. She just wanted a little space at first, and that was all right.

Or maybe she *had* seen him up on the hill, and was threatening him with the boyfriend. He tried to read her face, looking deeply into her eyes. He couldn't see any suspicion there, or any fear. She trusted him.

"I tried to pet Mr. Ackroyd's cat," he said, opening his hand now, "but the darned thing took a swipe at me. First time that's happened. We're old friends."

She nodded. "You ought to have someone look at it, old friends or not. Cat scratches as deep as those are dangerous."

"My car's just up the road," Pomeroy said, falling in beside her and heading toward where the Thunderbird sat at the turnout. "I've got a first-aid kit in the trunk. Maybe you could help?" He looked her over, his eyes stopping for a moment on her breasts. She glanced at him and he pulled his eyes away, embarrassed. "Where you headed?"

"Just out walking," she said.

"Like a ride somewhere?" He could sense that she understood him, or at least would be open to the idea of . . . He couldn't define it too clearly. He wondered if she lived nearby, maybe in one of the isolated houses out here in the canyon.

"No, thank you. I'm headed up toward the ridge, actually. I like to walk. Walking gives me time to think."

He considered asking her to drive his car for him. He could plead cat bite, say he was feeling shaky. But maybe it would be too much too soon. "What's your sign?" he asked.

"I don't know," she said. "I think it's neon."

Pomeroy laughed. He liked that, a woman who could joke. He had worked hard to develop his sense of humor. That was invaluable for a salesman. It was a very human thing, a sense of humor, and was attractive to people.

"You live out here?" he asked.

"No," she said. "My boyfriend does."

"How about you? Where do you live?" He pictured her in a small house, lace curtains, far enough from the prying eyes of neighbors so that she wasn't fastidious about her privacy. He wondered what her habits were when she was alone. Linda had been very free when she thought she was alone, very uninhibited.

"Locally," she said.

They were at the Thunderbird now, and he opened the trunk and took out the first-aid kit he carried. The canyon was full of hazards—snakes and animals. He liked to be prepared. It was the boy scout in him.

Beth dabbed the cut with a gauze pad soaked in liquid from a little spray can of antiseptic. The bite was ragged and deep, but the bleeding had nearly stopped. She covered his palm with another pad, fixed it in place with tape, and then wrapped his hand with a strip of gauze bandage.

Pomeroy barely noticed the throbbing in his hand now. Her face was close to his—closer than Linda's had ever been. Beth trusted him. She cared about him, *for* him. He cocked his head and smiled at her, putting his whole heart into it.

She stepped away. "There you go," she said. "You still ought to see a doctor. Bacterial infections are pretty common in cat bites."

He nodded. "I *will*. Thanks. You know, it's a pleasure to meet a beautiful woman out walking like this. Quite a surprise. Sure I can't drop you somewhere?"

"Very sure," she said. "Thanks for asking."

Near the parked Thunderbird she stepped off the road and onto a trail that angled down toward the creek. He could see that it wound away upward on the other side, and there was a cut in the steep mountainside where the trail lost itself in the brush. Pomeroy unlocked the car, and got in, watching her as she crossed the creek. Almost at once she was lost from view. He should have gone along with her. She would have enjoyed his company.

He started the engine, certain that he would see her again. Synchronicity had brought them together. He could sense it. This was *meant* to happen, to make up for . . . for what had happened before.

The cat bite throbbed worse than ever. Beth had been right about seeing a doctor. That had been good advice. He would keep an eye on his hand. Right now, though, he had a couple of other things to do.

He smelled dead rats and realized that the plastic bag was still tucked into his pants pocket. So he wound down the window and threw it out before driving away west, toward civilization. Things were going well. Even the damned cat bite had paid out. He grinned suddenly, anticipating his phone conversation with Lance Klein.

KLEIN WATCHED THE HILLSIDES THROUGH THE WINDOW. HE KNEW it was crazy, but something inside him, almost like a memory, whispered that at any moment she would appear. He'd been waiting for her, expecting her. He could picture her face clearly—the pale porcelain cast of her skin, her dark eyes and hair. Her name flitted into his head without his making any conscious effort to invent one for her, as if he had always known it.

The wind fell suddenly, and the shadows and trees were still, the hills empty. He imagined it was dark, late at night, the moon high in the sky over the ridge. Heavy with expectation, he walked toward the hills through the high grass. She appeared in the moonlight, and he went out to meet her, taking her hand and leading her to a room that smelled like pine and wool and tallow. Her clothes were a puzzle of ties and buttons, but with practiced hands he undressed her, the two of them moving together slowly in the sepia-toned candlelight. . . .

When the telephone rang he nearly knocked it onto the floor. It took a moment for him to recognize Pomeroy's voice.

"I think we've got a live one out at the end of the road," Pomeroy said.

"Which cabin?" Klein forced himself to look at the countertop, to yank his eyes and his mind around to business and away from the windy hillside.

"Thirty-five," Pomeroy said.

"They settled on a price?"

"Nope."

"You make any kind of offer?"

"Nope."

Klein waited. He did a lot of waiting when he talked to Pomeroy, whose pronouncements were full of pauses that seemed to imply things, except that Klein never knew if the pauses implied stupidity or secret knowledge. "So what did you tell them?" he asked, finally giving in. Two points for you, he thought.

"I told the woman to talk it over with her husband. My idea is to drive back out there in a couple of days, after they've had time to get worked up, and tell them I'm not interested. Then one of the new fronts can pick it up."

"All right," Klein said. "I'll go for that. Give me the name and phone number."

After listening for a moment he hung up the phone and shook his head, immediately punching in a number. The phone rang three times before a man picked up at the other end and said, "Callaway."

"Bob, this is Lance Klein, calling about that little real estate deal we talked about at the Spanglers' party. That's right," Klein said. "She was a riot, wasn't she? I *am* a lucky man. You don't know the half of it. Anyway, about that little deal, it's easy money, payment up front."

Klein nodded at the phone, peering out at the hills again. "Well," he said, "I'll tell you what. I've got the particulars if you're interested. That's right. Vacation home out here in the canyon, party name of Monroe. They've got a year-round home in Southgate."

Klein loved the view from the backyard, especially on a clear, windy day. The Japanese had the idea that you should build your house so that you couldn't see the view, so that you had to go looking for it. You wouldn't lose your appreciation of it that way. Sometimes the Japanese were purely full of crap.

Klein had cut, filled, surveyed, and built on the hills a hundred times in his head. It was a sort of mental exercise—creative thinking. Up behind the house there was a gradual slope for something like two hundred yards. Put in quarter-acre lots, ranch-style homes done right—plank floors, rock fireplaces, plenty of wood-frame windows. Nothing fake.

Call it "The Woods" or "Country Acres." Put out a couple of billboards along the Santa Ana Freeway—a painting of oak trees, the sun coming up, a creek, green grass, maybe a family of people hand in hand, watching the sunrise. Never mind that in ten years there wouldn't be any "country" left out here except for a few strips of what was sometimes called "green belt" by the used car salesmen who passed for city planners.

But then you didn't sell people with the truth. Not with that kind of truth, anyway. There was a bigger truth that had to do with inevitability. The best you could do was give people something for their money. They were on their way right now, those people were, getting out of the goddamn city, trying to find a little bit of breathable air. That's what the guy with the bumper sticker didn't get. You couldn't leave the canyons to the lions, not forever.

Prices were skyrocketing out in the foothills. A couple of years ago you could buy up a lot with a house on it for sixty thousand bucks. A hundred thousand would buy you a buildable acre. But those days were gone forever, and any serious real estate considerations, even out on the fringes of the county, were strictly for high rollers.

There was a lot of federally owned land in the county, though. The Cleveland National Forest stretched across most of the Santa Ana Mountains, and swallowed all of upper Trabuco Canyon. Most of it was wilderness. A dirt road ran back into the canyon, open to traffic for five miles or so. Some forty cabins were hidden back up in there, in Trabuco itself and in Holy Jim Canyon, which branched off and ran up toward Santiago Peak.

Right now you could buy one of the those cabins for pocket change. The same cabin in Modjeska, or in the little town of Trabuco Oaks, could set you back a couple hundred thousand. What accounted for that was partly that you couldn't *buy* the land out in the canyon. You got it for twenty years, and then had to renew the lease. Built into the lease was what the Forest Service called a "higher use" clause, which meant that the fed could buy you out at market value if they wanted to put the land to some other purpose—like a park.

Also, there was no electricity or phone out there. Water was sketchy, especially in drought years. What was worst was the bone-wrenching dirt road, full of potholes, that ran up into the canyon. Nobody went back in there casually. Klein would bet money that there wasn't one person out of a hundred in the county that even knew the place existed. Probably one in a thousand.

But it wouldn't take much to change that. Pave the road, say, and run a wire back in there, and suddenly, very damned suddenly, you could put your pocket change away.

In fact, Klein's canyon enterprise operated on the brink of out-right fraud. He wouldn't have used that word in the company of any of the consortium of investors and front men that he'd managed to peg together over the past months, but he had never been one to fool himself.

Just as soon as the county announced its intention of turning upper Trabuco Canyon into a wildlife park, something was going to happen to the value of the cabins back in there—something big. There were two ways it could go. The county could upgrade the road and run power into the area, and the value of all those fifteen-thousand-dollar hovels would increase tenfold overnight, literally. Or else the Forest Service would implement the "higher use" clause and eminent-domain the places, paying the owners off at market value.

Klein was betting on the second scenario. There were only the forty cabins back in there, in Holy Jim and Trabuco canyons combined—pocket money for the government no matter what happened to market value.

Somebody was going to make a piece of change, and the tax-payer was going to take it on the chin.

So far, Klein and his "consortium," as he liked to call them, had made offers on twelve cabins and had actually picked up six of them. It was Pomeroy's job to hunt for more, and then, when he found a possible sale, Klein passed the name on to someone willing to front for the consortium for a flat fee. You were prohibited by law from holding more than one lease, and that's why he needed the fronts—there were only a handful of investors altogether, looking to pick up something like twenty properties. Anyway, the consortium would ante up the money to buy each cabin and pay the front a flat fee to hold the lease.

Most of the longtime canyon residents had picked the places up years ago for six or eight or ten thousand bucks. If you offered them twice that they crumpled. Once you transferred the leases and picked up bills of sale, you sold the places back and forth among yourselves and drove the prices through the roof. In the end you'd divvy up, with a brokerage fee for Klein on top of his share.

If you were quick and clean and smart, you'd all walk away happy when the government bought you out. If you weren't, then the government would smell something—fraud, to be exact.

**11**

IT WAS NEARLY NOON WHEN PETER PARKED THE SUBURBAN IN the lot behind the city of Orange civic center buildings. Wishing he was anyplace else than where he was, he walked around to the front sidewalk, past a tile-and-concrete fountain that had four painted steel egrets standing on top of it, spitting water into the air. The water blew away in the wind, out onto the lawn and walkway. A half dozen sycamore leaves floated like boats on the fountain pool.

He had seen the fountain a thousand times, driving and walking along Chapman Avenue, but it looked strangely alien to him now. Abruptly he felt the urge to run—not in order to hide, but just to run, for the sheer sake of running, to make his legs work, to justify his heart. He found himself at the door of the police station without having run anywhere. His reflection in the glass looked back at him like a windblown ghost.

There was no one visible inside, no activity at all. A line of empty chairs sat along the windows to his left. Straight ahead was a long, silent hallway, and to his right lay a glassed-in reception office containing three cluttered desks empty of people. Maybe nobody got into trouble on Saturday morning. He ran a pocket comb through his hair and straightened his collar. There was no use looking the way he felt.

A woman appeared from a back room just then, carrying a cup of coffee into the reception office. He stepped to the window and said hello. She smiled at him, looking efficient and friendly, but her face changed when he explained what he wanted, as if she could read something in his voice and eyes. "If you could have a seat for a moment, Mr. Travers," she said, nodding toward the chairs by the window. At that, she turned around and went out again.

He sat down, although he didn't want to. Full of nervous energy, he was nearly compelled to get up again, to walk up and down the hallway or back and forth across the carpet, as if any movement at all would hasten him toward an answer. Eventually a man in a gray sport coat stepped into the reception cubicle. He patted his coat pocket and then paused for a moment to pull a pen out of a desktop penholder, looking out at Peter as if sizing him up before stepping out through the door. He carried a clipboard with several sheets of paper attached to it.

"Detective Slater," he said, introducing himself. "Ray Slater."

"Peter Travers," Peter said back to him.

"What seems to be the problem, then, Mr. Travers? How do you spell that? T-R-A-V-E-R-S?" the detective asked. The pen scratched across the paper on the clipboard. He sounded a little tired.

"That's right. My wife and child are missing. My ex-wife. We're separated."

"Their names?"

Peter reeled off their names and ages. He handed the detective a pair of photographs he'd brought along from Amanda's house as well as an inked set of David's fingerprints taken a couple of years ago during some sort of school safety program. After looking the photos over, the cop slid them under the papers on the clipboard, snapping the clip down across them.

"Missing since when?"

"A week ago," Peter said.

"A week?" He looked up now, a puzzled expression on his face, as if he must have heard something incorrectly. "Come with me," he said then, turning around and walking away up the corridor. He pushed open the door of a small room, furnished with a couple of upholstered office chairs and a desk. He gestured at one of the chairs, and Peter sat down. "Cup of coffee?"

"No, thanks," Peter said. This was the part that Peter didn't relish—admitting that Amanda and David had vanished last Sunday but that Peter was only now getting around to telling anyone. Either it would make him look guilty as hell or incredibly stupid. "As I said," Peter started in, "we're separated, and it was only this morning that I stopped by her house and found out that she and David were missing."

The detective nodded, tilting his own chair back, listening to Peter as if he were a psychologist and not a cop. Peter rolled the story out carefully, trying to make the whole thing sound a little less lame than it was. He left nothing out, though—the argument,

Peggy, the airline tickets and traveler's checks, the Honda still in the garage. He avoided any talk about premonitions and hallucinations.

Partway through, the detective abruptly sat up straight, looking as if he had just then remembered something, or as if Peter, finally, had said something that made a difference. Peter stopped talking.

"You live out in Trabuco Canyon?" the cop asked.

Peter nodded.

"Where? You mean Trabuco Oaks? Coto de Caza?"

"No, out in the canyon itself—Alder Springs area. Above the lower campground. Cabin with a Forest Service lease."

"Where do you work?"

Peter hesitated. The seeming irrelevancy of the question forced him to stop in order to process it. "Sycamore College," he said. "I'm a teacher. Architectural drafting."

"You were at school last week, Tuesday, say?"

"No. In fact I'm off right now. Lot of work to do on my house. I'm on half-pay leave until February."

"So where were you the first of last week, then? Down at the lumber yard?" The cop stared at him, waiting for him to say something good.

Surprised, Peter gaped back at him. He hadn't said anything yet about having gone to Santa Barbara to visit his brother. It had seemed irrelevant to him. "I was gone for a couple of days. Up north. Let's see . . . Monday through Wednesday. I stayed with my brother. He can—"

"I believe you," Detective Slater said, holding up his hand. "I don't want to talk to your brother. Wait here." He didn't sound irritated or suspicious, but he didn't look tired anymore, either. If anything, his voice held a note of compassion now, and the tone of it filled Peter with instant dread.

The detective stood up and pushed out through the door, taking his clipboard and pen with him, leaving the door open. Peter was suddenly nauseated. His fears and premonitions were like ghosts slowly growing visible in a night-darkened room. He closed his eyes and waited, wondering what the news would be, trying to anticipate it, to make himself ready.

The weight of the long morning oppressed the air of the room. The seconds ticked by. He nearly stood up in order to pace around the small room, but instead he forced himself to look out the window. Across the street people walked in and out of the savings

and loan, going about their simple business. The bushes in the
flower beds blew fitfully in the wind. A hook-and-ladder pulled
out of the fire department garage, turning on its siren and swinging around onto Chapman Avenue, followed by a paramedics
truck.

Detective Slater walked back in and sat down. "Change your
mind on that coffee?" he asked.

"No," Peter said. "Thanks."

After shuffling through the few papers on the clipboard, the
detective scanned a sentence or two. "Trabuco Canyon is out in
county territory," he said, looking up, straight into Peter's eyes.
He spoke slowly, seeming to choose his words carefully. "So we
don't have any jurisdiction out there. A lot of it lies inside the
Cleveland National Forest, where your house evidently is. Still,
it's the county sheriff that covers that area. If they find anything
back there that might concern us, the sheriff's department sends
out a notice." He paused, as if to establish that Peter was taking
all of this in.

"What did they find?"

"Nothing, really. Keep that in mind. What we've got is this.
A hiker claimed to have seen two bodies out there." He looked
at his clipboard, either reading or else pretending to read in order
to give Peter time to wrestle with what he was saying. "This was
back in a place called Falls Canyon."

"Right near my house," Peter said, nearly unable to breathe.

The detective nodded. "It was night. This hiker was back in
there with the idea of sleeping somewhere. I gather he was some
kind of transient. He claims to have heard a scream right as he
came around in sight of the falls, and there were the bodies,
maybe thirty feet away. He was alone, and apparently it scared
the hell out of him, and he hiked back out to the road and all the
way down to the ranger station at O'Neill Park to report it. One
of the rangers called the sheriff and then beat it back out there.
When they got back into Falls Canyon, the bodies were gone.
They just weren't there anymore."

Peter looked at him for a moment before asking, "A woman
and boy?"

"I'm afraid so."

# 12

POMEROY PICKED UP A FOIL-WRAPPED TOWELETTE FROM THE dashboard and tore it open, carefully wiping his face with skin freshener. Dust and leaves swept through the deserted schoolyard across the street, and he felt suddenly lonely and disconnected as he listened to the wind. It reminded him of playing alone on autumn afternoons in the empty field of his neighborhood school. What he remembered most keenly was the drone of distant, unseen airplanes. Somehow there was a world of loneliness in the sound of an airplane. It was sentimental weakness, though, thinking like that now. The past was simply past, and unless you could use it, it was nothing but a liability to recall it.

He tossed a bag full of videotapes into the backseat. He had spent longer in the video store than he'd meant to, looking at titles. Once, five years ago, he'd been at a party for a salesman friend of his that was getting married—not exactly a friend, really, just a man he worked with. They'd drunk beer, the rest of the men had, shown porno movies of the worst kind—women together, men and women committing perversions . . . He had walked out. There was no way he was going to sit around with a bunch of beer-swilling perverts and watch filth.

The video store had a whole section in the back full of movies like that. In the privacy of his own home a man might look into them. Some of them might be quite artistic, really, which was something you could appreciate if there weren't a lot of drunks shouting obscenities at the screen. There was no way he could check one out, though, not face-to-face with the clerk behind the counter. . . .

Even though there were a couple of hours to kill, he had no desire to drive back out into the canyon today. There was the chance that he could shoehorn another cabin owner into thinking about selling, but the cat bite in his hand throbbed, and the wind was just too damned wild, blowing straight down off the hills like that. And besides, there were other highly entertaining things to do.

He pulled into the post office parking lot and cut the engine, then took a padded manila envelope out from under the seat and slid a sheaf of papers halfway out of it. He shuffled through them slowly, stopping to scan a line or two on a page or to glance at a set of figures. He had made the copies in the fifteen-cent Xerox machine at the local grocery store, and some of them were so badly reproduced that they were edged with black shadows. Klein would get the point, though. It wouldn't take more than a couple of clear sentences and he'd get the point as clear and sharp as if he'd been hit with a pickax.

Pomeroy laughed silently, unable to make up his mind. Bills, transcripts, letters—everything he had was pretty good, although most of the letters and bills wouldn't mean much by themselves. They were substantiating evidence, really. Finally he decided on one of the best of the lot, a five-page transcript of a telephone conversation that Klein would no doubt rather not be reminded of. There were a couple of other choice articles among the papers; Klein could have copies of them in due time, if he needed them. The extortion business, if you did it right, was like cooking a bird. You didn't pour the heat to it all at once and burn it to a crisp. You let it simmer.

The transcript itself was ten years old—or at least the original was—and Klein had no idea on earth that it existed, although Pomeroy was willing to bet that Klein hadn't forgotten about the phone call itself. Pomeroy hadn't. He could remember every detail of it.

The shady little business meeting that followed the call had taken place at Angel Stadium: Angels versus Oakland, September 29, 1983. Pomeroy himself had been there along with old Larry Collier and a contractor out in Tustin who did core samples and geological surveys. It had even rained that evening, just a few big drops like a warning out of the sky before the clouds passed on. In the west a rocket had gone up out of Vandenberg, fizzling out and corkscrewing over the Pacific, painting the sky with a smoke trail that was clearly meant to be handwriting. Going into the game, the Angels had been contenders, two games out of first, and then lost that night to Oakland eight to two, sealing their fate on the very same night that Klein was sealing his. That was Klein in a nutshell, always coming close, but never quite making it to the series.

There was a certain synchronicity to things when the game was going right—or wrong, as was the case with Klein and the Angels. The universe played along, dealing out signs and symbols. If you understood the language, you could read your fate in the sky or on a baseball scoreboard.

From the glove compartment, he took a cassette tape of Klein's voice, recorded for posterity, and slid it into a fresh manila envelope along with the transcript of the recording. He had already addressed the envelope with rub-on letters, very neatly. It looked pro. Nothing to arouse suspicion in anyone but Klein himself, and Klein was already suspicious. Once he opened the envelope and took a good hard look at the contents, suspicion wouldn't enter into the transaction anymore.

Wind shook the car, and people up on the sidewalk turned their faces away from it, hurrying to get inside one of the open shops.

He moistened a sponge with water out of a plastic bottle, rubbed the gum on the flap, and sealed the envelope. Then he started the car, drove to the mailbox in front of the post office, and dropped the envelope into the chute. It would probably be routed through the main post office and get to Klein on Monday. By then Klein would have been simmering long enough, and Pomeroy could turn up the heat.

It was late in the afternoon, and the traffic was fairly heavy through Live Oak Canyon, mostly commuters driving home to Coto and Santa Margarita. Pomeroy owned a condo up there himself: athletic club, tennis courts, pool complex. It was close enough so that he could still make it home in time to put a fresh bandage on his hand and take a quick shower before his dinner meeting with Klein.

Traffic cleared, and he swung out onto the highway, heading northeast toward the turnoff to Trabuco Oaks. In his rearview mirror he saw a Volkswagen bus pull up behind him, signaling to make a left, up Parker Street, into the Oaks. A blond woman was driving, and he knew right away who she was.

"Beth," he said out loud. Linda's name only occurred to him afterward, as a sort of echo. He looked at his bandage-wrapped hand. Beth would heal both wounds! The sight of her sent a thrill through him now, and for a moment his breath caught in his throat as it had that morning, as if the mere sight of her would physically incapacitate him. Running into her twice in one day! What were the odds of that? He couldn't let the opportunity slide. It would be the easiest thing in the world right now to find out where she lived.

He breezed past Parker, watching in the mirror as the bus turned left, disappearing beyond the general store. Fifty yards farther, he made a quick U-turn across the left shoulder and pulled straight out onto the highway again.

DETECTIVE SLATER SAT IN SILENCE, LOOKING OUT AT THE STREET.

"What's being done?"

"Nothing," the cop said. "There isn't any case. Just the testimony of one hiker. It was night. The man was scared, alone. When the ranger got back in there he couldn't find anything at all. No blood, no broken-up bushes. Sheriffs looked the place over next day. There wasn't a piece of thread or a scuffed rock. Nothing. Locals back in there hadn't seen or heard anything."

"So what are you saying?" Peter asked. "What the hell happened to the bodies? Nobody was dead? What?"

The cop shrugged. "Hiker might have been full of baloney. Or else the people he saw might not have been dead at all. Maybe they got up and walked away. That's possible. Hell, we get reports of dead bodies around here all the time. Almost always turns out to be someone passed out drunk or a bag lady asleep in the Plaza. So I'm saying that nobody knows what happened out there in the canyon. Might be a half dozen answers for it. They've got the hiker's description of the alleged bodies, though—clothes, hair color."

"What clothes?" Peter asked, suddenly full of both hope and fear. If Amanda and Peter had disappeared out there, they would have been wearing the clothes they'd driven out in. They hadn't brought any others.

"Woman had on a long black dress. The hiker was close enough to see that. Apparently there was some moonlight. The boy . . ."

"He's sure it was a boy?"

"That's what it says here. The boy wore light-colored pants, maybe khakis. White long-sleeve shirt."

"That isn't what Amanda and David were wearing," Peter said. A wave of relief swept across him. "It wasn't them."

Detective Slater shrugged again, noncommittally. "Let's hope not. As far as the sheriff's department knows, it wasn't anyone. They don't have any bodies, just a man's testimony. What got me, though, was the coincidence of the whole thing. You lose your wife and boy out there, and a couple days later a hiker claims to have seen a woman and child dead. It's a small world, but it's not that small. I'm afraid I'll have to ask you to drive out to Santa Ana, soon as you leave here. Sheriff's office is down on north Flower Street, 550 block near the corner of Santa Ana Boulevard, by the courthouse buildings. I called them when I went after the report a few minutes ago."

Peter's head spun. He had spent the last hour processing what he knew, over and over until he couldn't see past it or around it. Now all of that was swept aside by these new revelations. "Am I under suspicion then?" he asked suddenly. "What, I just drive over to the sheriff's department alone?"

"That's the ticket. No crime's been committed as far as I know. Nobody's suspected of anything."

"What do I expect from them? Will they hold me on suspicion of something?"

"Of what?" Detective Slater shook his head slowly. "You shouldn't expect anything except a few questions. Like I said, nobody's under suspicion. If there's no bodies and no evidence of anything, then there's no investigation beyond the information taken from the hiker and the ranger a week ago. If bodies turn up, and if they're identified as your wife and son, then you can bet the sheriff's going to come looking for you. Right now all you've got to do is drive out to Santa Ana and tell them what you told me. I'll file two missing-persons reports and we'll see what comes up. Meanwhile I'll send them out copies of the photos and fingerprints you gave me. That's about it. If you think of something, though, or find out anything, come straight back here."

"Right," Peter said. "Thanks."

The detective stood up and put his pen into his pocket. It was over, this part was. He shook Peter's hand and walked him out to the door, explaining where the sheriff's department was again, where to park, who to ask for. Together they stepped outside, into a sheltered alcove between buildings. Even there, leaves and debris blew along the concrete and out toward the street. "Wind won't quit this year," Slater said.

Peter nodded. He couldn't think of anything to say. The small-talk center in his brain had been temporarily shut down. He wondered if that wasn't one of the things you lost forever if you became insane.

"You know, maybe there's other explanations for this," the detective said, making no move to go back in. "I don't mean the bodies out in the canyon, I mean your wife disappearing."

"What's that?" Peter asked.

"How about custody kidnap? What was the deal there? You say you were separated but not divorced. Was she happy with the arrangements? She got to keep the kid? The house?"

"She would keep David weekdays. He can go to the neighborhood schools that way. He stays with me weekends, holidays, summer vacations. My schedule's good that way."

"That's carved in stone?"

"It will be in another couple of months."

"And she likes that? Lot of mothers wouldn't give a child up that easily, you know. That's a pretty modern idea—sharing custody. Sometimes that kind of thing looks good in theory, but actually doing it is a different thing. How do you know she didn't just take the kid and go? Move to the east or something?"

"She wouldn't do that." Peter said this with conviction. Almost at once, though, he wondered how sure he was about it. "Impossible," he said, after a moment. "Why dump money into airplane tickets to Hawaii? Why leave a thousand dollars in traveler's checks behind, along with your luggage and clothes?"

"Why *not* do all that? If you're putting one over on the world, you want to do a job of it. Convinced the hell out of *you*, didn't it? She have any money? Enough to be independent of you?"

"She has enough. More than me, really—better job. It's me that'll have to tighten the belt. And she owns the house that her parents lived in before they died."

"The house here in Orange. Is that hers?"

"Technically it's both of ours still," Peter said. "It'll be hers when the papers are final."

"What I'd do, maybe, if I were her, is take out a big second, or a home equity loan on her parents' place. Lot of equity in that house. I'd guess, if she owns it outright? Then I'd throw a little of it away on airplane tickets and traveler's checks, set up my husband, and walk away with the kid. She could move out of state and do pretty well. It would cost her, but I'll guarantee you there's people all over the country doing it right now. It's a popular crime. Some states won't even extradite in cases of custody kidnap. Texas is a good bet for that. Living's cheap, too. She could buy a house with cash and bank the rest.''

''I don't think so,'' Peter said. ''I wasn't very perceptive about her sometimes. That's been part of the problem. But I think I would have seen that coming. She wasn't that good when it came to acting. In fact, she wasn't any good at all. She didn't play games. It wasn't in her.''

Slater shrugged. ''Maybe not. I just wanted to point out that there's other ways to look at it. You don't want to jump to any conclusions. Lots of missing people turn up again someday. She wouldn't be the first person to just walk away.''

''Well,'' Peter said. ''Thanks. I don't think so, but I'll keep it in mind. I hope you're right, or that it's something like that.''

''Call me if anything comes up.'' Detective Slater shook Peter's hand again and pulled open the door. ''Good luck,'' he said, and went back in. The wind pushed the door shut behind him.

THE LINE OF SOUTHBOUND CARS STOOD STILL THROUGH LIVE OAK Canyon, and Peter found that he could barely stand the wait. Almost nobody approached from the opposite direction; it was too late in the day for northbound traffic, and Peter was tempted, in order just to be moving, to swing into the oncoming lane and bolt past whatever was holding things up. His hand played across the steering wheel, brushing the horn without pressing it, and he turned the radio on again, listened for a split second, and turned it off.

Through some trick of inner acoustics, he could hear the blood rushing in his head, and he felt enervated, his thoughts scattered.

The wind was blowing hard again, and the air was electric and dry. He hadn't eaten lunch, or breakfast either, for that matter, and he was aware uneasily that he seemed to be letting himself slide, and had been sliding for months.

The morning's conversation with Beth returned to him. She had seen things in him that he himself had been denying, but which must have been obvious: getting up before dawn, wandering through the house, staring at photographs of his family . . .

A horn honked behind him. Traffic was moving again, but he hadn't noticed, despite having been full of nervous impatience only moments ago. He crept forward, edging around a bend and into the opposite lane, past the bumper of a pickup truck sitting sideways in the road, its broken rear axle visible beneath the truck bed. A man in a baseball cap stood at the truck's bumper, talking to a tow truck driver who was hooking the pickup to an elaborately painted towing rig. Peter heard them both laugh, and it occurred to him that the man who could laugh at his own broken-down truck lived an enviable life.

He swung back into the right-hand lane and stepped on the accelerator, watching the rear window of the car ahead, the shifting reflections of blue sky and oak trees in the sunlit sheet of glass. Into his mind slipped the image of a waterfall with two bodies lying at the base, broken and sprawled on the rocks, the dead woman's eyes staring upward toward the top of the cliffs. He saw it clearly, as if it were an etching in an old book that he had looked at countless times. More clearly than that, he *recalled* the face, as if the dead woman were the shadow of someone he once knew. . . .

"No connection," he said out loud. Then, startled by the sound of his own voice, he flipped on the radio again, loud, and rolled the window all the way down so that the wind blew into his face. After a moment he turned the radio off. It sounded like noise to him.

He had only been back into Falls Canyon once, hiking with Beth and Bobby. He knew where the mouth of the canyon lay, hidden by trees and by the overlapping contour of the hillside. There was a path that crossed the stream and angled up the little box canyon. It forked halfway up, a second path leading upward toward the ridge. Another little path ran down from the ridge trail to the top of the falls. He had passed it a number of times when he was hiking into Trabuco Oaks, but he had never followed the path to its end, to the top of the falls.

And yet now he could picture the canyon from above: the high narrow falls, the scattered boulders in the shallow pool, the night-black hair of the dead woman floating on the water, and the pale, moonlit complexion of her upturned face. . . .

He shook his head to wake himself up. They weren't dead. There weren't any bodies. Hell, it was probably a hoax.

At the sheriff's office he had learned nothing new. Detective Slater had been right. There was no "case," no investigation. He almost wished to God that Slater had never mentioned any bodies. It had severed whatever grip he'd had on his imagination.

On impulse he pulled off the road, stopping the Suburban alongside the river-rock wall that skirted the edge of O'Neill Park. He slid out, shut the door, and climbed over the wall, walking up a grassy hillside. Wind rippled the grass like a Kansas wheat field. Beyond the top of the hill there was no traffic noise, nothing at all but the sound of the wind and the cawing of crows somewhere off over the picnic grounds. He sat on a rock and looked down into a little grassy valley that had been cut by a seasonal stream. It was dry now, but a few willows grew up out of the rocky sand. He stared at the willows, trying to focus his thoughts. Beth and Amanda. He had known Beth for something like eight years, since right before she had married Walter. His attraction to her had always had to be tempered by his marriage to Amanda. As pretentious as it had probably sounded, he had meant what he said about being monogamous. That hadn't changed.

And that was the trouble. Clearly his life was still tied up in Amanda and in David and in the house on Monterey Street, in things as crazy and simple as Kool-Aid and Oreo cookies and playing Crazy Eights at the kitchen table, as if those things were magical amulets that carried the broken-off pieces of his soul. He had never come to terms with losing them.

He picked up a stone and threw it down into the sandy creek-bed. So what *did* he want? When he saw Beth again he would have to give her an answer. He owed her that. He owed himself that, which of course had been her point. He had fooled himself into thinking that his recent freedom meant not having to set a course at all, and so he had been drifting. And as was often the case with drifting, it hadn't gotten him anywhere.

Abruptly he stood up and hiked up the hill toward the car, the wind blowing the hair back out of his face now. What he wanted, what he had to do—at least for the moment—was to find Amanda and David.

**15**

POMEROY DELIBERATELY PREVENTED HIMSELF FROM CATCHING up with her. Instead he slowed down, casually checking driveways and side streets, his heart beating hard enough so that it seemed to be running on ahead of him.

He forced himself to be aware of everything—of cloud patterns in the sky, street signs, the faces of people in passing cars—anything that might be a warning. He knew that something had shifted in him, that minutes ago, when setting Klein up outside the post office, he had been full of careful calculation, arranging the future, stacking the deck. Now his mind was loose and staticky. He was full of anticipation, and yet the future, even five minutes away, was nothing but darkness to him. What he anticipated couldn't be expressed, and that could be a dangerous thing if he didn't take things very damned slowly. It was broad daylight, and that was a limiting factor that would protect him from himself, from the kind of rash mistakes that had got him into trouble the last time.

He switched that thought off and paid attention to what he was doing, realizing then that he was heading up toward Klein's place. He braked in order to turn around. He didn't want to spook Klein now. But just then he saw the Volkswagen, parked in the driveway of the house next to Klein's. Beth was halfway across the yard, heading for the front door. Pomeroy could see now that there was a child in the car, horsing around in the backseat.

On a hunch he swung around in a tight U-turn, then took an immediate left on a little dead-end street full of old houses. He turned around again and parked on the shoulder, cutting off the engine and reaching for a map in the glove compartment. He unfolded the map and watched Parker Street over the top of it.

Within a couple of minutes the bus reappeared, heading back down Parker. He reached for the key, thinking to follow, but the bus slowed and turned down toward him. He jerked the map up to hide his face. Would she recognize the car? He *had* to get something else to drive, something less showy than the T-bird. He watched in the mirror, wondering where the hell she was going. What had she been doing at the house up by Klein's? A friend's house? Her own? Or was she heading home now?

He turned on the ignition. He had to get out of there. His mind was suddenly chaotic. If she'd seen him and recognized the car, then he couldn't take the chance of compounding the error by lurking around. What could he accomplish anyway, until it was dark? He pushed the thought aside. He wouldn't ever again put himself at risk by . . . in that way.

But something prevented him from leaving—the barest chance that he would *see* something, *know* something. Human relationships were cumulative, a snowball effect. The more you knew about the person, the closer you got to her. He shut the engine off and studied the street behind him in the rearview mirror.

"Beth." He said her name out loud, almost tasting it. She had pulled into the nearly empty lot of a preschool. She got out of the bus now, together with a boy, and went inside. So that probably *was* her house then, up next to Klein's.

He wondered suddenly if perhaps he shouldn't drive back over there, have a look around while she was busy.

Not in daylight. Not with Klein at home next door.

He felt the familiar emptiness in his chest, the place left hollow when he was in danger of losing control. At the same time he knew he could control himself if he tried. Maybe he hadn't been able to in the past, but he had learned something from that. You could put your mistakes to good use if you paid careful enough attention to them.

After ten minutes, an old Chevy Suburban turned up the block, and Pomeroy knew right away who it was. He'd seen the piece-of-shit car back in the canyon. This would be the boyfriend. What a piece of junk—faded paint, beat-up rack on top. No way was this guy suitable for Beth. He raised the map to hide his face.

When the Suburban pulled into the school parking lot, Pomeroy started the engine and drove slowly away, forcing himself by sheer will to turn left toward the highway rather than up toward the top of Parker Street.

# 16

PETER TURNED LEFT ONTO PARKER STREET, WHICH WAS NAMED after the rancher who had lived at the top of the hill and had once owned most of what was now Trabuco Oaks. Back in the twenties, according to Beth, Parker's son had been murdered when a jealous husband had found his wife and young Parker together in the ranch bunkhouse.

Only a few years ago, the old, long-abandoned bunkhouse was torn down and the bloodstained floorboards hauled away with the rest of the debris. A new house sat on the property now, the lot overbuilt, expensive cars in the drive, all of it an example of the kinds of changes that were threatening to turn the canyons into suburbs.

A few years back the village was a Sleepy Hollow sort of place, with dogs dozing under the live oak trees and lots of vacant land. Now it was built up: old houses renovated, new houses selling for two and three hundred thousand dollars. There were still a few dogs shambling around, but they were wary, as if they knew that times had changed and things weren't quite so sleepy anymore.

Parker Street itself was only a half mile long, ending against a chaparral-covered hillside where the terrain got steep and wild enough to discourage casual development. Sometime in the future they would find a way to blast it into submission, but for now the hillside marked the point where civilization ended at the edge of the wilderness.

Beth rented one of the houses at the top of the street, the last house but one. It was unlikely that she would rent it much longer. She was thirty, nearly ten years younger than Peter, and was a graduate student in cultural anthropology. Bobby was six. Unless something compelling kept them there, they would almost certainly move on. Peter had isolated himself in the canyon in order to avoid moving on.

Bobby laughed a lot and acted silly. He couldn't sustain anger at all. He preferred a world in which things were cheerful and easy, starting with himself. Better to play than to sulk. Peter had learned more from Bobby's philosophy than from all the preachers and teachers he'd ever heard. But like all wise-sounding philosophy, the knowledge was nearly impossible to apply—easier for a kid, maybe.

He saw Beth's bus in the gravel parking lot of the day-care center, an old house that had been painted schoolhouse red and fenced with chain link. It was a cheerful-looking place, half the playground shaded by a pair of enormous sycamores. Plywood cutouts of *Winnie the Pooh* characters decorated one long wall. Peter pulled into the lot, cut the engine, and set the brake, but he didn't get out.

He watched the wind rustle the leaves on the playground trees. Five kids, one of them Bobby, burst out of the back door of the center, followed by a teenage girl in a ponytail who pulled a soccer ball out of the high grass alongside the fence and kicked it at them. The five kids chased the ball, pushing each other out of the way, and soon all of them were kicking it back and forth, using a set of parallel bars as goalposts.

Bobby wore his black cycling cap backward over his blondish brown hair, which dangled over his collar in back. He had on a pair of black sweatpants and an oversize black T-shirt with a skeleton on it, riding a skateboard up a concrete wall that folded over the skeleton's head like a breaking wave. The words "Bone to Skate" were scrawled on the wall in hatchet lettering.

Wind buffeted the quiet sun-warmed car, and the kids' voices, muffled by glass and metal, came to him as if from a great distance as he watched them play. They were completely abandoned to that business. He envied that kind of talent. A few more years and they'd trade it for a handful of beans, and they'd have to make do with the *memory* of playing soccer in a schoolyard on a windy autumn afternoon.

Bobby spotted Peter's Suburban, waved at him, and shouted something that Peter couldn't understand. Peter shrugged and shook his head. Bobby made eating gestures, then rubbed his stomach like a fat man contemplating a meal. Peter gave him the okay sign, and Bobby ran off, chasing the soccer ball.

Feeling almost cheerful, Peter picked up the spud guns from the backseat, took one of them out of the bag, and put the other one into the glove compartment. Then, thinking about it, he climbed out of the car and tossed the first gun back inside onto the passenger seat before shutting the door. It wouldn't be fair to give it to Bobby in front of the other kids. He didn't have a potato for it anyway. They could pick one up down at the general store later.

He stepped into the relative darkness of the day-care center. The low tables were covered with cut-up construction paper and scissors and glue. An aquarium bubbled against the wall, a half dozen rubbery-looking newts bumping their noses against the glass as if they were anxious to see who had come in. Beth stood in the kitchen doorway with her back to Peter, talking, probably, to Julie, the director and teacher. Their talk sounded serious, and so Peter waited in the empty room, not wanting to interrupt.

Beth's long hair was pulled back casually and caught with a clip of Navajo silver. She was wearing dark green jeans and hiking boots and a khaki, long-sleeved shirt like a ranger would wear. Peter sat down on one of the tables and stared at the linoleum floor.

Three weeks ago Beth had taken him on a hike, over the south ridge and down into Bell Canyon. She showed him a big granite rock full of *metates*—smooth holes where Indians had ground acorns hundreds of years back. Once she had found a few pottery shards back in there and a fragment of some sort of stone tool, treasures that were no doubt well worth the hours of scrambling around through scrub oak and sage and prickly pear.

On their hike they had discovered fresh mountain lion tracks along the streambed and Beth reacted as if she'd seen a Hollywood celebrity in a café. She insisted they follow the tracks up a little perpendicular canyon, just to see if they could catch up with the lion, and Peter went along without complaining because he didn't want to look like a city boy.

Tirelessly, she told him all about how California grizzlies with three-inch-long claws used to roam the Santa Ana Mountains, coming down into the ranchos and crippling full-grown cattle with a single blow to the back, then dragging the hundreds of pounds of meat miles up into the scrub to devour it. She seemed to think it was a terrible tragedy that the grizzlies had been hunted to extinction, and Peter agreed that it was a dirty shame, that he'd been looking forward to being devoured back in the scrub.

Bell Canyon was wild and empty. The north-facing hillsides were shaded by immense old oak trees, and the deep green heads of new ferns pushed up through the dark oak mulch. The trail finally more or less disappeared beneath a carpet of autumn leaves, and Peter lost all sense of direction and time as he followed Beth uphill, content merely to watch her move against the backdrop of rocks and trees and sky.

"Here we are," Beth had said to him finally.

They had come out of the woods onto a sunny patch of meadow grass that grew right down into the waters of a clear spring. A succession of mountains and ridges rose one behind the other in the east until they disappeared on the horizon.

Clearly she had led him on the hike with this lonesome destination in mind. She opened her daypack and pulled out a checkered tablecloth, unfolding it on the grass. The two of them lay down on their backs, listening to the silence. A distant pair of vapor trails materialized in the blue sky, the jets moving so high and fast that no sound at all fell to earth.

On the hike, Beth had been talking about bears and lions and edible shrubs, about how you could make soap out of yucca plants and leach the tannic acid out of acorns with lye and water. But as they lay in the grass there was nothing at all worth talking about, and they watched the vapor trails slowly turn into clouddrift and move off down the lazy afternoon sky.

To Peter she looked a little like a character out of a book, lying there in sunshine—maybe a princess who as a baby had been switched with a woodsman's daughter. She was five ten or so, and had a model's slender build. Her khaki shirt, unflattering as it was, couldn't hide her figure, and when she rolled onto her side as if to say something to him, the top three buttons of her shirt were loosened, although they hadn't been only a short time ago.

He lay still, waiting, almost afraid to touch her. When he felt the pressure of her hand on his thigh, suddenly it was unavoidable. Unhurriedly he traced the curve of her breasts above the lacy fabric of her lingerie. He unbuttoned the fourth button of her shirt, and then the fifth, and she sat up, shrugging out of it entirely, and then tugged his shirt out of his jeans as he knelt beside her. She pushed him away and untied her hiking boots herself, pulling them off and pitching them ten feet down the hill. He threw his after them, and both of them stood up, scattering their clothes around the meadow. He pressed against her, lost utterly in the warmth of her body, in the feel of her flesh against his, warming him while the breeze blew down off the wild hillsides at his back.

Leaves drifted down onto the meadow from the solitary trees, the ferns and high grass waved in the wind, the afternoon wore on slowly. Once a red-tailed hawk swooped down over the spring and snatched something up from the edge of the water, and for a moment the air was full of the sound of beating wings. . . .

Hearing her voice, he looked up now. She was saying something to him, looking at him a little oddly from the kitchen doorway, wearing the same shirt that he had helped unbutton that day on the meadow. Recollecting it had dragged him partway up out of the depressing rut his mind had been in all afternoon. At the same time it complicated things utterly, and he understood that despite his resolutions, there were some things he didn't want to lose. On that afternoon in Bell Canyon everything had been easy, but he knew that nothing that good ever stayed easy.

"You okay?" she asked.

"Sure." He managed a smile.

She walked out into the room. "Julie's been telling me that they've had some trouble here today."

"What sort of trouble?" Peter asked, forcing a look of interest onto his face.

"A strange boy hanging around," Julie said to him, following Beth out of the kitchen. She gestured toward the window. "Out there in the brush."

Through the glass Peter could see the trail that led up the hill and onto the ridge. It ran for nearly four miles before meeting up with the Holy Jim Trail. A couple of miles up the ridge, it skirted a hillside right above Peter's house. He and Bobby had hiked home that way from the day-care center once, racing with Beth, who drove down the canyon along the dirt road. Beth had beat them home, but not by much.

"He threw part of the carcass of a fawn over the fence," Julie said. "Hit Betty Tilton with it. She wasn't hurt, but it was pretty traumatic for her. We had to call her mother to come pick her up. He'd been hanging around this morning, I guess, making noises, mostly. Throwing rocks at the kids. One of the kids lost a glider over the fence, and the boy apparently picked it up and ran off with it. Then about an hour later he just rushed at the fence and pitched this dead fawn over."

"Do you think he *killed* it?" Peter asked. "What do you mean, *part of it*?"

"Doesn't look like he killed it," Beth said. "It's in the trash can out there. I'd guess a cougar killed it. Left the head and shoulders. Bones all splintered up. It's been dead for days, dried out from the wind. The boy probably found it up on the ridge and hauled it down.''

''I tried to talk to him,'' Julie said, ''but he just ran off. Later on I heard him crying off in the brush.''

The term ''crying off in the brush'' was startling. For a moment Peter could almost hear the crying, and he thought briefly about Falls Canyon, picturing the face of the boy now, lying beside his mother. . . .

He clipped the thought short. Probably there was nothing in this. Just a kid messing around.

''Couldn't have been foxes?'' Peter asked, looking at Beth. She rolled her eyes at him.

''I *guess* it was him crying,'' Julie said. ''Why he was out there on a day like this I don't know. The wind must have been blowing fifty miles an hour.''

''What can you do about it?'' Peter asked. The story had made him uneasy. There was something strange about it, something dark and suggestive. More coincidence.

''Nothing,'' Julie said. ''It's just a prank. Still, it was such a nasty one that it wrecked the whole day. Kids couldn't even play outside most of the morning.''

''Well,'' Peter said. ''Probably it's nothing. I remember we used to throw earthworms at girls when I was that age.''

''The world's changed,'' Beth said. ''Now it's dried-out deer carcasses.''

Julie walked to the door and shouted for Bobby. In a couple of moments he appeared, out of breath and smiling.

''What's up?'' Peter asked him.

''The moon,'' Bobby said. ''Did Julie tell you about the dead deer head?''

''Yeah,'' Peter said. ''She told us.''

''It's really gross. Can we keep it, Mom?''

''I don't think so,'' Beth said.

''I wasn't here,'' Bobby told Peter. ''I would have kicked his butt if I was.''

''He's lucky you didn't get at him,'' Peter said, ''but you shouldn't be talking about kicking people's butts anyway. The world's already too full of butt kicking. Probably he just wants a friend.''

''A friend?'' Bobby said, clearly unconvinced.

Nodding good-bye to Julie, Beth held the front door open, and the three of them went out.

"So what are you doing tonight?" Peter asked Beth as they walked to the cars. He winked at Bobby, who pretended to cut up food on a plate.

Before she could answer, Bobby said, "Want to eat at the steak house?"

"Sure," Peter said, answering for them both.

"I've got a load of stuff to do," Beth said doubtfully. "I should have gotten more done today, but nothing went right."

Peter shrugged. "You've got to eat."

"That's right," Bobby said. "We've got to eat. I'm as hungry as two dogs."

Beth looked hard at Peter. "You look beat," she said. "What's wrong?"

"Same thing," Peter said. "Nothing went right today." His throat constricted, and he suddenly found himself on the edge of tears.

"Then let's eat at the steak house," Beth said. "I've got nothing in the house anyway but frozen macaroni and cheese. And it's Saturday, we better get over there now, before the rush."

"Hey," Peter said, forcing himself to be cheerful, "I bought something in town today."

"For me?" Bobby asked, raising his eyebrows.

"Uh-uh," Peter said. "It's for your mother. A cooking tool." He pulled open the door of the Suburban and picked up the spud gun, showing it to Bobby and Beth.

"What is it?" Bobby asked.

"Potato laser," Peter said. "It's from a planet in the Milky Way called Idaho. They shoot potatoes there instead of bullets."

"Idaho's not a planet," Bobby said. "It's a state." He took the gun from Peter and pulled the plastic away from the cardboard, waving the gun around like a gangster and pretending to shoot his mother's car. "What does this shoot?"

"Potatoes," Peter said.

"You're kidding, of course." Beth took the cardboard backing from Bobby. She turned it over and scanned the instructions, then fixed Peter with a withering look. "It *does* shoot potatoes," she said flatly. "Pieces of them."

"Zucchini, too," Peter said.

"I think we can buy a potato at Emory's," Bobby said, opening up the passenger-side door of the Suburban and climbing in. "I'll drive down there with Peter, Mom. We'll meet you." He pulled the heavy door shut, and Peter shrugged helplessly at Beth, as if the world and its crazy affairs were beyond his control.

On the way down to the steak house Bobby talked rapid-fire about the deer head in the trash can and about how he wanted to take it and hang it on the wall like hunters did. But he said nothing about his flight back home from visiting his father or about the week he had spent there or about having to come back early because his father was a busy man.

Perhaps he had already bottled it up and put it away in the cardboard carton that people used to store that kind of thing, shoving it out of sight on some back shelf of their minds. Peter had been dumping stuff into his own carton for too damned long, closing the lid over it, carrying it around until the bottom had fallen out. If he could help it, he wasn't going to let Bobby do the same thing.

THE CLATTER OF PLATES AND BOTTLES WAS GIVING KLEIN A HEAD-ache. If he had been in any other company there wouldn't have been a problem, but he was eating at the steak house with Pomeroy, who had been explaining things in detail—gesturing, offering Klein unnecessary and unwanted advice.

There were ten good reasons not to be there listening to Pomeroy, and only one good reason *to* be there. Pomeroy was becoming a liability. It was necessary right now to humor him, and then to damned well think of some way to get him out of the picture entirely. Short of murder, Klein didn't have any ideas.

Pomeroy had even come up to the house today. Thank God Lorna hadn't been home. Pomeroy couldn't be persuaded that he and Klein shouldn't seem to be closely associated with each other, and he dropped by like an old friend, full of howdies, smirking around as if he had a secret that he couldn't share. Either he was the most happily self-deluded man Klein had ever met, or else he had a bigger agenda, and was running some kind of lowball bluff. He yammered on now, looking grave, talking about the world of car sales.

Klein had lost track of what the point was. He realized he hadn't eaten half of his steak, which was the size of a packing crate. Normally he could put away the sixteen-ounce sirloin without any problem, but Pomeroy had killed his appetite. He was nervous about simply being seen in the company of the man. The words *fraud* and *collusion* kept popping up in his mind like idiot cards.

The waitress appeared right then and Pomeroy couldn't keep his eyes off her tight jeans. Klein almost told him to quit being such a damned hormone case, but talking sense to him was like shooting peas into a can.

"Another beer?" the waitress asked Klein. She picked up his empty bottle.

"I'm fine, Peg, thanks."

"I'll have another glass of milk. A refill," Pomeroy said to her. "And *cold* this time, if you please. That last one was tepid. Check the date stamp on the dispenser. I think it's about to turn. If you start giving your customers bad milk, you won't have any customers left. That's a tip."

The waitress nodded at him. "Sure," she said, taking away his half-empty glass.

When she was gone, Klein said, "I used to work in a restaurant, back before I got into construction. There was a guy I worked with, a waiter, who used to hate that kind of thing."

"What kind of thing was that?"

"Advice from a customer. Complaints."

"Hey," Pomeroy said, holding his hands out. "The milk wasn't cold, period. It's another case of the customer being right."

"This guy I worked with, you know what he'd do to your milk?"

"What?"

"You don't want to know."

"That's disgusting," Pomeroy said, "whatever it was. Typical of small minds, I suppose."

Klein shrugged.

The waitress returned with the fresh milk along with a small stainless steel mixing bowl half full of ice. She sank the milk into the ice, winked at Klein, and left.

"What you have to realize," Pomeroy said, nodding at the milk, "is that if you can judge a person's character, eventually you can get what you want from them." He stared at Klein for a moment, as if he had said something significant and was letting it sink in. Then he turned away and watched the waitress work the tables along the far wall. Smiling faintly, Pomeroy spun the milk glass in the bowl of ice, cooling it off. Klein wanted to dump it over his head.

"This pal of yours . . ." Pomeroy started to say.

"What *pal*?"

"Your friend who . . . what? Spit in people's milk?"

"That was a guy I *worked* with. He was an asshole. He wasn't my *pal*."

"Well, he'd love this. . . ."

Klein listened with growing attention to the story of the rats in the water tank. Pomeroy seemed to have worked it all out very carefully. He knew just how sick you'd get from drinking contaminated water. No real damage if you got to the antibiotics in time. Little bit of a bug. Some gastrointestinal distress, that's all. Over in a day or two. Of course you'd have to drain the tank and disinfect it and fill it again. And you'd go crazy wondering how the hell rats had got in there in the first place. But really what it was was a minor sort of irritation, something to make an old man fed up with living out in the sticks, where you were at the mercy of every damned rat in creation.

Klein nodded, following the story uneasily. Peg walked past and he signaled her. "I think I need another beer after all," he said. He fought to maintain some self-control, but he was losing badly. Pomeroy was walking all over him. Why? That's what Klein wondered. Pomeroy was going to lengths here. Clearly he thought he had some kind of upper hand, but in regard to what? And what really frosted Klein was that he had seen it coming. He had known what Pomeroy was, that he was capable of this kind of vicious trick. This was his own damned fault.

Ten years ago he and Pomeroy had some dealings together, back when Pomeroy had been working for Delta Core Sampling, a Newport Beach firm that had finally been litigated to death. The building that housed the company had burned under mysterious circumstances, eradicating incriminating records.

Providing false core samples had been the issue in the litigation. A couple of houses out in Oceanview Heights had slid down a hillside that had turned out to be clay instead of bedrock. The core samples provided by Delta had been fakes, allegedly drilled out of an adjacent hill. Klein had built the houses. That was a few years before he married Lorna—part of a past that was better left in shadow. The owner of the drilling company, Pomeroy's boss, had died of a heart attack. Pomeroy had walked away and become a car salesman, apparently very successful, although there was no explaining the success.

So there were reasons that Pomeroy could sit here telling Klein about poisoning a man's water tank with dead rats, and Klein couldn't just hit him over the head with a beer bottle and do the world a hell of a favor. The second most regrettable thing in Klein's life was getting involved with Pomeroy again. The truth was, Klein had set the man loose on the canyon, bankrolled him, pep-talked him. Monsters by Dr. Kleinstein.

And that's where the trouble would come from. It wouldn't be fraud that would take them all down, it would be Pomeroy and his bag full of rats.

"So when I tried to pet the creature," Pomeroy said, showing Klein his bandaged hand, "it took a bite out of me."

"Can't imagine why," Klein said.

Pomeroy shook his head, as if he couldn't imagine why, either. "I've got a couple of other nice plans, too. Even better. We'll wedge the old man out of there yet. That's the nicest place in the canyon. I'm thinking of keeping it for myself. A little investment."

"Why don't you lay off the nice *plans*," Klein said, working to keep from shouting. "A checkbook ought to do the trick. We've had this conversation more than once. We've picked up a few places, we've got a lot of maybes, we've got twenty people to talk to still. All signs point to *success*. Leave the goddamned rats at home from now on. And as far as personal investments go, keep the bigger picture in mind."

"Relax," Pomeroy said, lowering his voice. "The beauty of this is that it's rats. They're a naturally occurring pest out there. Put arsenic in the tank, and they'll come looking for you. Put a rat in the tank and they put out a warrant on Mother Nature. It's foolproof. It's biodegradable."

"Clear it with me next time."

Pomeroy shrugged.

"Mr. Ackroyd happens to be a friend of my wife's," Klein said. "They used to work together. He's a nice old guy. Now what the hell am I going to do, just let him get sick? Shit." He looked around tiredly. With Pomeroy, if it wasn't one thing, it was another. The man was a grab bag of bad surprises.

"It's nothing personal," Pomeroy said. "It's business."

"It's *bad* business," Klein said. "You've got to remember that we've got a fairly heavy backer here. Sloane Investments, I mean. They prefer a soft touch. You don't have one. Take my advice and work one up before you wake them up, will you? This whole thing could dissolve in about a dozen phone calls."

"Sometimes a soft touch doesn't work. Sometimes you've got to push someone."

"Don't try to push me."

Pomeroy sat back in his chair. "There's pushing and there's pushing," he said. Then, widening his eyes, he rolled up a paper napkin, shoved an end into the candle vase, and let the paper catch fire. He dropped the burning napkin into the bowl full of ice and water alongside his milk glass, pushing it under the ice with his finger.

"Hey," he said, standing up. "There's someone I know. Small damned world, isn't it?"

Klein didn't look up. Any friend of Pomeroy's was sure to be worth avoiding.

"Thanks for dinner," Pomeroy said. "I'll cover the tip. Next time let's try a restaurant that's a little more upscale, though. All these chopped-up neckties hanging from the ceiling give me the creeps. That can't be sanitary." He threw two singles on the table and walked away.

"Anything more?" Peggy asked Klein a few moments later.

"What? No. I guess not," Klein said. "Look, I'm sorry about that guy. He's the king of the jerks."

"I guess I've seen worse."

"They don't come any worse," Klein said, taking the check from her. He calculated a twenty-percent tip, put the money on the table along with Pomeroy's two dollars, and got up to go. Then he saw that Pomeroy hadn't left yet. He was standing at a table near the front entrance, gesturing and talking. Seated at the table, not talking, was Beth Potter—Klein's next-door neighbor—along with her son and her boyfriend. Klein sat back down, looking away quickly when he saw Pomeroy point in his direction. In his mind he pictured card houses collapsing.

"Stupid," he muttered. "Really stupid."

**18**

"THAT ONE WAS MINE, I THINK," BOBBY SAID, POINTING AT A pink-and-yellow necktie that hung from the steak house ceiling. "My dad used to take me here all the time."

A party of a half dozen people sat at an adjacent table. Three of them wore loud ties that had been cut in half when they entered the restaurant. Yellow cardboard triangles had been stapled on beneath the knots, with the words "I lost my tie at a necktie party at Trabuco Oaks" scrawled across the cardboard in blue felt pen. Ten thousand severed ties hung from the wooden ceiling like multicolored bats. Peter realized that he had a hell of a headache, and that he was tensing the muscles in his jaw without meaning to.

"Take your hat off," Beth said to Bobby.

"How come?"

"Because it's polite."

"That guy over there's got one on," Bobby said, gesturing across the room at a man who looked like a lumberjack.

"I know him," Peter said. "He's got a condition. Otherwise he wouldn't be wearing it."

Bobby took off his hat unhappily and tried to smooth his hair down with his fingers. "Can I have some quarters?" he asked.

A video game stood just inside the doorway, around the corner in the waiting area. Peter dug five quarters out of his pants pocket and gave them to Bobby, who stood up, telling his mother to order him a cheeseburger and a Coke. No longer at the table, he put his hat back on.

"His father took him here *once*," Beth said when Bobby had gone. "Somehow Bobby always inflates it. He *promised* to take him all the time, but he never did. He used to call up and set up a time, but then he wouldn't show up. The first time it happened Bobby went outside to wait by the street. He must have sat on that eucalyptus log out front for two hours, waiting for his father, but the dirty bastard just never showed. He called the next day to explain. The first of many explanations.''

Peter found suddenly that he was crying—for Bobby, for himself, for a world that fell apart like a badly made toy. The tears had come out of nowhere.

He rubbed his eyes and forehead, shading his face, trying to hide his crying from the people around him. Then he forced himself to take a deep breath and tried to drink out of his water glass, but his hand shook and he spilled water on the tabletop. He forced a swallow past the lump in his throat and sat back in his chair, forcing a smile, as if to admit that he was a fool.

''What's wrong?'' Beth asked anxiously. She sat forward, lowering her voice. ''What's your condition? It's what I said this morning, isn't it? I didn't say it very well.''

Peter hesitated. He thought he could hear the wind blowing outside. The sound of it mingled with the clank of dishes and the drum of footsteps on the plank floor. ''Amanda and David have disappeared.''

''What do you mean 'disappeared'?''

He shrugged.

''Do you mean she took David and left? To tell you the truth, I considered that pretty strongly myself for a couple of weeks when it looked like Walter was going to insist on some kind of joint custody. He backed down, but I was ready to go. It can be a really bad mistake, though.''

He shook his head. ''I mean something's happened to them.'' He drained his water glass. Bobby reappeared just then, empty-handed. He hadn't been gone more than two minutes.

''Got any more quarters?'' he asked.

''Yeah,'' Peter said, smiling crookedly. He pulled out his wallet and found five singles. ''Get change from the cashier, okay? And put a couple quarters in the jukebox.''

''Five bucks?'' Bobby asked.

''Use it all,'' Peter said to him. Bobby left again, tucking the bills into his pocket. The look on his face brightened Peter up a little, enough for him to find the words necessary to tell Beth about Amanda's disappearance and about his trip to the sheriff's office that morning.

She sat silently, letting him talk. When he was done he shrugged, not trusting himself to say any more.

''And they're not going to do *anything*?'' she asked.

''Nothing they can do.''

"I heard about that incident in Falls Canyon. It's harder than hell even to find it, let alone to get back up in there. This time of year it's all choked with brush. Did Amanda like to hike? Would she have gone out of her way like that?"

Peter shook his head. "She played tennis if the courts were clean enough, but that's about it."

"Well, I think it's pure coincidence about what the hiker saw out there, if he saw anything at all. There's no way it has anything to do with Amanda and David."

"She might have tried to walk back here to the Oaks across the ridge," Peter said. "David knew about the trail. They might have . . ." He paused for a moment, looking for the right words. "They might have found the falls from the top. I don't know. She was pretty mad, I guess."

"Mad? Mad enough to what? Commit a double suicide with her son by jumping off the top of the falls? That's not mad, Peter, that's something different. You really believe that?"

He shook his head.

"How can you be sure she hasn't just taken off? Divorce screws people up. Being mad is like being drunk, you know. It makes you do things that you'd never do sober."

"Not a chance," Peter said, explaining about the traveler's checks and the plane tickets. "Nobody leaves their money behind when they skip town."

"What if she declared the checks lost," Beth asked, "and then picked up replacement checks at American Express? That's what I'd have done. Did you call the airlines? Maybe she did the same thing there. For that matter, who says she's not in Hawaii?"

Peter was silenced by the idea. The checks thing hadn't occurred to him. Still, he just didn't believe it. "I know her," he said. "That just isn't Amanda."

"You don't know Amanda mad," Beth said. "Believe me. I don't know her nearly as well as you do, but I know that much. I thought I knew myself, but I didn't. There were times when I could have killed Walter, and I'm not exaggerating when I say that. If you had seen Bobby sitting on that log waiting for him, trying not to cry as it got darker and darker out, you'd have killed the bastard yourself."

Before he could say anything more, their waitress appeared. "Peter," she said, looking surprised. Then she looked briefly and coolly at Beth before looking back at Peter again.

"Hi, Peg," Peter said. "This is Beth." Then to Beth he said, "Peggy's a friend of Amanda's."

"Glad to meet you," Beth said.

"I guess I'll have a Coors," Peter said.

"You sounded pretty screwed up on the phone this afternoon," Peggy said. "Everything okay?" She looked at Beth again, as if this had been said partly for her benefit.

"Yeah," Peter said. "Everything's fine."

"Something to drink?" she asked Beth.

"Iced tea, thanks."

"Right," she said. "A Coors and an iced tea coming up."

"And a Coke for my son," Beth said.

They ordered food then, and Peggy walked away toward the kitchen.

"Woof," Beth said. "Did you see the look she gave me?"

Peter shook his head. "She's not like that. That wasn't a look."

"That was an iron-clad look. You could have sailed it through a hurricane. She doesn't know about this, about Amanda disappearing?"

"I . . . ." Peter sat back and stared at the ties hanging from the ceiling. "I couldn't. I can't talk about it. I called a few people this afternoon just to see if maybe somebody would say something to clear things up. Everyone thinks she's in Hawaii. I didn't tell them anything different."

"To hell with it, then. Tell them some other time. What can you do, though? Did the cop suggest anything you can do?"

"Yeah," Peter said. "He told me that I can avoid leaving town. Hell, I don't know. I guess I'll go door to door. See if anyone out in the canyon recognizes them from a photo." Suddenly he was crying again. Going door to door with an old photo—the idea of it seemed pitiful to him, and the windy night outside was vast and empty.

"Shit," he said, wiping his eyes. "I just don't *do* this."

"Yes, you do," Beth said, reaching across and putting her hand on his arm. He was struck with how beautiful she was, with how much he wanted her help in this.

"You know," she said, "I came around to see you later on this morning, but you weren't there."

"When?"

"Ten, I guess. You were in town. I shouldn't have walked out on you like that."

"That's all right. You had stuff to do and all. . . ."

"Not that much stuff. I said enough to stir you up and then I left. Anyway, for what it's worth, I wanted you to know that I hiked back over later."

"Thanks," Peter said. "It's worth a lot. I have to say something about it, though."

"Say what you have to say."

"I've got to find Amanda and David," he said. "I have to get them back."

"Of course," Beth said.

"I don't want you to think . . ."

"What?"

"It's what you were talking about this morning. I've done some thinking since then."

"So have I," she said. "Why don't you do what you have to do? You don't need to make any excuses or apologies to me. Give yourself a little more credit. You're not some kind of villain in this. It's not your *fault*."

He sat there silently for a moment. There was no point in going into more detail, about the argument, about him driving away mad and leaving Amanda and David alone. "Still coming over tomorrow?" he asked.

"Bobby's looking forward to it."

There was a hand on Peter's shoulder then. It was Bobby, carrying a couple of dollar bills.

"I'm bored," Bobby said. "They ought to have more than one machine here. What's wrong?" he asked Peter, suddenly looking into his face.

Peter wiped his eyes again. "Nothing," he said. "I've got a bone in my leg."

"Me too," Bobby said. "It's nothing to cry about." Then he sat down and picked up a menu.

"Kids are too smart," Peter said to Beth. "My mother used to tell me about having a bone in her leg and I was perfectly satisfied. Now kids know all about human anatomy."

"I even know how the human heart works," Bobby said. "We learned about it. It's just a bunch of valves."

Peter stared at him, unable to think of anything to say, and right then Beth reached over and pulled Bobby's hat off. He tried to pin it to his head, but he wasn't quick enough. She put it in her lap, as if to guard it.

"Why can't *I* have a condition?" Bobby asked.

"You're not old enough to have a condition," Peter told him. "If you wear a hat at the table you insult everyone in here. None of them will be able to eat. It's too disturbing. The problem is that back when people were apes, they used to eat out of their hats. That was before they invented plates. So if people see someone wearing a hat at the table now, it reminds them that they used to be apes.''

"Your mother's side of the family was never apes," Beth said to Bobby. "We don't wear hats at the table because we've got too much class. So forget the hat." She looked around just then, as if searching for the waitress, but then suddenly looked back down at the table and said, "Oh, shit—shoot," and began studying her silverware.

"What?" Peter asked.

"*Ummm*," Bobby said to his mother, shaking his head, "that's *way* worse than my hat."

"That guy over there. Don't look up." She glanced behind her. "Never mind. He's seen me. Here he comes."

A man walked toward them, smiling like a television evangelist. His hair was perfect, not a strand out of place. "Well," he said, holding out his hand. "It's a small world, a helluva small world."

Peter shook his hand, which was rubbery. He was reminded of the joke chickens at the Sprouse Reitz that morning.

"Henry Adams," he said, and then he reached across and tousled Bobby's hair. "What's your name, fellah?"

"Bobby," Bobby said, and looked at Beth, who reluctantly handed him his hat back. He put the hat on, yanking it low over his forehead.

To Peter the man said, "I met the little lady out in the canyon this morning. You must be . . . ?"

"Peter Travers. You've got a place in the canyon?"

"No," the man said, "I'm shopping around, talking to a few people. I love this area. I'm interested in the environment."

"Good," Peter said. "So am I." There seemed to be a wall of dead air behind the man's words, as if Peter were talking into a vacancy. "It's end-to-end environment out here," Peter said. He found suddenly that he didn't like the man and was right at the edge of saying something outright insulting. He told himself to calm down. His patience was about one molecule thin. The man looked like the grinning salesman from hell, but that was no reason to pick a fight.

"Your place up for sale?"

Peter was struck forcibly by the thought. Selling his place

hadn't occurred to him, and he wondered for the first time what it was worth. Prices were going up like crazy out there, and lots of people were selling. His house was falling apart, literally. It had looked pretty rickety when he moved in, but since then he had really gotten a chance to take a close look at it. . . . "I don't know," he said.

"Here's my card." Peter took it, and Adams looked hard at Beth, smiling, but without any real emotion in the smile. "I'm certain I'll see *you* again," he said to her.

She hesitated long enough for the silence to become awkward, and Adams broke it by becoming hearty. "Think about making me an offer," he said to Peter. "That was cabin number . . . ?"

"Twelve," Peter said, immediately regretting having said it.

The man left, winking hard at Peggy, who just then showed up with their drinks.

"Friend of yours?" she asked Peter.

"Not mine," Peter said quickly.

"Creepola," Beth said. "I ran into him snooping around behind Mr. Ackroyd's place when I was heading back home this morning. I think he tried to put the make on me. He actually asked what my sign was."

"Him?" Peter asked.

"Yeah. I don't know what he was up to."

"He was eating with a guy in the back," Peggy said. "He's a regular customer, the other guy is. Lives right around here."

"It's Mr. Klein!" Bobby said suddenly, pointing toward the adjacent room. A man waved toward them, just getting up from his chair.

"That's him," Peggy said. She turned away, heading toward another table.

It seemed to Peter that Klein looked embarrassed, almost hunted, as if he wished there had been a handy back door, a way he could have avoided being seen. He'd only met the man a couple of times, but he knew Bobby liked him, and that was a good recommendation.

"Mr. Klein used to play baseball," Bobby said.

He approached the table. "Getting down in front of those grounders?" he asked Bobby. "Don't be afraid to dig 'em out of there. That's why God gave you a body, so you could get hit a couple of times."

"You remember Peter?" Beth asked.

"Of course," Klein said, putting out his hand.

Peter shook it. "Wife's not here?" he asked.

"This was business," Klein said, as if it were already clear that his wife wasn't welcome when it came to business matters.

"Who *was* that guy?" Beth asked. "I seem to be running into him all over the place."

Klein hesitated, as if he were surprised by the question. "He's just a guy looking for something to buy. He knew I was a contractor and he thought that maybe I had a lead on some kind of property out here. He's got good money to spend, but I told him I couldn't help him. I'm a contractor; I'm not in the real estate business." He winked at Bobby.

"What's his name?" Beth asked.

"What?" Klein said.

"I was wondering what his name was."

"I've got his card here," Peter said helpfully, and Beth rolled her eyes at him, as if he'd made some sort of blunder. " 'Henry Adams,' it says. Under that it says, 'Quality, an American way of life.' "

"What's that mean?" Bobby asked.

"Nobody knows," Peter said, throwing the card down on the tabletop.

"It means you don't go out to play ball unless you give it a hundred percent," Klein said. "Am I right?"

"Sure," Bobby said.

"Then keep it up, champ. With that arm of yours you'll make the majors." He looked at his watch, registered surprise, and said, "I better beat it, I guess. Nice talking to you folks." He hurried away toward the door.

"I wonder if that's the guy's real name," Beth said.

"Of course it is," Peter said. "Why shouldn't it be?"

The food arrived just then. Peter's steak covered most of the plate, and there were enough french fries and ranch beans to feed half the population of the county. "Let me show you how an ape eats," he said to Bobby.

**19**

BY EIGHT O'CLOCK THE SUN HAD GONE DOWN BEYOND THE RIDGE, and a broad black shadow had swept the canyon into evening. Above, on the ridges and the brush-covered hillsides, the chaparral shone pink and purple and gray in the waning light. Peter bumped along in the Suburban, edging around potholes and creeping across rocky, wind-scoured washes. Leaves blew across the hood of the car like tumbling black shadows in the darkness.

The lower end of the road cut through a gravelly section of river bottom where the canyon widened out. There were stands of sumac and greasewood and a few scrub oaks and stunted sycamores, but the low vegetation was upstaged by the hulks of stripped cars, rusty and shot full of bullet holes.

About a mile in, the canyon narrowed, and the steep walls rose away on either side, deepening the evening twilight. The Suburban navigated through the darkness, the headlights barely penetrating the black spaces between the heavy trees on either side of the road.

Peter was full of steak and french fries and salad, and could almost imagine being able to fall asleep tonight—something that would have seemed impossible to him a few hours ago. Beth and Bobby were coming over tomorrow. He would take things a day at a time.

The Suburban rounded a curve, its headlights momentarily illuminating the waters of Trabuco Creek, which was lined with alders and edged with enormous water-polished lumps of granite. Falls Canyon, where the hiker had supposedly seen the bodies, lay somewhere off to the left, and Peter slowed down, suddenly imagining the narrow, rock-strewn canyon again, littered with autumn leaves and fallen limbs.

Although no one had described the scene to him in any detail, he still pictured it with chilling clarity: the crumpled bodies of the woman and child, veiled by mist, lying half-submerged in the shallow pool at the base of the falls, their clothes buoyed up on the moving current, strands of the woman's hair trailing away from her upturned face like delicate waterweeds. . . .

The Suburban crept along as Peter looked out into the night, abruptly certain that he would be able to see something meaningful in the dark tapestry of the forest. The trees and the shadows were suddenly compelling, as if he were reentering the abandoned landscape of a long-forgotten dream. Something, an answer, a cipher, lay hidden in the windblown darkness. . . .

He suddenly saw a movement in the rocks along the creek.

He stopped the Suburban, shifted, backed up far enough for the headlights to illuminate the rocks again. Then, shifting into forward, he pulled off onto a grassy little turnout, shifted into park, and let the engine idle.

He had glimpsed it only for a split second—something, someone, moving along the trail. What remained in his mind was the memory of dark fabric billowing in the wind, just as it had billowed on the top of the pool of water in his memory only moments ago.

He watched, barely breathing, slowly growing more and more conscious of the wind-haunted darkness around him, thinking about the disappearance of Amanda and David, automatically putting their faces on the bodies in the pool. Beyond the glow of the headlights the trees were night black, their ponderous limbs swaying against an inky backdrop of vegetation and rocky canyon wall.

He switched the lights off, leaving his hand on the knob. The Suburban shuddered in the wind, and dry leaves and twigs ticked against the door panels and windows. Moonlight gleamed on the creek waters. As his eyes adjusted to the darkness, he could see farther into the trees, making out a grassy little clearing across the creek and a cave mouth in the steep hillside.

But now nothing moved aside from the wind-shifting vegetation. Whatever it was—probably an animal—had gone. That it had anything to do with Amanda's disappearance was impossible. His imagination was running him ragged. He pulled the lights back on, shifted into reverse, and glanced into the side mirror.

A face stared back at him, reflected in the mirror: a woman's face, her flesh ivory white in the moonlight, her long black dress and black hair tossed by the wind.

He slammed his hand down onto the steering wheel, accidentally honking the horn, then slammed the transmission into drive, jerked the wheel savagely to the right, punched the accelerator, and drove straight through the brush alongside the turnout and up onto the road before stopping and shifting again into reverse, the backup lights blinking on.

He swiveled around to look, gripping the steering wheel to keep his hands from shaking. The woman was gone. He slammed the door locks down one after another, catching sight just then of movement across the creek, someone—the woman in black—disappearing into the trees.

For one hollow moment he had been certain it was Amanda. He had *known* it. The sight of her ghostly face in the mirror had unnerved him. Now, although he could still picture the woman's face, he knew absolutely that she wasn't Amanda; and just as absolutely he knew who she was: the woman he had pictured lying dead at the base of the falls.

**20**

THE TELEPHONE WOKE BETH OUT OF A DEEP SLEEP, AND SHE SAT up in bed confused, her heart pounding, unable to identify the source of the ringing until the last remnants of her dream evaporated from her mind. Then she fumbled for the phone, wanting to silence it before it woke Bobby. There was something fearful about a late-night telephone call. Never good news.

After saying hello she waited. There was only silence at the other end. She could tell that the line was open, but that's all. Then a man's voice said, "I've been wanting to talk to you."

"Peter?" she asked, but when there was no immediate answer, she hung up. Peter didn't have a phone. It hadn't sounded like Peter's voice.

She sat for a moment, waiting for the phone to ring again. She was certain she had locked both doors. The wind blew outside, shaking the wooden screens on the windows and rustling through the eucalyptus trees that grew at the edge of the driveway. Moonlight shone through the wooden blinds, dimly illuminating the room. Probably the call meant nothing, a sick prank.

Wide awake now, she climbed out of bed and crossed the room. When the phone rang again she was almost to the door. She ran back to the nightstand and snatched up the receiver, not saying anything, but listening again to the airy silence of an open line. Then the same voice said, "I'm close by." The sound was muffled, like someone talking through a bundle of cloth. She could hear a metallic scraping—the sound of a steel telephone cord against the metal wall of a phone booth. "I was wondering . . ." but she slammed down the receiver, holding it against the phone as if it would jump off by itself.

She picked it up again and after listening for a dial tone, set the receiver on the nightstand, waiting out the thirty seconds it took for the recording to come on advising her to hang up. She muffled the receiver while it pulsed, then put it back down.

She walked out into the living room and checked the dead bolt, which was locked, just as she remembered. There was no sound from Bobby's room; he was still asleep. She went into the kitchen and looked out at her neighbor's house. It was dark, but she could see that their Jaguar was parked in the driveway, blocking the closed garage door. No doubt they were home. She found their number in the phone book and wrote it out on a piece of paper that she brought back into the bedroom with her, laying it next to the phone.

Completely awake now, she roamed through the house again, looking in on Bobby, who was sleeping among a heap of stuffed animals. After pulling his comforter over him, she went back into the living room and moved the blinds aside, looking out at the moonlit street. The wind had diminished a little, and the night was quieter than it had been.

Why had he said he was "close," unless he *was*? And why disguise his voice, unless he knew her?

Nothing more than to frighten her, probably. Well, it had worked. She dropped the blinds and went back to bed, where she lay with the light on, aware of the uncradled receiver on the nightstand, picking out and identifying stray sounds beyond the window. After a moment she opened a book and tried to read.

# 21

PETER THREW THE DOOR OPEN AND JUMPED OUT ONTO THE ROAD. "Wait!" he shouted, but the woman was already gone and the wind tore the word away so that he could barely hear it himself. He *had* to speak with her. He had seen her face in his mind a half dozen times that day. A single question . . .

Tree limbs lashed overhead, and the night was full of the sound of tearing and breaking. Shrouds of leaves rose from the forest floor, whipping into the air, whirling away down the canyon. He turned his head away from the onslaught, grabbing his leather jacket off the seat before slamming the door and loping down the hillside trail that led to the creek.

The woman had disappeared into the leafy darkness of the alders, moving upstream toward the foot of Falls Canyon. Looking for a crossing, he followed the creek until the trail was blocked by thickly growing willows. The water ran fast and shallow there, and he stumbled his way across, the half-exposed rocks shifting and tilting under his weight as he stepped from one to another.

The trees grew thick on the other side of the creek, old oaks with such a heavy canopy of limbs that their shadows were unbroken by moonlight. Darkness swallowed the steepening trail and there was nothing but night and wind. He peered into the gloom ahead, looking for movement issuing from beneath the trees at the verge of the steepening hillside. Here the trail forked, one path angling steeply upward toward the ridge, the other winding through grass and brush into the mouth of Falls Canyon, which lay hidden in the distance beyond a heavy tumble of rocks. There was nobody visible in either direction.

The wind fell off abruptly, the night quiet and still. He listened for the sound of footsteps, sliding rock, broken branches. Nothing. She had disappeared. She'd been hurrying, but so had he, and it struck him uneasily that she was close to him at that very moment, perhaps watching him.

When he had looked into the car's mirror he had seen Amanda, and although he knew it was crazy and impossible, it was Amanda's face, Amanda's presence, that he felt now, along with a wild, indeterminate fear for her safety. The smell of sage and oak leaves rose up around him as he stood listening, and in the momentary silence he heard from somewhere above him the plaintive sound of a child crying.

Fear slammed up into his throat, not for himself, but for the woman and her child, a wild despair, the certain knowledge that unless he found them, the dark dream of their death would become solid and real. Suddenly he knew that she had taken the path to the ridge, that she had somehow moved far ahead of him, too far. He ran, clambering up the trail, slipping and sliding on broken rock, scrabbling with his hands. The wind rose again, and the stiff brush on the hillside shuddered in the silver moonlight, animated like images in a jerky old film. There was the sound of crying again—faint, distant, muffled almost immediately by the rising wind and followed closely by an answering cry, a woman's voice, calling from somewhere above.

He threw his weight forward, grabbing the stiff shrubs along the trail, hauling himself up the scree-covered slope. Rocks scattered from beneath his feet and rattled away down the hill. He slipped, slid backward, rolled into the brush and caught himself, then immediately scrambled upward again, tasting dirt in his mouth, windblown debris stinging his face.

The path leveled again and he found himself on a broad, rock- and scrub-covered terrace, the trail running parallel to the canyon now, wind coursing unhindered out of the east. The trail switch-backed through the brush, so that the canyon was sometimes visible away to his left, sometimes hidden from view. Somewhere ahead lay the dense line of alders that shaded the stream at the top of Falls Canyon. He stopped momentarily, cocking his head to listen, and although it must have been impossible above the rush of wind, he thought he heard the sound of footsteps somewhere ahead. There was a smell in the air, traces of jasmine, like a woman's perfume.

He began to run blindly, the trail nearly level now, and in a moment he broke from the dense chaparral onto an empty, moonlit meadow some hundred yards across. Wind swept the meadow grasses flat, animating the limbs of a pair of oaks that stood on the far edge and cast a broad circle of dense black moon shadow. Shapes moved within the shadow. Peter's throat constricted, his breath jerking out in short gasps.

The woman in the black dress stepped from beneath the trees into the moonlight. She held the hand of a small boy. Peter was in plain view, but neither the woman nor the boy looked back. They disappeared beyond the underbrush again, still moving east along the trail.

Whoever they were, they weren't Amanda and David.

He set out warily across the meadow, following them, the trail narrowing again as dense brush closed it in on either side. He could see nothing ahead except darkness. There was no crying, no voices, just the sound of the wind and the noise of his shoes scuffing on the dirt and rock of the trail.

Suddenly a sharp, anguished scream rang out ahead of him, cut off with a chilling abruptness, like a snap.

The wind died. The night waited—one vast, dark silence for the space of five seconds. Then, with a wild shriek, the wind sprang up again without warning, slamming against him so furiously that he lurched forward, nearly falling, running toward the scream, knowing without any doubt what it meant. Ahead of him lay the dense stand of trees along the top of the falls. There was a dark hollow between the moving branches, like the mouth of a cave. He bent into the darkness, picking his way across the rocky streambed. The precipice itself was hidden by undergrowth, but the sound of cascading water rose from below, and he looked carefully out over the rocks into empty air. Creek water cascaded ankle-deep off the edge in a windblown spray, falling toward the rocky canyon floor nearly invisible in the shadows below.

Holding on to overhanging brush, he leaned out to see into the shadowy depths, trying to make out shapes, movement. He could just discern the gray-black outlines of rocks that edged the canyon floor, a glimmer of moonlight on the pool . . .

. . . and then, interrupting the spread of moonlit ripples, the twisted shapes of the two bodies that had fallen together a minute ago.

He screamed hoarsely. He was too late. As if carried on the wind, the thought rushed into his head—again he was too late, and for one anguished, desperate moment he was possessed with the wild urge to throw himself off after them.

Startled, he steadied himself, forced himself away from the brink of the cliff, and scrambled along the ledge, his footfalls knocking loose layers of weathered shale that tumbled off into the darkness. In order to descend, he was forced to angle away from the sharp decline of the canyon wall and to break his own steep trail through the sage and greasewood. The sound of falling water diminished behind him, masked by the wind.

Soon the hillside fell away so steeply that he hung on to the gnarled branches of hillside shrubs, lowering himself step by step, searching out footholds against roots and trunks secured in the decomposing rock. He chanced a look downward, surprised to see the trail twenty yards below, zigzagging up from the canyon floor. It was little more than a rain-scoured line, losing itself almost at once among the oaks that lined the lower canyon wall. As close as it was, it seemed to him that he would never reach it, and he was filled with the maddening, slow-motion futility of a dream.

He sat down and began to descend on his feet and the seat of his pants, braking with his heels, trying to keep his center of gravity far enough back to avoid tumbling forward. Within seconds he knew it was a mistake; already he was sliding downward in an uncontrolled rush.

He snatched at limbs and roots to catch himself, tearing the flesh on his palms. His hand closed on something and he held on, but his momentum cartwheeled him sideways, his face smashing against dried sticks and leaves. He let go, sliding again, and slammed to a stop against the broad trunk of a tree some few feet from the edge of the canyon.

For a moment he lay there catching his breath, looking up into the foliage, dazedly assessing damages. The palm of his right hand was scraped and oozing blood, but his leather jacket had protected his arms. He flexed his fingers and then sat up unsteadily, realizing that the wind had once again diminished, leaving the night warm and still.

The base of the falls was clearly visible below him now: the rock-strewn pool reflecting the starry sky, the falls tumbling into it and throwing up a veil of mist. Nothing more. Nothing even remotely similar to the broken, nightmare shapes he had seen from the ledge above.

## 22

A BUSY SIGNAL AGAIN, AND AFTER NEARLY TWENTY MINUTES HAD gone by. Clearly she had left the phone off the hook. If only she'd given him a chance to say something! Lonely women like that didn't know what they wanted sometimes. They were afraid of their own urges, their own unfulfilled needs.

He couldn't risk haunting the only pay telephone in Trabuco Oaks, not in the middle of the night. At least he had gotten rid of the red Thunderbird. That was a real eye-catcher in a hick town like Trabuco Oaks. He had managed to rent a Jeep Cherokee, which was about twenty times as practical as the Thunderbird when it came to negotiating the local dirt roads. Cherokees were common as acorns out there, too.

He dialed the number again—another busy signal.

He wondered how the conversation would go, how she would respond to him when she found out the depth of his feeling for her. He could only imagine it—gaining her trust, her interest. "I'm a little shy," he said out loud, then smiled just enough. She responded with a warm smile of her own, opening up to him. He took her hand. . . .

He tried one last time, got the busy signal, and regretfully hung the phone up. The wind blew dry leaves up under the back wall of the pay phone, and he closed his eyes, turning away. Then he climbed into his car and drove slowly up Parker Street, the headlights dark. He would just drive past her house one more time and then head for home. Maybe tomorrow he would see her again.

He turned around in front of Lance Klein's driveway, noticing now that there was a light on in the back of Beth's house. Without thinking, he cut the engine and coasted silently into the deep shadows of a stand of roadside trees. He set the brake, the car facing downhill. The street was deserted. Even the wind seemed to have died out. Except for a couple of porch lights, all of the houses were dark.

Even then he told himself that he would only watch and wait. When her light went out he would leave. He might risk another phone call, but nothing more than that.

The light was probably on in her bedroom. The window was too big to be a bathroom window.

He wondered what she slept in. Despite the wind, it was a warm night. . . .

The street was absolutely empty.

A person back in her driveway would be hidden by the corner of her house and couldn't be seen from Klein's, which was dark anyway. Across the street was an open field—high grass and trees. A redwood fence blocked the neighbor's view on the other side.

He released the parking brake, shifted to neutral, and coasted downhill. He was nearly to the general store again before he started the engine. Then he turned around and drove back up the street, pulling off onto the little road that led down to the preschool. He turned around again and parked near the corner.

He would give himself two minutes. That's all. Just a quick look. Would he knock? Of course it was late, but he was in the neighborhood and he saw that her light was on . . .

He smoothed his hair in the mirror, then took a bottle of breath freshener out of the glove compartment and sprayed his mouth.

A thrill of fear surged through him. He mustn't be caught. Not this time. They would never believe that he wanted nothing more than to *know* her. And he was on the edge of success with Klein— too close to screw things up.

He pictured her lighted window, the dark driveway.

Swiftly he unwrapped the gauze bandage around his hand. Then, carefully, he wrapped it around his face, leaving slits for his eyes and nose and mouth, tying the two ends behind his head and checking the result in the mirror.

Without another thought he climbed out of the car, leaving the keys in the ignition and all the doors unlocked. He jogged up the street, turning his face away from the few houses he passed. He slipped into the shadows of the eucalyptus trees that edged her driveway, and took one last look down the empty street, wishing there was more wind, if only to mask any noise he might make on the gravel drive. It would come up again any moment, but he couldn't wait. Even now she might be turning out the lights, and he would have lost an opportunity.

Carefully he walked toward the window, which was shaded by

louvered blinds. He barely breathed, stepping softly, keeping his hands off the windowsill. He crouched just a little, trying to see between the close-fitting slats, his heart pounding in his chest. He made out a dresser, the corner of the bed, the edge of a doorway.

The bed moved. He glimpsed a bare foot for a second as she shifted positions.

His breath caught, and a thrill ran through him that was nearly electrical. He swiveled his head around, again checking the driveway. He had to see more. He was intoxicated with the possibility of what might be revealed to him. The window was badly located, the angle wrong, most of the bed hidden. Unless she got up off the bed the night would be wasted.

He moved farther down the driveway, his crepe soles scrunching softly on the gravel.

Beth was aware suddenly that it was quiet outside. The wind had diminished, and the silence was eerie with premonition. She lay in bed, propped up on her elbow, trying to read herself back to sleep. She had set the phone on the floor behind the nightstand so that she didn't have to look at it.

Beyond the bedroom door the house was nearly dark. She could see the dim glow from the night-light in the hallway, but that was all. For a moment she considered turning on lights throughout the house, but that was foolish—the kind of thinking that worked you into a state once you got going with it.

A cricket started up outside the window, and there was a rustling of leaves in the eucalyptus trees along the driveway. Somewhere in the distance a dog barked.

She looked up from her book and listened. Silence again. And then the swish-scrape of a leafy branch against a window screen. She couldn't concentrate on the book, and found herself suddenly thinking about the disappearance of Amanda and David. Peter had been hit hard by it, full of pain and confusion. For the first time now she wondered what *had* happened to them.

It was crazy, of course, to think that these phone calls meant anything at all, and twice as crazy to think that there was some link between the calls and the disappearance. She wondered, though: if Amanda and David hadn't left the canyon, then where were they? What had happened to them?

The cricket abruptly quit chirruping. She had become oblivious to it, but she was immediately aware now of its sudden silence and of the low-key swish and rustle of the wind.

She heard something else.

Footsteps on the gravel driveway, the measured crunching of sharp rocks compressed by a shoe sole.

She held her breath, waiting. There was nothing more—only silence, the whisper of the wind and the scraping of dry leaves.

THE WOMAN ACKROYD HAD BEEN FOLLOWING HAD DISAPPEARED, perhaps literally. The trees cast heavy shadows across this part of the canyon despite the moonlight, and minutes ago she had vanished into the leaf-shaded darkness, utterly invisible in her black dress. He ascended the steep path that led from below the lower campground up toward the ridge, stepping carefully, planting the tip of his walking stick against half-buried roots and rocks. He had *no* business playing around like this in the darkness. If he fell he'd break a hip. God knows when they'd find him.

A half hour had gone by since he'd seen her through the window. He had been reading, the propane lamps off, no light but an oil lamp. The road beyond the front porch had been lit by the moon, and the wind stirred the dark trees opposite the house. When he read at night, he kept an eye on the road. It was common to see deer abroad at night. In the nearly fifty years he'd lived out there he'd probably seen every kind of animal that lived in the Santa Ana Mountains, and he'd gotten into the habit of watching the canyon at night like an astronomer watched the stars.

It wasn't only animals that he watched for. There were rumors of other things wandering in the canyon at night. A few days ago someone had seen two bodies at the base of the falls. It was a matter of the wildest coincidence—it had to be—although he would have been more convinced of that if bodies had been recovered. That would have ended the mystery. It was the inexplicable disappearance of those bodies that seemed to signify.

The wind shuddered through the canyon now, and when he

climbed out of the shelter of the narrow gorge and onto the open face of the hillside it nearly staggered him. He had a clear view of the trail for another hundred feet, and she was nowhere in sight. So she wasn't ahead of him. Or else she was so far ahead of him that it was hopeless. He made his way back down again, to where he was out of the wind and could rest. He was quickly tiring out, and if he had any hope of retracing his steps, perhaps following the trail up the creek, he had to do it now. In another few minutes he'd be winded.

He had recognized her—thought he'd recognized her—in that moment of utter clarity and certainty when she'd stepped out of the shadow of the trees and onto the road a half hour ago. She seemed not even to see the cabin, or to see him behind the window, even though he must have been clearly visible in the lamplight. He hadn't bothered with his coat, just picked up his stick by the door and went out, able to keep her in sight only for a few moments. After that he had listened for her voice on the night wind, guessing the direction she'd taken.

Faintly, from somewhere up the canyon, he heard it again, a plaintive wail. God help her, he thought, setting out again, working his way down the trail. She was searching for someone. It was what he feared—feared and hoped for. The trail leveled out, running down toward the creek. There it was again, her voice, even fainter now. She was below Falls Canyon! He should have guessed that she'd double back up the canyon.

He waded into the cold water, stepping carefully, pushing between the willows on the opposite bank. A little path edged the creek—a game trail, running a hundred yards down to where the creek crossed the road, then another fifty yards to the mouth of Falls Canyon. He stumbled forward, catching himself with the stick, climbing the steep bank and crossing the road, then half sliding down to the creek again and into a clearing at the edge of the old campgrounds.

Drifts of autumn leaves lay knee deep along the rocky outcroppings of the west wall of the canyon. He stepped through them carefully, probing with his stick, breathing heavily, already worn out, and the climb up to the ridge still ahead of him. Already it seemed to him that his imagination must have gone utterly around the bend. The woman he followed had died sixty years ago.

Abruptly he stopped, stepping back into the shadows. There was a truck parked at the roadside, a battered Chevy Suburban.

Moonlight shone on foil-colored window tinting, stenciled with some kind of desert scene. He recognized the truck. It belonged to his neighbor. Obviously the man had parked it and left it. But why? To follow her?

He hurried forward again, the trail angling upward now, rising between sandstone outcroppings. He had waited so *long* for this, watching, disbelieving the stories, captivated by them. He put one foot wearily ahead of the other, plodding upward, listening to his heart thump in his chest, knowing that it was futile to go on— far too steep. He couldn't hope to . . .

She screamed then—one long wail in the sudden stillness. He stopped and closed his eyes, waiting to hear something more, and yet knowing what the silence meant. Wearily, he turned around and headed home. He had no desire to confront his neighbor, to swap stories about what they'd seen and heard, about what it might mean.

"*No!*" KLEIN LURCHED AWAKE, SITTING UP AND THROWING HIS hands across his face.

"What?" Lorna shouted, startled out of a sound sleep and instinctively recoiling toward the edge of the bed.

Klein's chest heaved with exertion. Slowly he lowered his hands, looking around him at the dim room as if he only half recognized where he was.

"It's all right," Lorna said. She put an arm around him. "There's nothing there."

"There was someone. The wind. At the edge of the bed . . ."

"Don't *say* that," she said. "How *could* there be? You're not making any sense. You're still half-asleep."

"I . . . I don't know," Klein said. "I thought I saw . . ."

He lay down again. What Klein had thought he saw next to the bed was a man with an upraised shovel, his face a mask of

jealous, murderous loathing. There had been the sound of the
shovel cutting the air, the blade descending . . .

"Well, whatever you saw," Lorna said, "it was just a dream.
It's gone now."

"Yeah," Klein said.

But it wasn't gone. He had seen it too often for it to be anything
like gone. It was waiting for him. He had only to fall asleep again.
He looked at Lorna, who had shut her eyes and pulled the covers
over her, and with a quick surge of passion and longing he remembered the face of the black-haired woman who had lain next
to him in bed just moments ago.

He couldn't sleep any longer. There was too much wind, too
much moonlight. He lay still until he was sure Lorna was asleep,
and then got quietly out of bed, picked up his bathrobe from the
chair, and went out into the living room, where he poured himself
a glass of scotch out of the decanter. He filled the glass with ice
cubes and sat down where he could see through the french doors,
out toward the hills.

It would have been good to swim, but he didn't have the energy
to do anything but sit there and sip the drink. And besides, the
pool was full of leaves, the surface nearly covered with them like
some kind of autumn centerpiece.

The dream recurred on windy nights. Always it was the same:
the wind, the moonlit hills, the woman in black descending
from the shadows, him going out through the dry grass to meet
her. In the dream there was no pool, no wrought-iron fence. The
house and property were as they had been years ago, long before
Klein had torn down the remains of the old house and rebuilt.
There were horses on the meadow and a long wooden bunkhouse
where the stucco poolhouse now stood.

Only the hills and the sound of the wind were the same, the
sound of leaves scraping against wooden siding and curtained
windows. As he lay with her in the bunkhouse he could smell
tallow and wool, raw pine boards and the jasmine scent of her
perfume. The wind pressed on the door, tendrils of it skittering
underneath and moving the window curtains, finding its way
through knots and chinks in the siding.

It had been a long time—months since they'd been together.
She had tried to come to him, but she was a virtual prisoner. Now
and then they met in the woods, briefly, her husband's shadow
looming in both their minds.

On the bed in the bunkhouse they tore at each other's clothing, and she pulled the blanket up to cover them, her hands stroking his back, holding him as he kissed her bare shoulders, her neck, her breasts, the two of them moving together beneath the blanket. She curled her fingers in his hair, pressing him to her, wrapping her legs around his, clinging to him.

Then, always then, the door slammed open and something cast a black shadow on the moonlit floor. The wind rushed in, moaning, swirling, tearing away the loose woolen blanket. He scrambled forward, trying to cover her, the wind shrieking in his face, the shadow by the bedside coalescing into the form of a man holding a garden shovel.

The sod-caked blade lanced toward him, skiving down through the air. There was the sound of his scalp tearing, the shovel grinding against bone, slamming him backward against the mattress, and beyond that, as if she were already separated from him by a great distance, the sound of her scream. Then nothing but plunging darkness and the faint, momentary knowledge that she still gripped his arm. . . .

Klein stood up, shakily refilling his glass.

Lorna had given him a long article about hypnogogic hallucinations, waking dreams. They were apparently common. Nearly everyone had them at one time or another—nighttime visions of strange people and shapes and animals. They occurred when a person was perched right on the edge of sleep, eyes open but already drifting into unconsciousness. They were the source of ghost stories and stories of alien encounters, evidence of witchery, satanic visitations.

Klein had read the article carefully, almost desperately. When he had put it down he was very damned sure that it had nothing to do with him. His dream, if it was a dream, was too lush, too ordered, too much a product of all his senses. He'd had his share of sensual dreams over the years, nightmares too, but never anything like this. He couldn't begin to tell Lorna the details of it. It was the kind of thing a man kept to himself.

He listened for a moment to the silent house. Then, making up his mind, he drained his glass and set it on the coffee table. Tying his bathrobe shut, he unbolted the door and stepped out into the night, shutting the door quietly. He walked around the edge of the pool to the gate, where he stood watching the hills. Behind the poolhouse and outside the wrought iron fence stood a dozen small fruit trees, their leaves mostly fallen by now. Years ago there'd been an orchard there, and Klein had pulled out the last few stunted trees when he'd cleared the land. He'd found a scattering of old tools in the debris of the old bunkhouse—a rusted spade and some cultivating tools—which he'd kept even though they were mostly junk.

The wind blew softly now, stirring the meadow grasses, the moon drifting low in the sky. Beneath the leafless fruit trees the shadows of moving limbs intertwined like the avenues of a maze. The old spade stood against the crotch of a peach tree, its weather-silvered handle shining in the moonlight.

He thought of his dream again—the door swinging open, the shovel slicing toward his face . . .

He flinched and turned his head, and for one brief moment the stucco-and-aluminum poolhouse was gone, and what he saw was a long wooden bungalow, candlelight glowing through the windows, the door standing half-open. It swam in his vision like a desert mirage, and he staggered back into the fence, his fingers closing on the cold wrought iron. The wind rose in a howl, blasting the surface of the pool, blowing wet leaves into the air. There was a wild cracking noise from somewhere beyond the fence, and the sound of a limb tearing through shrubbery. The eucalyptus trees along his neighbor's driveway whipped like saplings.

Then the poolhouse was as it had been—no candlelit bunkhouse, no door standing open. He turned frantically to look out into the hills, sensing that for a moment she had nearly come to him. She had been out there, moving through the trees, drawn inexorably to him just as he had been drawn out of the house and into the windy night.

He waited for another minute, staring into the wind, knowing that the time had passed, that something had shifted and then had shifted back again. He pulled his robe tighter, retied it, and walked around the pool deck toward the back door, suddenly bone weary.

# 25

POMEROY ADJUSTED THE BANDAGE AROUND HIS FACE, WISHING he had tied it more securely. The knot was too tight to loosen. Wind stirred the trees overhead, and the moon, low in the sky, illuminated the backyard beyond the corner of the house.

There was another window, this one facing the bed. One slat was cocked open in the blinds, and a long blade of light shone through it. He peered between, his heart pounding.

She lay on top of the covers, her head propped up on her hand, reading a book. She was dressed in an oversize T-shirt that was pulled up over her thigh. Moistening his lips, he studied the shape of her body beneath the fabric and wondered what was hidden by the shirt's hem. If only she'd move . . .

He glanced around, charged with fear and expectation. He was visible from Klein's backyard, but to hell with that. The house was dark. Klein was asleep. He was safe. He could wait as long as he had to.

She shifted position suddenly, and he bent anxiously toward the window, nearly putting his face to the glass. Her nightshirt moved on her thigh. Filled with a wild frustration, he nearly knocked on the window. Then she was settled again, reading her book.

The eucalyptus trees overhead suddenly thrashed in a hard gust of wind, showering him with leaves and hard, pyramid-shaped seeds. Instantly the wind was howling, slamming furiously down from the hills. The tall trunks of the trees creaked ominously as they swayed under the onslaught.

Beth lay there oblivious to it in the quiet room, not moving, and Pomeroy was edgy with impatience. There had to be something he could do—tap on the window, break something—that would make her shift position, get up, anything. Then he would go. That would be it. There would be other nights, other visits. Right now he just wanted to *know* something about her, some-

thing that would make their relationship more intimate. He had
never had that, ever. Linda hadn't let him in, hadn't given him a
chance to relate to her on a deeper plane. . . .

A gust of wind pounded into him just then, nearly throwing
him into the window. There was a sharp crack from overhead,
and a limb tore its way downward through the foliage of the
eucalyptus trees, crashing onto the garage roof and sliding to the
driveway.

Pomeroy ducked away, scuttling out of the moonlight, deeper
into the backyard along the wall of the garage. The noise of the
falling limb had been tremendous, enough to wake the neighbors.
Fear slammed through him, and he wondered suddenly whether
there was a gate on the other side of the house, so that he could
get out to the street without using the driveway. He looked around
for a place to hide. If he had to he could go over the back fence,
into the hills. . . .

The light inside the room went out just then. The blinds shifted.
He pressed himself against the garage wall, out of the moonlight.
Beth looked out from inside the room, straight at where he had
stood just moments before. She could no doubt see the broken
branch, which blocked half the driveway. He held his breath
watching her. After a moment she dropped the blind, and he
moved forward along the garage, hurrying toward the window
again in case she turned the light back on. Maybe she would come
outside! He prepared for it, trying to think of the right thing to
say—that he was worried about her, the wind and all . . .

But the bedroom stayed dark. If she was going anywhere she
would turn the light back on. His anticipation drained away as he
realized that she was probably just going to bed. It would be
impossible for him to see her clearly inside the darkened room.
He knew that from experience.

The wind gusted again, howling through the trees. Beth heard the
sudden crack of a limb breaking, then the sound of it hitting the
garage roof and sliding in a leafy rush to the driveway. She
reached across and flipped out the light, got out of bed, and stood
by the backyard window. Carefully, she lifted the edge of the
blinds and looked out at where the broken limb lay against the
garage door. Moonlight shone on the leaves and across the lawn.

She dropped the blinds, then walked out of the bedroom
and into the dark kitchen. Through the window she could see
the hills and the fields beyond Klein's property. The dry grass

rippled in the moonlight. The wind shifted through the trees.

Something moved near the Kleins' gate, nearly in the shadow of the poolhouse. Beth froze, her hands on the sink. It was a person—someone standing, waiting.

Slowly she turned around and reached for the wall phone, the Kleins' number coming to her in a rush.

There was no dial tone. She remembered then that the phone was off the hook in the bedroom, and simultaneously the person moved, stepping out of the shadows. It was Klein himself, wearing his bathrobe. He turned and walked around the edge of the pool as if heading back into his house.

She thought of the footfalls on the gravel outside the window.

Pomeroy felt betrayed. Everything had come to an untimely ending because of the wind. He wasn't ready to leave yet. Not yet. Crouching, he hurried across the lawn toward the back door, treading as lightly as he could on the wooden stairs.

The wind that blew down off the ridges seemed to have gotten into his head, scattering his thoughts like leaves, and he couldn't see any farther than the next moment. His vision narrowed so that the door, the doorknob, the cheap locking mechanism filled his mind, drawing his hand forward magnetically, inexorably. Through the dark window he could see a washer and dryer, an old sink. His fingers tingled as he fondled the cold brass knob.

He pictured her rising happily off the bed, tossing her book aside. He was home! He'd been away—business. But he was home now. They'd brew a cup of coffee, talk, listen to the wind.

Gently, he leaned into the door, closing his eyes, watching it swing open in his mind, picturing the darkness that lay beyond, the woman lying on the rumpled bed in a moonlit room, the thin nightshirt. . . .

Surprised at first, she's relieved to see it's him. She's frightened of the wind, frightened of being alone. He touches her. He's home now. They'll be together, inseparable.

The knob turned in his hand.

Hanging up the phone, she walked past the table and into the service porch. She would check the dead bolt and then go to bed. It couldn't have been Klein in her driveway. Not wearing his bathrobe. Maybe he had heard something himself, and had come out to investigate.

The service porch was dark, but she didn't bother turning on the light. She reached for the dead bolt as she stepped in front of the door, and saw at that moment, just inches beyond the glass, a man's bandage-wrapped face, his hand rattling the knob.

THE SUBURBAN SAT ON THE TURNOUT WHERE HE HAD LEFT IT, THE keys in the ignition. He climbed in and sat for a moment resting, his head against the steering wheel, his eyes closed. The dark, shattered shapes at the base of the falls drifted into his mind again—the image identical to what he had imagined that afternoon, driving home from the suburbs.

He opened his eyes. It had been dark, and he had been spooked by the scream, by the windy night. It would have been easy to imagine shapes in the confusion of shadows cast by the rocks. . . .

Except that the hiker last week had seen the same thing.

Small comfort. He wasn't crazy; he was seeing ghosts.

He fired up the engine and drove toward home, keeping his eyes on the road ahead, not looking into the side mirror at all. Some distance up he passed the house of his nearest neighbor, Mr. Ackroyd, an old man who had lived in the canyon for nearly fifty years. The house was dark. The Suburban's headlights illuminated a climbing rose on a trellis that sheltered one end of the broad front porch. A profusion of white blooms overhung a couple of weathered rockers.

The comfortable look of the place made the solitude and darkness of the canyon settle on him like an increase in gravity, and he thought about the house on Monterey Street again—music on the stereo while he cooked dinner, David assembling Lego castles on the living room floor, Amanda working in her study.

A quarter mile farther on he turned down the drive through the trees, his house visible ahead. It was a canyon hybrid of a Queen Anne cottage, with high-peaked gables and decaying gingerbread, built on rock piers in order to survive the occasional seasons of heavy rain, when the creek flooded the narrow canyon floor.

Shaded by oaks and sycamores, the house looked as if it had never seen the sun. Despite the dry weather, the old roof shingles were green with a patchy carpet of moss that grew down into wooden rain gutters. The attic window yawned black and empty in the dirty white siding, ragged lace curtains stirring fitfully in the wind that blew in through the cracked panes. Sunlight and moonlight, Peter thought suddenly, were two distinctly different kinds of illumination. Maybe in the morning the place wouldn't look so much like it needed to be fumigated by a priest.

He locked the car and went in. Despite his having lived in and worked on the place for months, it had an abandoned, lonesome quality to it. Like a bat chased off by sunlight, the sensation fled only when Beth or Bobby were around. He pulled off his jacket and turned on the water in the sink, drinking a couple of mouthfuls right out of the tap. The cuts on his hands were nothing more than scrapes, the skin sandpapered off in a couple of dirty patches. He splashed water on his face and then shoved his head under the faucet, washing off trail dust and then rubbing his hair dry with the dish towel. Then he pulled a beer out of the old propane-powered refrigerator before going through the house and lighting every wall lantern he came to until there wasn't a darkened room left. The propane tank outside held 250 gallons. He could burn the lamps all night long for a month and not empty it.

He wandered aimlessly, too full of restless energy to go to bed, too fatigued to work. Finally he settled in the parlor, looking over the torn-up walls and the seedy old furniture. He could picture again the ghostly willow tree he had seen that morning. Then it had seemed like a psychotic episode to him; now it seemed like something else entirely.

Although the parlor had been built at the same time as the rest of the house, it had slipped further into decay over the years— the plaster falling off the ceiling, the floor settling out of level, the wall studs and moldings full of termite burrows. There was a stone-and-clinker brick fireplace with a broad hearth, but the joints had loosened, and now the fireplace floor was littered with chunks of broken mortar and decomposing brick.

The room was half full of old furniture: stuffed chairs, tables, bookcases, all of it crammed into the back corners and sitting on top of a Turkish carpet that Peter had rolled back in a vain effort to save it from plaster dust and wood chips. Open wooden crates held tarnished candelabras and books, odd pieces of crystal and broken art pottery, bug-eaten lace doilies, and cracked ceramic figurines. There was a dismantled Victrola, or at least parts of one, crammed into a crate along with random pieces of broken records and a half dozen framed prints of hunting scenes and of tree-shadowed cottages in somber forest glades.

The roof of the room had leaked for years while the house had sat empty, and much of the wooden furniture was loose-jointed and stained with dirty rainwater. Most of the pieces would take so much work to repair that it would save time and money just to junk them, except that in some vague way Peter had become attached to it, as if it were a collection of mementos from some dim, half-remembered life.

He could easily picture the room in its prime: the bookcases full of dark volumes, the chairs arranged in front of the fire, the Turkish carpet deep and plush, the plaster walls troweled smooth and hung with the dark-framed pictures. On the ceiling, the crumbling plaster filigree repeated elements of the carpet pattern, as if the ceiling were a dim reflection of the floor. The whole house had a pattern to it, a tediously careful design, like an ornately carved and assembled Chinese puzzle box. The man who had built it had clearly been obsessed, as if he'd had some higher or deeper purpose than mere shelter.

Looking around the room now, Peter was flooded with the sudden notion that all of it could be restored. In his mind he moved the old furniture back into its customary place, tightening screws, wiping the tabletops with lemon oil, draping the doilies over the arms of the chairs. Perhaps with patience and the right tools he could cheat time and chance and human frailty, repair the damage caused by a leaky roof and the passing years. There was a certain promise pending in the old room, as if everything he needed and wanted was right there, obscured by dust and age, and if only he could find the necessary order, the perfect arrangement . . .

As if the weather had suddenly changed, the room grew strangely cool, almost tomblike. Light headed, he leaned against the doorway and stared at the rubble in the fireplace. He listened vaguely to the wind blowing outside. The glow from the wall lamps diminished abruptly, and the room fell into shadow. There was the faint smell of jasmine on the air and the murmur of hushed voices as if from some far-off place. Slowly and languidly, a silver light began to leak out of the fireplace like drifting, moonlit fog—the same witchy light that had illuminated the room early that morning. . . .

POMEROY HEARD BETH SCREAM AT THE SAME MOMENT THAT HE saw her face through the window. He threw himself down the wooden stairs in a single, twisting leap, already running toward the driveway when he hit the lawn, hunched over, aware that he was illuminated by moonlight and wanting to distort whatever view she would get of him.

In the shadow of the house he straightened up and ran flat out toward the street, glancing at the still-closed front door. There was a light on in the living room. She was calling the police. Of course she was calling the police.

He leaped over a big eucalyptus log that edged the front lawn, ran across the street and into the darkness of the trees, unwinding the gauze around his face as he ran. Thank God he had wrapped his face up. She'd have got a clear look at him otherwise. It would have been over then, all of it.

The wind tore the night to pieces, blowing through the high, dead grass in the field. He ran straight into it, lit by moonlight again, still hunching down. No way he was heading straight back to the car. Ahead of him the field was scattered with bushes, all of them shaking and bending in the wind. He could lose himself pretty easily out there, hide as long as he had to.

He scrambled in behind a heavy stand of brush, pushing his way deeper into it. His hand was bleeding again from the cat bite. He tried to wrap it with the wrinkled strip of gauze, but he shivered so badly that he couldn't get it started. Suddenly enraged, he slammed the bleeding hand into the brush, driving it again and again into a limb until the pain receded behind a numb ache.

He was sobbing and sick, the wind clammy on his face, and

he fought to be quiet, to control himself, holding on to limbs with both hands as if the wind would blow him away. He was washed with remorse. Just like with Linda! He had nearly wrecked it all. Suddenly he was gripped by an impulse to betray himself, to walk across to Beth's door and admit everything. The very act of admission would make her understand what he wanted. He would beg her forgiveness, ask her to give him another chance. . . .

Someone was in the street.

Pomeroy held himself dead still. It was Lance Klein. Probably Beth's scream had awakened him, and he headed down the center of the street now, his bathrobe billowing around him. He was looking hard into the shrubbery of the few dark houses. The white Cherokee wouldn't mean anything to him.

As if unsure of himself, Klein stopped. Then he walked slowly across to the stand of trees along the road opposite to Beth's house. He stopped again, craning his neck, probably not wanting to get too close and be jumped by a prowler hiding in the darkness. Pomeroy nearly laughed out loud. No way Klein would head out into the field. Not on a night like this.

The police, though, were a different matter.

Klein turned around and hurried toward Beth's house, and Pomeroy pushed out through the brush, edging along behind it. He could hear Klein pounding on the door. "Open it," Pomeroy whispered. "Let him in."

He dropped to his hands and knees and crawled out into the wind, clutching the gauze in his damaged hand. The grass was high enough to hide him all the way to the street. Klein had quit knocking and was standing on the porch, shouting something. The door opened and he went in. The bastard, Pomeroy thought, still crawling toward the street. The dirty bastard. If he touches her . . . It was himself, Bernard Pomeroy, who ought to be inside that house comforting Beth. Everything had gone wrong. The damned wind. The moonlight. He should have read the signs. The wind didn't cover anything; it just woke people up, made them look out the window every ten seconds, hearing noises.

He was near enough to the street now. He stood up and ran, the air tearing in and out of his lungs in gasps. Tumbleweeds grabbed at his shoes. He expected a shout, the sound of doors slamming. His feet pounded on asphalt now, and when he reached the corner there was still no one in sight. Sliding into the car, he bent down across the passenger seat, just barely looking out at the road. Like last time, he let off the brake and the Cherokee moved off downhill, gaining silent momentum. He straightened up and checked the rearview mirror. Klein hadn't come back out.

He twisted the ignition key and switched the headlights on, rolling through the stop sign at the bottom of Parker and accelerating up the highway toward Coto de Caza. When he entered the first maze of suburban houses at the top of the hill, it dawned on him that he was safe. A vast wave of relief surged through him, and he screamed out loud. Fueled by the emotion, he screamed again and again until, winded and light headed, he forced himself to slow down and catch his breath.

It was two in the morning when he pulled into the garage, and he was utterly worn out, his shoes full of dirt and foxtails, the cat bite filthy. He stood in the shower scrubbing himself down with a loofah pad until his skin was raw and the hot water ran out. Then he loaded his shoes and clothes into three grocery bags and covered them up with kitchen trash, fastening the tops with twist ties. He took them out and locked them into the garage cupboard. There was no way he could throw them into the condo Dumpsters. That's where they'd look first. He would toss them out in two or three different spots tomorrow morning.

He washed his hands again and poured hydrogen peroxide over the cat bite before putting a wide Band-Aid over it. It struck him then, while he was looking at the palm of his hand, that he had touched the knob on Beth's back door. He had actually been standing there turning the knob! How in the hell had he let himself go like that? What had he hoped to accomplish? He had lost all regard for *consequences*.

That's what had happened to him last time. He had been lucky to pull a suspended sentence. Worse than that, though, had been the humiliation of being identified. It wasn't fair. She hadn't understood.

He had been fingerprinted, too.

Your whole life was nothing but consequences, lined up one after another, waiting to take a punch at you. When you looked away, even for a moment, one of them knocked you down.

# 28

THE SOUND OF BETH'S SCREAM DISORIENTED KLEIN AND FOR A moment he related it to the dream, to the final horrified scream of the woman beside him on the bed.

Then he yanked shut the half-open french door and ran to the fence, climbing up onto a deck chair and looking over. A man was just then rounding the corner of Beth's house, running hard, a strip of white cloth wrapped around his head, the loose ends trailing out behind him. The man threw his right hand out to catch the wall, braking his momentum and swinging up the driveway toward the street.

At that instant, when his hand was flattened against the wall of the house, moonlight reflected from the stone in his ring, and the brief glint of light resonated in Klein's mind. For a moment he was stupefied with disbelief, and he couldn't move.

Then he threw himself up onto the fence, trying to scramble over onto the lawn, levering himself around in order to drop down on his feet. The hem of his robe slid between two fence boards, wedging tight, yanking him back when he jumped so that he flipped around and sprawled on his hands and knees. The bathrobe cord wrenched loose and the sleeve nearly jerked his arm out of the socket.

"Shit!" he yelled, staggering to his feet and pulling savagely at the robe. It tore loose from the fence, and he hauled it back on as he ran past the back of the house, the wind cutting through his thin pajamas.

The street was empty by the time he got out there. He suddenly wished he had some kind of weapon, although at the same time he was certain he wouldn't need it. The man wouldn't show himself. The last thing the bastard wanted was a confrontation. He walked slowly toward the corner, looking into the shadows of trees and shrubberies, seeing again in his mind the reflected moonlight from the stone in the ring.

It was too weird to be true.

There was a Jeep Cherokee parked at the corner. It didn't belong to the Smiths, who lived in the corner house. Klein was certain of that. He stopped right there, twenty feet from the car, wondering how much he wanted or needed to know.

Deciding, he turned back, walking toward the empty field across the street and the dark bunch of trees at the field's edge, peering into the shadows they threw across the high grass. Someone had run through right there; Klein could see where the grass, brittle and dry, was mashed down. Following him would be nothing. . . .

He turned around and headed up toward Beth's door. He hadn't even checked to see if she was all right. And the kid . . . By God, if the prowler had hurt either one of them, Klein would track him through the field and rip his lungs out.

He pounded on the door and shouted to let her know who it was. After a moment Beth looked out through the window, saw it was him, and let him in.

"You all right?" he asked. She was pretty obviously shaken up.

"Yeah."

"How's the boy?"

"He didn't even wake up. He's still sleeping." Beth shuddered and sat down on the couch, holding her arms crossed in front of her. "I called the police."

"Good," Klein said. "There's no point in Bobby knowing anything; it'll just keep him up at night. If you've got to say anything to him, tell him there was somebody prowling around *my* house, and that I chased him off with a baseball bat. It's important that kids think the good guy won. Do you know what I mean?"

"Yeah," she said, smiling a little.

The smile instantly made him feel like a creep. But why should it? What did he really *know*? Half the men in the country wore big rings. "These prowlers usually don't come back anyway, once they're seen," he told her. "Scares the hell out of them to think they might be identified. No need for either one of you to worry about it."

She nodded her head. "Thanks," she said. "Thanks for helping."

Klein shrugged. Being thanked for things had always embarrassed him. This time it didn't; it just made him ashamed of himself. Still, there were things a man had to do. He could make it up to her. "The cops are going to want to know if he broke in," he asked. "Was he actually inside?"

"No," she said. "I saw him through the back window."

"It's important if he was inside. If you can identify him as having been inside, the cops'll take this very damned seriously."

She shook her head again.

"Well, good," Klein said, relieved. "Obviously just a peeper. I couldn't see any sign of him out front. Probably jumped straight into a car and was out of there before I had a chance to catch him. When you screamed, I was out back, having a nightcap. I couldn't sleep. Too much wind."

Klein walked to the window and looked out, not really wanting to see anything but an empty street. "Did you get a look at him? See his face?"

"No," Beth said. "Not a good look. He was turning the knob on the back door. He had something over his face—a bandage, maybe—wrapped around it. I panicked and ran back into the kitchen."

"Of course. That kind of thing scares the hell out of a person. I'll take a quick look out back. You be okay?"

Beth nodded.

"If the cops come tell 'em it's me back there."

"Right," Beth said.

The backyard was empty; Klein knew it would be. Unless the man was an utter fool, he was long gone by now.

He looked closely at the doorknob and at the crappy little twist-'em dead bolt holding the door shut. It had about a quarter inch of throw. One good kick, that's all it would have taken. Lucky Beth had seen him there and screamed. He might have been inside otherwise.

Klein looked back into the house. Beth was still in the living room, waiting for the cops.

He took up the corner of the hem of his bathrobe, spit on it, and very carefully rubbed the doorknob, polishing off any possible prints. Then he worked over the door around it before walking back down to the end of the house and rubbing down the dusty siding where the prowler had grabbed on when turning the corner.

It would look screwy that there were no prints of any kind at all on the doorknob, neither Beth's nor Bobby's, but that was the best he could do. Whether or not anyone could explain it, they would be sure to blame it on the prowler. There was no way they'd suspect him of anything.

A FIRE SPRANG UP IN THE RUINED FIREPLACE.

Peter stepped backward into the doorway, hearing his name spoken as if from a distant room. It was a familiar voice, the same he had heard that morning.

The heap of old furniture in the parlor receded into the shadows and became a black ill-defined mass. Four chairs sat before the fire now, two on either side of the butcher-block trestle table from the kitchen on Monterey Street. Two figures, a woman and a boy, slowly materialized in the firelight, sitting in two of the chairs and playing a game of cards. The woman was Amanda; the boy was David. Amanda dealt out the cards with a quick, staccato flickering of her hands, her body hunched forward as if she couldn't get close enough to the cards to read them clearly.

David rocked forward and backward on his chair, his unblinking eyes staring at the deck, his hands darting, picking up the cards that slid across the surface of the table. A glass pitcher of green Kool-Aid, beaded with moisture, sat beside two half-full glasses. A plate of broken cookies lay alongside the pitcher. Playing cards clicked and whirred like insect wings. The wind rose outside, drowning the low murmur of the cardplayers' voices, and the curtains blew inward on a sudden draft, and the cards scattered on the table.

There was a sudden movement among the shadows of the old furniture, only dimly visible, a darkened screen at the remote end of the room. A circle of light glowed against the darkness like a lighted tunnel. The figure of a man appeared, deep in the tunnel of light, as if walking straight at Peter across an immense distance, drawing closer and closer, his face lit by firelight. He wore a black

frock coat, a loosely knotted tie. His dark gray hair was the same
color as his eyes.

The floor seemed to recede, leaving Peter at the windy edge of
a cliff, and within the dark maze of furniture shadows he saw the
unmistakable shapes of the bodies among the rocks, water falling
into the black pool, the mist rising up, the woman's hair drifting
on the dark water. He felt the wind blowing against him, and he
was surrounded by black trees and the noise of falling water. He
groped his way forward in the windy darkness, listening in horror
to the sound of approaching footfalls, seeing through the trees the
measured approach of the man in the black coat.

And then, like an abrupt counterpoint to the wind, there was
the sound of crying somewhere off in the night, and like a heat
mirage, the man wavered for a moment in midstep and then
winked out of existence. The trees and the sound of water vanished on the instant. Peter stood in the parlor again, watching
Amanda and David play cards at the kitchen table. He could still
hear the sound of crying somewhere off in the forest.

The windows along the wall slammed open, and the wind tore
through the room, raising a cloud of plaster dust, shrieking up the
chimney, sweeping the table clear and sending the playing cards
end over end like leaves toward the fire. Shocked into movement,
Peter reached for the back of Amanda's chair, but his hand swept
straight through it. There was nothing there, no resistance at all.

The light dimmed and for one last moment he could smell
Kool-Aid and cookies, and he heard someone, David perhaps, say
something in a voice so creaky and slow that he couldn't make
out the words.

The chairs and the table were gone. David blinked out of existence. Amanda's face hung for a moment like a mask in the air,
her disembodied hands empty but still dealing imaginary cards.
Then, like David, she disappeared utterly.

The fire vanished, and the room was as it had been, the old
furniture ratty and dank and empty, the cold fireplace choked with
rubble. The wind blew fitfully outside, rattling the shutters. Peter
found himself crouched against the wall, staring at the dead fireplace.

# SUNDAY

It looks more to me as if this wind were made of dead men's souls. . . .
—John Ruskin
*The Storm Cloud of the Nineteenth Century*

□ □ □ □ □ □ □ □ □ □

**1**

PETER FIDGETED WITH THE PIECE OF MATERIAL THAT COVERED the arm of the sofa in Mr. Ackroyd's living room, drinking instant coffee that the old man had mixed in a teapot. Ackroyd was dressed for church, wearing a long-out-of-date coat and tie that were scrupulously clean and pressed, and Peter worried vaguely that he was holding the man up, asking strange questions about Amanda and David's disappearance. There seemed to be no hurry, though, and probably he wore his Sunday clothes all day long. Last Sunday he had been away from home all day—church duties—so he could offer nothing helpful about Amanda and David. But there was something in his response that Peter couldn't quite fathom, as if the story reminded him of something or had struck him in some odd way.

After an awkward silence the old man set down his coffee cup and said, ''Wind's dropped a little.''

''I'd just as soon it stayed that way,'' Peter said.

''Not much hope of that. Come nightfall it'll get worse.''

Peter nodded. The wind always seemed to be worse at night. He looked around at the forty or fifty years' worth of stuff that cluttered the room, although ''clutter'' was perhaps the wrong word. Everything was clean and in perfect order, and there was the smell of lemon oil on the air, as if the woodwork had been recently polished. Sunlight had bleached the rose-colored sofa fabric, but under the swatch of Navajo weaving that covered the arm, the fabric was like new. Two walls of the room were piled with bookcases full of books and art pottery, and the leftover wall space was hung with framed topographic maps and old photographs.

The largest of the photos showed a woman with bobbed hair standing among a grove of trees. Beside her stood a boy of around six or seven, smiling awkwardly. The woman had a clown-around look in her eyes and was holding the boy's hat out to the side, as if she'd just then snatched it off his head.

"That looks like Irvine Park," Peter said, pointing at the photo. "I'd guess the sycamore grove across Santiago Creek. I recognize that big sandstone formation. The water stain on it looks like a giant shoe print."

"Nineteen eighteen," Ackroyd said, pouring Peter another cup of coffee and then walking over to look closer at the photograph. "My sister and I." He gestured with the spout of the teapot and then set it down on a piece of ceramic tile lying on the dining room table. Next to the tile sat an oil lamp with a hammered copper base, and opposite the oil lamp stood a vase holding a couple of stems of roses from the bush out front.

The whole room had a homey look to it, as if the books and photos and flowers and Indian rugs were well satisfied to be there. Peter couldn't help liking Ackroyd for that. Over the years the atmosphere of a house came to reflect the inclinations of the people living in it, and the atmosphere of this house, with the breeze blowing through the bleached muslin curtains and sunlight glinting from the polished wood, said a lot in the old man's favor. It was the freshly cut flowers on the table, though, that signified the most. That sort of trifle was something he himself might do on a whim. But Ackroyd apparently did it seriously and steadily, as a daily routine, as if somehow he believed in the vase of flowers in the same way that he believed in putting on a coat and tie on Sunday morning.

Peter looked again at the woman in the photo. "She looks familiar, somehow," he said. "I can't help thinking I've seen her."

Ackroyd stared at him. "Where might that have been?" he asked. "She died a few years after this was taken."

"Sorry," Peter said, wishing suddenly that he hadn't opened his mouth. "I didn't mean it literally. You know—something familiar about her face. Beautiful, wasn't she?"

"More than that," he said.

Peter looked at the other photos. One, in a silver frame too large for it, had clearly been cropped in half. Someone had been cut out of it—a man. The sleeve of his coat hid part of a woman's arm. She stood looking downward, pensively, the same woman as in the other photo, but older and with her hair long, dressed in black now and holding a cut pomegranate in her hand. He knew suddenly who she looked like; she was a dead ringer for the woman he'd followed up onto the ridge last night. The resemblance was startling. She resembled Amanda, too—the smile, the unhappy look in her eye; Amanda when she was unhappy.

"What do you see?" Ackroyd asked.

"Nothing, really." The question struck him as odd. "I'd guess she had an arcane sense of humor, holding the pomegranate and all. Looks like Persephone in the garden, doesn't she?"

Ackroyd gazed out the window. There was no sign that he was listening. After a moment he said, "The woman you describe having seen last night sounds very much like a figure out of Mexican folklore. Maybe that's your answer." He turned away from the photos on the wall and sat down in a chair, pressing his fingers together nervously like a spider on a mirror.

Peter nodded. "Tell me about her. I'm ready to believe almost anything."

"Well, legend has it that there's a wandering woman, a ghost, named La Llorada. Always dresses in black, appears here and there weeping with remorse. There's a complicated story that explains the weeping—involves the loss of her children. It's very popular among the Mexican nationals living out here in the canyons. They'll tell you that La Llorada has haunted this area for years. In fact, it's funny you should bring this up, because Lorna Klein's maid spoke to me about it only last week."

"Really?" Peter said. "You know the Kleins?"

"Lorna worked for a couple of years at the library, right around the time she married him. When he got onto his feet financially, she gave it up. We'd become pretty good friends, though. Still are. I run into the maid every once in a while up at the general store in the Oaks."

"I'm friends with their neighbor," Peter said.

"That would be? . . ."

"Beth Potter."

"I know her," Ackroyd said, suddenly smiling. "Quite a naturalist. Her son's a good boy. Has she seen this wandering woman?"

Peter shook his head. He didn't think she had anyway. "Klein's maid saw her?"

"*She* certainly thinks she did."

"But you don't?" Peter asked. "You surely don't believe in this La Llorada character, do you? It's a long hike from Mexico, even for a ghost. She's probably got no green card, either. They'd deport her in a cold second." He smiled, but Ackroyd apparently saw nothing funny about it.

"I guess I rather *do* believe in such things, although I also believe that an overactive interest in the paranormal is massively unhealthy. Maybe you're better off scoffing at it."

"I'm not doing much scoffing these days."

"No, I guess you're not," Ackroyd said. "I can tell you absolutely that the woman and boy seen last week out in Falls Canyon were not your wife and son. That much I'm sure of, for reasons that would only strike you as nonsense. My advice is to leave it alone. Stay off the ridge at night. It's a dangerous place even during the day—areas full of sinkholes and dense brush. You're liable to walk straight over a precipice."

"It very nearly happened last night."

"There. What did I tell you? The most rational explanation is that the woman you followed moved into one of the cabins up in Holy Jim. Wilson's old place at the forks is a good bet. It's been empty for months. You're doing the right thing knocking on doors."

"Actually I don't think so. I told you I wasn't in the mood for scoffing."

"Well, my way of thinking is that if you get curious about that sort of thing, and start digging around in it, you'll unearth things that were better left buried, if you know what I mean. Probably there's nothing but grief there."

"I believe it, but maybe I don't have a choice. Under the circumstances, maybe I've got to start digging."

Ackroyd shrugged, then picked up the teapot and pointed it in the direction of Peter's cup.

Peter stood up and stretched, shaking his head. "Had enough, thanks." He looked out the open front door. The air outside was nearly motionless now, waiting for the wind to start up again. Something wasn't being said here. The old man was holding on to something. "What's this?" he asked, pointing to another photo, this one hanging near the door. It was a long stretch of tree-lined dirt road passing in front of a white, ranch-style house with chickens on the lawn in front. "Modjeska ranch?"

"Parker ranch. Nineteen twenty or so."

Peter looked closer. There was the edge of a low, wood-sided building beyond the house and what looked like an orchard beyond that. "Beth told me a little about it," he said. "Klein pulled down the old Parker place, didn't he?"

"Wind pulled it down," Ackroyd said, sipping from his coffee cup and letting the pause underscore what he'd said. "Klein just had it hauled away. There was a Santa Ana wind back in fifty-seven that blew the roof off the old ranch house. Knocked all the windows out. Wrecked the place. Wind blew for fourteen days. Maybe you remember that one.''

"I would have been seven," Peter said, "but I remember there was one wind back then that lasted about forever, knocked down some eucalyptus trees in our neighborhood.''

"Force twelve on the Beaufort Scale," Ackroyd said. ''That's hurricane force—a record breaker for Southern California. Hills were full of wildfires. Fifty thousand acres burned in the San Gabriels. They had to close the streets to the public after the wind blew a man right through a storefront window in Santa Ana. Toppled trees. Millions of dollars in property damage. Old Lydia Parker, of course, had been dead since the late thirties, and her daughter Anne had lived on there alone through the war. She was eccentric, a recluse. Passed on right around mid-century, and the place was abandoned except for the hired man who lived in the bunkhouse. He stayed on until the wind wrecked the place. By then it was beyond repair.''

"So this was after the murder?''

Ackroyd sat in silence, as if the mention of the murder had stopped him cold. "*Long* after," he said finally. "Parker's son was killed in the early twenties. Very bloody, terrible thing. They put a lid on it. These days the press would have a circus with it, but back then things were different. Justice was small time, much more personal. Often much less just.''

"What I heard from a waitress down at Cook's Corner is that my place sat empty for so long because it was built by the murderer. What was his name? Dr. Landry, I think. That's why it was cheap. No one wanted to buy a house with that reputation. My good luck, I guess.''

"Something like that. Landry left a certain amount of money in trust, actually, and a firm out in Tustin looked after the place for years, kept it locked up tight. Inflation ate the trust, though, and there wasn't enough in it to make structural repairs. There were no heirs. It was finally put on the market when the old lease ran out. I suspect that if you hadn't bought it, the Forest Service would have pulled it down.''

"You've been out here a long time. You must have known Landry. What happened to him?''

"Disappeared," Ackroyd said.

"He disappeared?''

"One day he was gone. Of course he might've been gone a month, and nobody would have known. He became a sort of hermit after the murder. A local pariah."

"And no one knows where he went?"

"Mystery was never solved. Some people think he wandered away into the hills and died."

"Why didn't they convict Landry for the murder?"

"Actually, they *did* convict him. They didn't jail him, though. Lewis Parker, the murdered man, was his wife's cousin. Dr. Landry caught them in a . . . dalliance late one night. Back then you could kill a man for that. It evened the score. Ended Landry's standing in society, of course, what there was of it. The marriage was what people called ill fated. Neither one of them did well by it, although she fared the worst." Ackroyd paused for the space of a long minute, as if lost in thought. "Maybe Landry tried, in his way, to make a go of it. Tried and failed. It was the child that pushed him . . . that he couldn't abide."

"It was Parker's child?"

"Maybe. People were certainly inclined to think so. *He* apparently thought so."

"That's why you said Landry had no heirs?"

He shook his head. "No, Landry had no heirs because his wife and the boy committed suicide on that same night that he hacked Lewis Parker to death with a shovel. Esther took the boy up onto the ridge. . . ." The old man stood up and turned around, examining the old photographs on the wall again. "The two of them jumped into Falls Canyon."

Peter was suddenly aware that the old man was crying. He sat in shocked silence. "I'm sorry if . . ." he started, but Ackroyd held up a hand and stopped him.

"It's nothing you did," he said after a moment. "I'm an old man who's lived here all his life holding on to a handful of memories like a child clinging to an old worn-out blanket." He sat still, recovering. Then, standing up and walking to the open front door he said, "Esther Landry was my sister."

**2**

THER WAS A CERTAIN COMFORTABLE ROUTINE IN GETTING BOBBY set up in front of the television on weekend mornings. He seemed to think that there was a magic in getting things just right, arranging his stuffed animals, wrapping up in his quilt. Beth wondered how long he would be allowed to believe in that magic. Last night he had slept through everything, thank God, even the visit by the police.

"Could you bring me a little smackeral of something?" he asked. Having a "smackeral" of something to tide him over until breakfast was a habit he'd picked up from Winnie the Pooh.

She put a coffee mug full of water into the microwave, and then poured Cheerios and raisins into a cup shaped like a hippopotamus head. She carried it out into the living room and handed it to Bobby, who sat with his legs crossed on the couch, surrounded by the menagerie of stuffed animals and covered by the worn-out dinosaur quilt even though he was already dressed.

"Here you go," Beth said. "Try not to spill, okay? Especially the raisins."

"Get cups for everybody, will you?" Bobby asked, taking the hippo head from her.

"Maybe not," Beth said. "I brought a lot for you, plenty enough to share. And put your shoes on while you're watching TV, okay? So you'll be ready to go."

"Sure," Bobby said. "You should have seen my dream last night."

"A bad one?"

"About Dad."

"Oh."

"I dreamed that King Kong picked Dad up, you know? And dropped him, like from the top of a building."

"How awful," Beth said. Actually she envied him the dream. She hadn't had any really pleasurable dreams in quite a while.

"Only Dad turned into a yo-yo, you know, on a string, and so he didn't hit the ground, after all."

Ah well, Beth thought, so much for happy endings. The microwave buzzer went off, and she went back into the kitchen, leaving Bobby to watch the last couple of minutes of "Sesame Street." After lifting the mug full of hot water out of the oven, she heaped about twice the recommended amount of instant decaf into it. She stirred it idly, and through the window she watched the wind blow through a distant line of eucalyptus trees. She felt dull, as if she were hung over from the iced tea she'd drunk last night at the steak house.

If Peter had a phone she'd call him up right now and say something to him, although she didn't know what.

How in the hell had she fallen in love with a man on the rebound, one who was so obviously blundering through an emotional mine field? There was no explaining it. And he danced like—what? There wasn't a word for it. Dreadful didn't cover enough ground. It was his eyes that had gotten to her first, years ago—always smiling and cheerful. That was partly it: he was easy to be around, comfortable. And in about twelve thousand ways he was different from Walter, her ex-husband. If Bobby had any dreams about Peter, they'd be good ones.

From inside her house she could see down into the next-door neighbor's backyard, and right then Lance Klein came out through their french doors and stood by the pool, holding a cordless phone. Beth couldn't help but like Klein, despite his being a little overbearing. He had called earlier that morning to tell her about how he was going to install new locks on her doors and windows. He was going to loan her the cordless phone, too, with his number in the memory dial. There was no use arguing with him.

Everyone, even his wife Lorna, called him Klein, as if he had never had a first-name sort of friendship with anyone. Lorna had been a blond bombshell once, but now she wore her bathrobe until the middle of the afternoon. She was a closet lush, too, probably to put up with his bullying. There was a lot to her, though, and maybe it would have been better if she'd kept her job at the library after marrying Klein. Doing nothing hadn't seemed to agree with her.

Lorna had told Beth that she herself had miscarried twice and then had never been able to get pregnant again. The doctor, Lorna said, had wanted Klein to provide a semen sample, but he had indignantly refused, and had said, out loud, right there in the doctor's office, that no one could *ever* question *his* manhood. As funny as it was, Beth had wanted to wring Klein's neck on Lorna's behalf.

Like Peter, Klein was almost always up for a game of catch with Bobby, and Beth liked him for that, too. Bobby's father hadn't ever had time for that sort of thing. And now, thank God, Bobby's father lived in New Bedford, where he had a real estate license and was married to a woman he had met when he and Beth were still married.

The woman was also "in real estate" as her ex liked to say. He was the king of jargon. The two of them, he and the bimbo, had been fond of having "lock box sex" in houses they were selling for people. They would meet at predetermined houses, let themselves in, and save the price of a hotel. Except that one afternoon the woman who owned that day's house had got off work early and found them rutting away on the fold-out couch in the den. Before she called the police and the Real Estate Board, she called Beth.

So now he lived back East, and sent child support but no alimony. To hell with his alimony; Beth didn't want his money when they broke up, and she didn't want it now. What she wanted was never to see him or hear from him again. She put the child-support checks straight into a bank account in Bobby's name. He could use the money when he went to college. In a just world King Kong would have dropped Walter onto his head.

Yesterday she had talked to Bobby about his having to come home early from New Bedford. Bobby acted as if it didn't matter. He was too cool to care. And besides, his father couldn't help it. He was a busy man, very important, tons of money. He even drove a Porsche.

She didn't want Bobby spending any time with his father anyway, even though Bobby still maintained some kind of love for the man, despite Walter's being a treacherous pig. Kids seemed to have that skill—loving people and things for reasons of their own, without any help from anything on earth. But like other kinds of magic it diminished as time passed. It had for Beth. Right now, for instance, Beth would just as soon her ex-husband dropped dead, if only because Bobby was so full of this selfless love, and yet the creep had sent him home early from his Thanksgiving visit.

To top it off, here it was almost two years later, and Walter still had the power to make her this mad. That's what *really* makes me mad, she thought, nearly laughing out loud. It didn't figure. Just yesterday morning she had lectured Peter about figuring out what he wanted, but it was the kind of advice she herself had never been able to put to use.

She wondered what was worse, to be two years out of a bad marriage and still want to murder your ex, or to be consumed with doubt about the divorce. Somehow, whether Peter wanted her to or not, she was going to have to set him up on the couch with a dozen stuffed animals and a hippo head full of Cheerios.

THE CABIN THAT PETER SAW THROUGH THE TREES WAS LITTLE more than a shack, what the locals called a "teardown." There was a mattress spring in the yard, stripped of stuffing and left outside to rust along with empty paint cans and old lumber, all of it overgrown with poison oak and covered in fallen leaves. What had happened to the paint in the cans was a mystery, because the cabin itself clearly hadn't been painted in years. The old rough-cut siding was full of woodpecker holes, and about half the windows were broken and filled with cardboard and aluminum foil.

Somebody was home, though. The front door was open, and there was a light blue Isuzu Trooper parked outside, nearly brand new and utterly out of character with the cabin. It was possible that Amanda and David had come this way last Sunday if they'd hiked up one of the trails to the ridge. *Somebody* must have seen them.

His conversation with Mr. Ackroyd this morning was making that harder and harder to believe. So this was it. If nothing panned out here, then he'd pack it in. He walked up the drive, and just then a scrawny little dog crawled out from under the porch and wandered toward him. It was some kind of pop-eyed chihuahua mix with a skin condition and a head the size of a golf ball. There was something weirdly possum-looking about it—maybe its tail, which was hairless except for a patch of fur at the end.

"Sit, Queenie," Peter said, bending over to pet it, and the dog sat down and raised its paw, then lowered it again without giving Peter time to shake it. It lay down and rolled onto its side, waving the paw in the air in a gesture of friendship. He scratched it behind the ear, and abruptly there was a loud voice from inside the cabin. Somebody was either angry or deaf. Peter stood up. To hell with knocking. Whatever this was, he didn't need it.

Just then the screen door banged open and a man strode out onto the porch, turning to say one last thing through the open door. Peter recognized him immediately—what's-his-name, Adams, the man who was "looking for something to buy" at the steak house last night.

"That's an attitude that some people can't afford to take," Adams said, in a tone that sounded as if the statement were meant as a piece of good friendly advice, and not as a threat.

"Shove off!" a voice shouted back.

"I'll consider . . ." Adams started, but then there was the sound of something heavy hitting the floor inside, and he clipped off his sentence and stepped quickly down the wooden steps.

"Think about *this*," the voice said, but whatever it was, Adams didn't wait to find out. He climbed into the Trooper, started the engine, and drove straight past Peter without taking his eyes off the road. There was fear and hatred in his face, which he seemed to want to take out on the car, slamming away across the potholes and throwing up a cloud of dust and leaves.

"That man's no damn good, Queenie," Peter said. The dog watched the car disappear around the bend.

Through the screen door someone shouted, "Freeway!" and the dog trotted toward the porch. A man stepped out and gave Peter a hard look. He was tall and thin, with white hair combed forward to cover a bald spot, although it looked as if it were combed that way by accident rather than vanity, and he clearly hadn't shaved for a couple of days. His flannel shirt was torn out at the elbows, and he wore it with the sleeves rolled up over long underwear even though the Santa Ana winds had already heated the morning air.

Peter nodded at him. "I think that guy might be trouble," he said. "I've run into him before."

"Run into him harder next time," the man said, wiping his mouth with his hand. "So who the hell are you? You want to buy me out, too? I don't even want to *hear* a price. I told that till I'm blue in the face to three people now. This cabin's about all I've got. Costs me three hundred a year lease from the Forest Service, and that's it. No rent. No mortgage. You can't live that cheap in jail. Why the hell would I sell out? Every damned week-end somebody comes up here looking to buy, but I ain't selling, and you can tell 'em that.''

"I don't want to buy your place," Peter said. "I've got one of my own down the road. I was just shooting the breeze with your dog.''

"That's old Freeway." The man relaxed, as if he could trust anyone who was a friend to his dog.

"Good name," Peter said. "I might get a dog one of these days.''

"He's half purebred. Champion stock. You don't want to get a whole purebred, though. Their brain's screwed up from the inbreeding.''

"I've always had a mutt," Peter said.

"And keep 'em in at night if you don't want the lions to eat 'em. It's all right they stay outside in the daytime, but night's a different deal. If you do leave 'em out at night, for God's sake don't tie 'em up. They ain't nothing but TV dinners tied up. Lion'll come down and eat a dog right off the chain, bones and all. Don't think it hasn't happened.''

Peter nodded. "I get the picture," he said, reaching down to pet Freeway again, who lay down and wallowed in the loose dirt. "I wanted to ask you a question if you've got a minute.''

"I got all day," the man said. "That's why I live out here. That stupid son of a bitch couldn't grasp that. You know what he did? Turned me in to the Forest Service for all this crap in the yard. I *know* it was him, trying to wedge me out of here." He gestured at the mattress springs and paint cans. "None of his damned business, and he calls the Ranger and turns me in. Now I got a notice that I got to clean it up. This morning he walks right in the door, like he already owns the place, and tells me that he knows I got my price, and he's willing to pay it. He comes around here again I'm going to set old Freeway on him. Freeway ain't got much hair, but he's got teeth like a saw blade. Hold on a second.''

He went into the house and then came straight back out carrying two bottles of beer. "Set down," he said, nodding at two old kitchen chairs on the porch.

"Peter Travers," Peter said, holding out his hand.

The man shook it, then put the beer into it. "Dooly Bateman. Which cabin?"

"Number twelve."

"I thought twelve was empty. Has been for years."

"Not anymore. I bought it."

"Twelve's been empty for years." He scratched his nose, as if he was calculating. "I'll be damned. Twelve. What'd it sell for?"

"Thirty thousand," Peter said.

He whistled and widened his eyes. "It don't seem like they could give it away. Nice place in its day, of course. I always wondered about it. Supposed to be haunted. They say a crazy man used to own it. Old Ackroyd could tell you about it. He's the only one's been out here long enough. I don't guess people want a place like that."

"I guess not," Peter said. "Nobody but me. What do you mean, haunted?"

"Oh, you know. Regular sort of thing. Old man who owned it was supposed to have died out there or disappeared or whatever. Anyway they never found him. People seen him through the windows, going around, doing all that worthless crap ghosts do. It's all lies, of course. Nothing to keep you awake nights."

"Doesn't sound like it," Peter said. He held up the photograph of Amanda and David. "I wonder if you've seen these people."

The man took it, holding it at arm's length. "What are you," he said, "some kind of cop?"

"No," Peter said, dreading this part. "I'm her husband."

"Swear to God?" Bateman said, widening his eyes. He paused long enough to drink the rest of the beer in his bottle, then looked at the photo again. "Now, I might know the woman," he said. "But the boy . . . I ain't seen the boy. What's the deal about 'em?"

"Lost," Peter said. "Last Sunday afternoon." That was the worst part. "When did you see the woman?"

"Well, at first I thought she was the one used to work up at the general store. Back a couple of years. But you say you're married to her, so you'd know that better than me. What was her name? Lu, I think it was. I didn't know she had a kid, though."

"That couldn't be her," Peter said.

"No, I don't guess so." He looked at the photo again. "You want another beer? I was just going to open me another one."

Peter shook his head. "Thanks anyway."

"You going to drink that one?"

"I guess not," Peter said.

"Then I'll go ahead and drink it for you. If I had a Coke or something I'd offer it, but I'm out. Cup of coffee?"

"No, thanks."

"Where they supposed to be, anyway?" He gestured at the photograph.

"Hawaii," Peter said without thinking.

He nodded slowly, as if that explained nearly everything. "I was married once. Lasted ten years. Two kids. She up and left me, too. Oh, it was my fault, I guess, come to think of it. You've got to treat a woman right." He looked at the photo again. "Nice-looking lady. No offense my saying so, I hope."

"No offense," Peter said.

"If it was me, I'd try to hold on to her a little tighter. I'd get the hell over to Hawaii, if I was you, not that I mean to be giving you advice. Either that or why don't you wire 'em money? You can do that nearly everywhere now. No problem to Hawaii. Tell her to get on the next plane out's what I'd do. Sometimes you've got to eat a little crow. It don't taste bad. A married man gets used to the flavor or he don't stay married."

"That's the truth," Peter said. Somehow a wire had disconnected in the conversation. He let it go for the moment.

"So what kept *you* home, anyway? Seems to me a man should go along with the family to a place like Hawaii. No offense meant again."

"I can't stand the heat," Peter said, taking the photograph back. "Haven't seen either of them, then?"

"Not unless that's Lu, and all I can tell you is that she worked over at the store in the Oaks, might have been, hell, three, four years back, come to think of it. Real nice gal. Same hair as this anyway. Dress kind of reminds me of a woman's been hanging around the canyon for the last week or so. Woman and boy. I don't know, though." He focused on the photograph and shook his head. "I guess that ain't them, either."

"Woman in a black dress?" Peter asked. "Kid's got suspenders and a striped shirt?"

"Them's the ones. I think they're some kind of homeless. That son of a bitch I just run off probably bought 'em out. That guy blows like big rats."

"That's the truth," Peter said, standing up. "Thanks, for the time.'' He patted Freeway again and stepped down off the porch.

''Sure you won't drink a beer?''

''Maybe later on.''

''Well, tell me, you ain't going up the road sometime today are you? My battery's just about as dead as it can be. You mind picking me up a couple of things? Just enough till I get going again. I could walk it, but I've got arthritis in both knees, and I'm about out of groceries.''

''Sure,'' Peter said. What the hell. He probably *was* going out sometime before the day was over, and if he wasn't, then he'd go out anyway. Bateman stepped inside and then back out again with a pencil and paper. He scribbled on the paper and handed it to Peter along with a pile of ones and some change. Peter shoved it all into his pocket.

''No hurry,'' the man said.

''Probably be later on this evening.''

''That'd be fine. And no offense on the advice, I hope. If I was you I'd think about wiring that money to the little woman, though. Soon, too. Western Union's the quickest, I guess. You wait too long like I did and you'll find yourself living out here like me with holes in your damned sleeves. Not that I don't like it.''

''Thanks for the good word,'' Peter said, turning around and waving over his shoulder. When he was out of sight down the road he took out the grocery list. ''Pabst Blue Ribbon, case'' was the first item, ''Pabst'' and ''case'' underlined three times. Then the words ''block ice.'' That was it. He didn't bother to count the money. If there was any change left he could wire it to Hawaii.

The sun had just climbed over the ridge and was baking the west-facing slopes. In the oak shadows of the canyon floor it was cool and perfect—the kind of day to open all the windows and doors and let the air in. The winds had diminished for the moment to a willowy little breeze that drifted out of the northeast, stirring the leaves high up in the alders and carrying on it the smell of chaparral. There were autumn colors in the sycamores, and except for that and the carpet of fallen leaves, it might have been summer.

Instead of heading toward home Peter hiked up the slope toward the ridge. If Amanda and David *had* gone that way then maybe there'd be something, some clue. If he had a dog like Freeway he could probably search out a broken twig or a wind-faded spoor. "Comb the hillsides, Freeway!" he said out loud, then laughed.

He stopped himself, closing his eyes instead, letting the breeze wash past him. If only he wasn't so damned useless! He'd had a wife and child, and six months ago he'd lost them, or thought he had. He'd spent those months twisting it in his head, arguing through it—whose fault it was, how it happened, this leading to that—as if the pieces of his marriage were a complicated jigsaw puzzle, and he could move the pieces around until they'd make a clear picture that he could study and make sense of.

Now he'd lost them again. Only this time it wasn't in any kind of figurative sense. There weren't any puzzle pieces now, nothing to argue through, nothing to protest, just some ghostly shapes in the darkness. What Ackroyd had told him hadn't made anything more clear, but had revealed an even deeper void, and he stood now on this windy hillside looking into it, trying to see something where there was nothing.

He opened his eyes. The canyon stretched before him, winding down toward the flatlands, disappearing beyond the ridges so that civilization might have been infinitely distant. He decided right then to hike as far as the top of Falls Canyon just to see what the falls looked like in the daytime. Maybe what he'd seen last night was some trick of shadow and perspective—just another illusion. Or maybe it was a picture in the darkness.

KLEIN HAD BEEN UP SINCE FIVE IN THE MORNING, PROWLING around the house, listening to the wind. He had cleaned and loaded his two pistols first thing—one of them for Beth, although she would probably try to argue with him about it. She didn't understand about Pomeroy, but he certainly couldn't explain him to her. Sometime this morning he would head down to the Builders Emporium in El Toro to buy a couple of decent dead-bolt locks for Beth's doors, and new sash hardware to replace the screwed-up stuff on her windows. He was going to lend her a cordless phone, too, in case the dirty little prick came back. She could haul the phone around with her from room to room and punch his number in the memory dial if she needed to. He pictured confronting Pomeroy—the look on his face when he saw the pistol in Klein's hand.

The telephone rang at nine. It was him, calling from the pay phone in front of the general store. Klein listened impatiently to the usual rundown on cabins, but he was distracted by last night. He had been half hoping that Pomeroy wouldn't call at all, that he would have pulled up stakes and moved.

". . . the old man again this morning," he heard Pomeroy say. "There was no action on the tank yet. I've got a couple of ideas for leaning on him a little harder."

"What?" Klein asked, listening now.

"I said I worked on Ackroyd again this morning. Only had a second, but you know me; I keep chipping away. I hate to push a friend of your wife's like that, but, hey, business is business. He'll end up with a good dollar."

Klein wanted to swear into the receiver, but he forced himself to stay calm. This *was* business, whether he liked it or not. "Maybe you better back off a little," he said. "You don't have to sell him or lose him today. He'll be there next week and the week after that. Maybe you ought to give it a rest for a little while, Barn. People are going to start wondering how come you're making so many strong offers and not buying anything."

"There's a time frame, Lance."

"I *know* there's a time frame. I set it up. It's *my* time frame. And I say to hell with Ackroyd. We don't want people asking questions we can't answer."

"I don't think we can afford to take that attitude, Lance. As far as the old man goes, I'll come up with something."

Like a rabid dog, Klein thought. Maybe there was nothing left to do but shoot him. "Clear it with me first, will you?" he said, forcing his voice to stay level.

"Sure," Pomeroy said meaninglessly. "But I think he smells something. Probably that woman I met out there yesterday said something to him."

"*What?*" Klein asked. "What *woman*?"

"The one I was talking to at the steak house last night. Her boyfriend's got a place out in the canyon. Number twelve, I think."

"Why would *she* have said anything to anyone? What the hell are you talking about?"

"I'm not sure, but she might have seen me fix up the old man's tank. You know, with the mousies." Pomeroy snickered.

"Jesus Christ!" Klein shouted into the phone. "What the hell kind of stupid—!"

"Whoa!" Pomeroy shouted back at him. "Relax. Don't worry. I'll chat her up a little bit. She'll get the drift." After a pause he said, "Problem is, I don't know where she lives. I think it must be around here somewhere. She acts like a local."

"That's what you *think*, is it?" Klein said evenly.

"Makes sense," Pomeroy said.

"Leave her alone," Klein said hoarsely. "I'm only going to warn you once about that. Don't say *anything* to her. Don't go near her. Get the drift?"

"I don't think *you've* got the drift yet," Pomeroy said. "You know, now that I think about it, maybe it was your wife who talked to the old man, since they know each other. What did you tell me, that they used to work together? You've got to watch what you say to her, Lance, or you'll turn your own wife into a liability."

I should have shot him last night, Klein thought. I should have followed him out into the field and got it over with, told the cops that the bastard jumped me. "My wife doesn't understand the first damned thing about this deal," Klein said evenly. "And if she did, so what? She's going to blow a hundred grand gabbing about it? Hell, she knows better than that. My advice, Barn . . . Are you listening?"

"All ears."

"My advice is that you don't talk to my wife, not even about the weather."

"Then you better send her out after groceries, Lance, because I think it's time you and I chewed a little fat face-to-face."

The line went dead. After a moment there was a dial tone, and it was only then that Klein understood that Pomeroy was on his way up to the house.

PUTTING DOWN THE COFFEE MUG, BETH WENT BACK INTO THE living room, where there was a cartoon on about a dog who was trying to parboil a cat, which escaped mutilation by making the dog step on a bear trap, momentarily crippling it. "This is awful," Beth said.

"It's a car*toon*," Bobby told her. "It's not real."

"Remember that," Beth said. And of course he would. He didn't have any trouble distinguishing between make-believe and reality. That was one of the main functions of a parent, though, to remind children about things they already knew.

"It's nearly time to leave," she said. "You about ready to go?"

"Yeah," Bobby said. "Where we going?"

"Over to the nursery. We've got to pick out a rosebush for Peter's house."

"Now?"

"In a few minutes. You were going to put your shoes on," she said to him.

Bobby kept his eyes on the TV screen. "I can't find them," he said. "I found my hat, though."

"They're right there," Beth said, "on the floor by the end of the couch."

Bobby said, "Oh, yeah," without looking up.

"Put them on. Now. You should eat something more, too."

He looked around for a moment, and then focused on the shoes. "I don't want those shoes. I want my new Airwalks if I'm going over to Peter's today."

"Then get your Airwalks. Just put on some shoes."

Bobby pushed his quilt around for a moment, finding a shoe underneath it. He held the shoe up in the air—eighty-dollar tennis shoes, a gift from his father. "Other one's gone," Bobby said. "I think it's lost."

Slightly irritated, Beth started across to turn off the television. The show was over anyway. There was a commercial just then coming on.

"Wait!" Bobby said. "This is great. Watch."

Beth watched as an ad came on for some sort of newly invented breakfast cereal with flying saucer–shaped marshmallow pieces in it.

"Can we get some?" Bobby asked.

"I told you about breakfast cereal with marshmallows in it."

"I know," Bobby said. "Marshmallows are just oil and sugar."

"That's right. No food value."

"Oil is good for you," Bobby said. "You've got to have oil. Just like a car."

"Who told you *that*?" Beth asked.

"Peter. He said that there's a part of your heart called a crank-case, and it needs oil once in a while."

"Peter's kidding."

"You saying there's no such thing as a crankcase?"

"Yes there's a crankcase, but it's not part of your heart. It's part of a car engine. Peter's just being crazy."

"I knew that," Bobby said. "I was seeing if you did."

"I know everything," Beth said. "I'm your mother."

"Then find my other shoe, will you?" Bobby stood up from the couch and wandered into the kitchen. "And find my trucks and my blue alien, too, okay?"

"If I can. There's a bowl of cereal on the table," Beth said. "Pour your own milk, but be careful."

"You always say that," Bobby said. "Like I'm going to spill on purpose or something."

"They pay me to say that," Beth said, and then went off to find his shoe. Bobby's bedroom looked like a wreck. He had too much stuff, and somewhere in it, hidden, lay the other tennis shoe. She got down onto her hands and knees and looked under the bed. Nearly every inch of space under there was clogged with stuffed animals. "Where did you find the shoe you've got?" she hollered at him. Sometimes she got lucky, and Bobby had taken off both his shoes in the same room of the house, so that if she found one of them she could find the other somewhere nearby.

"Under the quilt," Bobby shouted back at her.

"I mean *before* that."

"In the bedroom," Bobby shouted. Then, not quite as loudly, he said, "What is this stuff?"

Hopeful, she went back into the kitchen again in order to avoid shouting. She had bought a new breakfast cereal, one that had nothing to do with anyone's crankcase.

"It looks like Fruit Loops," Bobby said, "only they forgot to put enough color in them."

The cereal had no added sugar or salt. It was full of oat bran, too, and sweetened with fruit juice, which also provided the color. It was three-forty-nine a box, but what was money when your son's health was concerned?

"Looks okay," Bobby said, dousing it with milk.

"Yum," Beth said. "Good for you, too. What do you think?"

Bobby chewed up a spoonful, then laid the spoon back into the bowl and made an awful face. "It's *crap*," he said, and for a moment Beth thought that he was going to spit it back into the bowl. He choked it down, though, then picked up his milk and swallowed half a glass full. "*You* try it."

"I bet it's good," Beth said, picking up the spoon. "And I don't want you talking like that."

"Like what? What did I say?"

"You know. Just watch your mouth."

"All right. But you were the one who made me eat it."

"This is the sort of thing the astronauts eat," she said cheerfully, spooning some of it up. Bobby was in an outer-space phase right now, and so was susceptible to the mention of astronauts. Beth crunched the cereal up in her mouth, anticipating something that tasted at least a little bit like it looked. What she got was the flavor of sawdust mixed up with something like lemon extract. Poker-faced, she swallowed it, then drank the rest of Bobby's milk.

"Why would the astronauts eat something like that?" Bobby asked. "To lose weight? I mean, you wouldn't eat very much of it."

"That must be it," Beth said. She carried the bowl of cereal to the sink and poured it down the disposer.

There was shouting from outside. She looked out the window into the Kleins' backyard, where Lance Klein was striding back and forth at the edge of the pool, obviously mad as hell. He suddenly stopped, looked at the telephone, and then threw it hard into the bushes along the side of the house. She wondered whether it was the phone he had meant to loan her.

"What am I going to eat, then?" Bobby asked. "Can we go down to Emory's and get a box of Pop-a-Toast? Peter's never had Pop-a-Toast. Maybe we could buy a box of it and surprise him."

"Good idea," Beth said. "We'll bring him a box of Pop-a-Toast and a rosebush. Right now, though, try to remember where your other shoe is."

"It's under the bed. I just remembered."

She forced herself to ignore Klein, who was worked up into a frenzy and was kicking the hell out of a lawn chair. It was none of her business, thank heaven.

"What's it doing under the bed?" she asked, turning away from the window. "In fact, what are all those stuffed animals doing under the bed?"

"That's the zoo," Bobby said, using both hands to pour another glass of milk. "It's only the zoo animals under there." Without drinking the milk, he got up and led Beth back into the bedroom. He slid easily under the bed, hauling out animals until he found the shoe. A plastic man in a hat sat in the shoe as if it were an automobile. Bobby pulled the man out, pressed a lever on its back, and the man's stomach flew open to reveal sausage strings of plastic guts.

"See," Bobby said, "you can take his guts out too, and pretend to feed them to the lions or something."

"Fascinating," Beth said to him. "Put the shoe on and let's get going. And brush your teeth and comb your hair."

"I'll brush my teeth," Bobby said, pulling his shoe on, "but I don't need to comb my hair. I'm wearing my hat. Did you find the alien?"

"Not yet," Beth said, walking back toward the kitchen.

"I think maybe it's outside," Bobby said. "But I'm not sure." He disappeared down the hallway to the bathroom.

There was half a cup of cold coffee left, which Beth drank standing at the kitchen window again, staring out at the windblown hillsides. She realized then that all morning long she had been avoiding looking into the service porch, and she wondered if she would ever be able to look out through the back door window again without seeing that bandage-wrapped face in her mind.

A horn honked out front, and just then a blue Isuzu Trooper pulled into Klein's driveway. A man got out, slamming the door and carefully smoothing down his hair. It took a moment for Beth to recognize him.

**6**

"I'LL HAVE TO KILL HIM," KLEIN SAID OUT LOUD, SPEAKING to the empty backyard. "There's just no other way. Stupid damned . . ."

Then it occurred to him that Pomeroy's talk about Beth put a new light on things. If it *was* him last night, looking through the windows, then there was the chance he wasn't a pervert at all, that he was just trying to put the fear into Beth because he thought she'd seen him loading up Ackroyd's water tank with rats. That would be typical Pomeroy method—instant excess.

Either way, clearly Pomeroy was over the top. He had gotten to Klein bad last night and then again over the phone just now. Klein was running, and Pomeroy knew it. It was time to stop running.

There was the sound of a car pulling up, a door slamming. Klein ran along the side of the house and looked over the fence toward the driveway. There was no white Cherokee out there. Pomeroy was driving a blue Isuzu Trooper this morning. He could easily have ditched the other car.

A couple of moments later one of the french doors swung open and Pomeroy stepped out into the yard.

"Barney," Klein said, holding out his hand as if nothing had gone wrong over the phone. Pomeroy shook it. "You had me going for a second there, partner. What I want to know is that things are under *control*."

"You never have to ask me that, Lance. That's my middle name."

"Good," Klein said, gesturing at a lawn chair. "Then we're on the same wavelength." The two of them sat down near the fence where they were sheltered from the wind. "Glass of juice?"

Pomeroy shook his head.

"So give me the good news," Klein said, "if you've got any."

"Well," Pomeroy said. "All in all it was a good morning. I got out there real early. Lot of people working on their places. I managed to get prices on three out in Holy Jim. Number two, number five, and number twenty-eight. They'll all sell. Thirty-five thousand on number two.''

''That's gotta be bullshit,'' Klein said. ''We can get number two for twenty, max. Fifteen. Number two's nearly a teardown. I can't believe you're letting these people hose you like this. You're a goddamn *car* salesman, Barney. How about twenty-eight? That's a good item.''

''Forty K.''

Klein thought about it. Cabin twenty-eight was an easy thousand square feet, with solar equipment and a detached shed. There were leaded windows, a river-rock fireplace, and a thousand-gallon water tank. Propane tank owned, not rented. It was a good, solid cabin, unlike number two, which was a termite-eaten pile of crap. ''Name and number?''

Pomeroy pulled a slip of paper out of his shirt pocket and handed it to Klein. There was an address and phone number on it. ''Name's Newman,'' Pomeroy said. ''Oceanside couple. She's in and out of the hospital with some kind of heart trouble.''

''That's perfect. We'll take them down. How about number five?''

''Thirty-eight. And that's firm.''

''And you said cash?''

''Of course I said cash.''

''Then they're not serious. Give them a week to think about it. They'll come around. And, Barney,'' Klein said, talking evenly, trying to put an almost humorous edge on his voice, ''for Pete's sake quit talking about *leaning* on people, will you? I don't run a business that *leans* on people. That kind of thing isn't in my book. And if it was, then we *sure* as hell wouldn't want to talk about it.''

Pomeroy waited, smiling faintly, and Klein had to force himself to keep his temper.

''You know what I'm talking about?'' Klein asked. ''All you've got to do is make it clear that you've got cash and that you want to spend it. If they don't make a buck off you, then the guy next door will. That ought to be enough to get them thinking. Let the money do the talking, Barn.''

Pomeroy tilted his chair against the fence, still saying nothing, still smiling. Klein decided to wait him out. If he went on explaining himself he would start to sound frantic, and that was no good.

Finally, nodding heavily, Pomeroy changed the subject: "Hell of a nice place you've got here."

"It's a good investment," Klein said.

"No, I mean it's more than that. Nice pool. Sweet little neighborhood. Neighborhood looks like something off a Christmas card."

"Well," Klein said. "Lorna likes it pretty well." Immediately he wished he hadn't mentioned Lorna. Pomeroy seemed to light up at the sound of her name. He nodded as if that were just what he was driving at.

"What I mean is that it would be a dirty damned shame to pour this all down a rat hole." Pomeroy waved his hand around to take in all of it—the house, the pool, the view. He straightened his chair up and looked steadily at Klein. "Bad management could threaten it. We've both seen that happen."

"Yeah," Klein said. "I guess we have." This was it. Pomeroy was going to spring it.

"Poor old Larry Collier." He shook his head. "Still, a heart attack isn't a bad way to go. And they'd have screwed him, too. There was plenty there to convict him. Those fake perc tests and core samples. If that fire hadn't got the evidence . . ." He shook his head again, as if it were a hell of a shame.

Klein was silent. Finally Pomeroy had gotten around to the inevitable. What would it be, extortion?

"Does your wife . . . what's her name again?"

"Just leave her out of it," Klein said. "I told you that once. Don't make me say it again."

"Hey," Pomeroy said, holding up his hands in a gesture of innocence. "I was just wondering if she knew about those cheap-shit houses you built that slid into the ravine, that's all. Wasn't someone hurt? Man, I can hardly remember. A kid, wasn't it? It's a hell of a sad thing when a kid gets hurt. Paralyzed, I seem to recall."

Klein forced himself to sit still.

"I don't know if there's any statute of limitations on that kind of thing. It's worth looking into, though. You can't be too safe nowadays. World's full of people that would take you straight to the cleaners if they got their hands on all that burned-up evidence. And there's even worse things than *that*."

"I bet there are," Klein said. "Am I going to guess, or are you going to tell me about them?"

"Well," Pomeroy said, "it's a hell of a thing for a good

woman to find out that kind of thing about her husband. That was what happened to poor old Larry. You knew that part, didn't you?''

Klein watched his face.

''It took old Larry apart a piece at a time. He tried to hold it all together, but it was like the tide coming in. There wasn't a damned thing he could do. Information leaked out—Lord knows how. Then the lawsuits. He tried paying people off, and that didn't work. Next thing you know, his wife found out about all of it—all of Larry's little secrets. Just between me and you, Lance, old Larry had a thing for girls. And I do mean girls.''

''Barney, shut the hell up,'' Klein said. ''That was years ago. Larry's dead. If you've got something to say, say it.''

''No,'' Pomeroy said. ''Wait. This is a great story. You won't believe this, but there was a call girl service in Anaheim back in the early seventies, probably going on since who knows when. Girls nine, ten years old. The whole thing blew up back in—hell, when was it? My memory's gone. August twenty-fourth, 1974. Story broke the next day in the *Bulletin*. Maybe you read about it.

''Anyway, poor old Larry Collier got arrested along with a bunch of other businessmen—city-father types. Paid a hell of a fine, which he could afford, believe me. I really think that what finally killed him was his wife hearing about it. All the details. He really hustled to hush it up. No one knows how it happened, his family finding out like that. I'm certain that's what killed him, though, more than the bankruptcy. He'd had a bypass, too. Ate heart medicine like candy. I'm surprised it didn't explode when he was diddling one of those ten-year-old . . .''

Klein hit him in the face, a wild punch that caught Pomeroy's cheek and knocked him over backward. His chair hit the fence, skidded sideways, and dumped him onto the concrete. Klein stood up and grabbed a handful of Pomeroy's shirt, pulling him halfway to his feet. He threw his fist back to hit him again, but Pomeroy jerked loose, tripped over the fallen chair, and scrambled like a crab toward the pool. He stood up and held both hands in front of himself, backpedaling toward the poolhouse.

''Settle down, Lance,'' Pomeroy said. ''Think about the consequences.''

''You're dead,'' Klein told him. ''I swear to God I'll kill you. You don't come here again. You don't phone. You're through.

Do you understand me now? Or do you need another fist in the face?"

"Uh-uh," Pomeroy said. He shook his head slowly, a grin twisting his mouth. "*You're* the one who better get the picture straight, Lance. When you work outside the law, there's a *whole* new set of rules. One of them is this. We're partners. You don't let your partner down, or maybe he lets you down, hard. The second one is that you learn to accept things. Keep the consequences in mind."

Klein sat back down in his chair, suddenly tired. A gust of wind blew more leaves through the fence just then, scattering them across the surface of the pool.

"That's life, isn't it?" Pomeroy asked, patting his hair down and nodding at the leaves. "The wind blows and there's not a damned thing you can do about it except bend."

Then his face changed suddenly. He crouched down and looked hard at the fence, as if he'd seen something through the slats. He picked up his overturned chair and climbed up onto the seat, balancing himself on the bars on either side and holding on like Kilroy to the top of the fence in order to peek over the top.

Smiling broadly now, he looked back down at Klein and winked, as if this beat all, as if he'd never before been quite so pleasantly surprised.

SUDDENLY CURIOUS, BETH WALKED OUT ONTO THE SERVICE porch and looked down through the blinds into the Kleins' back-yard. What's his name—Adams—came out through the back door and he and Klein sat down out of the wind.

Carefully, she reached through the blinds and unlatched the window, sliding it open an inch. Their voices rose and fell, nothing but murmurs.

Strange that Klein would have lied about knowing the man. Well, he hadn't really lied; he had just played things down. Beth hadn't given much thought to what Adams might have been up to out at Mr. Ackroyd's yesterday, but suddenly she suspected that it wasn't anything good. It wasn't surprising that the cat had torn him up. . . .

She pictured the face at the window again—wrapped in what? Gauze bandage? She looked closely at his hand now—some kind of wide Band-Aid on it.

God, *could* it be him? Did Klein suspect it, and that's why he was being so solicitous with the locks and the phone and all?

She closed the window now, opened the back door, and stepped out onto the porch, careful that the wind wouldn't slam the door. Across the lawn, an enormous green plastic turtle sat near the fence, full of sand and leaves and scraps of eucalyptus bark and with a scattering of toys stuck in it.

The slats of the redwood fence had shrunk over the years as the wood dried out, and through it she could see the forms of the two men who sat with their backs to it. They would see her pretty easily too, if they turned to look. She moved as silently as she could. Half-hidden by the avocado tree next to the sandbox, she watched them through the fence.

Adams was talking, and it was clear from his tone that there was nothing friendly about their conversation. "I was just wondering," he said, "if she knew about those cheap-shit houses you built that slid into the ravine, that's all. Wasn't someone hurt? Man, I can hardly remember. A kid, wasn't it? It's a hell of a sad thing when a kid gets hurt. Paralyzed, I seem to recall."

The tone of the man's voice filled Beth with rage; it was so smarmy, so clearly false.

Klein didn't say anything, and Adams droned on, mixing up jocularity with threats, telling a story about some mutual friend. Obviously Klein was in trouble. Adams wasn't just talking to hear his head rattle; he was clarifying Klein's position.

Then, abruptly, there was the sound of a chair scraping, followed by a grunt and Adams's chair slamming back against the fence. For a moment there was nothing but hoarse breathing and someone scrabbling around on the concrete. Beth leaned toward the fence, trying to see more clearly.

"Settle down, Lance." It was Adams's voice, husky, but trying to sound controlled. "Think about the consequences."

"You're dead," Klein told him, sounding flat and final. Beth found herself suddenly wondering what to do. Was he serious?

She almost ran for the house, but the sound of Adams's voice stopped her. There wasn't any fear in it, just the voice of a man speaking the matter-of-fact truth. "When you work outside the law," he said, "there's a whole new set of rules. . . ."

She had the wild urge to cough or speak or somehow shut them up before they said something that she shouldn't hear. There was the scraping of chairs again, and Beth stepped out from behind the eucalyptus tree, heading for the house while they were busy putting things back together. Then Adams's face appeared over the top of the fence. He looked down at Klein, smiling like an idiot. It was all she could do not to run.

"Why, hello, Beth," he said. "I've been anxious to talk to you. What? You live here, next to the Kleins?"

"Yes," she said. "Small world. I'd love to chat, but I'm really pretty busy right now." She backed away toward the house, trying to keep her fear from being obvious.

"Maybe a little later, then? I'd like to get to know you a little better."

"That's *it*!" Klein shouted, and Beth could see him stand up, strobelike, through the fence boards. There was the sound of Adams's lawn chair spinning away, and then Adams abruptly slammed downward, his chin banging against the top of the fence. He grunted, then disappeared. Breathlessly, someone shouted, "Wait!" and then there was scuffling and the sound of someone getting hit.

Beth ran for the house and in through the back door, which she shut behind her and locked. She stood there until her heart quit slamming, and then went to the window again, looking out through the slats, ready to call the police if she had to.

Lorna stood by the pool, clutching her bathrobe shut even though it was already tied. Adams's hair was a mess, as if Klein had been yanking at it, and he stood at the edge of the pool, angrily straightening his clothes. They were talking plenty loudly enough now for Beth to hear them.

"Get the hell out of here!" Klein shouted at him. "Lorna! Get the gun out of the nightstand. Now!"

"Now, Lance . . ." Lorna started to say, but Klein shouted, "Now!" again, and then shouted, "Dirty son of a bitch!" and brushed past Lorna toward the doors, disappearing into the house. Beth could still hear him yelling incoherently. Adams headed up the side of the house toward the front, breaking into a run and going out through the gate.

A moment later Klein appeared by the pool again, carrying a

pistol, but by then the blue Isuzu was backing out of the driveway, and in a moment Adams was gone.

"What was all that?"

Beth jumped, jerking her hand away from the blinds, which clattered against the window.

"You spying on the Kleins again?" Bobby asked.

"I'm not *spying*. There was some kind of trouble, but I guess they worked it out." The sound of wild voices rose again from next door.

"I guess so," Bobby said. "Sounds like it. Did you find the alien?"

"No."

"It's not out back?"

"I don't know."

"Didn't you look? You went out there."

"I *looked*. I didn't find it." Suddenly she wanted to get moving, to talk to Peter, maybe to Mr. Ackroyd. She wondered if Klein was wild enough to hurt Lorna, but the idea of calling the police now didn't seem to be a good one.

Bobby opened the back door and went out. Beth went looking for her purse. She checked the locks on the doors and windows. She had given Klein the key that morning so that he could get in to work on the locks. Outside, Bobby had found a tomato stake and was sword fighting with a tree limb.

"Hop in the car," Beth said to him.

"We can't," Bobby said. "I haven't found the alien yet."

"Hop in the car. You can do without it, and you weren't looking very hard anyway." All her patience had drained away.

"No, wait," Bobby said, starting to explain his thinking on the matter.

"Get in the *car*," Beth said evenly.

Then, as with the shoe, Bobby remembered where the alien was. They found it in the sandbox, buried up to its neck. That was what pirates did to their enemies, Bobby said. They buried them up to their necks on the beach and then waited for the tide to come in and drown them.

"Sometimes I feel that same way," Beth said, rinsing the alien off with the hose. But her voice shook, and it wasn't as funny as it should have been.

**8**

INSTEAD OF ROLLING ON UP THE HILL TOWARD THE CONDO, POM-
eroy turned left up Trabuco Canyon Road for the second time
that morning. He touched his lip and winced. It was tender, maybe
a little swollen where Klein had hit him. He'd regret that before
they were through. Probably he already did. Klein didn't know
which way to jump, and it was getting to him bad. The Trooper
bounced along through the arroyo, past two dead cars and an
overturned refrigerator, all of them rusted and shot up. The dried-
out husks of yucca and sumac jittered in the wind, and the sun
was nearly blinding through the dusty windshield.

Even with the windows rolled up he could smell dust and vegetation mixed with the stale-cigarette odor of the inside of the
Trooper. There was the faint smell of something else, too, like
old lettuce, coming from the inside of the cardboard carton on
the passenger-side floor. He had made the rental agency wash out
the ashtrays and hose the upholstery down with some kind of
scented spray, but that had done nothing except add a sickening
miasma of roses to the car's interior. Probably he wouldn't keep
the car beyond a couple of days anyway. Still, he was going to
talk to the manager about it. That was no way to run a business,
renting a car like that to a non-smoker.

He braked carefully, grabbing the camera on the seat beside
him and easing the Trooper across a wash, past a swinging gate
made of rusty steel poles and old barbed wire. There was a
crudely drawn skull on the No Trespassing sign that hung from
the gate, and the word *trespassing* was missing an *s*. The bushes
around the gatepost looked like a graveyard for broken Budweiser
bottles, and it wasn't until the Trooper had bellied up out of the
wash that Pomeroy noticed a man kneeling in the brush near the
gate, jerking on the rope of a chain saw. He wore a dirty baseball
cap and a beard and there was some kind of tattoo on his bicep.
They locked eyes for a moment, and the man spit into the weeds

without turning his head. Pomeroy looked away, washed with a sudden abject fear. It was as if the man had seen straight into him, and made a judgment.

For a moment he was almost nauseated by the confrontation. It was a direct insult, the spitting into the weeds. He knew that with all his heart. He was sensitive in that way, almost psychic. He got it from grocery store checkers and waiters and people on the street. It was some kind of jealousy in people of a lower station; you could see it, plain as day, in their eyes and in what they said.

He shivered violently. Ignorant, damned white trash . . . The man hated him. His spitting told the whole story. For all he knew Pomeroy was the Angel of Mercy, but the man loathed him anyway. What was it? The new car? The fact that Pomeroy's hair was cut and combed? That Pomeroy knew how to spell and wasn't some kind of illiterate Okie beer-drinking . . . What did a man like that *want*, aside from more liquor?

He suddenly imagined Beth walking through the canyon alone. How would she *deal* with a man like that? It was unspeakable, first his eyes on her, then his hands, touching her . . . She'd be struggling, trying to jerk free, maybe pleading with him as he drags her out of sight of the road. One of the man's dirty hands is tangled now in her hair. She claws at his face, hurting him. Then suddenly the man stops, standing stock-still like a light-blinded animal. A dark hole has opened in his forehead, and a single line of blood trickles into his eye. He falls face first into the dirt as Beth jerks away, into Pomeroy's arms. She's crying, but it's over now. It's all right. He's come for her.

He straightened the steering wheel, bringing the car back onto the road. Reaching down, he flipped back the flaps of the cardboard carton on the floor. Inside lay a pellet gun. He'd had it forever, bought it at a hobby shop something like twenty years ago. The only living thing he'd ever shot with it was a parakeet. Next to the gun was a piece of twine, neatly looped, the loops tied with a bow. There was a can of tuna fish, too, packed in oil, and a can opener and a paper plate.

He wondered suddenly how much Beth had learned when she was spying at the fence. Klein, if *he* knew anything about last night, would have been a fool to tell her. His mind played through the conversation this morning. It couldn't have made any sense to her. Maybe she hadn't heard anything. He couldn't imagine that she was a snoop.

He suddenly realized that he hated it out there in the hills, and it wasn't only the trash dumped on the roadside or the crappy little trailers back in the scrub without decent plumbing and full of subhumans. As the Trooper rounded the long bend out of the open arroyo and into the green shadows of the high-ridged canyon, he knew that he hated the trees and the dark fern-covered hillsides even more. He hated the wind and the flying leaves and the goddamn broken-up road that went straight to hell no matter what was done to flatten it out. There was no order to anything, just a wild, threatening chaos, like in the filthy mind of the beer-swilling man with the chain saw, if "man" was the word he wanted.

He probed his lip with his tongue again, tasting blood now. Damn it! He slammed the edge of his hand against the steering wheel. Klein had made a *big* mistake, just like Larry Collier had made a mistake, too, all those years ago. And it would have been so *easy* to avoid, if only they could see who it was in their lives that was really *important*. Like the man just now by the roadside, they were too ignorant to believe that Bernard Pomeroy was a player, and look what it had cost Collier: his wife, his family, his *life*, for God's sake. That was the sad result of jealousy and ignorance.

That's what people had to learn. "Take this seriously," he wanted to say to men like Klein and Collier, like a father would say to a son. You couldn't always *explain* things—like for instance what it means that a stove is hot. A child learns respect fast when he touches the damned stove. After a while he doesn't ask why. If Pomeroy had a son he would go ahead and let him touch the stove, and get it right the first damned time. What he develops is *trust*. That's what Klein didn't have—trust. Collier hadn't had any, either. He hadn't trusted Bernard Pomeroy to come through. That was the modern world. For men like Klein and Collier, their own word on things apparently didn't mean anything *binding*, and so they didn't know that a man like Pomeroy meant what he said.

"Damn it," Pomeroy said out loud, slamming the steering wheel again, "if I say the stove is hot, and that somebody's going to get burned, then somebody's going to damn well get burned!"

The wind blew sand against the front end of the Trooper with a pinging sound. He passed a couple of empty cars parked at the creek crossing, and he could see two men fishing back down the creek despite the wind. Early this morning he had driven out to the airport and turned in the Cherokee at the Hertz lot, throwing the trash bags full of clothes and shoes into a trash bin behind a supermarket, which is where he had gotten the cardboard carton. He had only later realized that there might have been some identifying thing—thrown-out junk mail, say—along with the trash and clothes in the bags. He was getting sloppy. The whole episode last night was sloppy. He bit down on his lip, concentrating on the suddenly lancing pain.

He could see Ackroyd's place through the trees now. The driveway was empty. The old man had gone off to church. He swung the Trooper into the turnout across the road and cut the engine. Luck was with him. The Siamese cat lay sleeping in the sun, curled up on the cushion of a redwood lawn chair beyond the house. "Opportunity knocks," Pomeroy said out loud, and he opened the car door carefully, leaving it open. The road was empty in either direction. Despite the wind, he could hear the sound of a car engine in the distance, but that was a chance he'd have to take, even though it might be Ackroyd himself, coming home from church or from a run up to the general store.

Taking the box out of the car, he rehearsed what he would say if it *was* Ackroyd—a conversation that had played through his mind a hundred times: the price, the virtue in getting out while the market was good, a little bit of idle chat. Working through the conversation, he slipped open the lid of the box and groped inside, not looking in. Forty thousand dollars? That's right, probably it *was* more than the place was worth. A one-bedroom, after all, and on leased land.

The cat lay sleeping. His hand closed over the pellet pistol, still inside the cardboard box. Six feet, four feet. He stopped, listening to the wind, and conceded a point to Ackroyd. Yes, it was a big living room. And the built-ins were nice. You didn't find craftsmanship of that quality anymore. These old houses . . . Pride of workmanship . . . But of course the kitchen was small, and with all the Forest Service regulations nowadays, you really couldn't expand the place.

He pulled the pistol out of the box, aimed it, closed his eyes, and pulled the trigger.

**9**

THE WIND PICKED UP SUDDENLY, WITH A SOUND LIKE THE OCEAN sighing across rocks. It pushed through the chaparral in a wave, bending the stiff shrubs in a rustle of dry leaves, and Peter averted his face from a gust of flying sand.

In the moment that he shut his eyes, he saw a face in his mind—the face of the woman he had seen last night on the dark road, briefly framed in the rearview mirror. It was as if he glimpsed a snapshot of her, taken in a different time and place. He was suddenly swept with a memory of her, sharp and clear. She was younger, dressed in white, standing on a sunlit lawn, the wind blowing her hair. His life was full of a happiness that nothing could darken. . . .

Then the image faded. The wind fell and the picture in his mind slipped away, taking the happiness with it. He tried to recall it, but couldn't. It was simply gone. Whatever he had seen or felt had abandoned him. It was as if some elemental thing had rushed past—something of actual material substance, like a memory built of moving air—and had disappeared into the shadows of the oak-woods that lined the canyon walls below. For a moment he stood there watching the trees in expectation, still possessed with the notion that something had come, or better yet, returned to him out of the past—a cool breath of autumn wind that had left him strangely regretful and empty for its passing.

He nearly turned back. The open ridge above seemed suddenly solitary and lonesome and strange. From somewhere he heard the solitary cawing of a raven. Far down the canyon the wind still stirred the tree branches, and he could see a dust cloud rising along the empty road. Then, with a premonitory rustling, the wind began to blow along the ridge again, steadily now. Peter started up the trail. To hell with going back down. If relics of old memories haunted the morning air, then maybe it was best to follow them. He leaned forward as the hillside steepened, the trail winding between outcroppings of sandstone. Sage and greasewood, shuddering in the wind, grew out of cracks in the rocks.

Soon he was out of sight of the canyon, very near the top of the ridge. The trail was almost level, and the shrubbery grew so thickly on either side that it would take a machete to hack through it. He had the disturbing feeling that the wind was almost an animate presence, rushing at his back, and the myriad noises, the rustling and grating of the wind in the dense brush, sounded like the exhalations and utterances of a living thing. Suddenly he was anxious to get out of the thick chaparral and into more open land. He quickened his pace, now and then getting a glimpse of the dense trees below. The top of Falls Canyon lay only a short distance to the southwest.

Then suddenly, from somewhere in that direction, lonely and distant, came the now-familiar sound of a child's crying.

Peter stopped, listening to hear it again, and right then the wind grew suddenly still. In the lingering silence he heard the faint echo of the woman's voice in return, calling anxiously. Peter hurried upward, breaking into a run. The wind slammed into him, shrieking up the narrow path, pushing him forward as the trail steepened again, rising the last forty or fifty feet toward the ridge.

He broke out into a clearing—the same one where he'd seen the woman and boy last night—and ran headlong toward where the trail disappeared into the chaparral again, overwhelmed with the certainty that they were just ahead of him. A knot of leaves and twigs swirled up into the air a few feet in front of him, sweeping along in a dusty cloud. The mass of debris rose head high, buoyed up by the wind, seeming almost to expand and contract like a lung. There was the heavy hum of buzzing flies or bees, and the sound of hurried footfalls from ahead of him, unnaturally loud, the feet of the woman and boy scuffing on the rocky path, the woman's breath sobbing in and out of her throat, the boy wild with fright, crying aloud. . . .

It was dark night. The moon and stars shone in the sky overhead. Peter felt the wind sweep through him, hastening him along as if suddenly it would lift him above the rocky landscape like a clutch of dried leaves.

He shouted with a wild desperation, but his voice was hoarse, again as in a nightmare, and the wind swept him across the darkened landscape. He saw them ahead of him, knew that they were running from him, the two of them possessed with a desperate terror. The moon shone on her black dress and pale skin, and illuminated the white of the boy's shirt. The distance between them shortened, and for a brief moment he thought he might overtake them. He shouted again, reached toward him, the dark shadows of his arms and hands stretching away like the shadows of ragged tree limbs across the gray sagebrush.

The thicket of alders stood like a dark wall along the rocky streambed. There was a moonlit hole between the wind-lashed trees that led like an open door into the moving shadows. He could hear the rush of water that plunged in a torrent over the clifftop. His breath came in ragged gasps. His hands in the silver moonlight were streaked black with dried blood and dirt, and at the sight of them he was gripped with revulsion.

The rage that had driven him through the last hour, the jealousy and the loathing, turned to raw fear. In his mind he saw two dark shapes lying dead at the base of a cliff, and he knew absolutely what she meant to do. He had driven her to it, just as surely as if he had led her by the hand to the edge of the precipice.

He saw the inside of the bunkhouse then—the candles burning, the moving shadows, the flesh of her uncovered flank along the edge of the quilt, the man's face turning in sudden horror toward the swept-open door, the rush of wind and leaves swirling into the still air of the room, the feel of the weather-roughened handle of the spade in his own upraised hands, the shock of the shovel blade scraping across flesh and bone. . . .

The dark arch in the trees opened before him, still impossibly distant but seeming at the same time to rush forward as if he were falling into a yawning black pit. Moonlight shone on the hem of her black dress as she slipped into the darkness ahead, pulling the boy through with her, glancing back at him with eyes filled with such fear and terror that he groaned and looked away, stumbling and falling to his knees on the rocky path. Over the sound of the wind and water he heard her scream, and then, in the abrupt silence, the moon and the stars were swept as if by a hurricane into the deep void of the night sky.

Peter stared at the dirt of the path. His hand was pressed into a sharp pebble, and he lifted it to brush the pebble away before looking around him, vaguely surprised at the daylight. Somehow it ought to have been dark. Or maybe not. He remembered her scream, and he had a perfect memory of Amanda's face, looking back at him out of the darkness of a cave mouth.

He stood up shakily, his head pounding. It was the first time in his life that he'd fainted—if that's what had happened. The line of alders stood out against the sky some thirty feet ahead of him, leading back up the ridge along the streambed above Falls Canyon. Somehow he had walked, or run, the last quarter mile along the ridge, but he could barely remember any of it, just ragged images of the moon in the sky confused with a man's bloodied face against a dark wall, and the dim memory of Amanda running away from him into the darkness.

He lurched forward, nearly sick, and sat down on the trail again, fighting just to breathe evenly. There in front of him lay the shadowy hollow like an arched door in the thicket of alders. Gray limbs bowed and danced across it as if beckoning him to step through into the shadows. He stood up and walked slowly toward it. The certainty that he had seen Amanda's face in the darkness there was too crazy to believe. The morning sun shone through the trees, illuminating the stream with glinting diamonds of light. There was nobody among the shadows.

The miner's lettuce and nettles and grasses that lined the creek had been smashed down, and there were depressions in the soft dirt on the opposite side of the creek that looked like boot-heel prints—his own, from last night. The creek gurgled along, a clear brown like tea because of the dead leaves on the stream bottom. He stepped carefully out onto the rocks and looked over the edge of the falls, but there was nothing now, no bodies lying broken in the shallow pool. The narrow gorge fell away steeply, choked with dead limbs and leaves that were barely disturbed by the wind, and he could hear the sound of car engines down on the road.

Suddenly in his mind he saw once again the moonlit image of his own bloody hands. The picture flitted away, replaced by the dead man's eyes, open in horror where he lay entangled in the bedclothes, and he was flooded with a jealousy and horror so loathsome that it was nearly inhuman. He pushed himself away from the precipice and lurched back out into the sunlight. Staggering forward, nearly falling again, he caught the limb of an alder and held on to it, forcing his mind clear, tasting the residue of the bitter emotions as if he'd eaten burned food.

He realized that his shoes were soaked, and the knees of his jeans were scuffed and dirty from where he'd fallen forward onto the trail. He looked at his shaking hands, then abruptly turned around and started back down the trail. The wind blew fitfully now, innocently, and the morning was spent. Bobby and Beth would probably be at the house already, and suddenly what he wanted more than anything else in the world was to be there with them.

PARTWAY UP THE RIDGE TRAIL BEHIND HIS HOUSE, KLEIN STOPPED to pull foxtails out of his socks. The Colt pistol was heavy in his pocket, as if it were going to tear right through the thin fabric and fall onto the dirt. He half wanted to pull it out and fire all six bullets into a tree, or whatever the hell else presented itself. But that was crazy. He was going to be in deep *kim chee* if he didn't get a grip.

He had screwed up badly again with Pomeroy. Larry Collier wasn't worth more than about a nickel's worth of anger, but somehow Pomeroy, with his smart-ass tone and his pervert mouth, had managed to turn Collier into some kind of issue. Klein shouldn't have hit him, no matter what, but the *real* mistake had been the gun talk, especially in front of Lorna. Lorna would know he wasn't kidding. He had told Pomeroy to leave Lorna out of it, and then he had involved her in it himself by losing control. And here he was now, loafing around out in the hills, carrying the loaded .38 that he'd promised to use to blow a man's head off.

And even if it came to that, even if that was the *only* way, finally, to deal with Pomeroy, it was the stupidest thing in the world to talk about it, especially when it might be a real option. As far as Klein knew, Pomeroy didn't have any family. Nobody would miss him aside from the shysters down at the car lot where he worked, and they wouldn't miss him much. Probably they'd have a celebration and burn the contents of his desk in the middle of the showroom floor.

But he wasn't serious about killing anyone. Not yet, not as long as Pomeroy was all talk. When he produced something real, then Klein could get serious. Part of Pomeroy had to be a little bit worried. There was sure as hell fear in his eyes when his lip was bleeding and he was crawling across the pool deck like a crab. But the thing about psychopaths like Pomeroy was that time and experience didn't change them. They were locked too deeply into their own twisted point of view, and they thought the same thing was true about everyone else. In that way they were nearly blind.

That was what would screw him up. When push came to shove, Klein would hand him his head on a plate. That's what Bobby next door had said once. Klein brightened up, thinking about it: "Cut off his head and make him eat it." That was it. Christ, that was funny—something like that coming out of the mouth of a six-year-old. Kids were so full of beans these days that he couldn't get over it. Times had changed.

He thought suddenly about Lorna. He had laid into her pretty good back at the house. It was true that when he was in trouble she'd stood there blinking like a blinded rabbit, but then what the hell did he expect, that she'd chase Pomeroy down and kick his teeth in? "Here's your gun, dear, I've loaded it myself. . . ."

Right now she was probably drinking a Bloody Mary for breakfast, putting down a little hair of the dog. Well, he couldn't really blame her. Not this morning. If he hung around Pomeroy much longer he'd become a damn sight bigger drunk than she was. He had always figured live and let live, as the saying went, and he had applied that to Lorna, too. She was free to have her own opinions, which she could keep to herself. The thing about wives was that they wanted to control you, and that was something he'd never been able to stand. He didn't want a nanny, thank you very much.

And for that reason he had always given her the same break: if she wanted to sleep till noon, so what? If she took a dip in the vodka bottle at breakfast, fine. She was a big girl. He wasn't going to tell her how to spend her time.

It occurred to him now, for the first time since they were married, that there was another way of looking at it—as some kind of *failure* on his part. He tried to wave the thought away. It suggested too much. It was so big that it threatened to knock him over. He had always believed that running a marriage was like putting together a plan for a home: you drew things out the way you wanted them, adding in enough doors and windows, moving the pencil and straightedge yourself, so you didn't turn out with some kind of mess.

He couldn't stand uncertainty, which was why he attended to his own business and let Lorna attend to hers. The way she talked sometimes it seemed like she wanted him to *submit* to the marriage, or something, and that sounded to him like drowning. Maybe he just didn't have the faith—in her, in marriage itself. Faith had always seemed like a sucker bet.

He looked around him, feeling a gust of wind on the back of his neck. The grass on the hillside billowed as if a wave had run through it, and he thought suddenly of the woman in the black dress. Was that why he was out there? Waiting for her? Christ, he was one doomed son of a bitch, crazy and criminal both. He started toward home, looking one last time at the nearby oaks and sycamores. The shadows were merely shadows. He couldn't wait all day for something that wasn't going to happen anyway.

Lorna wasn't in the kitchen. He opened the cupboard under the sink and checked the trash. There was an empty V8 can that he was pretty certain hadn't been there earlier. For a moment he half thought he'd fix himself one—a shot of Tabasco, stick of celery. It might make Lorna feel better about things if he had a little belt, too. She wouldn't be drinking alone.

He let it slide. Drinking during the day cut into production. He'd promised Beth that he'd install the dead bolts, and he still had to run down into El Toro to buy the damned things. There was no use muddying the water with alcohol, so to speak. That was almost funny, except that he had the feeling that somehow he'd slipped around the issue again. And he was already sick of feeling that way. Why couldn't Lorna just put a *lid* on it?

Shutting the study door behind him, he sat down at his desk, opening the top drawer and sliding the pistol into it. Later, when Lorna was awake and out of the bedroom, he would return it to the nightstand. There was no use letting her see him with it. Tilting the chair back, he pushed up the lid of the Rolodex, then flipped through the cards until he found Dale Winters's telephone number. Winters was his contact, call it his go-between, with Sloane Investment Services. Sloane was an investment "consortium" that seemed to finance a number of cash-only restaurants and import-export businesses that shipped merchandise to South America. That's all Klein knew about it, the only thing he *wanted* to know. Winters had arranged the loan in return for a percentage, and Sloane's money spent as well as anyone else's, although they expected a good return—a damned good return when you added Winters's to it. That's something Pomeroy couldn't get into his head: that if he took Klein down, and the deal collapsed, Sloane would be the unhappy loser, not to mention Winters. It was high time that Pomeroy was "leaned on" himself, by someone heavy enough to make it count.

Winters had an office in Irvine, and sometimes he worked on Sundays. It was a good day to call, because there weren't any secretaries there, and if Winters was working, then Klein could get straight through without being put off, which wasn't always easy. He remembered Winters laughing at the Begin joke at Spangler's party. He was one of those oversized people who hugged everyone. He got awards for giving truckloads of toys to kids down in Mexicali or somewhere. He didn't owe Klein any favors, but there was a good chance, if Klein pitched it right, that he'd have something valuable to say about Pomeroy.

He punched in the numbers and the phone rang three times before it was picked up and a voice said, "Yeah."

"Dale!" Klein said. "This is Lance Klein."

There was a moment of silence and then Winters said, "What's the difference between a man and a bottle of wine?"

Klein thought about it, but nothing came to him. After a moment Winters said, "Wine matures," and Klein laughed out loud, even though it took him a moment to get it. He forced another laugh, wondering vaguely if the joke was meant to apply to him.

"You know who told me that?" Winters asked.

"I give," Klein said.

"A waitress in a restaurant in Laguna Beach. Can you beat that?"

"I could think of a dozen to hit her back with," Klein said, "especially if she was a blonde."

"Well," Winters said, "my wife was there, and she's a blonde. I'm not big on blonde jokes, I guess."

"Me either," Klein said quickly. "Lorna's blonde, too."

"That's right!" Winters said. "*She* was the life of the party the other night. What was that joke she told? Something about the elephant and the Hindu."

"Something like that," Klein said.

"So what's on your mind? Want to hack a few divots?"

"I haven't shot a round in a year," Klein said. "I wouldn't know how to hold my club."

"Hold your *club*? Sounds like that joke about 'Madame Thumb and her four comely daughters.' Hey, listen to this, speaking of holding the club. There's a Yale man and a Harvard man taking a leak. They zip up, see, and the Yale man heads for the sink. The Harvard man, though, he heads for the door. The Yale man says to him in this old-boy accent, 'At Yale they taught us to wash our hands after urinating,' and the Harvard man turns to him and says, 'At Harvard they taught us not to piss on our hands.' "

Klein snorted into the mouthpiece, then thrust the receiver away, holding it at arm's length he was laughing so hard. He thumped it down onto the top of the desk and stamped his foot, trying to regain control of his voice. "*Hoo*, that's funny!" he said finally, then laughed again. Winters was dead silent on the other end, as if letting Klein get it out of his system.

"You're a hell of an audience, Lance," he said finally.

"And you tell a hell of a joke, I guess." He waited for a moment, but Winters didn't say anything more. The joking around was apparently over, just like that.

"I just wanted to run a little business matter past you," Klein said. "Nothing much."

"Shoot."

"You met Bernard Pomeroy the other night, didn't you? That party at the Spanglers' house."

"Can't say that I did," Winters said.

"Sells Mercedes Benzes out in Newport Beach. He didn't hit on you to buy a car?"

"Not that I remember."

"Well you *would* remember. He'd have sold you one."

"I'll watch out for him."

"He's doing a little sales work for me, out in the canyon."

"Out in the canyon?"

"That little enterprise of ours that Sloane financed."

"Oh, sure. Of course. Some kind of problem with it?"

"No," Klein said. "We're not doing bad. Not bad at all. Pomeroy's tenacious."

"Well, I'm glad to hear that. He sounds like a good man. You take care of things out there."

For a moment Klein thought he was going to hang up. "I intend to," he said, trying to work things around to the point. "We've got a timetable, but I don't want to rush things, for all the obvious reasons."

"You're the boss," Winters said.

Klein could hear him rustling papers. "You know, it's funny you should say that. If Pomeroy's got one fault it's that he's a little—what the hell?—overanxious, maybe. Do you know what I mean?"

"Not yet," Winters said. "What *do* you mean?"

"Well, let's just say he's not subtle. He could sell raincoats in the desert if he set his mind to it. But he has a hard time taking no for an answer. Tries to jerk their wallet out of their pocket. He's kind of a purse snatcher when he gets impatient."

"I'm still in the dark," Winters said. The paper rustling had stopped. He was paying attention now. "What are you saying here?"

"Nothing, really," Klein said, easing off. "I'm just a little concerned that if he goes around acting like a cowboy . . . You know . . . He might piss on his hands." He laughed weakly.

"I think that would be a large mistake, Lance."

"That's what I'm saying. I agree with you on that."

"Tie him down, then. I don't have to tell you how important it is for this whole thing to work."

"Of course not," Klein said. "Everything I've got is tied up in it."

"Other people have things tied up, too. Your creditors are my creditors. Don't drop the ball on me."

"Hell no," Klein said. "I appreciate what you're saying to me."

"And you can appreciate how a man has a reputation in the financial community, especially in regard to investment consortiums like Sloane."

"We're rock solid. I didn't mean to imply that . . ."

"And Sloane isn't interested in your man Polaroid or any of his affairs. They don't care about your gardener, either, or your grandmother's niece. This is a question of where the buck stops, Lance. That's the bottom line. Do you follow me?"

"Absolutely," Klein said. "Loud and clear. I just thought that some weight might be brought to bear. . . ."

"I'm virtually certain you don't want that," Winters said flatly.

Klein was silent for a moment. There wasn't a single thing he could say. He was fairly sure he'd been threatened, and there was no way in hell he wanted it spelled out more explicitly. The conversation was over. He'd never in his life engaged in a conversation that was more clearly over.

"Well, thanks for letting me yak in your ear," he said. It sounded weak, but he hurried on, trying to finesse things. "Sometimes it's good to talk things through. You see things from a different point of view." He could hear Winters's voice, but it was muffled, as if he was holding his hand over the phone and talking to someone else. Klein waited him out.

"Go ahead," Winters said finally. "What was that?"

"I guess nothing much," Klein said. "I just wanted to touch base."

"Always happy to hear from you," Winters said. "My best to the wife."

"Thanks, and tell . . ." Klein started to say, but Winters hung up before he had a chance to finish his sentence. He listened to dead air for a moment. When he hung up the phone his hand was shaking. What an incredible blunder! He should have seen it coming. Winters was up to his eyeballs in the whole deal, and here Klein had called up and set off every bell and whistle in his head. It almost seemed like a good idea to call back right now and clarify things. He didn't want Winters thinking that there was some kind of problem when there wasn't. No use worrying about trifles.

He reached for the phone again, but didn't pick it up. Instead he stood up and headed toward the door. It was damage-control time. A drink made some sense, after all. Something would come up to answer the Pomeroy question. What the hell, he could tell Pomeroy any damned thing at all about his conversation with Winters, tell him a story about a guy with a baseball bat. . . .

He opened the door, and there was Lorna, standing right there, a surprised look on her face. He couldn't believe it. She'd been sneaking around in the hallway, listening at the door.

**11**

THE CAT SEEMED TO SCRAMBLE FOR A MOMENT ON THE CHAIR cushion as if trying to get up. Pomeroy dropped the cardboard box, pumped the gun, and fired again, hitting the cat low on his side, just in back of the ribs. The animal pawed the air now, and he reached down and pressed it to the cushion, holding it there. Die, he thought. For God's sake . . .

There was a noise out on the road right then, like a car door shutting, and Pomeroy stiffened, careful not to spin around like a guilty man. He bent over, picked up the box, and upended it, spilling the contents out onto the dirt. Then, before turning around, he put the box over the cat, which lay still now. No one could have heard the little popping noise that the pellet gun had made, so unless they'd *seen* him there was no problem. He set his face in a smile and looked casually back toward the Trooper, ready to say something sad and philosophical about the poor cat. What was it that cats died of? Cat fever. Was that it? The cat was dying of it, suffering terribly. . . .

There was no car on the road but his own. At first he couldn't see anything. Perhaps it was just the wind, his imagination. Then there was a movement in the front seat, and suddenly he saw a face staring out at him through the dusty windshield, half-obscured by the glare of the sun.

He couldn't believe his eyes. There was a kid in the goddamn front seat!

The camera! Pomeroy understood it at once. The little bastard was ripping off his Nikon. Pomeroy had left the door open and the camera was sitting there on the seat, plain as day. . . .

He lifted the box and pushed the cat into it, then picked up the tuna fish and can opener and twine. He slid the gun into his pocket and then looked at his hand. Somehow there was blood on it; from the cat? Or was it his own blood, from where the damned thing had torn him up yesterday?

"Hey!" he shouted, picking up the box now and heading along the side of the house. The kid was in no particular hurry. He was rummaging around in there, probably going through the glove compartment. There was the toiletries kit in there, but nothing valuable. Holding on to the box with both hands, Pomeroy began to run. The boy was looking out past the hinge side of the open door, waiting till the last possible moment.

"Hold it right there!" Pomeroy shouted. He might as well save his breath. The boy backed out through the open door, turning and running down toward the creek and into the deep shadows of the alders beyond. The camera dangled from his hand. He was dressed weirdly, like Tom Sawyer, another backwoods hick in the making.

Pausing just long enough to shove the box into the car, Pomeroy slammed the door and took off down the trail. He was damned if he was going to let the kid have a five-hundred-dollar camera. At the edge of the creek he paused, listening to the wind, to the tree limbs brushing together in a leafy rush of sound that seemed to fill the canyon from side to side. The kid was gone, just like that. But if he had crossed the creek there'd be wet footprints beyond, and there weren't; no way he could have jumped across. The creek was too broad.

Without waiting, he pushed through a thick stand of willows, breaking down the little pencil-thick stalks. The kid must have headed upstream. Downstream the vegetation was too thick. He wouldn't have had time to get through it. Upstream, beyond the willows, there was a nothing little trail, mostly stamped-down grass. The wind shrilled through the alders, the tall straight trunks swaying ominously. Dead leaves blew into his face, and he covered his eyes with his forearm, pushing shrubbery aside with his arm. The damned place was full of poison oak, but he didn't know what it looked like, and if he was going to get the Nikon back there was sure as hell no time to study it now.

He climbed over a fallen tree and slid to the ground on the other side. Something caught on his pants pocket. There was a small tug, and he felt the material tear. Cursing out loud, he clambered out into a clear area again. The stream ran swift and narrow ahead of him, with broad, solid-looking rocks sticking up out of the water. That was it. That's where the kid would have gone across. The trail went on up the hill on the other side, disappearing within the moving shadows of close-growing oak trees. The kid probably had some kind of hideout back there. The walls of the ridge were pocked with caves, mostly played-out old tin mines that had never amounted to anything. He stepped across the rocks in the creek, leaping the last three feet to the trail, then sprinted uphill toward the sheer canyon wall. The wind would hide the sound of his running, and if he hurried he could catch the kid before he had a chance to get to his hiding place.

Beneath the oaks the ground was soft with a heavy layer of mulch, and it was damp and very nearly still. The trail simply ended there. The canyon wall rose steeply above, so that the limbs of the trees brushed against it, and a person could easily have climbed up the loose rock and scrub in order to walk straight out onto a limb. He searched the trees overhead, but there was nobody up there. There was nothing—no indication that the kid had come that way at all. If he had, he would have had to be a mountain goat to go any farther.

Pomeroy turned around, heading back. It occurred to him for the first time that the kid might have seen him shoot the cat. He hadn't checked before he shot. He'd just blasted away like some kind of idiot. But if the kid *had* seen him, why steal the camera? Pomeroy could use that to advantage—I won't tell on you if you won't tell on me. . . .

Had the kid picked up the damned camera and taken a picture? Pomeroy started to run toward the road. That was *just* what he needed. He leaped across the creek, leaving the trail and struggling up the loose dirt of the hillside, taking the shortest route back to the car. He saw the blue paint of the Trooper through the trees.

At first it didn't dawn on him that something was wrong with it, but then, just as he staggered up and stopped by the bumper, breathing heavily and sweating, he realized that the door was open. Five minutes ago he'd slammed it shut, but it was open now.

He looked around, wary, glancing into the interior of the car and then jerking his head back. It was empty. If the kid had come back after something, he was gone now. Quickly, he walked around to the opposite side of the car to shut the door. Then he saw it: his camera lay in the weedy dirt, beaten to pieces. The case was cracked and the lens was gone entirely, probably having flown off into the bushes. The back of the camera had sprung open, and the film was gone.

That was no good. The kid had snapped a picture, then taken the film with him and wrecked the camera out of spite.

He noticed then that the front fender of the Trooper was dented in. The little bastard! He'd smashed the goddamn Nikon against the fender until the strap had broken! Pomeroy picked up the broken camera and tossed it into the car, onto the front seat. Insurance would . . .

The *box* was gone—the cat, the goddamn tuna fish, all of it. He had put it on the front seat and shut the door. The kid had come back after the box. Why? He must have seen *everything*. Pomeroy rested his face in his hands for a moment, massaging his temples, then stepped back and kicked the fender. This was unbelievable. Set up by a *kid*. But for what reason? The kid couldn't even know who he was.

It didn't make sense. Stealing the camera made sense, just like stealing anything made sense. But the rest of it—wrecking the camera, stealing the body of a dead cat . . . Unless it was a local kid.

That had to be it—a kid who *did* know who Pomeroy was . . .

He climbed into the car, fired it up, and swung around in a wide U-turn, heading out of the canyon again. He picked up speed. If he was right, then he might even catch them. He put it together in his mind, how it must have happened. . . .

Say he'd been followed after stopping off at Klein's place. He'd never know it after getting out into the canyon, with all the curves and dips. Following him would have been easy. And there was the car he'd heard back up the road. What if they'd stopped a hundred yards down and simply come up along the creek? *Clearly* Klein was involved in this. He'd sent the kid in to do the dirty work because Pomeroy would have been recognized Klein in an instant, and it would have been all over.

He grinned and shook his head. Who'd have thought Klein would move that fast? You had to hand it to him. Maybe the Larry Collier threat had spooked him. The stove was so damned hot that he'd gone after a firehose.

So who was the kid? The answer to that was obvious, although Pomeroy hated to think it. Beth's kid? It had to be. And that was a dirty shame, because Pomeroy would have liked to be the kid's friend. That was the trouble with a broken marriage. He had read an article on the dysfunctional family, and here was evidence of it. What the boy needed was a positive male role model. Beth would *have* to be made to see that. Klein had really lowered himself to use the boy like that.

He passed three other cars getting back out to the highway, but he didn't catch up to Klein. Probably they had too much of a jump on him. He'd wasted ten minutes in the woods and another five minutes with the wrecked camera.

It struck him suddenly—what he'd do was make a phone call to Klein's lovely wife. Tit for tat. If the rest of the damned neighborhood was involved, there was no reason to leave her out. And there was no need to rake up some scandal from Klein's past, either, even though there was plenty of it lying around. *Any* allegation would do where a wife was concerned, especially if it involved sex. Never mind that it wasn't true; the trick was to make Klein *deny* it.

"WHAT THE HELL IS THIS?" KLEIN ASKED. "HOW ABOUT A little privacy here?"

"What are you talking about?" Lorna wasn't in her bathrobe. She was dressed and made up.

"You know damned well what I'm talking about. You were listening through the door."

"I was *not* listening through the door. Give me some credit."

He looked at her for a moment, breathing hard. There was no way he could put up with this kind of thing, not with this Pomeroy business looking more and more like a powder keg. Probably she was lying, which was the kind of betrayal he didn't need right now. Still, he'd tiptoed around so much when talking to Winters that there was no way she could have understood any of it.

"Well," he said, "it's just that a man in my position can't put up with . . ."

"With *what*? What is it exactly that a man in your position can't 'put up' with? This man comes around here this morning and starts a fight, and you're talking about shooting him, for God's sake. *Shooting* him! And that's not my business, too? You can't understand my thinking that might concern me?"

"I got a little hot-headed, that's all," Klein said. "The last thing you should do is worry about it."

"I've *been* worrying. Now's a fine time to tell me not to. You don't sleep at night. You don't say six words to me. You roam around like you're waiting for something to happen. Don't treat me like a fool. You didn't used to be like this. *Something's* wrong, and I don't have to be some kind of shrink to see it."

"So you're saying I need a shrink?"

She stared at him. "That's not what I said. It isn't even close."

"Fine. I accept that. Now I'll say it again: *don't worry about it.* It's just business. It stays in the office."

"Except when you take it to bed at night."

"And what the hell's that supposed to mean?" He felt a cold fury. She was pushing him too hard, and she wasn't even drunk. He was pretty sure she was stone sober. Maybe that was the damned problem.

"You can't ever take *anything* at face value, can you? You've always got to fly off the handle about what you *think* I mean. And that's because what I'm saying is true, isn't it? And you're so defensive about it you jump all over me when I say the most obvious things. *All* I'm saying is that something's eating you up. I'd have to be an idiot not to know that."

He looked at her for a moment. She was really wrought up. This was exactly what he didn't want. "Times are tough," he said, lowering his voice. "I'm going to ask you, though, one last time, not to worry. What would help is for you to relax on the issue."

"Should I relax about the phone call I got when you were out?"

"What are you talking about?"

"While you were out walking in the hills, getting some air."

"What phone call, damn it!" But he knew suddenly what she was talking about. He could guess it. Pomeroy! The bastard couldn't let well enough alone. . . .

"I think it was him, the man who was here earlier." She crossed her arms in front of her as if to shield herself, and her voice went up an octave. "I think you ought to tell me what the hell is going on!"

"Don't swear at *me*!" Klein said. "Simmer down. That clown's *nothing* to worry about, nothing at all. What did he say?"

"He just asked if I knew what you were up to."

"That's it?"

"That's it. What you were up to."

"Ignore him. He's a horse's ass."

"So what *are* you up to?"

"I said ignore him. Don't play his game. That's the kind of tone he *wants* you to take."

"What game am I supposed to play? *My* game? I'm tired of it, sick and tired. I've been playing it long enough. Either you can let me in on *your* game, or—"

"Or you'll what?" Klein asked. "Mix another drink?"

Immediately he was sorry he'd said it. Her face was frozen in stunned disbelief, as if she was working hard to grasp the notion that it had finally come down to this—insults and betrayals. She brushed her hair back from her face. Her hand was trembling. For a moment he thought she was going to say something more, but instead she turned around and walked away down the hall and into the bedroom, quietly closing the door behind her.

"Aw, hell!" Klein said, and he punched the wooden door casing with his fist. He couldn't believe it how she backed down so damned fast! If she had slapped him, at least it would have shown some guts. He shook his hand, kneading the knuckles, and knocked on the bedroom door, but she didn't answer. "C'mon," he said. "When I say we shouldn't worry about something, this is exactly the kind of thing I'm talking about."

Still she said nothing.

"You know I don't like ultimatums," he told her. "Married couples shouldn't hand each other ultimatums. That's why I flew off the handle." He listened for another moment, but it was too late. He'd screwed up. Using the drinking against her! He'd sworn he'd never do that. Hadn't he just been thinking the same thing a half hour ago, up on the hillside? That it was her life? She could do what she pleased? What a mess.

"Look, I'm *sorry*," he said. And when again she didn't respond he said, "I can't say any more than that, can I? I don't know what else you want from me. I'll say it one more time: I . . . am . . . sorry." After a moment he started down the hallway, but then turned around and came back. "If that jerk calls again, hang up on him. What you don't want to do is listen. He's playing a game here. It's all psychology. Just hang up as soon as you recognize his voice. Treat it like an obscene call. Don't say anything and don't give him a chance to talk." He left again, going out through the kitchen door and into the garage in order to get his power screwdriver.

Pomeroy and Lorna—he had to deal with both of them now: kid gloves for Lorna, something worse for Pomeroy. But what? He wondered when the bastard would make his next move. Probably it would be some kind of demand. This phone call was meant to show Klein that Pomeroy was serious. It was just a nudge to show him that there was some kind of precipice ready to open up. But Pomeroy wouldn't try to push him over the edge until he'd made his money. Blackmailers were predictable that way. They didn't wreck the guy they were setting up. That didn't make any sense. Klein would bet ten dollars that there wouldn't be any more phone calls that day. One was enough.

He slid a fresh battery into the screwdriver and grabbed a little can to dump parts into. If he could, he wanted to replace that old sash hardware on Beth's windows with something similar. Maybe they still made something the same general size. It wouldn't take more than an hour and a half to run down into El Toro and pick the parts up. By then Lorna would have simmered down, maybe found some words to say. It was flat-out impossible to discuss anything when she wouldn't even speak.

It struck him right then that probably it would kill the day putting on the new dead bolts and all. Lorna was always ragging on him to spend the day with her, which usually meant going to the mall or something, so he hardly ever found time for it. And now here he was giving another woman a hand while his wife sat around in a funk. He couldn't win. There weren't enough hours in the day anymore.

He had a friend who divorced his wife—big long list of "irreconcilable differences," like he wouldn't do housework or quit smoking or lose weight or whatever the hell it was. Then a year later he'd met someone new, and had quit smoking and lost all that weight. Even gave up beer. Now he vacuumed the house like J. Edgar Stinking Hoover, twice a week, and they washed dishes together at the sink, wearing matching aprons. His ex-wife was probably stupefied over it. Ironic, that's what it was. Your marriage started out like a mutual admiration society, and then went downhill like a coaster wagon.

He almost put the screwdriver down and went back into the house. But Lorna would want answers he couldn't give her. Not yet. And he'd promised Beth about the dead bolts and the windows. Hell, that maniac had nearly broken in last night. Lorna would understand that. And if she didn't, then she was simply dead wrong. That's all there was to it.

He let himself in Beth's back door and counted the windows throughout the house. They all had the same kind of hardware on them, old as hell and bent up and with loose screws. A couple of the windows you could shake in their tracks, and the two pieces of the sash lock came right apart. Might as well replace it all. He moved a small table out of the way and eased the screws out of a set in one of the rear windows, put it in his pocket, and went back out, climbing into his truck in the driveway. What the hell would he tell her about "what he was up to" that wouldn't just make things worse?

PETER COULD HEAR BETH INSIDE THE HOUSE, MOVING AROUND IN the kitchen, clanking pans. The teapot whistled, and through the open door there was the smell of bacon cooking on the stove. It was past noon, a little late for breakfast, but according to Bobby that made breakfast an even better idea, especially on a Sunday, which wasn't an ordinary day anyway.

Somehow Bobby was as solid and clear as a diamond, in contrast with the murky twilight of what Peter had seen last night and up on the ridge this morning. He wondered again how he was going to tell Beth what he had to tell her. Probably she'd advise therapy. If *anything* was certain, it was that what he had seen could not have been real. The confusion of day and night, of faces and thoughts and emotions—all of it argued some kind of terrible pathology. Except that apparently he shared part of that pathology with Detective Slater's "hiker" and with old Bateman up the road. . . .

"How deep?" Bobby asked him, coming around the corner of the house. He carried a shovel that was taller than he was. Beth and Bobby had brought Peter a redwood trellis and a climbing rose in a five-gallon pot. It was covered with crimson blooms. The idea was that Bobby and Peter were going to plant it while Beth fried bacon.

"Deep," Peter said. "Up to your knees."

Bobby scraped a depression in the dirt near the corner of the porch. He stood on the shovel, trying to force it into the rocky ground. "I can't," he said. "The ground's too hard."

"Sure you can," Peter said. "Think about how the ants dug the Grand Canyon—one grain of dirt at a time. It took them years."

"Mom said we had to get the hole dug before we can eat, so that won't work. We don't have that long." He jumped on the back edge of the shovel blade, pogo-sticking it into the dirt, then he dusted clods out of the hole with his hand.

Beth had done this same kind of thing twice before when he had taken her out to dinner. She didn't argue about him paying the check or buying movie tickets afterward, but then the next day or the day after she showed up with some sort of very practical gift, as if she wanted to keep things balanced, or as if it was easier to invest money than to be expected to invest emotion. He hoped that wasn't it.

"It's got to be deep enough to fit the whole pot into," Peter said to Bobby.

"There's rocks here," Bobby said. He skittered a little more dirt out of the hole before dragging the heavy plastic pot into it, checking the result.

"Another foot and a half," Peter said. "We need extra room for the root mulch."

"I think you're smoking dope," Bobby said back to him.

"*What?*" Peter nearly laughed, but he restrained himself. He probably shouldn't encourage that kind of talk.

"Nothing," Bobby said. "That's what my friend Caleb says when he means you're talking stupid. You know."

"Yeah, I knew that. I was just wondering if it was a *good* thing to say."

"It's not dirty, is it?"

"No, it's just . . . it's just not the kind of thing to say around people who wouldn't understand you were just being funny."

"I don't care what they think," Bobby said. "You said people like that were hosers."

"Well," Peter said, looking for some way to change the subject. "Dirt's pretty hard, eh? You know what I'd do?"

"Buy a six-pack and draw up plans?"

Peter gave him a mock-threatening look. "I'm telling you to lay off that kind of thing. Maybe you don't want to let your mother hear you talking that way. Where did you get that? Caleb again?''

"No, I heard it on television. *I* was the one who told it to Caleb."

"Well, do your mother a favor and don't tell *her* things like that. There's some things mothers shouldn't hear. You wouldn't say that kind of thing to your teacher, would you? It's kind of smart aleck, isn't it?''

Bobby shrugged. He hacked at the hole with the spade again. "Maybe *I* wouldn't say it to her. But Caleb got in trouble yesterday for saying something worse."

"What?" Peter asked.

"The *S* word."

"The *S* word?'' Peter could only think of one.

"Sex," Bobby said.

Mildly relieved, Peter shook his head, as if he couldn't quite believe anybody would say such a thing. "Did your teacher give him detention? What's her name again? Mrs. Cheese, isn't it?''

"Mrs. Crumb. He didn't exactly say it, but he got in trouble for it anyway. It was Mrs. Crumb, really, who said it."

"*She* said the *S* word in class? What grade are you in?''

"Second."

Peter shook his head. It was a brand-new world, full of mysteries. "So why did Caleb get in trouble?''

"Well," Bobby said, "Mrs. Crumb was talking about Columbus, you know? And she was talking about sailing to America, and how they were lost and all. And she said that they found their way by using a sextant. It's one of our spelling words. Off the special list. And anyway, when she said sextant, Caleb said, 'What kind of tent?' ''

Peter started laughing. He couldn't help himself this time. Of course he ought to act as if the whole thing were shameful, so he pretended to be clearing his throat. "Right out loud?" he asked.

"Yeah, and Mrs. Crumb really lost it."

"I bet. Nobody laughed, did they?"

"Of *course* everybody laughed," Bobby said. "Wouldn't you laugh? You just did."

"I was coughing. And anyway, the thing is that you can't say that kind of thing in front of grown-ups. They can't take it. Kids can take it, but grown-ups have trouble with it."

Bobby looked at him suspiciously, as if he found Peter's statement intriguing but probably a lie.

"It's true," Peter said. "I'm not kidding about this. There's things you better not say around adults. Now *I* don't really care, mostly. You can say almost anything around me. But I'm what they call a deviation from the norm. Most people have a thing in their inner ear. You know about the inner ear?"

"There's bones in it. Little ones. The hammer and something."

"That's right. Well, you understand then. I don't have to tell you about that part of it. There's a delicate balance there that mustn't be upset. Mrs. Crumb's ear bones upset easily, and you don't want to start talking dirty in front of her and make her get dizzy and fall over."

"There's nothing dirty about what I said about the six-pack."

"You know what I mean. Dig that hole deeper. You'll never get to China at that rate. Here, let me take a stab at it." Peter stepped down off the porch and kicked at the shovel, which clanked against a rock. He jammed at it and wiggled it, managing finally to unearth a piece of granite about as big as a lemon. Around it the dirt was hard and dry. They'd need a pick. Better yet, a jackhammer. "Does Caleb talk like that all the time in class?"

"Yeah. He got in trouble on Wednesday, too."

"What did he say?"

"The *D* word."

"Damn?" Peter asked.

"No, 'dick.' "

Peter started laughing again, despite himself. "Dick! He said that? What? In a joke or something?"

"No," Bobby said. "Just out loud. He stood up, too."

"He just stood up and said, 'Dick'? Then what did he do?"

"Sat down again. He yelled it, actually. Mr. Brown heard him, too."

"Who's Mr. Brown again?"

"The principal. Caleb was dead meat."

"I bet he was," Peter said. "That's what I've been warning you about. Principals can't stand that kind of language. They can't take it. It's a threat to them. It's worse than the chicken pox. Worse than head lice. It gets into their eustachian tubes and they get dizzy and sick, like they just got off a bad carnival ride. People who say words like that in front of principals end up in the penitentiary half the time, picking oakum." Peter tilted the shovel against the wall. It was no use even trying to dig the hole any deeper.

"What's oakum?" Bobby asked.

"I don't really know," Peter said, wiping his forehead, "but in jail they make people pick it."

"Do you know what I'd do?"

"About what? Caleb talking like that, or picking oakum?"

"About this hole. I'd fill it with water, you know. And then you let the water soak in and maybe fill it up again. Then the ground's softer, and you can dig in it."

"That's a brilliant plan," Peter said. "Get the hose."

Bobby trotted off around the side of the house. A moment later Peter heard the side door slam shut in the bus, and Bobby reappeared, dragging the hose and carrying a box full of toy trucks and alien-looking plastic figurines. "I'll hold it," he said. "You turn it on."

"Sure," Peter said. He headed around to the back where the water spigot was. "Holler for me to shut it off!"

"It's not even on yet!" Bobby shouted.

"I know. I mean when it *is* on." He cranked the water on and waited until Bobby hollered. When he got back around to the front, the basinlike hole in the dirt was brimming with muddy water, and Bobby was dropping the aliens one by one into it. He picked up a couple of boards nearby, blocked one of them up into a ramp, and drove one of the trucks up the ramp so that it sailed into the water.

"You want to do one?" Bobby asked hopefully.

"Sure," Peter said, picking a big truck out of the box. "Watch this." He put one of the aliens into the cab, then drove the truck up the ramp. It sailed off into the hole, sinking until only the front bumper and the top of the cab stuck out.

"We've got to get him out," Bobby said, "before he drowns." He ran off again. Peter heard the bus door slide open and shut, and then Bobby was back, carrying a tow truck with a little winch in back wound with string.

Pretending to be the trapped alien, Peter made drowning noises while Bobby tied the end of the string to the bumper of the sunken truck and began turning the crank on the winch. The truck bumped forward a couple of inches, exposing the head of the sorry-looking alien. Bobby picked up the rock dug out of the hole and dropped it into the water by the open truck window. A little wave washed into the cab, momentarily submerging the alien again. Peter made noises like a man talking underwater while

Bobby scooted the tow truck forward, hauling the drowned truck out onto dry land.

"He's dead," Bobby said, looking in the window at the creature behind the wheel. He poked at it with a finger, and the alien fell over sideways.

"Maybe we can revive him," Peter said.

"No chance. He's drowned. He was a bad guy anyway. He stole the truck."

"Oh," Peter said.

"We need more water. This is soaking in."

"What we need is a bigger hole," Peter said.

"And a river. There should be a river leading somewhere. Into the bushes. That over there is the jungle. Can we use any of those boards in the pile? We need a base."

"A base? We used to call it a fort."

"We call it a base now. Can we use them?"

"Sure," Peter said.

Together they salvaged a dozen short pieces of lumber out of the scrap pile and built a base for the good aliens. Peter remembered doing that countless times as a kid. Once he had spent all day building a fort out of sticks in the soft dirt of a flower bed, fashioning a jungle compound like the one destroyed by King Kong. After dark he had wanted to go back out with a flashlight and work on it some more, but his mother hadn't let him.

Somehow he had never done that with David—built forts in the dirt. All his memories of that kind of thing were left over from his own childhood. Thinking about it now wrecked his mood, and suddenly all the magic went out of the boards and the waterways and the aliens. There was a time when that kind of thing looked like the kingdom of heaven, but somewhere along the line it had lost its glow. Maybe that was just the cost of growing up. And maybe the cost of growing up was too high.

Those were easier days, he thought, but then suddenly he remembered David. What might he be going through? Nothing *easy*. He pushed the thought back into the darkness, and just then Beth came out of the house, carrying two plates.

"Did you dig the hole for the rose?" she asked doubtfully.

"We're conditioning the soil first," Peter said, taking one of the plates from her.

"Ah," she said. "That's what it is. I can see that now."

"We just drownded the bad alien," Bobby said. "Now we're setting up a base. What you do is put your guys around inside and then knock it down and then see whether they got crushed or not.''

"Seriously," Peter said to Beth. "The ground's too hard, so Bobby suggested we soak it with a little water. I think it's a brilliant idea.''

"I do too," she said, picking up the shovel and scooping wet dirt out of the hole. She pried out a couple of rocks, chopped more dirt out, and sent Bobby around back to turn on the hose again. She worked silently, and Peter knew she had something to say and was waiting for the right time.

"I brought the spud gun," Bobby said to him. Peter hadn't seen him return from the back of the house. Beth went back inside to get the coffee. Bobby pulled the gun out of the cardboard box along with potatoes in a paper bag. "Four potatoes," he said. "Too bad we only have one gun."

"We have two," Peter said. "I bought one for me at the same time I bought yours." He stood up and walked over to the Suburban. There was no use letting the spud gun sit around in the glove compartment. So what if he had bought it for David? He'd done it out of guilt, and he could do it out of guilt again. When all this was over, he'd buy ten spud guns and a sack of potatoes for each one, and really make the guilt count for something. He opened the car door and twisted the glove compartment latch. When it sprang open, Peter stood there looking at it, not quite believing what he saw.

The spud gun was gone, along with a tire pressure gauge and a ball-point pen. He rummaged among the insurance papers and maps. What else? There had been something else along with the spud gun. . . .

David's flute. Damn it! To hell with the rest of it, David's flute *meant* something. He couldn't believe he'd been robbed, right in broad daylight. It must have been this morning, or maybe late last night. He checked the back: his toolbox was there along with a bundle of road flares. The notion was almost too preposterous. Between last night and this morning, someone had stolen four dollars' worth of junk and left a hundred bucks' worth of tools.

**14**

"Why do you think it's this guy Adams?" Peter asked.

"I don't know," Beth said. "Something. Intuition. I guess because he's the only one I've met lately that would do something like that. I don't believe it's just some guy out walking in the neighborhood."

"Could you tell anything from his voice when he called?"

"No. I don't know what he was doing to it, but I didn't recognize his voice. Probably he was talking through a towel or something."

Peter stood up and looked out toward the creek. Bobby had finally gotten bored with the aliens and their base and had gone for a hike. The wind was blowing hard again, and Peter was edgy even though Bobby had promised not to go very far. "You'll have to get a line trap on your phone, whatever they call it," he said, sitting down again. "A line I.D."

"That's what the police said. Now that I've got a case number from the police, Pacific Bell can hook it up. The only trouble is that he's calling from a pay phone. I could tell that much. So the best thing I can hope for is that if he keeps calling he's stupid enough to keep using the same pay phone. I don't think he will, though. And even if he does, then the police have to stake out the phone, and how long are they willing to do that?"

"Probably not at all. Why don't you think he'll use the same phone? One near your house?"

She shrugged. "That's what he said—that he was nearby. But he's obviously not just a telephone freak, not if he called twice and then came right over. I think he used the phone to call me just like anyone else would do."

"That's a little bit scary."

"A *little*," Beth said, wrapping her arms around herself as if she were suddenly cold. "It's not quite as scary as your story, though. I think you win the prize."

"I don't know. I think I'd rather have ghosts than maniacs. Anyway, I don't like the idea of your being in the house alone," he said, steering the conversation away from himself. "If he calls again, leave. Go to a hotel. Drive out here."

"And if you get a call from any ghosts, *you* leave. We can meet halfway and camp in the woods like refugees."

"I'm serious."

"I know. So am I. Anyway, Klein's putting new dead bolts on the doors right now."

"*Klein* is?"

"Uh-huh. New latches on the windows, too."

"I could have done that," Peter said.

"I'm not even sure it's all necessary, but he wouldn't take no for an answer. I almost think . . ."

"What? You don't think it was *him*, do you?"

"No." She shook her head. "Absolutely not."

"Why not? It would be easy as pie for him. Think about it. He's out in the middle of the night and notices a light on in the neighbor lady's bedroom. It's too much temptation, and he sneaks through the gate and looks in the window, and when she sees him and screams, he simply pretends to be chasing the bad man off. Then he's terrificly helpful afterward, and the neighbor lady ends up saying, 'Thank God for Mr. Klein.' "

"I can't believe that."

"And to top it off, he ends up with copies of the new dead bolt keys."

"Too crazy."

"That's what I'd do if I was him. I mean, I wouldn't do that in the *first* place, but if I did, that's exactly how I'd explain being out and about in the middle of the night. Why did *he* say he was out there?"

"He couldn't sleep. He was having a drink."

"Not very original."

"That's why it's probably true. You don't know him as well as I do. He just *wouldn't*—especially the breaking-in part. *Especially* not with Bobby in the house."

"And there were no fingerprints on the doorknob?"

"Nothing but a smear."

"So the guy was wearing gloves."

She shook her head. "No. I saw his hand when he turned to run. He wasn't wearing any gloves."

"Why did you say you 'didn't know' a moment ago when you mentioned Klein? What don't you know about him?"

"Just that I don't know how he's mixed up with our friend Adams, but I know he is. He was lying about that last night at the steak house. And I think he's lying for some good reason."

Peter listened as Beth told him about the overheard conversation that morning, but he was distracted by the wind and by Bobby's being gone. Brown leaves blew out of the woods, carpeting the drive nearly ankle deep in places.

"I thought Klein was going to kill him," she said. "I'm not kidding. If Lorna hadn't got in the way, I think he would have shot him. He threatened to."

There was a blast of wind just then that rattled the house, picking up the fallen leaves and filling the air with them. The trees creaked and swished in an orchestra of wind noise. Beth paused for a moment and then went on with what she was saying. But Peter barely heard her now. He stood up again, listening for stray sounds, for human voices on the wind. There was something urgent in the atmosphere, something wound tight.

The dense shadows of the alders along the creek moved rhythmically, casting over and over again the shapes of swaying, gesturing limbs across the ground. There was the suggestion of animation in the shadows, of arms sweeping the sunlit spaces, of someone running forward only to be pulled backward again into the dark formless spaces among the trees.

He heard a noise behind him, light feet scuffling along a carpet, and he turned and looked through the window into the dim house. A light was burning in the parlor—an oil lamp; he could just see it beyond the edge of the open door. The light dimmed as a shadow passed before it, and in that moment a man walked out of the bedroom, carrying an open book, his dark form a moving silhouette on the curtains.

"Are you listening?"

"What?" Peter asked. The man was gone, vanished, and the oil lamp with him. "Listening for what?" The air was full of whirling leaves. He tried to recall what they'd been talking about, where they'd left off.

"To whom, you mean, not for what."

"Oh," Peter said. "Of course I was listening. What were you saying? I was distracted for a second. Sorry."

She looked at his face. "Are you all right? You *look* distracted."

"Yeah," he said. "It's nothing."

"I was asking why, if it was Klein, and he just happened to see my light on and get this crazy idea, why would he call me on the phone first?"

"I don't know. I guess he wouldn't. Unless he was trying to throw everyone off the scent." He rubbed his forehead. His head ached vaguely and he felt drugged, as if he'd just waked up from an afternoon nap. He looked back through the window again, into the empty house.

"I don't quite get it," she said.

"You know." What? He couldn't think. "It wouldn't be a bad ploy, Klein doing something that didn't make any sense so that you'd think it couldn't be him, because it didn't make sense that he would do something like that."

"I think you're not making any sense. What the hell's wrong with you?" She stood up, cupping her hands against the window in order to peer in. "What did you see in here?"

"An old man walking across the room."

She stepped away from the window. "Don't *talk* like that."

"I'm not kidding." Then, seeing the look on her face, he added, "It might have been a reflection."

"Of what?"

"Something . . . I don't know. Maybe the leaves blowing."

"Is that what you think it was?"

Peter shook his head. "He came out through the parlor door, carrying an open book. I heard something, too, a scuffing, like I could hear him walking. You hear anything?"

"I was talking too much." She looked in the window again. "The parlor door's shut now. Did he shut the door behind him or leave it open?"

He shook his head again and gestured helplessly. "He left it open, I think, but . . ." A movement near the creek caught his eye. "There!" he said, pointing at the dark stand of alders and willow. Beth stepped closer to him, both of them looking out toward the wind-lashed trees. The dense shadows were alive with movement as the wind scoured leaves and twigs from the forest floor and tore them from the limbs overhead. A small cyclone of autumn debris rose and fell near the ground, spiraling in a slowly eddying pool, expanding and contracting as if the mass of dead verdure were a living, breathing thing. The wind sculpted it, tearing away clumps of leaves, stretching and bending it into the form of a human—someone bent forward, as if struggling to get up, its mouth and eyes merely black shadows like small windows into some infinitely dark place.

Beth gasped and clutched Peter's arm, and right then there was movement in the darkness beyond the struggling thing, something shifting among the alders as if a fragment of shadow had come loose from the rest. There was a sound like a cry from a human throat, and the thing made of leaves, standing nearly upright now, burst into fragments, the wind picking them up and flinging them out into the open air.

A woman stood now where the moving shadow had been. She looked back at the house, the hem of her black dress whipping in the wind. Her face was contorted with fear and anguish as she turned and hurried away up the creek-side trail, the wind carrying back to them the sound of her voice, crying out the name of her lost child.

"That's *her*," Peter shouted, and just then the wind slammed into the house with enough fury to make the walls shake. There was the sound of a shutter banging and then of breaking glass. A scattering of shingles hit the dirt of the driveway, skidding out toward the road, and Peter grabbed Beth and dragged her back up under the shelter of the porch roof.

"Bobby!" Beth said, yanking away and then pushing past him and down the couple of porch steps. The wind blew frantically now, churning up dust along the road, whipping the heavy branches of the oaks and sycamores. The house thrummed with the sound of it, the wind whistling under the porch and through the latticework that enclosed the cellar.

Peter followed Beth out onto the drive, grabbing her shoulder and leaning in toward her ear. "Upstream or down?" he shouted, but she shrugged helplessly, shaking her head. Of course Bobby hadn't said where he was going. He might be anywhere—up along the ridge, visiting at one of the other cabins. . . .

"He knows he's not supposed to go past the Forks," she shouted, pointing west, down the canyon. Her hair blew out behind her in the wind, and she sheltered her face from flying debris. Reaching out for his arm, she turned him around, shouting into his ear. "You go that way, and if he's not there, turn around and come find me." She turned and ran then, down toward the creek, disappearing in seconds into the dark shadows of the trees.

# 15

POMEROY TURNED THE ISUZU AROUND IN KLEIN'S DRIVEWAY AND headed down Parker again. Klein's truck was gone. If Lorna was home and saw him, so much the better. The phone call this morning would have unnerved her, especially with her husband still out of the house, probably chasing around through the hills with the woman next door. Maybe later in the day he'd call her again and let her in on that aspect of Klein's life, too. It would certainly be doing her a favor.

He wondered suddenly if he were right about Klein and Beth. The idea had been bothering him all morning. Beth wasn't like that, but of course Klein was exactly the kind of man to take advantage of a lonely single woman burdened with a child. What Beth didn't need was the poisonous influence of a degenerate like Klein who would take advantage of her being lonely and unprotected. He searched his mind for some contrary explanation: what had happened to him out in the canyon was just too damned weird not to be connected to Klein and their little enterprise.

He passed the general store and turned left onto the highway, driving slowly, watching the wind play through the dead grass at the edge of the schoolyard. As had happened last night, the car seemed to want to navigate, to lead him somewhere for reasons he couldn't quite settle his mind on. He saw that a high white streak of cloud-drift angled down the sky, disappearing behind the hills.

Follow it. . . .

The thought came to him like the wind whispering, and he turned the wheel hard to the left, across the highway in the direction indicated by the sky. A car honked and swerved around him, and he bumped across the far shoulder and back up onto the road that led down into Rose Canyon, pulling into the deserted parking lot of Señor Lico's Mexican Restaurant.

In the back of the lot he cut the engine and sat for a moment in the quiet car, letting the afternoon speak to him. Against the glare of the windshield he saw the reflection of the slats of wooden siding on the wall of the restaurant, lying one over the other like the slats of the window shade that hid the interior of her bedroom. He bent his head just a little, peering into the bar of light where the one slat was caught open, revealing Beth's bed and the soft curve of her leg, revealing a world that was separated from him by nothing more than a thin pane of window glass, and yet was as remote as the make-believe world of a television program. He stood outside in the windy darkness while Beth lay there reading and thinking, her mind examining bright objects that he couldn't see or touch.

What separated them, two sensitive people alone in the world? Mere window glass? Chance? Hadn't chance brought them together at last? He pictured her shifting her weight on the bed, getting comfortable. The boy was out of the house, gone to his father's for a month. Pomeroy stood just outside the partly-open bedroom door. He could feel her loneliness reaching out to him, yearning for him. She saw him finally, and sat up smiling, pulling modestly at the hem of her T-shirt. . . .

The few houses in Rose Canyon ran nearly parallel to the village of Trabuco Oaks, with just a low-lying ridge of hills in between. The little day-care center near where he'd parked last night couldn't be more than a quarter mile northeast of where he sat right now. The cloud-drift in the sky had moved on, but had led him to this spot minutes ago as surely as an arrow on a road sign. The dry grass and lone sycamores on the open land between the two canyons were probably national forest property, and there was no law against his being out there hiking around.

He got out, holding a topographic map that he unrolled across the hood, flattening it to the blue metal with his hands to keep it from blowing away in the wind. His heart raced, and he licked his lips and looked furtively around, settling his mind again on a picture of the back door of Beth's house, on the shadow that the doorknob had cast across the pale paint in the moonlight.

The house was empty right now. And its emptiness lent a note of urgency to the afternoon that was heightened by the wind and the silence. A car turned up the street, and he stared at the map, tracing the contour lines of a set of hills with his finger. He watched the car turn into a driveway opposite and disappear behind a hedge of oleander. The driver hadn't even looked up. Pomeroy waited for the sound of the car door slamming before rolling up the map and tossing it back onto the seat of the car.

He would take a quick look around and then go home. That's all. It wouldn't hurt anything to see what things looked like from the back of Klein's house. Ignorance in that kind of area could be fatal if things heated up, like last night, for instance. He clipped the thought off, rolling up the window in the Trooper and locking the doors.

Abruptly he turned and walked the fifty yards to the end of the road, vaulted the barbed wire fence, and headed straight through the tall grass up the hill, walking quickly but with his hands in his pockets. He ducked in behind a broad sycamore tree and stood with his back to it, breathing heavily. Ahead of him was nothing but scrub-covered hills and lone trees edging up toward where the hills steepened, angling away toward the ridge.

And if she came home while he was there? His heart quickened its pace. He licked his lips and set out again, reminding himself that he was merely going to have a look around, nothing more than that.

THE WOODS WERE FULL OF NOISES. THE WIND BLEW THROUGH THE treetops with a continual rustling sound, and small things scratched through the dry leaves. Something as tiny as a bird sounded like a bear. Bobby wondered if there *were* bears out there. His mother said there weren't, but how did she know, *really*? There were plenty of places for bears to hide. He knew there were mountain lions around. He had seen one once at the zoo in Santa Ana. Its fur looked like an old rug and its eyes were drippy and it always slept in the corner of its cage. What you did if you saw one was throw your arms over your head so that you looked bigger. Mountain lions didn't like big things.

He looked back behind him, down the creek, but he couldn't see Peter's house at all anymore. Ahead of him lay the fallen sycamore tree, and he could easily climb up onto it and have a better view of things. Although the tree had fallen across the stream, maybe years ago, it was still alive, and you could walk across the trunk like a bridge. He could tell a sycamore tree because of its leaves shaped like hands, and because it had bark that you could peel off like paper, in sheets. He and his mother had made a treasure map out of it once.

Something hit him in the shoulder just then and fell to the path. Somebody throwing rocks? He looked around, listening hard, but he couldn't see or hear anybody. The wind had fallen off, and the forest was nearly silent. A big acorn lay beside his shoe. It hadn't fallen from the trees above, because they were alders and they didn't have acorns. He picked it up, in case he had to throw it back at someone, and suddenly he wished he'd brought his spud gun along. But he'd left it back at Peter's, and if he went back after it they'd probably make him stay.

The wind sighed through the treetops again, and the willow leaves shivered along the edge of the creek. He climbed out onto the fallen sycamore and sat down, dangling his feet above the moving water. He peeled two little pieces of bark off and tossed them into the creek a few feet upstream, and immediately they were swept up in the current and came racing back down at him, bumping around rocks. One of them got caught in a little whirlpool and slowed down. The other one sailed beneath the fallen tree and out of sight behind him. Next time he'd bring out a couple of boats to race, with two of the aliens for riverboat captains. Maybe he could follow them all the way down to the arroyo.

A woodpecker landed in the branches of an alder next to the creek. It stood there nearly upside down and began knocking a hole in the bark. Maybe the woodpecker had hit him with the acorn. After it made a hole in the tree it would come back and stuff an acorn into the hole, like a cork, and then the acorn would rot and bugs would get in it and the woodpecker could eat the bugs. His mother said that all those little holes were like woodpecker TV dinners.

He leaned back against the branch and listened to the creek water burble around the rocks below. His mother knew the names of every little thing out there, and was always talking about them as if she liked to hear the sound of their names. She could spend a half hour following a newt around. There was nothing wrong with newts, but there were at least ten million of them out there, and they all looked exactly alike—little gumby things made out of root beer–colored rubber.

Out of the corner of his eye he saw something move—something white down among the oaks along the base of the ridge. He sat perfectly still, holding on to a branch, ready to run if he had to. Whatever it was, he could be up the bank and out to the road before it could catch him. That was the quickest way back to Peter's house.

It darted into the open now, from behind a trunk—a kid, throwing acorns! One pinged off the branch that Bobby leaned against and plopped into the water below. The kid disappeared, back into the shadows, then appeared again farther up the canyon, heading across a clearing toward the abandoned cabin. Bobby could barely see it through the trees—just the front corner of it and the edge of one dark broken-out window.

He jumped down onto the ground and began picking his way up the creek again. There were a couple of big oak trees not far ahead. He could fill up his pockets with acorns just in case the kid wanted to start a war. The creek turned in toward the ridge right there, and straight ahead of him was a sort of clear space, overgrown with weeds and autumn-colored poison oak and partly shaded by big, low-limbed trees. A stone chimney sat all alone in the clearing, half-crumbled and with weeds growing out from broken places and from holes between the bricks.

Bobby poked around in the leaves with a stick, picking up the biggest acorns he could find. He looked for the kid again, but couldn't see him. A scattering of leaves lifted in a clump on a fresh gust of wind and blew away up the canyon, and the wind began to blow strong and steady. He grabbed a couple more acorns and then set out cautiously toward the empty cabin, which sat on the other side of a little grove of nearly bare fig trees. That's where the kid would be, maybe inside, maybe outside. Bobby held his biggest acorn in his hand, ready for the kid to pop up and throw one.

He could see the house clearly now through the branches of the fig trees. Although the walls were still standing, the roof was caved in at the front corner and the porch had fallen into the dirt. A couple of boards had been nailed across the black rectangle of a broken-out window, and tendrils of wild grapevine grew up the wall and over the sill, the leaves yellow and falling because of the season. If the kid was hiding inside, that wasn't really fair. There wasn't any other cover around the outside of the house except for the concrete shell of an empty cistern twenty feet or so from the front door.

At the edge of the trees there was a barbed wire fence, rusted and broken, the wire lying along the ground and most of the posts fallen over. Bobby stepped carefully over the wire, watching the house and listening for sounds, but all was still and quiet except for the deep drifts of leaves shifting and whispering in the wind. The kid was around somewhere. Bobby could feel it—eyes watching him. He crossed the driveway, making his way toward the cistern. The driveway was disused, overgrown with dead grass and scattered with branches.

Warily, he crouched behind the cistern for a moment, then broke from cover and ran across to the wall of the house, ready to turn and bolt for the cistern again if the kid stood up to throw an acorn. He should have brought more ammunition, especially if he was going to be trapped so far from any oak trees. Maybe the kid had a whole pile of it in there and was leading him into a trap.

Cautiously he looked through the hole where the window had been. Inside, the dirty wooden floor was covered with leaves and bottles and torn-up magazines. Clearly someone had been there off and on, but right now the place felt empty and was utterly silent. If the kid was there, he was in the back somewhere.

The wind blew hard just then, and a flurry of dust and leaves drove down along the side of the house, straight at him. He turned away, hiding his face with his jacket. It would only get more windy as the afternoon turned into evening. Santa Ana winds always seemed to blow hardest at night, just like it always rained more at night, or like it was almost always sunnier on Sundays than on any other day of the week.

The wind blew harder now against his back, pushing at him, and the sound that the wind made blowing through the broken-out windows of the house was almost like a voice whispering. Inside there was shelter. The leaves and trash on the floor barely stirred. It was quiet and warm. He walked slowly around to the front again, where the door yawned open now on the wind. He stepped to the doorway and listened.

"Hello!" Bobby yelled after a moment, but there was nothing but an answering silence. Stepping completely into the room, he tried again. "I *know* you're there."

Again there was nothing but silence. Then, with a wild gust, the wind threw the door open wider, and it banged off the side wall of the porch and slammed shut with enough force to shake the old house. Bobby spun around, grabbing the rusty doorknob,

and turned it. A rush of leaves and paper blew up from the floor,
whirling around the walls of the room and clinging to his clothes
and hair, and right then the doorknob twisted off in his hand,
scattering a shower of rust flakes onto his shoes. He dropped the
knob and looked at his open hand, stained the color of dried blood
with the rust.

He was trapped. He knew there was a back door, but finding
it meant going through the rest of the deserted house. He looked
over his shoulder. Opposite the front door was another door into
the back—maybe the kitchen. It was open about an inch and
revealed a vertical line of shadow. He stepped toward it, trying
to see through. If he had a stick or something he could push it
open without getting too close.

There was nothing around to use, and when he reached out a
hand toward the dirty white panel, the door swung partway open
by itself, revealing boarded-up windows beyond, sunlight slanting
through the gaps between the boards and more vines growing
through into the dim room and curling down onto an old wooden
countertop littered with yellow leaves. Then the door creaked entirely open, and a boy stepped slowly out from the shadows behind it and stood looking silently at Bobby, his gaunt face a shade
of pale white like the color of a moth.

POMEROY WAS OUT OF SIGHT OF ANY OF THE HOUSES AT THE BACK
of Rose Canyon. The wind swept through the grasses, making the
landscape doubly lonesome and alien, and he stopped for a moment
and looked behind him at the perfectly empty hills. Overhead a vul-
ture circled slowly. He might have been the last man alive in the
world. The thought thrilled him and horrified him both.

Hurrying now, he set out through the grass again. He didn't
have the luxury of daydreaming. There wasn't time. Beth might
return at any moment, and Klein along with her. Pomeroy wasn't
afraid of Klein, except in the sense that you'd be a fool *not* to be

afraid, say, of a rattlesnake or a cocked gun. A man like Klein was liable to go off without warning, and so you had to be certain you were in control when dealing with him.

Sweating, he climbed to the top of a hill, glanced over his shoulder again, and jogged down into the little valley beyond. Dust rose around him, and he wiped his face with the back of his hand, then tried unsuccessfully to flatten his hair back down. A dry creek bed ran between the hills, edged by willow scrub. He pushed his way through it, the soles of his shoes scrunching in the crusted sand of the creek. Flies rose from a muddy little pool, swarming for a moment around his face, and he broke into an uphill run, fanning himself with both hands.

From the next hill he could see another barbed wire fence off to the left, stretched along a windbreak of eucalyptus. It had to be the back of one of the little streets running off Parker, probably just north of the steak house. He angled west, climbing along a cattle trail that edged a thicket of greasewood and castor bean. The shrubbery shook stiffly in the wind, hiding him from the eyes of people in backyards. Another couple hundred yards to go, maybe less.

The trail abruptly cut upward, rising steeply toward the ridge in exactly the wrong direction. He pushed his way into the scrub, crouching down and peering through the dry foliage. He could see Klein's backyard now, the poolhouse and the blue rectangle of water enclosed by a wrought-iron fence. There's where he'd have to watch himself. He couldn't allow himself to be seen. That would introduce a hell of an awkward variable.

When he was sure the yard was deserted, he stepped boldly out through the bushes, half running and half sliding down the hillside toward the redwood fence that marked the perimeter of Beth's yard. And then, just when he was entirely exposed, striding through the dead, knee-high grass, he saw something move off to the west, among the trees beyond Klein's place.

He dropped flat onto his stomach and lay there breathing hard. Cautiously he pushed his head up and peered over the waving grass. The wind poured down off the ridge now, making a weird thrashing noise in the eucalyptus trees at the edge of the field. It was a woman that he'd seen. She stood near the fence now at the back of Klein's yard. She was dressed in a flowing black gown of some sort, although it seemed at least as likely that she stood in some kind of dark and inexplicable shadow. Even from that distance the skin of her face looked as pale as milk. He realized that she wasn't in the yard after all, and neither was anybody else. Like him, she had come down out of the hills.

But what the hell for? Dressed like that, she must be some kind of local hippie or something. What did Klein have going here? Pomeroy watched her carefully. Slowly he became certain that she didn't pose any kind of threat to him. She was dressed too strangely, and she looked through the black wrought iron as if she were utterly lost and only half recognized the place, perhaps as somewhere she'd once been. Abruptly she turned around and walked toward the hills again, lifting the hem of her dress above the windblown grass. When she reached the shadows of a stand of sycamores she disappeared utterly from view. He waited another moment, but she didn't reappear. Apparently she'd gone on up toward the ridge.

He stood up and ran toward the fence behind Beth's house. It had been twenty minutes since he'd checked her driveway. Maybe she was home already. Time suddenly seemed desperately short, but he couldn't quit now, not after having come so close to his goal. One quick look over the fence and that would be it. He would satisfy his curiosity and then go.

But at the rear of the yard, just at where Klein's wrought iron tied into the redwood corner post of Beth's fence, there was a huge avocado tree. A heavy limb reached over the fence boards there, arching down nearly to shoulder level. The fence had been built with the rails facing out; that was a mistake. A fence like that was easy to climb, an invitation to any passing burglar or child. Pomeroy stepped onto the bottom rail and peered over.

Nothing. No sign of anyone home. He could see straight across her yard to where the driveway ran into the detached garage. If she had gotten home, she'd parked the bus near the street instead of pulling it up. Only she hadn't gotten home. He could feel it. The house was quiet and closed up tight.

He grabbed the big limb with both hands, pulling and kicking his way into the foliage until he stepped onto the top of the fence. Crouching, he looked out along the side of the Kleins' house. There was the tail end of Lorna's Jaguar in the drive. Klein's truck was still gone.

Without waiting another moment he dropped to the ground and straightened his clothes, then tried to brush off the dust and foxtails he'd picked up crawling around out in the field. With a shaking hand he smoothed his hair, abruptly wishing he had his toiletries bag with him. He wanted to look his best in a situation like this, not disheveled like some kind of tramp.

Keeping low, he loped across to the back of the house. Without giving an instant's thought to what he was doing, he pulled his shirt out of his pants, wrapped his hand in it, and grasped the doorknob. The knob turned. He pushed on it, but the door held fast. Bolted! One good kick . . . He rejected the idea, letting go of the knob and turning away, heading toward a pair of windows that looked out onto the backyard. Beyond them was a rectangular bay, probably a bedroom closet, and beyond that lay the window he'd peered into last night. There was no way he was going around the corner of the house, not in broad daylight.

He had three shots at it, and that's all. There would be no breaking windows, no evidence that anyone had been there. The lawn ran all the way up to the foundation of the house, so he wouldn't leave footprints, and he was careful this time to keep his hands off the dusty siding. The first window was clearly latched. He didn't bother to touch it, but moved on quickly to the second window. It didn't have any latch at all.

He looked through it, into what must have been the living room or dining room. A door on the left led into Beth's bedroom. Hesitating for one last moment, he let his mind spin, waiting for something to appear—some warning, some sign, some reminder of the absolute desperation of what he was doing.

Instead he pictured what lay on the other side of that inner door—things that were a part of Beth's secret world, things that Lance Klein could only imagine. Real intimacy, that was what he and Beth would share. . . .

Quickly he thrust the palm of his hand against the top of the lower half of the window. It slid open easily. He pulled off his shirt, laid it across the sill, and boosted himself through, careful of his bandaged hand. He lowered himself to the floor on the other side, touching nothing but the carpet. It was then that he saw the power screwdriver lying on a small table that someone had graciously pulled out of the way for him.

Klein again. It had to be him. He had been there tinkering around, trying to make sure that the house was safe from prowlers. Pomeroy smiled. "Thanks, Lance," he said out loud, but the sound of his own voice in the empty house startled him.

He pushed the window closed with his shirt, and then put the shirt back on, tucking it in haphazardly. Forcing himself to breathe evenly and deeply, he stepped across the carpet and shouldered open the door to Beth's bedroom.

**18**

BOBBY WHEELED AROUND, READY TO RUN BACK INTO THE FRONT room.

"Wait," the boy said. "I want to show you a thing that I have."

Bobby stared at him. He wasn't very big. His clothes were weird, as if he was poor and couldn't afford anything better, or maybe was religious. Leaves swirled up around his black leather shoes, which looked tight and uncomfortable, and he wore suspenders and a shirt with sleeves like a pirate might wear. His voice was thin and frail, sounding almost as if he'd been hurt or had been sick for a long time.

"I saw you in the woods," Bobby said to him. "I thought maybe you wanted to have an acorn fight."

"I saw you, too."

"My friend Peter's coming in a couple of minutes. I've only got till two." He checked his watch.

"Me, too," the boy said. "I've only got till two." He smiled, showing uneven teeth. There was something in his voice, almost a buzzing sound like a voice out of a machine or as if he were talking through a swarm of bees.

"So you threw the acorns?"

"I threw the acorns," the boy said.

"Don't copy me. I don't like copying."

The boy said nothing, so Bobby said, "You were the one at the day-care center yesterday, weren't you? The one that threw the deer head over the fence." He suddenly knew it was true, even though he hadn't been there at the time.

He shook his head slowly. "That was my brother. I didn't throw dead things."

"You've got a brother?"

"Sometimes I pretend to be him."

"Where is he now?" Bobby asked, looking past him into the kitchen. This sounded like a lie.

"He's lost. He can't play. Ever."

"Then how did he throw the deer head over the fence if he's lost?"

"He threw a deer head over the fence."

"I guess I better go," Bobby said. "Peter and my mom will be out looking for me. Probably they're right outside now."

For a moment the boy said nothing, and then, as if he suddenly remembered to speak, he asked, "Do you want some Oreos and Kool-Aid?"

"Sure," Bobby said. "If you really *have* any."

"It's what I always have. Do you want to see my treasure?" He turned around without waiting for an answer and headed back into the kitchen. Bobby followed him out through the back door and into the windy sunlight.

"It's down here," the boy said, leading him around the side of the house where it was partly sheltered from the wind. A profusion of wild grape grew against the wall, the vines curling into the eaves of the house and spreading out along the ground, half covering the plank door of a storm cellar that sat in a raised frame of rotten-looking boards. A rusty hasp and stick held the door shut, and the boy tugged the stick out and dropped it into the weeds alongside the frame. Bobby helped him pull the door back to where it leaned open, resting against the mass of vines.

A shower of yellow grape leaves drifted down onto a set of wooden stairs illuminated by a rectangle of sunlight. There was a room beyond the bottom of the stairs, and a cool wind drifted up out of it, carrying on it the earthy, musty smell of closed-up places. Bobby could just make out dusty wooden shelves against a far wall. Beneath them on the dirt floor lay a scattering of broken glass and a couple of rusty lids, as if long ago someone had stored food down there.

"I'll go first," the boy said, almost eagerly, and stepping down the wooden stairs, he disappeared into the shadows toward the far end of the room.

Bobby hesitated before following. He waited on the second step, trying to see. If he had a flashlight it wouldn't be so bad. "Just bring the Oreos up here," he called down into the room, but there was no answer. He heard a scraping then, as if the boy were pulling a box across the floor, and he stepped onto the next stair and bent down to see. There was just enough sunlight so that he could make out shapes—the boy at the far end of the room and a box of some sort at his feet.

As his eyes adjusted to the darkness, he could see that the opposite side of the small room opened onto a low crawl space under the rest of the house. He could make out the exposed wooden substructure of the house itself, sitting on concrete piers in the dirt, and a couple of little patches of sunlight shining in the distance, maybe through broken places where the old front porch had fallen.

Just then someone called outside, a woman's voice from some distance away, barely audible above the wind. The wind stirred the chalky dust beneath the house, moving strings of cobwebs that drooped from the floor joists.

"Hurry," the boy said. "This is only one of my treasures. I've got them hidden around. Sometime I'll show you the rest."

"Where's the Oreos?" Bobby asked, stepping down to the floor, but for some reason still not eager to look into the box. He was almost certain the kid was lying.

There was the sound of the woman calling again, closer now. It might be his mother, although she didn't usually sound as creepy as that. He looked at his watch. He was only late by a couple of minutes. . . .

"I'll only show you if you promise you won't tell," the boy said.

"Course I promise," Bobby said, just as the calling started up again, the voice closer now. She was hollering somebody's name, half moaning and half crying. It *sure* wasn't his mother.

"Don't take anything," the boy said suddenly, pulling open two of the flaps of the cardboard box.

"I wouldn't," Bobby said. "I don't steal things. I thought you said there was Oreos and Kool-Aid."

The boy started crying then. He stepped away from the box, brushing past Bobby to the base of the stairs where he stood for a moment and listened. "Green Kool-Aid," he said, trying to catch his breath and speaking out into the wind and sunlight. "We call it bug juice."

"Is that your mom out there?" Bobby asked. "Are you in trouble for being down here?"

Suddenly crying out loud, the boy stepped past Bobby and up the half dozen wooden stairs, stopping at the top and looking back down into the room. He looked wildly around himself, as if he couldn't make up his mind to stay or go, and then abruptly turned and stepped completely outside, disappearing past the edge of the tilted-open door.

"Wait," Bobby said. "I'm coming too." Hurriedly he took a step closer to the half-closed box, bending over to look inside, just to get a glimpse of what was in there. The cardboard flaps hid most of the interior, and he could just make out a scattering of things pushed against the far corner: a couple of glass things and a dog collar and what looked like some kind of weird flute. A plastic-covered square of cardboard lay beneath the flute, and on the cardboard were the words "Spud Gun" and a picture of three boys shooting at each other with red plastic guns just like the ones Peter had bought, just like the one stolen that morning out of Peter's car. . . .

"Hey!" Bobby shouted. No wonder the kid didn't want his mother to find him down there. He'd been stealing stuff from people and hiding it under here. He pulled the flaps of the box open all the way and reached for the potato gun, but then suddenly stopped and drew his hand back slowly.

A cat lay curled inside, up against the wall of the box. It might have been asleep, except that its head was pushed down at a funny angle and its cream-colored fur was streaked with blood. A gust of wind blew down into the cellar, scattering dead leaves across the packed earth. Just then the door swung inward, falling in a rush. Bobby turned and scrabbled toward the wooden stairs as the sunlight blinked out and the door banged heavily into its frame. He threw himself against it, pushing as hard as he could push and at the same time hearing the sound of the stick scraping into the iron ring of the hasp. Then there was nothing but darkness around him and the sound of dry vines skittering and scraping across the wooden planks overhead.

**19**

KLEIN LET HIMSELF INTO BETH'S HOUSE AGAIN AT THE BACK door without going home first to let Lorna know he was back. Probably she would have heard him pull in anyway, unless she was still hiding out in the bedroom. He had decided to tell her the truth, or at least that part of it that she could deal with: that he had made a mistake hiring a man like Pomeroy, and that he was going to let him go with some sort of commission for the work he had already done—a one-time commission based on setting up the sales of five houses. That was it for now, just what Klein owed him. If everything clicked, and the cabins eventually resold at a good profit, and they all made their percentage, then there'd be more in it for Pomeroy. But in the meantime, if there were any more phone calls, any harassment, any trouble at all, then Klein would go to the police.

By God he would, too, if it came to that, if Pomeroy forced him to. But of course it wouldn't come to that.

He put the bag of door and window hardware on the kitchen table. It had cost him nearly sixty bucks, but he would let that slide. He could afford to chip in that much in recompense for bringing Pomeroy into the neighborhood. Except if Beth brought it up, which she would, it would be tough to explain not taking her money. He pulled out a dozen cardboard-backed sets of window latches and started peeling off the stiff plastic fronts. He'd have to go back into the garage for a couple of drill bits and a hole saw before he could install the dead bolts, and when he did, then he'd set things straight with Lorna. One thing about her, she usually didn't bear a grudge. She got mad quickly enough, but her anger evaporated in a few hours. All she needed was time.

The screw holes in the new window latches matched the old holes perfectly. Klein anchored them with slightly oversized screws, then closed the window he'd left unlatched and tried it. It was solid, no movement at all. It would be easier for a burglar to break the glass than to jimmy the thing open. Short of installing bars over the windows, that was the best he could do.

He shoved the little table back into place before replacing the hardware on the second window. Then he moved on to the service porch and the kitchen, working quickly and methodically. He missed this part of the business—the handwork, the craft. Your eyes and hands developed their own brains if you worked at it long enough, and you could tell the size of a screw at a glance or cut a square edge with a handsaw or feel whether a tabletop was planed smooth.

That was the way it was—the things worth knowing were the things you couldn't be *told* how to do; you had to put years into them. And when you finally had them right, you hired a bunch of other guys to work for you and you moved on to the desk work, doing crap that any kind of idiot could do, half your time spent in the car, running around from job to job, sweet-talking city inspectors and aggravating your ulcer and your wife.

He nearly laughed out loud, sinking the last screw in the kitchen window. For ten cents he'd be a carpenter again, where he'd started—except there goes the house and the pool and Lorna's Jag. But hell, they were on the line anyway if Pomeroy screwed up the canyon deal. He'd probably lose the whole nine yards and Lorna into the bargain. There was some kind of poetic justice in life—karma, whatever you called it—and he'd just come face-to-face with the ugly bastard, sneaking around the backside of the barn.

He pushed open the door to Beth's bedroom and very nearly shut it again. The bed was littered with underclothes. He stood at the threshold for a moment, as if the things on the bed might explode at any moment into a whirlwind of lace and elastic. Hell, he wasn't even sure he knew what it all *was*. He hated walking through lingerie sections in department stores. *Most* men did, if they weren't deviants of some kind, although Lorna could never understand that. Women had a different attitude about it—obviously they had, or else Beth wouldn't have left it strewn all over the bed. Damn it, she *knew* he was coming over to fix the doors and windows. . . .

Then the thought crossed his mind that she *wanted* him to see the stuff, but he quickly brushed it aside. That was crazy. He wouldn't let himself think like that. Moving into the room, he glanced at the bed again. Clearly she'd been particular in picking things out to wear, laying them out like a man might lay out shirts

and ties. And hell, there was nothing wrong in that. It was what
women were *supposed* to do; although maybe men weren't supposed to see it. She was a grown woman, with a kid, for God's
sake, and she had a boyfriend who seemed like a hell of a nice
guy. If she treated him right, more power to them both. . . .

"Lance!"

Klein leaped forward at the sound of the voice, a strangled
sound gasping out of his throat. Throwing out his hands to catch
himself, he pitched the screw gun into the wall, and it bounced
back onto the bed. He scrambled around, flailing through the un-
dergarments and bedclothes, grappling for the fallen screw gun.
He clamped his hand around it, waving it in front of him like a
weapon as he staggered to his feet, stupidly pulling the trigger so
that the gun made a little whirring sound. The closet door opened
and Pomeroy stepped out, grinning like a cartoon pervert.

"Put the gun down, Lance," he said, holding both of his hands
in front of him and shaking his head theatrically. "Calm yourself
a little bit. Look at the mess you've made out of Beth's things."
He looked like hell, his hair blown straight toward the ceiling and
his face streaked with sweat and dirt. The knees of his pants were
soiled, and one was torn, a little triangle of material flapping open
to expose a patch of hairy, pale skin. One of his hands was
wrapped in dirty gauze that was streaked with dried blood.

Klein was still gasping so hard for breath that he couldn't
speak. He lowered the screw gun slowly, slipping his whole hand
around it so that if he had to he could slam Pomeroy in the
forehead. Jesus, he looked screwball as hell, with his mouth slack
and half-open and his shirt wrinkled and loose. He stood there
gaping, licking his lips, blinking a little too fast and often. It only
took Klein a few moments to put it all together.

"You sick bastard," he said finally.

"Why do you say that, Lance?" Pomeroy widened his eyes,
as if he sincerely wanted an answer to a simple question.

Klein waved the screw gun at the disheveled bed. "Did any of
it *fit*?"

"What are you talking about?" Pomeroy blinked hard a couple
of times.

"The underwear. About your size?"

Pomeroy's face fell, and he frowned deeply, narrowing his
eyes. "Beth and I have an intimacy that a man like you can't
*begin* to understand," he said.

"You're damned right I can't understand it," Klein said. His heart had slowed down finally, and he managed to keep the edge out of his voice. He wasn't going to lose it again, not like he had that morning. He waved at the open closet door, at the stuff on the bed. "You'd need a wheelbarrow full of shrinks to make sense out of any of this crap. Does this pass for sex with you, playing with a woman's underwear?"

"You know *nothing*," Pomeroy said, nearly spitting out the last word. "What were *you* staring at anyway, the wall? If I'd let you go on another minute there's no telling what you'd have done with Beth's things. I couldn't have you handling them! I want you to stay away from Beth from now on out. Do you hear me? Your hippie in the black dress was lurking around outside your fence an hour ago. Isn't *she* enough for you? You've got to follow Beth around, too, corrupting her?"

"Say that again."

"*You* know who I mean. Did you think you could keep something like that hidden from *me*?" He poked himself solidly in the chest. "What does Lorna think of your hippie friend?"

Klein stood silently, trying to take this in. How the hell had Pomeroy come up with it? The man was some kind of devil. . . .

"What?" Pomeroy said. "You're surprised I know about that? I'll tell you what. You go about your handyman chores here, but then that's *it*. Stay away from Beth from this point on."

"Sure, Barney," Klein said. "Whatever you say." He smiled and nodded.

Pomeroy tried to mash his hair down, but it was a failure. "Does Lorna know about your other woman?"

"Yeah," Klein said. "That's the maid's sister. They rent a little place at the back of Rose Canyon. But, hey, listen to me. I've got a hell of an idea. I'm going on over to the house to get a framing hammer. That's a big one—head weighs a couple of pounds and has waffle ridges cut into it. The claws are *just* about as long as my first two fingers." He waggled his fingers in the air to illustrate his point. "You with me so far?"

Pomeroy was silent.

"Good," Klein said, "you're listening. Here's the important part: I'll be gone five minutes, more or less. Why don't you tidy things up here—put this stuff away, close up the drawers, straighten the bed. When I come back I'd like to see things *really* neatened up. And I'd like to see you gone. If you're still here, then I swear to God I'll drag you back up into the hills and take you apart with that hammer."

Without another word Klein stepped toward the door. Pomeroy glared at him, opening his mouth to speak. Klein feinted toward him as if to hit him right then and there, and Pomeroy stumbled into the half-closed closet door, slamming it shut with his back.

"Five minutes from now," Klein said. "Better check your watch. It'd be a *hard* way to die, Barney."

PRETTY SOON THEY WOULD FIND HIM. BOBBY REMINDED HIMSELF of that again and glanced once more toward the opposite end of the room, where the cardboard box was a dark shadow on the dirt floor. Strangely, a vague and filmy light shone from within the box, just a faint glow, like a lantern muffled under a blanket. A flashlight left on? Or some kind of glow-in-the-dark toy? Bobby wished he had a flashlight, any kind of light, but he wasn't ready to look into the box again even if there was something like that in there.

He pushed himself closer to the stone wall of the cellar. Over his head the vines scraped across the trapdoor, falling silent for a moment and then scraping again, as if they were very slowly trying to claw their way through the old planks. Sunlight shone between two of the boards where the wood had splintered out, the light appearing and disappearing as the vines shifted with the wind.

He glanced again at the box. He knew whose cat it was, and abruptly he wondered if the kid had killed it or just found it. Maybe he went around killing things, like the deer at school. The deer head was all old and stiff, but that didn't mean anything. He might have killed it a long time ago and saved it just like he was saving the cat, and now he had locked the cellar door and was saving . . .

He pounded on the boards overhead again with the side of his fist, but even *he* could barely hear it. With all the vines and the wind, they'd *never* know he was down there. They might never find the door at all under the dead leaves.

He thought about the glass things he'd seen in the box, whatever they were called, heavy lumps of glass that came from telephone poles. He and Peter had gone out picking up rocks in the arroyo once, and they'd found two of the glass things hidden in the weeds near a telephone pole that had fallen over. One of them was green and the other one was purple because of the sun. Peter said it was worth ten dollars.

He folded his arms and leaned forward, resting his head and picturing him and Peter walking up the arroyo, picking up rocks and rolling them into the back of the Suburban. They'd found some round white rocks, and Peter said they were dinosaur eggs, and they'd found water that bubbled up out of a sandy place and then soaked back into the ground again. There'd been a garter snake near the water, but Peter couldn't catch it, and there was a horned toad, too, which you hardly ever found anymore, although there used to be thousands of them and they'd ride around all day in your shirt pocket and look out at people in grocery stores and things. They ate ants.

He looked up, cocking his head to the side. The vines had quit rustling across the wood, and it sounded for a moment like a voice shouting. He yelled and then right away stopped to listen again. There was silence now, but he was certain more than ever that he'd heard someone, and not the crazy kid's crazy mother, either. He pounded on the door again, then leaned back and kicked it hard with the toe of his tennis shoe. The wooden planks jumped, and dirt sifted through the cracks between them. He turned his face away, closing his eyes and mouth and kicked again, then put his hands to the narrow sunlit opening and yelled as loud as he could.

He listened again, to the swishing of vines and the sound of the wind blowing around the frame of the loose-fitting door, sounding almost like a faint and distant music. It couldn't be the wind; there was a melody to it, but not like a radio song, more like someone whistling, or playing the flute, off in the woods somewhere or inside the house above his head. He recognized the tune, and it slowly dawned on him that it was coming from the inside of the cardboard box. The wind died and the vines fell silent, and the music dwindled away.

**21**

THERE WAS NO SIGN OF BOBBY AT THE FORKS. THE FEW CABINS around the fire barn were apparently unoccupied, and the road was empty and blowing dust. Peter followed the course of the creek toward home again, hollering Bobby's name, although even if he were nearby there was probably no way he'd hear anything above the wind. The alders bowed beneath the onslaught, brown leaves scattering from the branches and rising high into the air. He broke into a run, thinking of Amanda and David. There was something desperate in the wind and in the suddenly empty afternoon, and he was struck with the irrational idea that if he didn't find Beth and Bobby quickly, he'd never find them again at all. That the wind would take them, too.

It was a crazy fear, and he knew it, but he didn't slow down. Leaping over rocks and debris, he ran toward the north wall of the canyon, away from the creek and its more dense vegetation, shouting Beth's name and looking hard into the silent shadows of the old oaks, where dust and leaves stirred in little swirling circles, protected from the wind. There were no cabins visible now, no people or cars. He shouldn't have let her go on alone. Never mind that she knew the woods better than he did; he was certain right now that neither one of them knew anything about what was going on here, about what had happened to Amanda and David. . . .

And then he caught up with her near the abandoned cabin. He skirted a stand of willow, and there she was, limping, her tennis shoes and pants legs wet and dirty as if she'd fallen in the stream. "Hey!" he shouted, out of breath, and she turned and shook her head, instantly cutting off his questions. Then she tilted her head and cupped her hand to her ear, listening to the wind, and Peter right then heard the last couple of notes of a pounding sound coming from somewhere nearby, probably from inside the cabin. Leaving Beth to catch up, he jogged through knee-high foxtails toward where the rear door stood partly open.

Inside, out of the wind, he shouted Bobby's name, and right away the pounding started up again, suddenly louder, sounding as if it came from inside a closet. There was a short hall, most of its old wallpaper long ago peeled away and holes knocked in the lath and plaster, which littered the dirty wooden floor. At the end of the hall hung a ragged curtain, nailed to the ceiling and making a door across the only bedroom. He shoved the curtain aside and looked in, but there was no closet in the room, only a mere depression in the wall with a single tottering shelf. He ducked back out through the curtain and looked around helplessly. There was literally no place in the house to hide, so he headed back out into the kitchen, listening to the pounding and to Bobby's voice calling for help.

"Out here!" Beth hollered, knocking once on the back door, and suddenly it was evident to him that the pounding wasn't coming from inside the house at all, but from under the floor, from some kind of cellar or crawl space. He ran out again, into the wind, and Beth was just then rounding the corner of the kitchen. He jumped down from the wooden step and followed around to the side of the house where a wooden cellar door, fixed shut with a stick, jumped in its frame as something thudded into it. Beth yanked the stick out and wrenched the door back, flooding the dark room beneath with sunlight and a rush of yellow grape leaves.

Bobby stood in the light, shading his eyes from the sudden glare. Abruptly he started crying, and Beth limped down into the cellar and scooped him up, hugging him tightly for a moment before leading him back out into the daylight. The three of them went back into the cabin and out of the wind, leaving the back door open.

"Who locked you in there?" Beth asked, kneeling in front of Bobby. Peter could see that she was furious, and was trying to keep the fear and anger out of her voice, but without much success.

"It was just a kid," Bobby said with sudden indifference, "messing around, you know. It's no big deal."

"*I'll* show him about messing around," Beth said. "Who was he? Have you seen him before?"

Bobby shrugged. "I didn't ask his name. He was dressed funny, like he came from someplace. I think he was the kid who threw the deer head at school yesterday. I heard he was dressed funny then, too.''

"What do you mean?'' Peter asked. ''Why do you say he was dressed funny?'' But even then he knew what the answer would be—who the kid was—although he didn't know at all what it signified.

"He had on this shirt,'' Bobby said. ''You know, it looked like he was in some kind of old movie. And suspenders, too, and these really ortho-looking black shoes.''

"Let me guess,'' Peter said calmly. ''He started crying really loud, and his mother came for him?''

"Yeah, how did you know? She was really mad, or scared or something.''

"So you know this kid?'' Beth asked Peter.

Peter nodded. ''So do you, in a way. You remember the woman we saw when we were standing on the porch? When the wind really got going?''

"You said she was 'the one,' '' Beth said, nodding. ''*That* one?''

"This was her son, I think.''

"And you think they're the two you told me about? Up in Falls Canyon?''

He nodded. ''I *know* they are.''

"Who *are* they?'' Bobby asked. ''They're really geeks or something.''

"You got it,'' Peter said. ''They're a couple of weirdos. Stay away from them. I don't think they'd hurt you, but stay away from them anyway, like you'd stay away from a snake if you didn't know what kind it was.''

"*He* would,'' Bobby said. ''He'd hurt someone. He killed a cat. It's down there, in a box.'' He pointed out the door.

"Oh, no!'' Beth said, putting her hand on Peter's arm.

Peter stepped outside again, striding around the side of the house and down into the semi-darkness of the cellar. He saw the cardboard carton immediately, and bent over to pull the flaps back, dragging the box into the sunlight through the door. There inside, just as Bobby had said, lay a dead cat. It was a moment before he recognized it—Mr. Ackroyd's cat, Sheba. If her eyes were shut she would have looked asleep, but her eyes were wide open, staring at the low wooden ceiling.

Next to the cat, piled up on the floor of the box, was stuff that had been stolen out of his car and yard—a couple of insulators, the spud gun, David's flute. . . . What the hell did it mean? Things were weird enough without this. This kind of thing made it vile, too. And he'd bet that the two of them, the woman and the boy, were even then up on the ridge, making their way down toward Falls Canyon, repeating the horrible scene that they'd played out at least twice before over the last couple of days. What they'd left here were more pieces to the puzzle, but the picture they seemed to want to form had the incongruous and unpredictably changing shape of a nightmare.

He carried the box up the stairs and back into the kitchen, setting it down on the old linoleum. Beth looked in and then quickly looked away.

"The kid killed it," Bobby said. "I know he did. Just like the deer head."

"I don't think the kid did this, champ. Someone's shot her. Probably the kid found her and put her in the box."

"Actually," Beth said to Bobby, "I'm pretty sure it was a lion that killed the deer. You could tell that from the bones. Something killed it to eat it. The kid just found what was left, that's all. He probably found Sheba, too. Maybe he even wanted to help her. How do we know?"

"How could he help her?" Bobby said. "She's dead." He pointed at the box. "That flute there . . ."

"Yeah," Peter said. "He stole it out of my truck along with the spud gun. I *guess* it was him that stole it."

"Well, it was playing music."

"What do you mean?" Beth asked, her voice tight. "The kid was playing it?"

He shook his head slowly. "No. It was *ghost* music, playing all by itself. And there was this green thing, like a floating glass thing. I think it was a pitcher of green Kool-Aid, only not real. The kid called it 'bug juice.' "

Beth hugged him around the shoulders. "You probably heard the wind," she said. "The wind whistles like a flute when it blows hard."

"Wait a minute," Peter said, crouching in front of Bobby and looking him in the eyes. "You thought it was what?"

"A real song. The flute was playing a real song."

"Not the song, the other thing. What did you say it was?"

Bobby shrugged, stepping away from him as if he thought Peter had turned into a lunatic. "I don't know." He crossed his arms and chewed on his top lip, then looked down and shoved the box with the toe of his shoe.

"He said it was lime Kool-Aid," Beth said. "What's the deal? You look . . . You know how you look—like your usual self lately." She shook her head a little, as if she wanted him to ease off.

"I guess nothing," he said, standing up. "Tell you later." Maybe he was wrong anyway. Maybe it was coincidence, synchronicity, whatever. He breathed deeply and tried to smile. Bobby was in bad enough shape already. There was no use going haywire on him. "So what was the song, champ? 'Blowin' in the Wind'?" He forced himself to laugh.

"Probably not," Beth said. "It couldn't have been anything half that silly. Probably it was that nitwit seventies song, 'Dust in the Wind.' "

"No, it wasn't," Bobby said. "And it wasn't funny, either. It was that song from *The Wizard of Oz*, when they get to the Emerald City and everyone's dancing. . . . "

And suddenly Peter walked out through the open door and sat down on the wooden stoop. The wind blew through his hair. Leaves skipped and danced their way across the dead grass, which was bent nearly flat. For a moment he seemed to hear the buzzing of flies again, and for some reason he was desperately thirsty.

Whatever notions he might have had that morning about talking again with Detective Slater evaporated utterly. He heard Beth's voice, speaking softly to Bobby inside, still cheering him up. " 'Merry Old Land of Oz,' " she said, and right then he realized that what he wanted to do more than anything else in the world was to gather them both up, climb into the Suburban, and drive away—to anywhere, it didn't matter. Somewhere out of the wind, out of the canyon, maybe to the ocean or the desert, where there were vast, open sunlit places. He made himself stand up and go back inside.

"Could you close its eyes?" Beth asked, gesturing at the box. "We ought to take it back to Mr. Ackroyd, and I think it would be easier if it weren't staring like that."

"Sure," Peter said. He bent over the box and touched the cat's eyes, one eye with either hand, and right then, unmistakably, the cat blinked. Startled, Peter stood up.

"What?" Beth asked.

"It *blinked*. I swear it blinked." He knelt by the box, sliding his hand under Sheba's chest. She was warm. Where the hell did you find a cat's pulse? There it was, her heart beating faintly. He could just feel it.

"She's alive," he said, picking up the box and heading for the door. "In some kind of shock."

Bobby bolted past him, around the side of the house toward the road. "Hurry!" he shouted, and Peter ran after him, cradling the box and holding it as steadily as he could. He should have taken the rest of the stuff out of it, but he didn't want to stop to do it now.

Bobby crossed the creek ahead of him, leaping from rock to rock, but Peter slogged straight through the water and up the steep driveway to the road, jogging downhill toward Ackroyd's place. Beth was out of sight behind him, and he stopped suddenly and turned, mentally telling her to hurry. He still wouldn't leave her in the woods alone. But just then she appeared out of the trees along the creek, and seeing him there, she waved him on. He turned and jogged down the road in wet shoes, past his own place and rounding the last bend that would lead past Ackroyd's house. He could see it now through the trees. The old man stood on the porch, listening to Bobby, then looked down the road at Peter before turning around and going inside. In a moment he was out again waving the keys to his car and heading around the side of the house.

"I'm going with him," Bobby said, running back to be with Peter. "We're taking Sheba to the vet and save her life. Come with us."

"I guess not," Peter said. "You can do the job." He set the box down and hauled out the rest of the debris, piling it by the roadside.

When Mr. Ackroyd opened the car door, Peter slid the box onto the backseat and Bobby climbed in beside it. "She's been shot," he said to the old man. "With what, I don't know. Maybe a pellet gun. We thought she was dead at first, or we'd have brought her quicker. No telling how long she's been in the box—at *least* an hour, probably longer."

"The dirty bastard," Ackroyd said quietly, shaking his head. "If I knew who did this . . ."

"Do you know a vet?"

"Dr. Stone out in El Toro. Open for emergencies on weekends. He saved her once before when she got mixed up with a coyote; maybe he can again."

"Hurry. Let's go," Bobby said from the backseat of the car. "Let's pick up my mom."

Mr. Ackroyd got in and started the car, backing out onto the road, gunning the engine and sliding to a stop next to where Beth was just then coming over the hill. After saying something through the window, she climbed into the front seat, and the car jumped forward, braking again in front of Peter.

"I'll take your car home!" he shouted through the window.

"Keys are in it!" she said, and Mr. Ackroyd gunned the engine and drove off, the car disappearing around the bend.

KLEIN WAS SHAKING SO BADLY WHEN HE WENT INTO THE GARAGE that he had to sit down on a pile of lumber to compose himself. He looked at his watch: two minutes to go. He stood up and pulled the framing hammer off the wall. Push had come to shove. If Pomeroy was utterly out of control then he'd still be there, screwing around in the house, not about to let Klein scare him off and get one up on him. Klein hefted the hammer, feeling the weight and the balance of it. One halfhearted blow would crack a man's skull like an eggshell. He set the hammer onto the bench top, checking his watch again, surprised that only thirty seconds had ticked past. If Pomeroy had *any* kind of brains he'd be gone.

There was a noise, and he glanced up. Lorna stood outside the open garage door, looking in at him.

"Where'd you take off to?" she asked.

"I didn't 'take off,' " Klein said. "I went down to the hardware store in El Toro. I'm replacing the latches on Beth's windows for her." He picked up the hammer and walked out onto the driveway.

"That man that tried to break in last night—the one you chased off. That was him, wasn't it?"

"Who?" Klein asked. "What are you talking about?"

"The same one that called me today. I think this is worse than you're saying it is."

Klein looked at his watch. In a couple more seconds he'd be late for killing Pomeroy. He shook his head. "Nobody knows who the prowler was. Probably just some vagrant or something."

She stared at him, clearly unconvinced.

"I've got one more thing to do next door," he said, nodding in the direction of Beth's house. "I'll just be a second." If he didn't keep his word to Pomeroy now, he might as well kiss it off. It was time for the showdown.

"I thought maybe we should really talk about this," Lorna said. "Without all the anger and saying stuff we don't mean."

"I won't be more than a minute," Klein said, hoping he was right. "You go on inside, and I'll be right there. Beth's house is wide open. I'm just going to close things up."

She looked at him and then looked at the hammer. It didn't take any kind of genius to know what she was thinking—that he was up to God knows what kind of thing, and that whatever it was, it was more important to him than she was.

"Look," he said, "this is all really simple. It won't take three minutes to clear it up. I was way off base with what I said inside, and—"

"It was what you were thinking," she said, interrupting him. "So you couldn't have been that far off base, could you? And I got defensive about it, didn't I? Both of us have been doing that, like we're on different sides in some kind of war or something. But really we're on the *same* side. And we've got to slow down and realize that before something happens to us."

She was nearly pleading with him. And she was dead right. But he had to take care of Pomeroy first. Pomeroy was like a fire about to go out of control. You put the fire out first, then you could sit down and talk about it. He turned away, giving her the high sign with his fingers and thumb. "We'll talk," he said, winking at her. "But give me just a minute first." She stood silently, watching him jog off toward the gate into Beth's backyard. He felt like the creep of the world.

He searched through the house, walking from room to room, looking into closets and corners, constantly aware of the hammer levered loosely between his thumb and the palm of his hand. The house was utterly silent except for the creaking of floorboards and the sound of the wind swishing through the eucalyptus trees along the driveway. Outside each closet door he gripped the hammer handle and raised the hammer head high, half expecting Pomeroy to be standing inside in the darkness, waiting for him.

The door to Beth's bedroom was nearly shut. With the toe of his shoe, he pushed it open hard so that it rotated all the way around and into the door stop. The bed was remade and empty of lingerie, and the room appeared to be deserted. The closet door was standing halfway open, probably the way Beth had left it.

Relief surged through him. Pomeroy had backed down! The bastard was scared, and he damned well *should* be. Maybe this would satisfy him—the simple knowledge that he'd pushed Klein too far. If Larry Collier had tried paying Pomeroy off, then he'd made a mistake; he'd lost the game. Once you showed them the inside of your wallet, they had you. The stakes got higher and higher. It was better to show them a closed fist, right from the get-go. Klein reached for the top dresser drawer, but then stopped himself. Pomeroy wouldn't have left any clues. He was criminally psychotic, but he wasn't stupid. And there was no reason for Klein's prints to be all over the drawer pulls.

He took a last, quick walk-through, then let himself out and headed home. He would have his talk with Lorna, and this time he'd hold on to his temper. Somehow they'd hash through things, just like they always did, and then he'd come back over and at least get the dead bolts out of the way before the sun went down. In the garage, he set the hammer on the bench and immediately went into the house, phrasing in his mind what it was he would tell her.

Stopping at the sink to get a glass of water, he hollered Lorna's name. There was no answer. The house was silent. Abruptly worried, he walked down the hall and into the empty bedroom, then back out into the living room, where he could see through the french doors into the deserted backyard. A big tumbleweed had blown down out of the hills against the fence, and the deck was a mess of broken twigs and leaves. A lawn chair had blown over, and the wind had nearly scooted it into the pool. The backyard was empty.

For a moment he stood there looking at it, thoughts of Lorna dwindling away as he searched the moving shadows on the hillsides, anticipating the approach of the woman in the black dress. Clearly Pomeroy had seen her that afternoon. She was no figment. . . .

He shook his head, driving the thought of her out of his mind. "Lorna!" he shouted again. But he knew it was futile. There was nothing but silence in the house and the swish and scrape of the wind outside, the sound of dry leaves blowing across concrete. She'd left. She hadn't waited for him. He felt betrayed. What did she want from him? What could he have told her, that he was going next door to beat Pomeroy to death with a hammer? That Pomeroy had been inside Beth's house, going through her things, but that there was damn-all he could do about it because he was up to his earlobes in fraud and all the rest?

Slowly he walked out through the front door to verify what he already knew. Her Jaguar was gone. She'd run off without even leaving a damned note.

PETER DROVE BETH'S BUS BACK INTO TRABUCO OAKS, THEN hiked home along the ridge trail. In a couple of hours he would walk on back up to Ackroyd's place and find out how things went at the vet's in El Toro. The wind drifted out of the east, skimming through the dry leaves and grass with now and then a gust driving down off the ridges, blowing hard for a minute or two before falling slack again. He listened for human voices on the wind, but the late-afternoon shadows were deep and empty, and the woods were quiet.

It was nearly dark when he got home, and, looking at the dimly lit parlor, he thought of Mr. Ackroyd's warning about "unearthing things better left buried." The idea was full of suggestion.

It took him two hours to sweep the parlor and clear away the tools and debris. He cleaned the rubble out of the old fireplace and then started a new fire with eucalyptus logs and the antique newspapers that had been stuffed into the wooden crates as packing material decades ago. He unrolled the carpet, swept it clean, and retrieved the tarnished candelabras, filling them with candles from the kitchen drawer. It was important that the candelabras be full—a matter of effect. He didn't want the hiss of propane light or the white glow of burning gas mantles. He wanted to hear the wind, the variety of its tone and expression, and he wanted a flickering yellow light, dim and full of shadow—the light that had illuminated the room years past, when the room was newly built. That's how he pictured the room in his mind. And as he worked, arranging and rearranging, reassembling the parlor bit by bit, that picture grew more clearly detailed until it became as whole and vivid as a memory.

He set the two chairs before the hearth with a small table between them and filled the bookcases with old books from the crates. The books were water-warped and terminally dusty, but empty bookcases wouldn't have worked; they would have stood out like holes torn in a stage curtain. Slowly he was filled with an artist's instinct for where each piece of furniture had to stand and each print had to hang—what the entire room must look like. As he worked he found the subtle depressions of table and chair legs in the old carpet, like marks on the boards of a stage, and once he saw them they seemed to become even more pronounced, like slowly developing images on photographic paper. The room was a theater that had waited long years for the reenactment of a drama in which he was an understudy—an understudy with a lifetime of anticipation.

He fed the fire, watching the smoke whirl away up the chimney, listening to the crackle of the wood as the flames rose. Handfuls of dry leaves altered the yellow color of the flame, tinting it an autumn red at the edges. The air had turned chilly, and despite wearing a sweater he couldn't seem to get warm. Finally he was drawn to the chair before the fire. He sat down wearily, looking around the room. The decayed furniture was shabby, the glass in the bookcase doors cracked, the wood stained and warped. But the old bookcases hid the crumbled plaster, and the flickering candles and fire threw a veneer of shadow and light over the room that muted the ravages of time and weather.

The chair opposite him was empty. Somehow it was a lonesome sight, a symbol of all the things he'd had and lost. He pictured her in his mind, sitting with a book in the firelit room, the wind moving through the trees outside. He recalled the shape of her cheekbones, the color of her hair, how much like Amanda she had looked in the melancholy photograph on Ackroyd's wall. Somewhere, back in the recesses of his mind, he heard the scratchy, weirdly toned music of an old Victrola, and he tried to identify the melody. It was familiar to him, but at the same time alien, and it mingled confusedly with a dozen other random sounds—the clinking of glasses, footfalls on the carpeted floor, the rustle of papers, the wind, the mewling of a cat. . . .

Until this evening he had never really *lived* in the house. He had been an outsider, an interloper, an audience. That had been his mistake. Amanda and David had become players in a strange masque to which he thought he had been denied a role. But he knew now that he had merely to submit to it to gain access. He understood why grieving parents maintained a dead child's bedroom just as it had been when the child died—the clock stopped, the door closed, the dusty pages of the calendar stirred only by the passage of ghosts. The precise arrangement of things was as full of suggested magic as were the things themselves.

He watched the space in front of the empty chair, seeming now to see a shadow there, and he forced himself not to think, but to allow himself to see. Perhaps the pieces of the puzzle had been available to him all along; he had only to quit looking so hard. . . .


"It's late for that, isn't it?"

The question seemed to irritate her, though there was no reason it should. A wife's place, after all, was with her family. Running out after dark, leaving her husband and son alone, that was something so independent as to be almost immoral. What about your wedding vows, he wanted to ask her.

"I promised Aunt Lydia that I'd read her a chapter. Remember? I told you a couple of days ago. She's expecting me."

"Well, she'll have to find a way to bear your absence just this once."

"That's a little ungenerous, don't you think?"

"Tell me, why is it that the woman continually calls on other people to be *generous*? We need a clearer definition of the word." He sat there seething. Over the past eight years she must have read through half the English novelists to the old woman. It was an act of philanthropy—that was the implication—and he was a humbug if he denied it to either of them. Well, he'd see who was the humbug. If she was determined to leave, he'd at least make it sting a little.

He watched her face as she stared at the fire, his mind falling under the same shadow that had darkened it for weeks now—the knowledge that things had changed between them, that *she* had changed. He had remained constant, but he was losing her. And after what he had sacrificed—his practice, his time, his very life.

That was the irony of it; he had mortgaged his life for her, hadn't he? And now he would lose her. She was still young, only twenty-five, and yet in most ways hadn't managed to grow up, but had retained the flighty, silly mannerisms and enthusiasms of her girl-hood, a lily of the field.

And that was something that had attracted him—how long ago? Nearly seven years now. He would freely admit that his building the house in the canyon, inconveniently far from town, had been designed to remove her from the things in the world that would inevitably change her. But that which had been cheerfully frivo-lous in the girl he had married had transmuted into a baser metal over the years, losing its luster. The look in her face just now had been insolence, pure and simple. What else could he call it when she made her every trivial dissatisfaction apparent to him with a look or a toss of her head or a heavy sigh?

"There's a gale blowing. It'll get worse." He opened his book, as if the issue were settled. He knew it wasn't, and didn't bother to focus on the words.

"I'm not afraid of the wind or the darkness, and it's not really very late, is it?"

For a moment he stared at the book in silence. It was clear that she had made up her mind. "Why on earth can't that woman have books read to her during the day?" he said, and already he knew he was defeated.

"She sleeps during the day. She's an insomniac, remember?"

"My memory isn't the issue here. Surely the woman has fits of wakefulness during daylight hours."

"You might at least have the courtesy not to refer to her as 'the woman.' "

"And you might do me the courtesy not to be insolent. I'm your husband, and you should treat me as such."

There it was again—the change in her features that made it clear what she was thinking, her indifference to him, to his needs and his rights.

"It's barely seven-thirty," she said. "I'll be there and back before ten." She busied herself unnecessarily now, slipping her book back into the case, straightening the pillow on her chair, making it clear that she was preparing to leave.

"I suppose I'll start up the sedan."

"I don't *want* you to start up the sedan." For a moment she looked irritated, out of patience, but then her features softened and she said, "Really, I'd rather walk. I love the canyon at night.

This isn't the first time I've been out after dark, is it? It's very nearly routine.''

He said nothing. That was the point, wasn't it? Short of tying her up, what could he do? Aunt Lydia! Of course the old lady *was* her aunt, but what did that signify? Simply that Esther was at her beck and call, apparently twenty-four hours a day. "What about Lewis?" he asked. "Is the boy an illiterate? He can't read to his own mother? Did the war deprive him of his faculties?"

She closed her eyes, as if she were counting to ten. "I know nothing about the extent of his literacy. I suppose that in your eyes it was an act of betrayal that he didn't die at Flanders. Perhaps you're wrong in that. But as for Aunt Lydia, she read to my brother and me when we were children and now I read to her. You should come along, too. We're reading *Middlemarch*."

He waved his hand at her and shook his head. "I don't need a soporific. *I'm* not the insomniac."

She moved toward the door, the conversation having ended. He wondered what she would say, what she would do if he simply refused to let her go. He had that right, as her husband. But he watched in silence as she left, his eyes on the back of her head, trying to make her feel the full weight of his stare. Moments later he heard the door to Jamie's bedroom close. The boy was already asleep, thank God. The back door slammed shut, and he was struck with the knowledge that he smelled the scent of jasmine on the still air of the house. She'd put on perfume before going out.

"Amanda!" Peter said, standing up out of his chair. He reached for the glass on the table, but there was nothing there. Momentarily confused, he looked down, expecting to see the faceted crystal glass, the decanter beside it. The empty table was scarred and discolored, part of its veneer peeled away.

The sound of the door slamming echoed in his head, which throbbed with pain at his temples, as if he were hung over. Impossibly, he could taste the whiskey on his tongue, and he felt disoriented, not quite clear how long he'd been sitting there or why he was angry. But even as he thought about it, the anger dwindled away, leaving him chilled and empty. The moon was up now, the fire was burned down to a few glowing coals, and the candles were within an inch of burning out.

He rejected the idea of going out into the kitchen to check the door. Why had he thought it was Amanda going out? It was so obviously just the wind. And just as this thought concluded, the fire sprang up in the fireplace again. The embers flared, licking at the bottom of the flue. He watched the leaf shadows dance on the wall, and his hand strayed across the tabletop and settled on the top of his restored glass. For a flickering moment he knew that the glass was wrong, and that the lingering scent of jasmine on the air simply couldn't exist. But he picked up the glass and tasted the whiskey. The headache diminished as he thought about Lewis, home at last from the war, long awaited. Esther putting on perfume, going out on this wind-haunted night . . .

HE DIDN'T LIKE LEWIS. IT DIDN'T MATTER THAT HE WAS ESTHER'S cousin; the man was a parasite. The war-hero talk was nonsense. The man had avoided death—hardly something that could be construed as heroic. The least such a hero could do with his idle time was read to his invalid mother, but instead he wrote poetry, or rather a bad imitation of poetry, a grown man looking out at the world through big moony eyes with too much white showing under the irises as if he were drowsy with opium. He had a slight tubercular build and was no good at conversation. And he meddled, giving Jamie the damned cat. The damned thing had scratched the furniture to pieces. There was only one thing more intelligent than simply shooting it, and that would be shooting Lewis instead.

Esther had prevailed upon him to let the boy keep it, but he could see now that it had been a mistake. He wanted no part of Lewis in the house. He was a slow poison, the single ruinous thing in their lives, and there was no doubt at all that he was the chief engineer of the change in Esther. He stared into his glass now, the heavy crystal making the half inch of whiskey seem far deeper than it was. The night blustered beyond the windows, and the floor was stippled with moonlight.

There were things that a man could overlook, things he could outright deny in order to have peace, to maintain the sanctity of his home. But when a man's wife threw these things into his face, then he had to admit that his home had come undone. That was the dark truth. There came a point when he could deny it no longer, and either he acted decisively or else he admitted defeat and crawled off beaten.

He sat scowling at the fire, full of self-loathing now as well as the rest. Damn the cat, and damn Aunt Lydia, too. The question had become as plain as a red flag: was she going to Aunt Lydia's to read *Middlemarch*, or was she going to pay a visit to Lewis? That was what it had come down to. And now that it had, the question must be answered, the truth revealed.

There had been an incident years ago that had planted the germ of the idea in his mind. He could trace his dwindling unhappiness to that day—the two of them, Esther and Lewis, embracing as if . . . He couldn't put words to it, although these several years later the scene was etched in his mind in the clearest sort of detail. Esther had laughed it off, waving her hand at him. Of all the silly notions—she and Lewis were *cousins*. They had grown up together. He was going off to war. A kiss was a natural thing between cousins. Never mind that it had occurred in an otherwise empty room and that the look of shocked surprise on her face had been as expressive as the novels she read to her aunt.

And her laughter. What had once appealed to him chilled him now, roiling up dark billows of regret and loathing within him. He forced himself now to picture the face of his son—the dark eyes, the narrow build. People remarked on his resemblance to Lewis. Aunt Lydia herself had cackled over it more than once, no doubt with a good deal of nasty calculation: "Why, look at the two of you," she'd say, seeing them together. "Who wouldn't think you were father and son?"

And for Esther he had given up the world! She might as well have slapped him in the face when she left a half hour ago. That's what the slammed door meant; that much couldn't be argued. He swirled the faceted glass in front of the candlelight, the smoky amber whiskey catching the light. Then he tossed it off and poured another, his hand shaking as he set the decanter down.

He abandoned his thoughts abruptly and tried to read again, but he couldn't. The words meant nothing. He could concentrate on nothing but the picture of the two of them together, Esther and Lewis, childhood companions, their names falling inexorably together. He stood up unsteadily and put the book down next to the glass, staggering just a little as he picked up the candelabra and stepped to the door.

Right then he caught sight of his face in the mirror over the mantel, and for a moment he scarcely knew himself. He drew back in confusion, his mind a jumble of contradiction, his features so twisted by evil passion that his own face was alien and loathsome. The glass in the mirror was cracked and hazed with dust and reflected only a vague outline of the candlelit room behind him.

Then a door slammed, or a shutter, and the noise revived him like cold water. He swept the glass and decanter onto the floor, his confusion gone, his mind suddenly clear and purposeful. He walked through the front room, pushing open the door to Jamie's bedroom, holding the candelabra over his face and trying to read something in his features that would deny what was becoming more apparent by the month—that their marriage was a travesty, that he was a cuckold, and that the boy sleeping before him was a bastard.

There was a movement at the foot of the bed—the cat, Lewis's cat, shifting on the mattress. It stood up and stretched, clawing at the bedclothes, catching at the loops of thread and yanking them to pieces. Without thinking, he swung the candelabra at it, but the cat scampered toward the top of the bed, and the candelabra cracked into the edge of the doorframe, half the candles pitching out onto the floor, still alight. One landed on the bed cover, burning a hole in it, and he pinched the flame out with his fingers, cursing, and stomped out the flaming candles on the floor, turning in a rage to find the boy awake, staring at him, holding the cat to his chest. The wind shrieked under the eaves outside, and dark leaves flew in the moonlight beyond the window.

The eyes, the damned eyes. You couldn't get around them. He turned away, his chest heaving, then leaned down and clutched the cat by the fur at the back of its neck, yanking it out of the boy's hands. The boy cried out, scrabbling across the top of the bed. "No!" he yelled. "Daddy, no! Don't hurt it!"

"Get dressed," he said, his voice husky. He held the cat at arm's length, letting it kick. Hurt it? He'd kill it and return it to its owner. Right now. Sometimes what a person needed to change a bad habit was a shock to the system.

The boy dressed hurriedly, trying to smile, as if it would make a difference. Just like his mother—the smile that would turn the world right. Well, not this time. "Come along," he said, his voice cold, and he pinched out the couple of remaining candles so that the house fell into darkness.

LORNA HAD COME HOME LATER THAT EVENING, IN NO MOOD TO talk. He knew better than to ask where she'd been, but he could see that she was stone-cold sober, so she hadn't been off drinking with a girlfriend. Her smile was forced, and the couple of pleasant things she had said to Klein set his teeth on edge. She'd pretty much gone straight to bed. He wrote the whole day off as a bad investment and decided to wait until morning to confront her. Now that he'd gotten the upper hand with Pomeroy things had steadied out a little; tomorrow would be a little brighter for all of them.

Meanwhile he would bunk down on the couch. He poured out a glass of scotch and iced it up, lying down in his bathrobe and watching the wind blow across the top of the pool, herding the leaves into the shallow end and making a kaleidoscope picture out of the moon's reflection. If anything, the wind was blowing harder than it had all week.

From where he lay he could see through the wrought-iron fence, out to where the dry grass waved on the moonlit hillside, the wind flattening it out in sheets and runnels. He sipped his scotch and waited, not sleepy, but full of sharp anticipation. It occurred to him that it was a perfect night for Lorna to be sore at him—him on the couch and her holed up in her bedroom—but then he thrust the idea aside, getting up to refill his glass.

He stood at the window, watching the shadows, listening to the night. He could almost hear her voice, the woman's voice, on the wind. "Come on," he said softly, picturing her in his mind, the two of them together in the dimly lit room of his dreams, the smell of jasmine and tallow and pine . . .

And then he saw her.

He closed his eyes for a moment, and when he opened them again she was gone. He searched the shadows with his eyes, his breath stopped. He set his glass down quietly on the coffee table and opened one of the doors, the wind blowing into his face. She had been descending along the ridge trail, and perhaps had slipped out of sight beyond the poolhouse, even then crossing through the orchard toward the gate. He flipped on the outdoor lamp, and in that moment she appeared beyond the fence, stopping in the darkness of the poolhouse shadow, just at the edge of the circle of light. He flipped the light off and went out through the door.

For a second he couldn't see her, but he knew she was there as he hurried to the fence, grasping the cold wrought iron. She stepped out of the shadow then, the moon shining on her face and hands. "Esther," he said, her name materializing in his mind. She smiled at him, and he reached up to unlatch the gate.

THE NIGHT WAS A TORRENT OF NOISE AND MOVEMENT. THE CACO-phony of wind and of blowing leaves and creaking limbs shattered the cold deliberation that had settled on his mind minutes ago, reducing it to a broken glass jumble of rage and jealousy and suspicion. He turned his face away from the wind and strode out into a circle of moonlight that played across the top of the low stone retaining wall behind the house. The cat, as if panicked by the wind, snarled and kicked, and he tried in vain to grapple the writhing thing around the neck with both hands, forgetting utterly about Jamie until, with a wild cry, the boy grabbed his arms and hoisted himself off the ground, trying to force his hands apart and save the cat.

He flung the boy aside, staggering sideways with the force of it, and in that moment the cat twisted loose, dropping to the ground on all four feet and disappearing in an instant into the windblown darkness beyond the rock wall. Cursing out loud, he lunged after it, climbing onto the wall, pushing into the tangle of vines that crept out of the edge of the forest. Picking up a broken limb with both hands, he flailed at the bushes, beating them to pieces in his rage to punish the cat. He felt Jamie's hands on his arm again, dragging at him, and heard him sobbing, pleading with him to stop. The crying filled him with an inexpressible anger, and he swung the limb sideways as the boy jerked away, ducking beneath it. He saw the cat reappear in the moonlight along the top of the wall, nearly at the end of the house, then dart away into the darkness of the open cellar. In his rage he slammed the limb against the stones, snapping it off short. He flung the leftover piece into the darkness.

Jamie cowered against the wall of the house now, shrinking away, afraid to look at his face. The boy broke and ran along the wall, dodging out of the way, calling for the cat. Dr. Landry let him go. Neither the boy nor the cat was of any interest to him any longer. He was wasting his time here. He had to hurry if he wanted to catch them together. In his mind he pictured Lewis, and then Lewis and Esther together, embracing in a dimly lit room. His breath whistled in and out of his lungs, and the wind stung his eyes as he staggered back into the house, searching for the door key, yanking out cupboard drawers and spilling their contents onto the kitchen floor.

He found a can of lamp oil, and for one wild moment he considered setting the house on fire, pouring the oil over the wooden floor and setting it aflame. That would put an end to it forever— the ruins of their marriage, the irony of his building her this house in its idyllic setting, a place where they would make each other happy forever. He laughed out loud, the laughter nearly doubling him over.

Then he saw the key, hanging on a nail inside a cupboard door. He plucked his watch out of his pocket—just past nine o'clock. She'd still be there. He forgot about the lamp oil and methodically checked to see that the windows were not only shut but locked. The thought of bringing his rifle occurred to him, but instantly he knew he wouldn't need it. That wasn't the way it would happen. . . . .

An image sprang into his mind: a door blowing open, swirling leaves, the man rising before him on the white sheets, his face welling blood. He looked about him at the dark furniture, at the dancing shadows on the windows. The wind howled, rattling the front door, moaning through the eaves. Lurching forward, he threw the bolt to lock the front door, then turned to go out the back again, into the night, locking that door, too, and pocketing the key. The boy was gone, the little bastard, for good and all. The house was ridded of his presence, of Lewis's presence. That was the beginning of putting things right.

Lewis's face appeared before him again like a ghostly projection against the trees, drawing him along the trail, into the darkness of the woods.

POMEROY SWUNG THE CAR INTO THE LOOP FOR THE THIRD TIME—out Portola to Alicia Parkway, hooking up onto the San Diego Freeway south, then off at El Toro and all the way up to Cook's Corner, where he turned up into Live Oak Canyon, drifting past the mouth of Trabuco Oaks and up the hill again. Sometimes he did his best thinking when he drove. He wanted to be doing something, but he didn't know what, besides drive, waiting for instructions. Something would suggest itself if he was open to it—the stars, the wind, the pattern of headlights coming toward him on the highway.

Something in the wind was lonesome and empty tonight, and the quiet interior of the car was a barrier against it—that loneliness, and although it wasn't something you wanted to think about, aimless movement was better than no movement at all. Tomorrow morning Klein would get the letter and cassette in the mail, but Pomeroy had no patience with tomorrow. Today had been too curious, too full of suggestion for him to let it end early. The night still held promise.

Klein had reacted hard to the mention of the woman in the black dress, clearly lying about her being related to the damned maid. Hell, the maid was a Mexican, and this woman was as white as snow, literally. There was something here to take advantage of, but he didn't know what.

On impulse he pulled into the parking lot of a Ralph's grocery store. An idea had come to him—something so evident that he was astonished it had only now occurred to him. He got out of the car, holding his hair flat with both hands as he jogged to the double doors, which swung aside to let him in. In the produce section stood a wooden cart covered with potted plants and surrounded by bouquets of flowers.

He didn't want anything cheap, like one of the bundles of daisies and fern leaves. The roses were sorry-looking, which was too bad, since roses had romantic connotations. Finally he settled on a mixed bouquet, mostly purple and yellow with a lot of iris and marigolds, already arranged in an attractive glass vase.

The checker smiled at him, obviously aware that the flowers were for someone special. He smiled back after counting the change, then plucked a violet-dyed carnation out of the bouquet and handed it to her. "A pretty lady like you is one of God's little flowers," he said, winking broadly, and strode out smiling and self-satisfied. She'd remember him for that—the gallant stranger who thought enough of another stranger to show her an act of kindness. What he had said sounded like poetry to him. It had just come to him—an inspiration. Maybe later this evening he would tell Beth about it, playing it down a little bit so he didn't sound conceited. Or maybe it would be better just to say it to *her*, as if he'd just then made it up. That was a side of him she didn't know about, a sensitivity that would be attractive to her, she being a woman and all.

Twenty minutes later he passed O'Neill Park, which was dark and deserted. The post office slanted past on the left, and he could see the sign for the steak house ahead and the little cracker-box general store beyond that. He slowed down, making up his mind finally and forever.

It would be stupidly dangerous going back up to Beth's tonight and just hanging around, waiting. She might expect that, be listening for it. If she caught him outright it might mean the end of their relationship. She wouldn't give him a chance to explain. And if she brought the police in, the whole deal with Klein would be in jeopardy.

The flowers, though, would be his ticket. That had been the idea that had struck him on the highway, right before stopping at Ralph's. What he had to do, obviously, was knock on her door, not as a stranger but as a friend bearing a thoughtful gift. There was no law against that. He would explain that he happened to be in the area, and that he was still interested in hearing about the place owned by her boyfriend. That was good—his using the word *boyfriend*. He wasn't any kind of threat that way. The flowers weren't meant as some sort of romantic ploy; they were a gift from one seeker after beauty to another. If he could merely talk to her, she would see what it was he felt, what he was willing to sacrifice for her.

He pulled off to the side of the road a block below her house and cut the engine. Very neatly, in his best hand, he wrote "From an admirer" on the little square card that thrust up out of the bouquet on a plastic prong. Immediately he regretted it, thinking that probably there was something better, something that implied more of the deep feelings he had for her. But it was too late, and he climbed out of the car, walking up the road and carrying the vase full of flowers, trying to shield them from the wind. Her son would be already in bed. The two of them could have all the privacy they needed. Still, he looked behind him down the street, relieved that as usual it was empty.

He realized he was nervous, that it had been years since he'd come calling on a woman like this—making love to her, in the old-fashioned sense of the word. Perhaps a little bit of nervousness on his part would appeal to her—a woman liked a man who was shy, a little unsure of himself. But his hands were shaking, and that wouldn't do. It looked too much like fear. And he had to have something in his mind to say—something quick and good. What? The thing about the flowers? What he had said to the checker at Ralph's? He tried to get the sentence right in his mind, to be able to say it in a way that sounded spontaneous.

He decided that it would be good to check things out first, have a look around, see what lights were on, what she was doing. . . .

In a moment of uncertainty he loped across the lawn and into the shadows along the driveway. His heart pounded, and he broke out into a cold sweat, like a teenager asking a girl out for the first time. Part of his mind warned him that he was risking it all again, that he had to control himself, that there was a right and natural way to do this. But he took a couple of steps down the driveway anyway, then, despite the danger, he stepped out onto the moonlit gravel to see whether the light was on again in her bedroom. It wasn't. The house looked dark, as if she weren't home. But her car was there in the drive; she *had* to be home.

He hurried down toward the backyard, keeping to the shadows, until he could see past the corner of the house. Moonlight bathed the backyard, and in order to stay in the shadows he was forced along the wall of the garage toward the back fence and the shelter of the big avocado tree. Somehow his certainty that she would appreciate a late-night caller had abandoned him. How late was it, anyway? He looked at his watch—nearly ten.

Then he saw that there was a light on, after all—in the kitchen. She was up and about still, probably doing domestic chores. He angled up along Klein's fence, thinking that maybe he could see her through the kitchen window, just get a glimpse of her. . . . He knew right then that there was no way he could deliver the flowers himself. That was presuming too much this late at night. He would leave them for her—a bit of romantic mystery.

There she was, moving in front of the window, working at the sink. The window was elevated above the narrow side yard, and the angle made for a bad view. She evidently hadn't changed into her night clothes yet. If only he could get up onto the fence . . . It was possible, but he'd be too damned visible in the moonlight. She'd see him, and that would be it. What *was* she wearing? He didn't recognize her blouse, but it clearly was too masculine for her. And the colors were all wrong. He shook his head. That was something he could share with her—his knowledge of colors vis-à-vis one's astrological sign and basic physicality.

She moved away, out of the window, and he stood for several minutes holding the flowers and staring at the kitchen cabinetry above the stove, waiting for her to return and worried that by waiting he would miss something going on in some other part of the house. She might even have gone into her bedroom. . . He hurried out of the side yard, pressing himself along the wall of the house, ducking under the curtained service porch windows and running quickly through the ring of porchlight. He stopped, in the shadows again, his mind flying at the sight of the back door. He set the vase down and got down onto his hands and knees, crawling across the grass to the porch, up the concrete steps. With a trembling hand he reached up and tried the knob.

The door was locked. He pushed on it a little to see if it would give, careful to make no noise, but it was firm now, no play at all. A wave of relief swept through him, the knowledge that the lock had prevented something from happening that shouldn't happen, something that was dangerous, that wasn't at all what he wanted to happen. He started to picture it in his mind while he crawled backward into the shadows again: Beth coming out of the bedroom carrying her night things, heading, probably, for the bathroom, surprised to see him, but pleased. . . .

Then all at once he realized that he hadn't covered his hands when he tried the door. Fingerprints! Hell! Crouching in the shadow of a pair of bushes, he fought to control his sudden panic. The worst damned mistake! Jesus, he had to watch it! Another slip like that . . .

He decided to take the chance of wiping the knob clean, but just then the light came on in Beth's bedroom, and he stood up carefully, pressing his lips together, suddenly light-headed. He *must* see her tonight. He'd spent all this *time*, taken risks! He picked up the vase and tiptoed across to the back porch again, setting it down at the corner of the landing. It was fairly well sheltered from the wind. She'd find them in the morning, and if she was as bright as he knew she was, she'd put two and two together. Maybe it would be the perfect icebreaker after all.

He would chance one look through the window. Nothing risky. With blinds like that there was almost always a place to see through; he knew that from experience. This time he'd be careful. No more surprises. He started out, moving in a crouch, the wind blowing his hair back. The bedroom light blinked out. Damn it! He bit his lip in frustration. Momentarily another light blinked on—the bathroom? Could he reach the bathroom window? It would mean revealing himself in the driveway, but he was willing to risk that. He looked around for something to stand on, then remembered the couple of broken-down redwood chairs beneath the avocado, and set out across the yard after one.

At that moment a light came on in Klein's yard, and then just as quickly went off.

He scrambled into the shadows behind a low-hanging limb. Damn Klein! If the bastard was out snooping around again and screwed this up . . . The flowers! Christ, he'd find the damned flowers and wreck everything!

He listened, watching the fence hard. There was enough moonlight so that he'd easily see someone moving beyond it. Was there movement? The sound of voices? He was suddenly certain that whatever Klein was up to had nothing to do with him, that this had to do with what he'd seen that afternoon—the hippie woman in the black dress. He eased out of his hiding place, scuttling along the fence to the side yard again, where he could get a better view of Klein's. Carefully, very carefully, he stood up, peering over the top of the redwood slats.

Klein stood near the pool, his hands grasping the wrought-iron

fence, looking out onto the windblown hillsides. Beyond him the
hills were alive with moving shadows. He stepped toward the
gate, unlatching it and swinging it open just as the woman in
the black dress appeared, obviously having made her way down
along the trail from the ridge. She hesitated momentarily—perhaps the two of them were speaking—and then she followed him
down the concrete path toward the darkened poolhouse. Together
they went in, closing the door behind them.

Pomeroy licked his lips, thinking for a moment. Then he turned
around and ran, moving as quietly as he could, straight past the
bedroom and bathroom windows, both of which were dark now.
There was a light on in the kitchen again, but it didn't attract
him. Another brilliant idea had come to him, and he needed a
telephone, right now.

HE STRODE UP TOWARD THE RIDGE ALONG THE WEED-EDGED
track of sand and rock, sweating despite the wind that swept down
off the ridges and filled the night with a rush of sound that had
an almost physical presence, like the shifting of rocks deep in the
earth. The forest canopy danced against the moonlit sky, and the
trail was littered with the brittle, broken-off limbs of alders and
sycamores.

Soon he climbed above the trees. The chaparral on the hillside
was a jittering sea of dry vegetation glowing silver in the moonlight. He saw the canyon stretching away behind and below him,
swatches of it dark with trees, the road a dusty ivory. His breath
wheezed in and out of his lungs, and his shoes bit into his feet.
The trail slanted downhill, and he broke into a run, slipping on
the loose dirt and scree, falling backward and catching himself
on the palms of his hands, barely feeling the rocks rasping against
his flesh. He scrambled to his feet and went on, running again,
dark within himself, his mind open to the night and the wind like
a derelict, roofless house.

• • •

The village of Trabuco Oaks lay below the ridge, a half dozen lamplit houses clustered near the general store. A narrow dirt lane wound between them, turning into the carriage drive that led to the gates of the Parker ranch. The ranch house itself was dark, and the sight of it unlit filled him with suspicion. Was the old lady even home, or was she away in Los Angeles on one of her outings? The bunkhouse sat at the edge of the orchard, a short distance behind the house. It was a rough structure of unpainted pine boards, with long eaves overhanging a porch. A light shone through the side window—the flickering glow of candles.

His bones felt dry and brittle, like sticks, and dry leaves swirled around his feet as he hunched forward, half running and half sliding down the slope. It was as he had feared. All of it true. By Christ, it would all come to an end now! He looked at his hands. The moonlight made his flesh look ghostly white, and for one vague moment he wondered why his hands were empty. He ought to be holding something. Whatever it was he could almost feel it there, pressing into his palms. He looked around, possessed with the dreamlike feeling that he had been there before, stumbling down this rocky slope toward some awful destiny. In his mind he could see the shadow of that destiny—a man's profile against a candle-lit wall, a scream in the darkness. . . .

The moon and wind seemed to make the nighttime flicker, and he saw things in a fluttery half-light. Leaves jerked past and the landscape wavered in a staccato dance. He found himself at the edge of the garden, his feet half-sunk in the newly tilled soil. He heard a horse whinny and fought against dizziness as he crept past an irrigation standpipe half-full of moonlit water. He leaned against the rough wooden wall of the bunkhouse. There was the sound of a woman's voice within, low, almost a whisper, yet audible above the wind. He strained to hear what she said, but heard a man's laughter instead.

Stealthily, he crept to the window and peered into the bunkhouse through a narrow gap in the curtain. There were three beds, two of them empty. The floor was strewn with clothes.

Esther lay on the center bed, partly covered with a sheet, her hair pulled back in a red ribbon. Lewis kneeled on the wooden floor, leaning over her, his hand under the sheet, his lips on her neck. She shifted on the bed, moving one of her legs so that her foot touched the floor. Her hand played across the back of his head. He heard their sighs and their breathing, the two of them moving in the lamplight as the wind blew in a perfect frenzy now, hammering against the sides of the bunkhouse, slamming at the bolted door. She bent at the waist, pulling herself toward him, her hand snaking around his shoulders.

He flung himself away from the wall of the bunkhouse, striding toward the ridge, screaming at the wind that blew into his face. A shovel stood tilted against a leafless fruit tree, its blade caked with dirt. He closed his hand around the wooden handle, feeling the familiar, weather-raised grain against his palm. Hefting it with both hands, he turned slowly toward the bunkhouse again, hearing their voices in his mind, stepping up and across the wooden porch, his feet echoing on the floorboards, and raised the shovel over his head, driving it against the wooden door with all his strength as the wind shrieked behind him, filling him with rage and desperation.

THE PHONE WOKE LORNA FROM A DEAD SLEEP. SHE SAT UP IN BED, still only half-awake, thinking it was the alarm clock and that Lance had set it for some reason. It was on his side, so she reached across to shake him and found the bed empty. It rang a second time and she remembered: he was asleep on the couch. The telephone was ringing. She fumbled it out of the cradle and said hello.

"Hello, Lorna?" a voice said. She recognized it—him again. Instantly she was awake.

"Do you know where Lance is?" the man asked. His voice was almost sad, as if he were performing a tragic duty. For a moment she wondered if he really wanted to know. Perhaps it was business; it wasn't all that late. She stayed silent anyway, growing more tense as the moments passed. Slowly she became fearful for her husband. She'd known that afternoon that there was something dangerous going on. Lance had been tense. . . .

"What do you want?" she asked.

"I want you to know that he's entertaining female guests in the poolhouse."

There was a dial tone then. No laughter, no threats, just this matter-of-fact statement expressed in a voice full of earnest concern.

She got out of bed and parted the blinds, looking out the window. The poolhouse was dark. Of course the man was a filthy liar. She pulled on her robe and slippers and went out through the door, suddenly regretting that she'd rebuffed Lance so hard that evening. It was only lately that they'd started taking their arguments to bed with them, and she'd told herself this afternoon that it was going to stop, along with the rest, the drinking.

The couch in the living room was empty and the french doors stood open to the wind. There were newspapers scattered on the floor from where they'd blown off a chair, and the curtains were blowing away from the wall, billowing up like bedsheet ghosts. The backyard was empty in the moonlight, and the pool was full of leaves.

The gate was open. So that was it. He'd gone out into the hills again. Or had he? Had the man on the phone been right? There was a movement just then, a stirring of the curtains in the poolhouse window. She sat down on the couch, where she had a clear view of both the gate and the door to the poolhouse, noticing for the first time the glass of scotch on the coffee table. The three or four ice cubes in it were only half-melted. He must have poured it ten or fifteen minutes ago.

How could the man on the telephone have *known*? She stood up, carried the glass to the sink, and dumped it down the drain. Then she rinsed it out and put it away in the cupboard. Going out to the poolhouse would be idiotic. What if *he* was there, waiting? The same man who'd been prowling around Beth's house last night. She peered past the edge of the drape, looking at the poolhouse again. There was a movement, out toward the hills. Her breath caught, and she stepped back out of the window. A man had appeared out of nowhere, out of the old orchard, carrying what looked like a shovel.

# 30

THE INTERIOR OF THE POOLHOUSE WAS DIM, VAGUELY ILLUMI-
nated by moonlight through the partly open curtains. The wind
hummed in the caves and things whirled past beyond the windows, their shadows flickering briefly across the walls and floor.
The scent of candle tallow and jasmine and dusty pine came to
him, and Klein let himself imagine that the soft light playing
across the floor was cast by the pair of candles burning in his
dreams. He glanced at the woman, nearly invisible in the soft
darkness. He could see her moving, hear the rustle of her dress,
her shoulders showing pale white in the light of the moon.

It was the dream again. He toyed with that idea—that he was
dreaming, asleep in the house. It wouldn't be the first time that
he was conscious of dreaming but still lost in the dream itself,
and he forced himself deeper into it, picturing the candles, the
bed against the plank wall, the scent of her perfume. He didn't
want to lose it, this dream that was a sheltered place, dark and
secretive, the rest of the world nothing but an abandoned illusion,
reduced to the sound of the wind.

The candle flames flickered. He knelt on the floor at the edge
of the bed, tracing the curve of her elbow through the woolen
blanket. "Esther," he said out loud, noticing for the first time
that she had a red ribbon in her hair. She turned to him, her hand
on the back of his neck, pulling him to her, and he knew that he
had come finally to a place he was destined to be, that they had
found one another again at last.

But just as this thought came to him, the walls shook with a
gust of wind, and he looked up uneasily, listening to the door
rattle, hearing something in his head like the drone of flies. "The
wind," he whispered. She sat up languorously, wrapping an arm
around his shoulders, sealing his lips with her fingers, her black
hair a shadow, a scrap of nighttime darkness, her pale skin a
clever reflection of moonlight. He had the feeling that he was

falling, not quickly, but drifting like a leaf, free at last from something he could neither see nor define.

The door rattled again, as if there was a hand on the latch. He sat forward, listening. The room shook with wind. The night outside was alive with a crashing and rustling. Something chunked solidly into the door, scraping down the length of it, and suddenly all his night fears sprang in upon him—the horror that inevitably shattered his dreams, hidden from him until the end. The woman sat up, clawing at his shoulder now, trying to hide herself with the covers as if she, too, knew what it was that had found them there. The door panel bowed inward with the force of the wind, quivering and thrumming.

With a shriek it tore itself open, slamming inward. The air was suddenly full of leaves and dust, the wind blowing full into his face with such force that he turned his head away, cowering backward against the wall. He opened his mouth to scream, and dry particles of windblown debris choked him, filling his throat. There was the heavy banging sound of a table turning over, and in the moonlight he could see the curtains flailing against the windows.

A shadow moved through the swirling, wind-driven debris, a dark wraith that was partly human, partly animate rage. Klein turned his head away, not wanting to see it, knowing that in his dream he turned his head away, and that he saw it anyway, and he knew each time that the shadow would take the form of a man, of Esther's husband. As if the room had tilted sideways, he felt himself sliding, and he grabbed frantically at the bedstead with his right hand, realizing at the same moment that there was no bedstead, and clutching a sofa cushion instead. He threw his left hand and forearm across his face as the shadow moved past the edge of the door, the moonlight glinting on the steel blade of the shovel. Klein slid onto the floor, curling into a ball and covering himself, looking wildly around for a means of escape but driven against the wall by the tearing wind.

The man raised the shovel over his head—dark hair and eyes, his clothing torn and dirty, his mouth open in a scream that was either silent or was lost in the wind. Klein saw the blade slash downward, heard the woman's screams. The room reeled around him. As if from the vantage point of a dream, he saw the dying man on the bed—not himself, but a man young and frail seeming with wide, terrified eyes, his hands flailing in front of him, the woman scrabbling away across the sheets, and the blood-flecked pine boards behind them white with moonlight. Klein *knew* this man, as if they shared some common history, but like water fading into sand, the knowledge dissipated and was gone.

Something brushed past him in the dim light, a moving shadow that trailed across his flesh like cobweb. He heard a shuffling noise and saw, standing against the white panel of the poolhouse door, a man holding a shovel—not the murderer from his dream, but someone he vaguely recognized, blurred behind the veil of swirling leaves. Klein pushed himself backward, clutching the sofa cushion in front of him as the man staggered out into the night. A moment later he heard the clatter of the shovel hitting the pool deck, and then, almost at once, an explosion that sounded like gunfire.

Slowly the door swung shut, the wind fell off, and the leaves and dust settled in the room. He sat in the darkness waiting, pressed into the corner and listening to the slow scraping of feet on the concrete outside.

THE DOOR STRAINED INWARD WHEN HE PUSHED ON IT, THE WIND howling around him, pounding against the wood siding of the bunkhouse, straining the old iron door latch. He stepped back, raising the shovel over his head, his mind a chaos of broken images like the moon's reflection shivered by a stone. Throwing himself forward, he drove the shovel into the door. The wood deflected the blade and it slashed down across the door panel, the sound grating in his ears like a shriek. In his mind rose the picture of a man's visage, eyes broad with terror, blood welling out of an open gash. He struck the door again, along the edge now, and felt the latch snap, the door slam inward, the wind sweeping him into the room in a wild rage.

The candles guttered and went out. Moonlight glittered on a rustling vortex of leaves that tore through the room, the silver light shining on Lewis's face, betraying the craven terror in his eyes. Esther was a dark shadow above a dim white blanket.

His mind veered away from her, flickering with staccato images like the stuttering frames in an antique movie: the quick, narrow vision of a face rushing toward him down a tunnel; the moving hands of two card players at a moonlit table; a dead cat in the bottom of a box; a wooden flute lying on the cracked tiles of a fireplace hearth; a narrow, rock-walled, night-dark canyon alive with the rush of water and wind; two broken shadows in a pool of moonlit water. . . .

He reeled forward, gripped by the sudden throat-seizing fear of falling, overwhelmed with the anguished knowledge of who lay dead or dying in that black pool. He reached out to grip the corners of the table before him, saw playing cards spinning past far below in a dark void. "Peter . . ." He heard her whisper, knew her voice. . . .

And a shadow moved away from him like a torn-off shred of darkness. He staggered back, released suddenly by the wind, and through the litter of leaves and dust he saw the dark figure of a man—separate from him now—raise the shovel into the air. He heard the woman scream and the groan of effort from the man's throat as the shovel hatcheted downward. . . .

He turned and plunged out through the open door, into the night, nearly stumbling into the leaf-choked swimming pool. He looked around with the wild, empty fear of a suddenly awakened sleepwalker, hearing the sound of a woman's scream tear through the wild night air. An empty chaise longue, propelled by the wind, skidded toward him across the concrete deck, spinning around and dropping into the pool, and he could hear the clicking and husking of dry sycamore leaves as they blew against the wrought-iron palings, gripping the black metal like paper hands.

Abruptly he knew where he was—the dark, rocky hills rising behind him, cut with the black ribbon of the ridge trail. He saw movement in the lighted window next door—Beth, her kitchen window. He was suddenly conscious of the weight of the shovel in his hands. The poolhouse door slammed shut behind him and then blew open again, and he saw the long scar in the white paint. He threw the shovel down and sprinted toward the fence, leaping up and grabbing the redwood boards and propelling himself upward, feeling the fence shudder as he boosted himself over with his elbows, a splinter of wood scraping his cheek.

Something exploded behind him like the crack of a firecracker,

and he threw his hands over his head even as his feet jarred with
the impact of hitting the ground. Gunfire! They were *shooting* at
him! He crouched down and sprinted across the leaf-strewn lawn
toward the back porch, praying that the door would be unlocked.

WHEN SHE SAW THE MAN WITH THE SHOVEL, LORNA DUCKED
back out of sight behind the drape, throwing her hand to her
mouth. He was half-obscured by windblown leaves and dust, but
he clearly wasn't the man who'd been over to see Lance that
morning. A jealous husband? In a sudden panic she turned toward
the bedroom. The wind howled outside with a power that nearly
took her breath away, and a hailstorm of leaves and twigs pelted
the doors and screens. There was a fearful pounding just then,
like someone breaking down a wall, and she looked out just as
the poolhouse door slammed inward, the man with the shovel
silhouetted against the darkened interior. She saw him raise the
shovel with both hands and heard simultaneously a woman's
scream and the hoarse shouting of a man's voice.

She ran back into the bedroom, snatching the phone off the
hook and punching the 911 button on the keyboard. She found
the gun in Klein's nightstand when the operator answered. "This
is Lorna Klein at 242 Parker in Trabuco Oaks," she said. "Top
of the road. It's an emergency." Lance made a point of keeping
the gun loaded. "My husband is being assaulted by an armed
prowler. Send the sheriff as quick as you can. I'm leaving the
phone off the hook."

Without waiting for an answer, she tossed the receiver onto the
bed and ran out into the hallway and through the living room,
pushing open the screen door with her shoulder. The wind blew
her hair around into her face, and she brushed it away as she
charged straight across toward the poolhouse door. It had been
broken in, and it turned now on the wind, swinging slowly outward, hanging from its bottom hinge. The night was full of noise

and movement, tree limbs lashing and spray blowing out of the storm-tossed pool. Lawn chairs scraped across the concrete, animated by the wind, and one overturned in front of her, sliding in a rush into the water.

Then she saw him in the moonlight—climbing over the redwood fence, into Beth's yard. She saw the castaway shovel, knew she was too late. She threw the gun up wildly and pulled the trigger, turning her head aside and closing her eyes, but even so she could see the muzzle blast through her eyelids, and she flinched at the explosion of the gun going off in front of her face. She looked up just in time to see the man disappear from the top of the fence, dropping out of sight beyond it like a stone. She screamed then, hearing the wail of police sirens above the wind. The sheriff's substation wasn't a mile away. They'd be here any moment.

She looked at the pistol in disbelief, only now really *thinking* about having pulled the trigger. It was heavy and cold, blue-black in the moonlight like a thing of evil. She nearly threw it into the pool. But that was stupid. Hide it? What the hell good would that do if a dead man lay on the other side of the fence? Who would they think shot him if not her?

She thought about Lance and made herself move, pushing a fallen chair out of the way and walking toward the poolhouse, not letting herself picture what she'd find there. For a moment she stopped breathing, swallowing down the stuff that rose in her throat, staring out at the moving hillside through the fence. Someone was running up toward the ridge—a woman in a long black dress like a shadow. She thought she heard a scream trail down toward her as she ran toward the broken-in door of the poolhouse.

It had been a hell of a long day. Bobby had fallen asleep in Mr. Ackroyd's car on the way home from the vet's and had dropped into bed at about eight, totally zonked, as he put it. The keys to the new dead bolts sat on the dining room table, and next to them a shoe box with the words, "Beth, Personal and Confidential" written on it in the careful kind of lettering that draftsmen learn. She'd left the box lying there while she put Bobby to bed, and it was just as well. Inside lay a gun—a little .22 rimfire pistol, big enough to cause a rat considerable grief if you shot it between the eyes. It looked like a toy—tinny and without a trigger guard, like Bobby's sparkler pistol or Peter's potato gun. She'd put the top back on the box and left it on the kitchen counter. Tomorrow morning she'd give it back to Klein.

She washed the morning's few dishes at the kitchen sink, watching the wind blow the night to pieces outside the window. The Kleins' yard, backing up to the hills, was a dervish of leaves, and she watched as a tumbleweed blew across the hillside in the moonlight and slammed into the wrought-iron fence, scattering debris across the pool deck and into the water.

She looked at the shoe box and then looked away. She and Peter had hardly had a chance to talk today. This wind . . . Maybe when the wind stopped they'd get clear of all this. The thought had come into her mind a dozen times today—if only the wind would die down—as if the wind itself was some sort of dark spirit coming down off the deserted ridges to manifest itself in their lives.

She put the last dish away and dried off the counter, then wiped the chrome faucets clean of water spots before sliding the towel through the refrigerator door handle. She looked at a picture that Bobby had drawn at day care a couple of weeks ago and hung on the refrigerator door with magnets—a surfer wiping out on a wave that looked something like an iceberg. His head was cut off at the neck and was flying through the air, the eyes wide open in surprised wonder. The caption underneath read, "Eating It Big." Walter, her ex-husband, used to surf, back in his salad days, and before their breakup he had always talked about it with Bobby, but hadn't ever found time to take him to the beach. She wondered if the headless surfer was Walter and what a shrink would say about it. Immediately she decided it *was* Walter, just for the fun of it, and that she didn't care what the shrink would say. She straightened the picture, trying to neaten the impossible mess of taped and magnet-stuck papers.

Bobby's Halloween drawings were still hanging on the side next to the stove, along with a crayon rendering of a Fourth of July rocket, a comical dog, and a construction-paper envelope containing the valentines Bobby had gotten last spring in school. There were outdated dental-appointment reminders and telephone

numbers and awards for good grades and Little League achieve-
ments and who knew what-all else. The entire refrigerator was
buried beneath layers of paper like some kind of weird collage.
There was a sort of Velveteen Rabbit effect to it, though, the
refrigerator coming to life because of all this attention it got from
Bobby and her. She couldn't any longer envision it clean and
white, like her sister's refrigerator, which always seemed dead to
her and metallic, like an alien monolith out of a science-fiction
movie.

How long would it be before Bobby grew up a little and the
refrigerator went back to being nothing more than a machine?
Suddenly she was struck with the desire to have another child, if
only for the sake of keeping the refrigerator happy and alive. She
nearly laughed, except that she realized that it wasn't funny; it
was true. She thought about Peter again and about how everyone
needed a second chance—a chance to do things right.

When she reached for the light she noticed the shoe box sitting
there like a reminder of all the world's horrors, another machine
with an agenda of its own. What had Klein said last night? Not
to worry, prowlers don't usually come back anyway. . . . And here
he was switching out all the door and window hardware and leaving a gun, for God's sake, on the dining room table.

She pictured the man at the back door, the gauze-wrapped face,
the hand on the knob, and then thought about the creep Adams
that morning out at Ackroyd's, his hand torn up where Sheba had
scratched him. Suddenly it dawned on her, cold as gunmetal—
Adams had gone back out there and shot the cat. Of course he
had.

Abruptly she took the lid off the shoe box and picked up the
box of cartridges inside, sliding it open and looking at the flat
little brass disks. She eased one out with her fingernails—a little-
bitty thing about the size of a Good 'n Plenty. You don't threaten
a man with a loaded gun unless you're willing to use it. That's
what her father had taught her. And you surely didn't threaten a
man with a gun that wasn't loaded.

Her father had taken her target shooting a lot when she was a
kid. She liked that, putting holes in pieces of paper, and was pretty
good at it. He had made her help clean and oil the guns when
they got home from the range. So the pistol wasn't strange to her.
She knew she could empty the gun into the creep in a half second
if he threatened Bobby. That was what was dangerous—feeling
that way. She wasn't any kind of pacifist. But she wasn't any

kind of cowboy, either. And she was damned if she was willing to admit that she needed to be. If Southern California had gotten that bad, even out here in a quiet village like the Oaks, then she was taking Bobby and getting the hell out.

She thought about Amanda and David's disappearance then, about Klein's argument with Adams that morning, and Dr. Stone taking the pellet out of Sheba's spleen. . . .

Just a prowler, scared away now. No threat of his coming back. Klein confident enough to lend her a gun . . .

She put the cartridges back into the shoe box and carried it into the bedroom with her, setting it on the nightstand. Then she slid her dresser drawer open, glanced inside, and on impulse turned away, picking up the phone. She listened for a dial tone, then laid the receiver down on the nightstand. If the bastard called tonight he could damned well talk to the busy signal.

She realized that she was staring into the open drawer now, trying to puzzle something out. Tired as she was, it took her a moment to see it.

Her nightshirt, somehow, wasn't on top where it should be, where she had dumped it this morning. It was an oversized T-shirt with a picture of Sleepy the dwarf on it, a Christmas present from Bobby. Then she saw it, folded beneath her lingerie, down toward the bottom of the drawer.

The lingerie was folded, too, neatly, arranged in little rows. Lying among her things was a stem of wildflower, a sprig of blue aster, as fresh as if it had been picked that afternoon.

She pulled her fingers away from the side of the drawer.

Somebody had gone through her things. Today.

She spun around, looking suddenly at the door, half expecting to see the man standing there, already inside the house. There was no one. Only the sound of the wind in the eucalyptus trees, the eternal swishing and scraping out in the darkness.

Klein? She remembered her conversation with Peter, his suspicions about Klein. He'd certainly have had the opportunity to go through her things. She almost hoped it *was* Klein, but something told her it wasn't. This was too crazy—folding things up and all. The flower. Whoever did it wanted her to know he'd been there.

She pulled the sprig of aster out, tossing it into the trash can, then shut the drawer and tipped the lid from the shoe box, opening the cartridge box before picking up the pistol. Her hands shaking, she disengaged the little rod beneath the barrel and snapped out the cylinder, then loaded four bullets into it, leaving the hammer over an empty chamber for the sake of a safety. She wouldn't change her clothes at all. She'd sleep on the couch, dressed. She thought of calling the police, but rejected the idea. Maybe in the morning. If Peter had a damned telephone she'd call him, and she wondered suddenly if the Kleins were still up, and whether it wouldn't be a good idea to let Klein know about this.

She heard something then, from outside—what sounded like a woman's scream. Tense, she waited to hear it again, disbelieving her own ears, and almost at once there was the sound of gunfire— a single shot from somewhere out back. She ran out of the bedroom and into the kitchen again, carrying the pistol with her trigger finger along the barrel, hoping that Bobby wouldn't wake up, and flipping out the kitchen lights as she headed onto the service porch.

The moonlit backyard jumped into clarity through the window in the door, and her heart flew into her throat at the sight of a man hunched and running straight across the lawn toward the steps. Forcing herself silent, she stepped back against the clothes dryer, bracing herself, and raised the pistol, clicking the hammer back.

CAUTIOUSLY, WITHOUT LOOKING VERY FAR IN, LORNA FLIPPED ON the light inside the poolhouse door. What met her eyes looked like the aftermath of some kind of battle involving trees. Leaves and trash from the hillsides littered the floor and furniture, clinging to the curtains hung over the windows on the back wall. The Ping-Pong table was flipped onto its side and her ceramic elephant lamp lay smashed into pieces on the floor. Over all of it lay a carpet of twigs and dry mulch and autumn leaves.

She looked past the edge of the door toward the end of the room where there was a sofa, two chairs and a Franklin stove. Her husband sat on the floor beside the sofa, leaning against the wall. He was wild-eyed and scared, as if he expected God-knew-what to be coming in through the door, and he hugged one of the sofa cushions in front of him, his naked legs thrust out from underneath it. There were leaf fragments and twigs in his hair and stuck to his chin so that he looked like someone escaped from a madhouse. He swallowed several times as if he wanted to speak but couldn't, and then looked around with the mystified air of a sleepwalker just waking up in the wrong place.

He noticed the gun in her hand at the same time the police siren cut off short out front.

He stood up, clutching the cushion to his abdomen and looking around. "A gun. What . . . ? What did you *do*?" He shook his head back and forth, then spotted his bathrobe, lying against the opposite wall and entangled with his pajama bottoms, both of them covered with dead leaves and dirt.

"What did *I* do?" she asked, and tossed the gun onto the couch. "I don't know what I did."

As she turned toward the door he set the cushion on top of the gun and hurried toward the bathrobe. "Wait!" he said. "I can explain."

She nearly laughed out loud. His voice was husky, as if he was about to start crying, and there was a begging tone to it that right at that moment enraged her more than what she now *knew* had been going on in there just minutes ago. The woman, clearly, had gone out the window and through the orchard. Lorna forced herself to walk to the fence and look over into Beth's yard. There was no dead man. He was gone.

Two policemen came around the corner of the house just then, their revolvers drawn. One of them was big, like he'd played football ten or fifteen years ago. The other was a small Hispanic man, handsome and neat and with brushed-back hair that was apparently impervious to the wind. His uniform looked tailored.

The sight of the two of them looking around the backyard made her suddenly aware of where she was—of how things had declined over the last couple of days, and she put her hand to her mouth inadvertently, suddenly weary with shame. Lance came out of the poolhouse, tying his bathrobe, trying to brush the leaves off it. His hair still looked like he'd combed it with a branch off a dead tree and he had a horrible fixed grin on his face, worse than any car salesman.

"Freeze," one of the cops said. "Hold it right there." Lorna looked at him in surprise. "Put your hands where we can see them."

She held her hands out in front of her, looking quickly at Lance to make sure he wasn't too baffled to cooperate.

"Could you please identify yourselves?"

"I'm the one who called you," Lorna said. "This is my husband. . . ."

"Your names?"

"Lance Klein," Lance said. He looked at Lorna as if she'd committed the ultimate betrayal, as if the whole world were a sudden fearful mystery.

"I'm Lorna Klein."

"Do you have any ID?"

"In the house," she said.

"If you wouldn't mind my going in with you to get it, ma'am. . . ." the big one said.

He followed her in, and she collected both their driver's licenses, handing them to him. Then the two of them filed back out into the night, past the couch made up with blankets, the scotch decanter on the coffee table. Outside he held the photos under the lamp, stared hard at both of them, and handed them back to her.

"Why don't you tell us what the trouble is." He looked at Lorna instead of at Lance. The wind had diminished now, and the moon was high in the sky. Both of them glanced around the yard again, taking in the overturned furniture and the windblown mess. She saw then that the chaise longue was in the pool, its wheels hanging on the edge of the deck and its front end, cushion and all, submerged beneath a solid layer of floating sycamore leaves.

"I don't know," she said finally. "I honestly don't know."

They waited for a moment, as if that wasn't what they expected to hear, then the other one said to Klein, "How about you, do you know?"

He shook his head hard, then managed to say, "A little quarrel, that's all."

The big cop nodded his head. "Someone put in a call to 911 and reported an assault in progress. You said that was you, ma'am?"

Lorna nodded. She wasn't going to lie.

"Then why don't you start from there? Tell us why you called 911."

"Because I thought my husband was being assaulted. I woke up and heard a noise, and when I looked out the window I saw a man with a shovel."

"A *shovel*?" the cop said.

"This one?" His partner pointed to the old shovel lying near the redwood fence.

She nodded.

"What was he doing with the shovel?"

"He was . . . he was standing in front of the door there." She pointed at the poolhouse door, which tried to swing shut just then, dragging its bottom edge across the floor inside. There was a long gash in the wood, the white paint skived away where the shovel had bit into it.

"He was beating on the door with the shovel?"

"No. Well, yes. I didn't *see* him hit the door. I heard it. But by the time I looked out, the door was already open, broken like that."

"It was mostly the wind," Lance said, "breaking the door like that."

The big cop nodded at him, then asked Lorna, "What was he doing? You saw him assault your husband through the open door?" He sounded tired and there was an edge to his voice, as if he'd already figured out that he wasn't going to get any straight answers.

"No, I turned around and ran for the phone."

"So you didn't actually see anyone assault anyone?"

She shook her head.

"Were you assaulted, sir?"

"No, sir," Klein said quickly. "This was all a mistake. I was out here in the wind, you know, trying to get things straightened out. Wind was blowing the damned lawn furniture into the pool and all. Anyway I go into the poolhouse to switch on a couple lights, and when I turn around there's this guy outside the door, like Lorna said, holding the shovel."

"Just holding it?" the smaller cop asked. "Getting ready to dig a hole or something? Maybe he wanted work."

Klein shrugged. "Stealing it, I'd guess. People steal any damned thing around here anymore. I guess I surprised him at it."

"There was some activity out here last night, wasn't there?" the smaller cop asked. "Somebody put in a call right around this same time. This related in any way, or just coincidence?"

"Coincidence," Klein said quickly. "Could have been the
same guy, of course—the prowler. Maybe he saw something to
steal and came back after it."

"So what did you and the missus have a quarrel about?"

"What?" Klein asked.

"You said you had a quarrel. That's what all the uproar was
about."

"Oh, yeah. Well, that was before. Hell, I don't want to get into
personal stuff, but I guess I was pretty teed off when I came out
here. And anyway, when I saw that this guy was in the yard, I
started yelling. Anybody would have. I guess he thought I was
going to take a shot at him or something and he started waving
the damned shovel around. Then he dropped it and took off."

"What do you mean 'take a shot'?" the big cop asked. "Did
you have a gun with you?"

"No! Christ, no!" Klein said. "Hell, I meant *hit* him, take a
punch."

Lorna almost told them about the gun. If someone heard the
shot and reported it, then it was worse to lie, then the whole story
would look like a lie. But she waited, and the cop went on, talking
in a voice that made it clear that the whole story already looked
like a lie.

"Uh-huh." He nodded, looking hard at Lance. "So what we've
got is that this stranger was stealing that shovel. Maybe it's some
kind of antique?" He grinned.

"Well, yeah," Klein said. "You could say that. It's *old* anyway. Maybe, like I said, he picked it up to break down the door.
Probably he wanted to steal something out of the poolhouse."

"I thought you were already inside the poolhouse," the smaller
cop said. "Wasn't the door already open?"

"I guess the wind blew it shut."

Both cops looked at him as if he'd lost his mind, neither one
bothering to ask him anything more. Then the big one said to
Lorna, "Do you have anything to add to that?"

"Only that he jumped over the fence," she said, nodding at
Beth's yard. "He threw down the shovel and jumped the fence."

The smaller cop walked over and looked down at the shovel,
then walked over to the fence, jumped up, and grabbed the top,
and easily pulled himself high enough to rest his elbows on the
top. He looked around Beth's backyard for a moment before kicking himself back and away again. He looked at his partner and
shook his head, as if to say that there was nothing to see.

The big cop looked at both of them for a moment, as if sizing them up. To Lorna he said, "Ma'am, maybe you could get things straight next time before calling 911. We respond to assault calls with what's called a code three. It doesn't make us happy when we have to draw our weapons for no good reason."

She breathed deeply, trying to keep her temper, telling herself even then that it wasn't the cop's fault. She had to keep a lid on it, get it over with. Get out of there and breathe a little, out of the wind. But damn it, she saw what she saw—a stranger in her own backyard. And the phone call. She couldn't mention that without really tearing things up, but she was damned if she was going to pretend that this was going to be about a lunatic stealing a rusty shovel and her being some kind of panicky nut.

"It didn't look like a man stealing anything to me," she said, stony voiced. "I honest-to-God thought he was going to attack my husband, and *that's* why I dialed 911. Whoever he was, he shouldn't have been in our backyard. That's trespassing at the very least, isn't it?"

"Yes, ma'am," the big cop said politely.

"Well . . ." She wasn't sure what to say. "I don't like that. I . . ." She found that she was crying all of a sudden. All of it hit her, just like that—the phone call, the gun, the woman running away up the hillside, Lance stark naked, hiding behind a sofa cushion on the poolroom floor, his hair all full of leaves. She turned away, closing her eyes, the wind blowing softly into her face. She felt a hand on her shoulder and jerked away. Lance could put his hand on someone else's shoulder from now on. This was it, the last humiliation.

She heard the police say something to Lance, but she couldn't make out what and didn't care. Then one of them said, "Why don't you two call it a night. Close up and go to bed. Call us if something more happens."

She stood there looking out at the blowing grass, listening to the wind as Lance showed them out through the house.

# 35

THE CLOTHES DRYER SLID BACKWARD AN INCH, JAMMING AGAINST the wall, and Beth nearly stumbled sideways, frantic, thinking *Shoot through the window*. And then, as he ran into the circle of porch light, he threw his head back, reached forward, launched himself up the few stairs, and hammered on the door.

It was Peter. Lunging forward, she threw the dead bolt and swung the door open, flipping on the inside light again. His face was bleeding, and he was breathing so hard that he was almost wheezing. Immediately he reached past her and turned the light back off, and right then she heard Bobby's voice from what must have been the living room. "Mom?" he said, sounding scared. The police siren was winding out now, coming up the hill.

"In here!" Beth shouted. Peter looked like . . . she couldn't say what he looked like. His face and clothes were dirty, his jeans filthy to the knees, like he'd waded through the creek a couple of times and then kicked dirt all over himself. The blood on his face was mostly dried, smeared across a ragged cut, dripped and smeared down the front of his shirt, which was torn open at the sleeve and with a blood smear there, too. His eyes were haunted, confused.

She twisted the dead bolt again, locking the door, and said, "Wait here," then opened the dryer door, set the gun inside, and shut it again. Heading back into the kitchen, she met Bobby coming around the corner, sleepy looking and mussed up. She put an arm around his shoulder and turned him back into the living room, looking back to see whether Peter was following. He stood in the shadows, waiting. The police siren stopped abruptly, and through the curtains on the front window she could see the revolving blue light.

"What was that noise?" Bobby asked.

"Nothing," she said. It sounded stupid to her.

"I heard someone banging. And a siren."

"There was something going on at the Kleins' house," she
said. "I don't know what, but that's where the police were going.
See, there's the light on top of the police car, through the curtains.
See it?"

"Uh-huh," he said. "Can I look out?"

"One look and then back to bed," she said to him, steering
him toward the window. The police were already out of the car,
moving up the Kleins' driveway. "Doesn't look like much is
going on," she said. "I think maybe it was some animal got into
his backyard—coyotes, probably."

"That's because of his fence," Bobby said.

"I bet that's it. He needs one like ours. Now, time for bed."

"But I heard someone, like, knocking on the back door or
something."

"That was just Peter."

"Peter? He's over?"

"Yeah. He stopped by for a little bit to find out about Sheba."

Bobby scooted away from her, straight into the kitchen, Beth
following, trying to think what to say, wondering whether to grab
him.

Peter was standing nonchalantly by the service porch sink, rubbing his hands with a dish towel out of the clothes hamper. The
light over his head was still off, but there was kitchen light shining in, and she could see that his face was clean and his hair was
wet and smoothed back. He didn't look happy, but the look of
crazy confusion was gone from his face.

"Hey, man," he said, holding his hand out, palm up.

"Hey," Bobby said, slapping his hand. Then he said, "Man,
your jeans are *dirty*!"

"I worked hard to get these jeans dirty like this. That's the
style now. You don't like them?" He edged toward the kitchen,
positioning himself so that he couldn't be seen through any of
the windows.

"Sure," Bobby said. "I don't like wearing jeans. What happened to your face?"

"Walked right into a tree limb. You ever do that?"

"I had three stitches once from broken glass."

"That's worse than a tree limb," Peter said. "This is just a
scratch."

"What are you looking at? The Kleins'?" Bobby boosted himself up on the washer and looked out through the side window.
"You see better with the light out, huh?"

Beth looked past him. The two policemen stood in the Kleins' backyard, one of them gesturing toward the fence. Klein and Lorna were both in bathrobes, and the door to their poolhouse was hanging crazily, the paint scarred off in a long slash. She almost looked at Peter, but didn't. He needed time to get around to telling her about it. She felt cold, though. Something had gone out of control tonight. She had half prepared herself to deal with a prowler, but this was something beyond her. She glanced at him, and he smiled and shrugged and shook his head slightly. She took the dish towel from him and dabbed the line of fresh blood on his cheek.

Bobby drummed his feet on the front of the washer and then hopped down. "Where did the coyotes go?" he asked Peter.

"What coyotes?"

"The ones that were in the Kleins' backyard," Beth said to him. "We think that maybe they got in through the bars of the fence. I was thinking that it was a good idea we didn't have bars. They can't get into our yard."

"That's right," Peter said. "There were a couple of them, I think. Probably they went back out through the fence. They aren't going to hurt anybody anyway, unless you're a cat."

"Yeah, but there *are* a couple holes in our fence," Bobby said. "One goes into the Kleins' yard. It's where that possum was going back and forth, remember?"

Bobby looked out through the window in the door now, into the backyard, apparently seeing nothing interesting. Then he looked down toward the porch and said, "What's all the flowers?"

"What?" Beth asked, looking out herself. There, at the corner of the porch, sat a vase of flowers. Out of curiosity she started to open the door, then realized what it was, turned to Bobby, and said, "Time for bed now," in a no-nonsense voice.

"Aw," he said. "Can't I stay up with you guys?"

"Nope," Beth said. "Hit the sack. Peter and I want to talk."

Bobby rolled his eyes. "Adults *talk*," he said, as if it were the stupidest, most pointless activity in the world.

Beth propelled him forward, through the kitchen and into the bedroom, thinking all the time about the flowers on the porch. There wasn't any doubt who left them. He'd been there again. She had come in through the back door when Mr. Ackroyd dropped them off late that afternoon, and the flowers hadn't been there.

"And *stay* there," she said, tucking Bobby in and settling the quilt over him.

"Read me a story," he said.

"No story. It's too late for a story."

"Then put in a tape. 'Baby Beluga.' "

"All right." She searched through the tapes in the tape box, found the right one, and slid it into the tape player, leaving the volume turned up a little higher than she usually would. There was no use Bobby listening to her and Peter talk, and he'd fall asleep anyway, no matter what the volume was like. His eyes were at half mast already, and he yawned wide, turning over onto his side and shutting his eyes as the music started up.

By the time she got back out onto the porch, Peter had brought in the flowers. He stood in the darkness, peering out the window. The police were still in the Kleins' backyard, and one of them walked over to the fence, boosted himself up, and looked over. He dropped, walking back toward his partner and dusting his hands off.

"Let's go into the kitchen," she said. "I'll put on some coffee."

"I'm going to stay out of the light for another minute," he said. "Till the cops leave."

He handed her the flowers. "You've got an admirer," he said, then abruptly shivered as if he'd suddenly gotten a chill.

"I know I do," she said, and kissed him on the scratched cheek. In a while she'd tell him about it.

"Don't tell me you're a vampire," he said softly.

"Only in the dark." She set the flowers down on top of the washer and put her arm around his shoulder, pulling him close to her. Together they watched the night through the window.

**36**

THE POOL LIGHT GLOWED THROUGH THE DEAD LEAVES THAT
covered the water. Klein had pulled the chaise longue free of the
pool, but he didn't bother trying to net out the leaves. There were
too many, and he was too tired. He swam slowly, pushing clots
of leaves away with each stroke, watching them swirl away into
the lamplit depths and not bothering to peel off the limp leaves
that clung to his face when he raised his head to breathe. A lawn
chair sat on the bottom of the deep end, squarely over the drain,
lamplight shining between the plastic strips on the backrest like
the sun through clouds.

He moved his arms mechanically, letting his feet trail behind
him, pushing off the wall and plowing into the leaves again. Lorna
was gone; he didn't know where, probably to her sister's. She
had put a few things in an overnight bag and then left without
saying anything to him except that tomorrow was Imelda's day
off, as if that piece of trivia had been worth opening her mouth
for.

He couldn't even pretend that he blamed her—her going away
like that, giving him the silent treatment, and he wondered how
much she knew, what she'd seen. He thought of her finding him
like that, hugging the goddamn sofa pillow, and he flushed with
shame.

He stopped swimming and leaned on the coping, looking out
into the hills. What had Lorna said about them acting like they
were on different sides in a war, when really they were on the
same side? Sometimes she could say things just right, but he
couldn't see the rightness of it until later, after he'd blown off a
lot of steam and managed to hurt her. He had never thought about
whether there was such a thing as *too* late, and he wondered
abruptly if he was scared a little by the idea of Lorna sober. Up
till now it had always been easy to win.

Why the hell hadn't he told her about things this afternoon

when she'd pleaded with him to get it out in the open? Hell, because this—this thing in the poolhouse—wasn't what she meant, that's why. He couldn't tell her about something that he himself didn't understand, something he couldn't foresee. He wondered if she had seen the woman leave, known what he was doing out there? He wasn't sure himself if the woman had left at all, or had simply evaporated into the shadows.

His thoughts and fears trailed away into nothing, into fatigue, and he pushed off the wall and set out tiredly again. How long had he been swimming? An hour? Two hours? The moon was halfway across the sky. He felt loose and enervated now, and out of nowhere came the memory of something he'd read once, about someone who dived to the bottom of a pool, curled his fingers into the drain cover, and then drowned, unable or unwilling to pull loose.

When he lifted his head to breathe, he could feel that the wind was starting to blow again. Little wavelets pushed the leaves into the shallow end, and the water slapped his face, getting into his mouth. He submerged his head, treading water over the sunken chair, then let himself sink, exhaling slowly, settling into the chair and gripping the aluminum arms to hold himself in. The leaves curling down into the water looked black from underneath, and the wind churned the surface so that clusters of leaves and twigs were stirred under, drifting in slowly moving currents.

His lungs ached, and he closed his throat and watched the leaves swirl. They caught the pool light and turned from black to gold. He wondered if it was physically possible to open his throat and fill his lungs with water, and what Lorna would think if she found him that way tomorrow, dead at the bottom of the pool, sitting in a lawn chair.

Christ, he nearly laughed out loud. He *would* drown if he didn't quit acting like some kind of stupid . . . He pushed off hard with his feet, hanging on to the chair and carrying it with him to the surface. He sucked air into his lungs as he kicked toward the side and with both hands managed to push the chair up onto the coping. Immediately it tottered in the wind, nearly falling back in. "No, you don't, you dirty bastard," he said, talking to the wind rather than to the chair, and he gave it a shove that propelled it into the flower bed along the wall of the house. Then he climbed up the ladder, nearly falling back into the pool, surprised at how bone weary he was.

Inside the house he caught sight of the half-full decanter of scotch. The glass was gone. He picked it up and carried it into the kitchen, pulling the scotch bottle out of the cupboard and dumping the contents of the decanter into the bottle before rinsing the empty decanter at the sink and putting the bottle away. He went into the bedroom, where he left his wet trunks in a heap on the floor. After a moment's hesitation he climbed into bed on Lorna's side and shut his eyes, breathing her scent, his face on her pillow.

# MONDAY

. . . trifles make the sum of life.
—Charles Dickens
*David Copperfield*

1

KLEIN WOKE UP FAST OUT OF A DEAD SLEEP NEXT MORNING AND
bolted out of bed, standing in the middle of the bedroom floor
and looking around, breathing heavily, overwhelmed with sudden
fear. Then he saw his swimming trunks on the floor and the sunlight through the curtains. He moved the trunks with his toe, grim-
acing at the pink stain that the fluorescent nylon had left on the
white Berber carpet. He'd get Imelda to scrub it out, except that
it was Imelda's day off. He looked at the alarm clock—nearly
noon. No call from Pomeroy, thank God.

He knew without having to look that the house was empty.

He got dressed and went into the kitchen, sitting down in front
of the phone. After a few moments of thinking he punched in
Lorna's sister's number. She answered after the fourth ring, just
as he was about to hang up so that he wouldn't have to listen to
the phone message.

"Joanne?"

"Speaking," she said, then waited. She knew who it was.
Lorna was there, or had been.

"Can I talk to her?" he asked.

"She's not here now."

"Yeah," Klein said. "Just let me talk to her."

"She's not here, Lance. She was here but she's gone. If I were
her I'd be scouting out lawyers, after what you did to her."

"Whoa," Klein said. "Wait. What the hell did she tell you?"

"She had to tell *somebody*, for God's sake. She could hardly
talk it over with *you*. She was a goddamn wreck when she got
here."

"What'd she say, Joanne?" Klein asked tiredly. "I need to
know. There was a lot of confusion last night. I'm not even sure
*I* know what happened. She wouldn't say two words to me."

After a silence she said, "Okay, Lance. I'll tell you. She
opened up with the whole story—the phone call, the jealous hus-

band, you out in the shed or wherever it was you took the bimbo
to have your way with her while your wife was asleep right inside
the goddamn house, for Christ's sake. You want more? If you
had *any* kind of shame at all you would have died there when
she found you. She even told me what you said: 'I can explain.'
She started laughing so hard when she told me that I nearly had
to slap her. Then she curled up on the damned couch and
wouldn't say anything more, just laid there and cried herself to
sleep.''

There was silence again, but he could hear her breathing hard
on the other end of the line. He stood with his eyes closed, his
mind stuttering. "What phone call?" he asked.

"What?"

"A phone call. You said something about a phone call and a
jealous husband. What phone call?"

"From the guy. The one that's *been* calling her. One of your
friends or something, called her up and ratted you out. What'd
you do? *Brag* about it to your pals beforehand?"

Klein counted slowly to ten, composing himself. "No," he said
finally. "I didn't brag about it. There's so much . . . so much
Lorna doesn't know."

"Thank God, I'd say."

"Where is she now?"

"Why don't you leave her alone, give her a little space?"

He fought down the urge to tell her what to do with her advice.
"Give me a break," he said. "Give us both a break."

"And what are you going to do if I give you a break, if I tell
you where she is? Run over there and yell? Push someone
around? Get into someone's face?"

"Please," he said.

After a moment Joanne said, "All right. I'll give you a break,
but for God's sake, don't screw it up this time. She drove out
into the canyon. There's that old man out there, the one she
worked with at the library. She wanted to cry on his shoulder, I
guess."

"Yeah," Klein said. "I know him. Thanks, Joanne."

"Uh-huh," she said. "Just try to do the right thing this time,
will you, Lance? And let me tell you something, because I know
you're thinking about it. No, she didn't drink anything last night
when she showed up. I offered her a drink and she turned it down
flat. What she told me last night was *her* talking, not alcohol.''

"Yeah," Klein said again. "Thanks." She hung up then, and

he listened to the silence until the dial tone started up. At loose ends now, he walked to the front door, picked up the mail, and shuffled through it, pulling out a padded manila envelope with something sliding around inside—some kind of junk mail, maybe a real estate come-on. But it was full postage, mailed locally, and there was no return address. The lettering on the front had been rubbed on, a couple of the letters already peeling away from the paper.

He closed his eyes, feeling his forehead tighten with a sudden tension. This was it; this was why Pomeroy hadn't given him a wake-up call—what all his talk yesterday morning had been leading to. He tore it open, scanning the contents of the several pages of Xerox. It took him a couple of moments to understand what it was exactly. Inside the envelope lay a cassette tape. There was no letter of instruction, no list of demands. Pomeroy wasn't a hasty man; he was working this into a long-term investment, like some kind of carefully built-up tax-sheltered retirement.

Klein walked into the living room, bent down, and turned on the automatic ignition in the fireplace. The gas burner whooshed on, flames curling up around the cleverly painted concrete logs. One by one he fed the Xerox pages into the flames, picking up the unburned scraps and feeding them back in until nothing but ash remained. He tore up the envelope then, and tossed it into the fire, too. Then he snagged the tape out of the cassette with his fingernail and jerked it out, yanking yards and yards of it onto the living room floor. Slamming the plastic cartridge down onto the brick hearth, he pulled out the ornamental fireplace poker and beat the little rectangle of black plastic until the iron head of the poker flew off its spindly brass pole and clunked into the leg of the coffee table.

He heaped the tape into the fire, watching it flare up and disappear, then snapped each half of the cassette shell apart with his hands, getting up finally to throw the pieces away in the trash compactor. He washed the ash off his hands at the sink, over and over again with Ivory soap out of the squeeze bottle as if it were Pomeroy and all his filth that he was washing away.

He had told himself not two days ago that although he had been guilty of crimes, of big mistakes, all of that had been in the past, years ago. He'd met Lorna since then, started a new life. But suddenly he was neck deep in it again, complicit in Pomeroy's breaking into Beth's house, in the rats in the damned water tank, in every single damned twisted crime that Pomeroy was out there committing in both their names. And the insane truth of it was that he hadn't even needed Pomeroy's help in what happened last night. What Joanne said was true; he'd screwed things up with Lorna entirely on his own.

Help fighting the war—that's what Lorna had offered him yesterday. And he'd turned away from her and gone off to fight it himself, with a claw hammer. Maybe it would have been better for all of them if he'd had a chance to use it.

Outside it was sunny and almost hot, the wind fallen. The poolhouse door still hung open, and he realized that he could barely look at it. He pushed the button to open the garage door, then went out through the back, fetching the screw gun off the bench along with a box of wooden kitchen matches before heading for the poolhouse. One by one he jammed kitchen matches into the stripped-out screw holes in the doorjamb, snapping the matches off flush with the wood. He tilted the door back into place, forcing it upright with his knee against the knob, then ran the screws back into the plugged-up holes. He opened and shut the door a few times, then looked at where the bolt had splintered free of the wood. He'd have to chisel it out and scab in a piece, then fill the door panel and repaint the whole thing.

There were leaves and trash strewn everywhere, under the sofa and chairs, heaped up in the corners. He took down the curtains and shook them out, then hung them back up. Then he turned the Ping-Pong table upright, opened the closet door, and took out the broom and dustpan. Methodically he swept the place out, filling the trash can and hauling the leaves out to the fence. The room needed to be vacuumed but, like the painting, that could wait. He'd get to it. Bit by bit he would erase and eradicate his errors. . . .

He put the broom and dustpan away and was on the verge of going back out into the sunlight when he remembered the gun. Slowly he walked to the sofa and lifted the cushion. Beneath it lay the .38 from his nightstand—the gun that Lorna had brought out to shoot the man she thought was assaulting him.

The guy who needed to be shot was probably out in the canyon right now, leaning on people. He slipped the pistol into his pants pocket and went after his car keys on the kitchen counter.

**2**

POMEROY SLOWED THE ISUZU, PEERING INTO THE WOODS AND brush along the creek, trying to spot the boy again. He'd caught a glimpse of him a moment ago, walking among the trees. The wind moved through the vegetation now, stirring the willows and alder saplings so that the forest was full of movement. It *had* to be the same kid that had wrecked his camera; there was no mistaking the thrift-store clothes. He had given up on the idea of its being Beth's son, though; a woman like her simply couldn't have a kid that far out of hand.

There he was! Heading up along the creek, in no particular hurry. Pomeroy stepped on the accelerator, and the Isuzu banged along to the closest turnout, where he pulled in, cutting the engine and setting the parking brake. He jumped out and clambered down the bank, through the dry grass and into the willows along the creek, shouting, "Stop right there!" as he ran, even though the kid was out of sight again.

Pomeroy slowed down, getting his bearings and making up his mind. He wasn't about to back down. There was no excuse for kids to be running wild like this, stealing things, doing malicious damage to other people's property. . . . There was a movement ahead of him, beyond the willows, and he crouched in the shelter of a tangle of roots where the creek had eaten the bank away. Hadn't the kid even *heard* him? The wind wasn't making *that* much noise. It made him suddenly nervous, the kid fooling around like that, as if maybe he *wanted* him to catch up.

Pomeroy looked around carefully, making up his mind about going on. Then the boy stepped across the creek and headed up the other side of the canyon, kicking his way through the tall grass of a clearing toward what was pretty clearly a cut in the wall of the ridge, maybe a little side canyon, its entrance obscured by a stand of oaks. Keeping low, Pomeroy followed, finding a rocky ford where the kid had crossed the stream. A little section of trail lay exposed on the hillside above, some distance above the top of the oaks, and he suddenly wondered if it led up to the trail that wound back down into Trabuco Oaks.

Beth had headed up that way two days ago after he'd chatted with her in front of the old man's house. When he saw the boy climb up onto the section of exposed trail, vanishing beyond the rock and brush, he set out at a run, leaping over fallen limbs and ducking into the deep shade of the big oaks. The wind blew straight into his face as it funneled down out of the side canyon, and a little leaf-choked stream trickled through scattered rocks from a spring somewhere above.

He found the trail and set out hurriedly, then stopped in his tracks, listening to a strange noise that seemed to float down toward him on the wind. He could swear it was the sound of a child's crying. After a moment came the clear sound of a woman's voice, clearly calling out a name. The wind picked up just then with a rush of creaking and rustling, but Pomeroy had heard enough. In a rush of understanding he connected the boy's strange clothing—the suspenders and out-of-date shirt and pants—with the hippie-looking woman out at Klein's fence.

Of course! He felt ashamed of himself for suspecting that Beth would have anything to do with a man like Klein or would use her son for any such purpose. A woman like her! It was Klein and this hippie woman all along, conspiring against him. Good God, maybe the kid was Klein's son! A little bastard!

He pushed on, not knowing what any of this meant, but knowing that he could *use* it. He had to meet the woman, follow her, speak to her. He would automatically have a certain power over her. . . . As he climbed he watched the trail ahead closely, so as not to come on them unawares. Better to seem as if he were just out hiking. The kid would be knocked sideways seeing him, but so what? He'd keep his mouth shut.

There was the woman's voice again. She sounded pretty worked up, and there was the crying again from the kid. The wind slammed down the trail so suddenly and so hard that he staggered backward, nearly pushed off his feet. He had a sudden vague premonition that he was reading this wrong, that there was something involved here that he didn't understand. Was the wind trying to turn him around? He searched the sky. It was cloudless, clear blue, as if inviting him to climb higher—at least up onto the ridge.

Heavy dry brush closed in from either side, and the trail was so steep, and it switched back so often, that he couldn't see far enough ahead to gauge how close to the top he was. He was sweating freely, and the flies swarmed around his face in the heat, buzzing infernally. He wiped his forehead and listened for footsteps ahead, but the wind blasted through the vegetation and he heard only the sound of the flies and of his own feet scrabbling across the broken rock.

Then suddenly the trail opened out ahead of him, the ridge leveling off some distance above into a nearly flat scrub-covered plateau. Mountains rose again beyond it, rough and dense with vegetation, but the trail he was following wound away to the west now along the edge of the plateau. He stepped out into a broad clearing and then stepped hurriedly back again, hunching down behind the edge of the brush. There she stood, Klein's back-door bimbo, not twenty yards away, dressed just as she had been yesterday afternoon and last night. Her hair was a windblown frenzy, and the dress, clearly, had seen a lot of wear. Clearly she was some kind of local white trash, a drug case or something. He knew that Klein was low, but taking advantage of a woman like this . . .

She took the boy's hand and was hurried forward, the boy crying now for all he was worth, and the wind blowing her skirts up around her legs. Surprised, Pomeroy stepped out into the open and shouted, setting out after them. The wind threw his words back into his face. If they heard him, they didn't care. Ahead lay a dense stand of dark alders clustered along what must have been a spring—the source of the little creek at the bottom of the canyon.

Making up his mind, he set out at a run, overtaking them near the trees. They were tangled and dense, heavy with undergrowth, and even with the sun high in the sky, the interior of the little copse was dark with shadow. There was the sound of water splashing somewhere below, weirdly clear despite the rush of wind on the unprotected ridge. The woman hesitated for a moment before a dark hollow in the branches, an arched window of moving shadows. Lunging forward, Pomeroy grasped her shoulder with one hand and the boy's elbow with the other.

"Whoa up there, little lady," he said, trying to sound pleasant even though he had to raise his voice to be heard.

She slipped from his grasp like smoke, not even turning to look at him. He realized that she was weeping—something was going on here; something more than he understood. The boy pivoted

around and looked Pomeroy full in the face, his wide-open eyes
staring and dark with fear as if he were looking into a pit. Clearly
he comprehended nothing. His face was almost idiotic with fear.
Pomeroy stepped backward in sudden alarm. The boy clutched a
cat to his chest, cradling it in his right arm, and for one terrible
moment Pomeroy was certain that the cat was the same one he'd
shot yesterday, that the boy had been carrying the dead cat around
for the past twenty-four hours. Then the darkness of the overshadowing trees swallowed the two of them, and Pomeroy was
left alone with the wind.

Recovering a little, he shouted, "Wait!" and bent forward
warily, shading his eyes from the leaves and dust that the wind
raised into the air around him. He groped into the darkness within
the trees, stretching out his arms to fend off the moving branches.
There was the sound all around him of wood snapping and of the
roaring wind, and then suddenly, piercing through all of it, the
nightmarish sound of a woman's scream.

Pomeroy edged forward, pushing out through bushes to find
himself suddenly at the edge of a cliff, looking downward over
the edge at cascading water. He reeled backward, stepping into
the shallow creek, realizing then what the scream had meant,
what the woman had done. Even then he wondered if he could
use it against Klein. The dirty bastard! Clearly what had gone on
last night had driven this poor woman to suicide.

He turned back into the darkness, covering his eyes against the
dirt and leaves that flew into his face, trying to grope his way
back out toward the arch of sunlight, which glowed now like the
mouth of a cave. Creek water filled his shoes. The gale lashed
through the foliage, and a heavy spray of wind-whipped water
and leaves slapped his pants and shirt and face. He slipped on
wet rocks, falling forward, reaching out to break his fall with his
hands and opening his mouth to shout, plunging into water up to
his elbow. His mouth filled with grit and wet leaves, and he
clamped his teeth down, gagging on the debris in his throat.

Pushing himself to his feet, he lurched forward out of the creek
bed, groping for something to hold on to. The tree limbs flayed
themselves leafless, whipping at his face and back and arms.
Something hit him on the back of his head—a broken-off tree
branch, slamming down with all the fury of the wind behind it.
He staggered like a drunken man, looking wildly around, trying
to breathe, but sucking in dirt and fragments of leaves. The wind
crashed and hummed, and the arch of sunlight and open air was

obscured by windborne stuff, swirling tighter and tighter until it looked to Pomeroy like a dense curtain of leaves and twigs and branches that was roughly the height and shape of a man.

He took a step backward, grabbing onto a limb to steady himself. He could almost imagine that the black void in the thing was an open mouth, the focus of the terrible humming of the wind. A shower of pebbles and dirt flew toward him suddenly, cast from within the whirling mass of forest trash, forcing him farther back into the trees and undergrowth. Behind him—ten feet? twelve?— lay the edge of the cliff. The thing tottered forward, groping toward him, broken branches thrusting out from its side like rude arms. Mulch and dust dribbled from the open hole of its mouth and were sucked back into the revolving mass. Pomeroy heard the sound of the waterfall at his back as the thing drew near. With a desperate scream he lunged blindly toward it, flailing with his arms, trying to sweep it aside and escape once again into the sunlight.

He tripped on a limb and fell hard, the broken stump of a branch tearing his shirt and chest. He felt his face peppered with dirt, and he squeezed shut his mouth and eyes and groped blindly forward on his hands and knees. A twig wiggled down into his ear like an insect antenna, and he snatched at it, suddenly terrified, screaming despite himself and feeling his mouth fill instantly with muddy leaves and mulch. He pushed himself to his feet, coughing and spitting and windmilling his arms in front of him, pressing his chin into his chest. Something hit him hard in the small of the back, and he staggered forward, barely keeping his feet, bursting out of the trees and into the open air.

Without looking back, he lurched through the high brush, into the clearing where he'd first come upon the woman and boy. From behind him he heard the snapping of branches and a sound like dry leaves being crushed in a box. He screamed, redoubling his pace, angling down the path, the wind driving at his back now, hurrying him forward. He plunged down the steep hillside, and within an instant he was running headlong, the vegetation along either side passing in a blur. Still he could feel the awful rush of wind pushing at his back like hands, and he could hear the humming of it in his ears and the snapping and breaking of vegetation.

He looked wildly over his shoulder now, and in that moment he tripped and was flung face forward. He threw out both arms to catch himself and felt the unmistakable snap of bones in his right wrist as he tumbled downward, smashing to a stop against an almost vertical wall of stone, his breath slamming out of him as if his lungs had collapsed. Wheezing for breath, he managed to stand up for a moment and stagger a few feet forward before his ankle gave out and he collapsed onto all fours, only to be jolted by the rushing storm of tumbling, windborne debris that had followed him down from the top of the falls. He was jerked to his feet, the sticks and limbs and wind working his arms and legs as if he were a spastic puppet, forcing open his eyes and mouth and nostrils, stopping his breath with dry leaves and sand. Staring up into the sun, he tore at the stuff in his mouth with the fingers of his good hand, unaware now of the roaring of the wind, of anything but the desperate need to breathe.

PETER AWOKE THE NEXT MORNING TO THE SOUND OF A CAR ENgine shutting off nearby. A door slammed, and there was the sound of footsteps on gravel. He looked around in confusion before knowing where he was—at Beth's, where he'd collapsed into dreamless sleep some time after midnight. He opened the blinds, and daylight flooded the room.

"Awake?" Beth asked, pushing the door open a crack.

"What time is it?"

"Eleven. I've been down to Benny's doughnuts. Coffee in a second."

She shut the bedroom door, then opened it again. "Why don't you take a quick shower?" she asked, closing the door again.

Peter got out of bed. He was still dressed in his clothes. He glanced in the mirror, unhappy at the reflection. He looked as if he'd been dragged through the forest by wild pigs.

Beth had a tray set up in the bedroom, the windows open, sunlight streaming in. He sat on the bed and picked through the box of doughnuts. "No jelly?"

"All out," she said. "You don't get to be picky this late in the morning."

He pulled out a glazed and a strawberry frosted, and Beth took a chocolate-chocolate. "We're going to get crumbs on the bed," Peter said, licking the sugar glaze off his fingers before trying to dust doughnut crumbs off the bedspread.

"Let's not care about that," she said. "Let's eat these doughnuts as if we were millionaires and could buy a hundred bedspreads."

"Millionaires eat doughnuts different than we do?"

"They just eat more," she said. "Unlimited doughnuts. That's one of the attractions of being rich."

"Where's Bobby? He ought to be in on this, eating like a rich man."

"School," she said. "It's Monday. Holiday's over. I arranged for him to spend the night with Julie and Simon. That way you and I can investigate your house for monsters."

Peter didn't say anything. That wasn't exactly what he had in mind, mixing Beth up in everything. "We'll see," he said.

"That's right," she said. "We'll see together."

"That wasn't exactly what I meant."

She shrugged, as if she didn't care what he meant.

After a moment he asked, "Why'd you get a dozen?"

"Cheaper."

He didn't ask the obvious question, but picked up another doughnut just to do his part. It was going to take a major effort to make this pay. He looked at the doughnut but couldn't bear the thought of eating it, so he put it down, noticing just then a wooden, three-tiered Chinese box that lay on Beth's dresser. It was lacquered a dark blood-red and painted with white flowers and viney-looking gold leaves.

"Treasures?" Peter asked her, gesturing at the box with his coffee cup.

"Probably not the kind of treasures you're thinking of."

"May I?"

"Knock yourself out. Nothing very exciting to anyone but me."

It dawned on him suddenly how little he really knew about her—her day-to-day habits, the things that made her laugh and cry. He removed the lid from the top box. Inside lay a little collection of baby toys—a plastic rattle in pastel colors, a comical stuffed dog with the name "Binky" embroidered on it, a chewed-on pacifier, a fuzzy rabbit with a missing ear, a baby's ID strap from the hospital. He lifted the first box and looked at the contents of the second.

"More of the same," Beth said. She picked up a baby bottle with a picture of a duck on it. "This was his last bottle. One day I told him that when he threw it into the trash he would turn into a boy, with all the baby gone out of him. So he did. Right then. Didn't wait more than three seconds. He walked straight into the kitchen and jammed it into the can under the sink. I started crying, and as soon as he wasn't looking I took it out and kept it."

Peter sorted through the dozen or so photos that had lain beneath the bottle—Bobby in all sorts of moods, wearing little hats, grinning up from his bath in the kitchen sink, toddling across the carpet. "This was taken on his third birthday," she said. "I made him a three-layer cake with three colors of frosting." The photo was cut neatly in half lengthwise. Whoever had been sitting next to Bobby at the table had been trimmed.

"Cutting-room floor?" Peter asked, remembering the photo on Ackroyd's wall. Somehow he had never wanted to cut Amanda out of his life, not that way.

She nodded. "It was Walter. Later, when we were splitting things up, I sent him his half of the photos. I should be ashamed, shouldn't I?"

"Clear and effective statement, I'd say."

"Maybe. But it's the kind of statement you make when you're out of your mind. Later on you wish you'd kept your mouth shut. I've got the negatives. Someday I'm going to have a new set printed up."

"For Walter?"

"For me. I'll mail him the other half of the ones he's got."

Peter picked up a pair of baby shoes, the laces tied together. He could have worn them on his thumbs. "First shoes?"

"They look like little cartoon shoes, don't they? Like mice would wear. Check out this bib with the duck on it. He used to bring this to me when he wanted to eat. He'd just walk up and hand me the bib." She laughed softly and shook her head. "Don't ask me why I save all this stuff. Just nostalgia. Even Bobby thinks it's silly."

"I don't think any of it's silly," he said.

"I guess it is a little like a treasure chest or something."

"Remember the end of 'Pandora's Box'? When she lifts the lid and all the evil spirits fly out into the world, and she just sort of takes it in stride because at least she got all of them out of her house? 'Now our house harbors only hope,' she says, and that's the end of the story. I wrote that on a piece of paper once and carried it around with me. Finally lost it somewhere. Turned out not to be true in my situation anyway.''

''I always thought 'Pandora's Box' had an *un*happy ending.''

He shook his head. ''It looks that way, but then she manages to hold on to the good thing and let go of the rest.''

''She was lucky. With me, all this stuff is more like *The Velveteen Rabbit*. That's a story I can believe in. I think that all these baby trinkets have a kind of magic power because they belonged to Bobby. Crazy, isn't it?''

''No. It's not crazy at all. You're right.'' He watched her stack the boxes and set the lid on top, and at that moment he realized that he loved her. Whatever indecision he'd been muddling through during the last couple of days and weeks vanished. He sat looking at her, as if he were just now seeing her clearly.

''What's so funny?'' she asked, seeing his face. ''You look goggle-eyed all of a sudden.''

''I love you.''

She blinked at him. Saying nothing, she turned toward the dresser, moving the box carefully so as to position it to precisely cover the dust-free square of mahogany where it had sat ten minutes ago.

He was suddenly sobered. She had no humor at all in her eyes, just a sudden thoughtfulness, as if she'd been reminded of some long-forgotten regret.

''You'd better say just what you mean,'' she said after a moment.

''I just did.''

''You've been a little doubtful over the last couple of days.''

''I had the right to be.''

''Probably so. But what happened to all the doubts? Where did they go? Out the window with the bad spirits? Now there's only hope left?''

He shrugged, suddenly not trusting himself to speak. ''I figured out what I want—what you told me to do yesterday morning, remember?''

Abruptly she smiled. ''Did I advise that?''

He nodded.

''And so this is like the first day of the rest of your life?''

''Absolutely,'' he said. ''Yours, too. Look how it started—

sleeping late, waking up to doughnuts and coffee. Not a bad life."

"That's what you've got planned? You sleep in while I go out for the doughnuts and brew the coffee?"

He picked up the doughnut box and held it open in front of her. "Now this box harbors only leftovers," he said.

She took it out of his hands and set it on the dresser. Then, shaking her hair back out of her face, she pushed him over backward onto the bedspread.

THERE WAS SOMETHING RESTFUL ABOUT THE CANYON—THE BLUE sky rising above the gray ridge, the north-facing wall dark green with fern and oak. On a Monday morning the place was empty. It struck him for the first time that he wouldn't mind having a little cabin back in here himself, maybe along Holy Jim Creek, although if the park deal went through and the cabin owners had to clear out, then the whole idea would be bust anyway. And if the park deal *didn't* go through, well . . .

He almost wished it wouldn't now. He could hardly face the months of dealing with the scheme as it got more and more top-heavy. And as for Pomeroy, he *had* to be . . . dealt with somehow, once and for all.

He put the idea out of his mind and waved at a bearded man working next to a rusty gate that blocked a road into a little side canyon. The man nodded to him, taking off his cap and wiping his face with his arm, and Klein shouted, "Must be Miller time!" at him, hearing the man yell some kind of affirming comment back as the truck rounded the bend. Klein waved once more out the window, passing the rusted, beat-up hulks of a half dozen abandoned cars and refrigerators and rusting debris that you couldn't quite recognize anymore.

He realized that he felt strangely good—clear and sharp. He couldn't say why, after last night. He seemed to have lost weight or something, gotten rid of baggage. And he had the feeling that he knew something now that he hadn't known before, something he'd learned from Lorna, maybe even from Pomeroy in a round-about way. He didn't feel like that very often, which was probably a character defect. But it was probably a worse defect to think that you didn't have any defects. Of course it was a defect thinking like that, because you were secretly proud that there was at least one defect you didn't have.

He almost laughed, drumming his fingers on the steering wheel, the truck dipping across the creek, which ran across the road some six inches deep. There was a sheer drop of three or four feet on the right, where the creek pooled up into a still pond. There was something beautiful about it—the dark water beneath the over-hanging oaks and alders, a scattering of leaves floating on it like boats. Probably he was about to be screwed from every conceivable direction, but at least he didn't have any illusions about it anymore.

The truck angled up the rise, then swung to the left as he followed the road past the old lower campground. Maybe it was better to let Lorna do the talking—the demanding—whatever it was she wanted. He would tell her straight out what he knew about last night, which wasn't one damned thing, really. There was a lot he hadn't told her over the years, but as far as he remembered, he hadn't made a habit of lying to her, and maybe she'd appreciate that now and take him on faith.

He caught sight just then of a light blue car fender, and he slowed down, creeping up next to an Isuzu Trooper parked just off the road. Pomeroy. It was a rental, without a doubt the same car he'd been driving yesterday morning. Klein braked to a stop and sat there considering things, the wind suddenly kicking up dust in front of his bumper. Why out here? The lower campground lay a good mile or so below the first cabins. There was no way in hell that Pomeroy would park out here and walk up. He had to be up to something. . . .

A bee flew in through the open window just then, and Klein noticed that there was a swarm of bees just across the road, buzzing around a hollow tree. He rolled up the window and pulled off onto the turnout, cutting the engine and looking around at the silent woods. There was no sign of him. The air was quiet, just the wind whispering. Across the creek lay the trail that led back into Falls Canyon, its entrance nearly hidden by vegetation. That was really the only place Pomeroy could have gone, unless he was hiding in one of the caves in the hillside. . . .

Wait him out? Klein got out of the car and walked across to the Isuzu, looking in the windows before opening the passenger-side door. He tripped the glove compartment latch and rooted around inside, pulling out what looked like a toiletries kit. There was all kinds of crap inside the kit, including some kind of face makeup or cover-up or something. Maybe that wasn't any kind of surprise, given Pomeroy's antics with the underwear yesterday. He flipped through the few papers, finding nothing but a map and rental car folder containing registration papers and a Triple A pamphlet.

The rest of the car was clean. He shut the door and leaned against it. If Lorna left Ackroyd's she'd have to drive right past him to get out, in which case he'd stand in front of her car till she agreed to talk things out. Meanwhile, if Pomeroy showed up . . .

He took the .38 out of his pocket, remembering what he'd said to Pomeroy yesterday about dragging him out into the woods and killing him. The hills were rugged, full of dense brush, thick with coyotes and carrion birds. Even now he could see a half dozen vultures circling up over the ridge, high in the sky. Nobody paid a damned bit of attention to that kind of thing out here.

He let his mind run, calculating how much of his life was about to come down in a smoking heap: his house, his marriage, his financial security. Of course the truth was he'd set himself up for it; all it took was a monster like Pomeroy to knock him down. It occurred to him again that Pomeroy himself was very nearly the perfect victim—secretive, no family, certainly no friends. . . .

He put away the pistol and let the idea slide away from him. For fifteen minutes he stood by the roadside, leaning against his truck, listening to the sound of the creek and the rustling of leaves. A car went by, but it wasn't Lorna. The wind gusted a couple of times, and the day grew increasingly lonesome and empty. Klein began to feel fidgety, wondering if he was waiting in vain. Or worse, if he was waiting around while Pomeroy worked more of his creepery on someone.

What the hell *was* Pomeroy doing up there? He was the last man on earth to take a damned hike. Had he followed some-body up there? Klein set out toward the creek, in a sudden hurry now that he had decided to move. At the edge of the water he stopped, full of indecision, his hand on the gun in his pocket. He turned around and jogged back to the truck, putting the pistol away in the glove compartment, locking up, and then turning around and heading down the hill again.

He picked his way across the creek and up through the oaks that led to the mouth of Falls Canyon. The narrow defile was nearly choked with broken alder and sycamore limbs, fallen from trees growing up the canyon walls. Drifts of leaves covered the tangle of brush, and he was forced to clamber partway up the steep cliffside to find the trail again where it rose above the floor of the canyon.

He picked up his pace when the way was clear, the soft dry dirt rising around him, dusting his arms with grime. Here and there he could see the marks of crepe-soled shoes, the kind Pomeroy wore when he was out here conducting business. He stopped to listen, damned if he was going to let the bastard come upon him unawares. There was nothing but the morning silence, though, barely disturbed now by the wind.

He wiped his face on his sleeve and continued up the trail, stepping over fallen branches. Soon the trail forked, and he took the upper fork on instinct, knowing that it led to the ridge. The lower fork led to the falls—an unlikely destination for Pomeroy unless he was just out sightseeing, which was nearly unimaginable. Thick brush overgrew the trail, and he pushed through it sideways, climbing into the shade of a granite ledge and resting for a moment, wiping the sweat off his forehead. A big lizard darted across the path just then, running for the shelter of a heap of sticks and leaves and brush, nearly shoulder high, that blocked the trail ahead.

Klein stepped toward it, wondering whether he'd have to leave the trail and climb around it, and at the same time reaching for the broken end of a branch. He stopped suddenly, then reversed direction and trod backward, shouting inadvertently and bumping up against the cool granite behind him.

A man's face, dirty and bruised, eyes and mouth wide open, stared out at him from the interior of the tangled debris. One upturned hand and arm lay parallel to the broken branch Klein had just reached for. A dirty gauze bandage dangled from where it was wrapped around the lifeless hand, and the hand itself, supported by the tangle of brush, clutched a knot of dead leaves.

# 5

IT TOOK KLEIN A FEW MOMENTS TO REALIZE THAT THE DEAD MAN
was Pomeroy. The skin on his arms was discolored from bruises
and dried blood, and his face, visible through the mass of debris
and vegetation that nearly covered the corpse, was distorted with
terror. His eyes were wide open and seemed almost to bulge, as
if he'd been suffocated or strangled. It was the big ring on the
finger of his outstretched hand that was unmistakable.

"Jesus," Klein said out loud, turning away and looking back
down the trail. For a moment he held his breath, and then he let
it out slowly. He couldn't fathom this—who could have done it?
There were probably plenty of people in the world who wouldn't
mind seeing Pomeroy dead, but why out here, up on this God-
forsaken ridge? What, had he been *lured* up here?

Then he knew suddenly that there couldn't be any such explanation. He looked at Pomeroy again, at the leaves clutched in his
hand, stuffed in his half-open mouth. What the corpse reminded
him of was himself, last night, crouched in the corner of the
poolhouse while the wind pounded at him, choking him with dead
things.

It was the wind that had killed Pomeroy.

He nearly turned back down the path, full of sudden fear. The
breeze only whispered through the chaparral now, vaguely stirring
the dirty gauze that hung from Pomeroy's wrist. Klein closed his
eyes for a moment, forcing himself to think clearly. Why did it
*have* to be the wind that had killed Pomeroy? The path leading
up to the ridge was steep. Pomeroy had tripped on loose brush,
tumbled forty or fifty feet, probably broken his neck. That was
all—a stupid accident, bad luck for Pomeroy, but good luck for
the rest of the world.

Klein was free of him. The realization was like the passing of
a cloud shadow. He nearly laughed out loud, and for one giddy
moment he almost reached out and shook Pomeroy's limp hand.

The corpse's discolored face sobered him, though, and it dawned on him that whatever had happened to Pomeroy, he couldn't let the body be found. That much was obvious. They would think Klein had killed him. They would *know* it. He'd been yelling it out loud for the last couple of days, wandering around the hills with a loaded pistol. He'd screamed it at Lorna. Beth had over-heard him say the same thing. And Winters . . . Christ, he'd called Winters yesterday morning and advertised that Pomeroy was out of control and had to be stopped. Winters would hang him out to dry. And to top it off, his truck had been parked for the last hour alongside Pomeroy's Isuzu, down at the damned turnout. When push came to shove, there was enough circumstantial evidence to drown him. And when the rest of it came out—the scheming, the blackmail—it would all be over except for the prison sentence.

The wind was still now, and the air had grown hot. In the silence he listened for the sound of footsteps on the trail, for hikers taking an afternoon stroll to the top of the falls. He had to hide the body, and the quicker the better. He pushed against a broken branch that hooked around Pomeroy's back and neck, dig-ging into the flesh of his cheek. Dead leaves and twigs cascaded to the ground, and Klein jerked his hand away when the body moved and the head abruptly fell sideways and dangled at an unnatural angle.

Klein steeled himself, grabbing the branch with both hands and yanking it free, throwing it as far into the scrub as he could manage. He hauled away a clot of loose limbs, tumbling the corpse into the brush beside the trail. Methodically he pulled the rest of the debris to pieces, scattering it into the chaparral, scoop-ing up handfuls of twigs and leaves and tossing them into the wind.

Finally the corpse lay on its back, its face staring at the sky. He crouched next to it, holding his breath while he twisted the ring from Pomeroy's finger. Then he went through his pockets, pulling out his wallet, car keys and a small address book con-taining the names and phone numbers of canyon residents.

"Good," he said when he saw the book. He sighed heavily, starting to breathe again, and slid all of it into his own pockets before grabbing Pomeroy by his belt and shirt collar. Slowly he began to drag him up toward the ridge, setting his feet, hauling the corpse a yard or so, and then setting his feet again. Down would have been easy, but down was no good; there wasn't any part of the canyon that wasn't hiked through by boy scouts or picnickers or somebody. Up on the ridge, though, some distance off the trail . . .

Halfway to the top he stopped to rest, thinking suddenly that he could throw the body off the top of the falls, make it look accidental or something. But just as suddenly he abandoned it. What would they make of the stuff in the corpse's mouth? How long had he been here? A couple of hours? *Any* competent coroner would know that he died first, had choked to death, and then been tossed over the top, and they'd be on Klein like a pack of dogs within a couple of days. Getting clever like that would be the worst thing to do.

He looked toward the top of the trail, another twenty or thirty feet up, then slid the body farther across the scree-covered dirt. Both its shoes came off almost at the same moment. Klein cursed, dropping Pomeroy and hurrying down to retrieve them. He tied them together with the laces and hung them around Pomeroy's neck before grabbing his wrists and starting again, trying not to look at the bloated face, which lolled back and forth. The loose gauze bandage dangled nearly to the ground, and when Klein finally dragged the corpse onto a level spot, he let it lie, bending over and wrapping the gauze around the wrist again, brushing off the clinging oak leaves.

He rested his hands on his knees finally, catching his breath. Pomeroy was a little man, thank God. Maybe that had been his problem. Klein remembered then that Pomeroy had described himself to someone at the Spanglers' as the ''Napoleon of car sales.'' When the hell was that? Only a few days ago, and here the poor son of a bitch lay dead with one hand flopped across his chest. After a moment he set out up the ridge trail, jogging slowly and looking to both sides for a break in the dense shrubbery. Soon he came to what looked like a kind of deer trail—a narrow opening in the chaparral that led away into the interior, toward where the hills rose again toward an even more elevated ridge. Beyond that lay the Santiago Truck Trail, which traversed the high, wild ridges leading up to Santiago Peak, but between here and there was nothing but a couple of miles of unbroken and untraveled wilderness.

He made his mind up and jogged back down, hurriedly now. The day was wearing on. It'd been a couple of hours since he'd talked to Joanne, and it all of a sudden was more important than ever that he find Lorna and try to set things straight. Picking up the shoes, he set out again, pulling the corpse by the feet now. Pomeroy's head bounced on the trail, dust rising around it, his hair gray with the dust. Flies settled on the bruised face, were dislodged almost at once, and then buzzed around and settled again.

At the game trail Klein didn't hesitate, but hauled Pomeroy through the brush, jerking him along, unmindful of broken branches. Hell, there was no way to be tidy, to hide his trail. When he came to a stop, finally, Pomeroy's shirt was shoved up under his armpits, and Klein reached down and yanked it over the white, hairless belly. He rolled the corpse over, turning away at the sight of the back of Pomeroy's head, scraped clean of hair after being dragged up the path. He noticed then that there were already vultures overhead, circling in long, declining loops. Pulling and dragging the corpse deeper into the greasewood and sage, the flies swarming around now, he managed finally to wedge it beneath a clump of heavy brush, shoving the shoes in with it. He considered searching out sticks or pulling up plants in order to hide the body even more thoroughly, but then abruptly gave up.

"That's it," he said out loud, stepping out toward the trail. The thought occurred to him then that taking Pomeroy's clothes off would hurry the process of decay, make things easier for the flies and for the carrion eaters that would find their way down off the ridges. But the idea was too ghoulish, and he set out again, the stiff chaparral plants springing into place behind him, dense enough so that unless someone happened to stray off the trail and wander into the scrub, the body might never be found. He headed down the ridge trail, back toward the cars, aware that the wind was rising, the dense vegetation shifting around him like the surface of the sea.

HE DROVE POMEROY'S CAR INTO THE CREEK AND LEFT IT THERE, the keys in the ignition, and walked the half mile back up the canyon to the truck. Within a few days the Isuzu would be stripped, shot full of holes, turned into another rusting hulk. Six months from now the county would haul a crane and a flatbed truck up the canyon clearing out wrecks at the taxpayers' expense.

When they got around to it, they'd trace the car to Pomeroy. But so what? That was inevitable. There was nothing in the wrecked car to indicate there'd been any violence, nothing in it of any value. What it looked like was a typical car theft—joy riders ripping off a new four-wheel-drive vehicle and driving through the canyon like maniacs, abandoning the car after they'd wrecked it. There was nothing in it to suggest that Pomeroy was dead, that his body lay decomposing beyond the top of Falls Canyon. . . .

He unlocked the truck and slid into the driver's seat, taking a look at Pomeroy's wallet and at the little notebook. Inside the notebook, after the several pages of names and phone numbers and figures, there were half a dozen blank pages and then another page containing a couple of sentences written in very careful handwriting, full of flourishes and curlicues and loops. "I might compare thee to the flowers," the first line read, but then the word *thee* had been crossed out and replaced with *you*. The sentence was repeated, the *you* replaced with the words *my Darling*. The rest of the page was filled with doodles of flowers and lightning bolts and question marks trailing off into nothing.

"Poetry," Klein said out loud, shaking his head. It was unbelievable, Pomeroy trying to write this kind of trash. It didn't jive with the Pomeroy that Klein knew. He dropped the notebook on the seat and sorted through the stuff in the wallet. There were a dozen credit cards and an assortment of business cards. Tucked in among the credit cards was a library card issued by the city of Irvine and a couple of membership cards to video stores. There was nearly eighty dollars in cash along with a couple of store receipts, including a computer-printed receipt for a two-dollar video rental—*Way Out West*, the old Laurel and Hardy movie.

Klein was dumbstruck. One of his own favorites! Somehow, of all the excesses in Pomeroy's personality, this was the most incongruous, even stranger than the damned poetry—the notion of him sitting around alone, drinking cold milk and laughing at Laurel and Hardy. There was something depressingly pathetic about it. Suddenly he was sorry he'd paid any attention.

He closed the wallet. The less he knew about Pomeroy the better. For God's sake, *he* hadn't killed the poor creep. He started the engine and moved slowly out onto the road, leaving Pomeroy's stuff beside him on the seat. Almost at once he saw the bees swarming around the oak tree again, and on impulse he stepped on the brake and slid the transmission into park. He got out, leaving the door open and carrying the wallet, address book, and ring. Calmly and slowly, he walked in among the bees, which hummed in and out of the hollow trunk, disappearing down into the shadows. It was impossible to say how deep the hollow was, but the interior of the tree was dark as night, and he couldn't see the bottom.

Abruptly making up his mind, he pitched all three objects into the yawning mouth of the hollow tree, turning at the same instant and sprinting toward the truck. He threw himself in through the open door and slammed it behind him, half expecting a swarm of angry bees to bang into the closed window. There was a dense cloud of them buzzing around the dark hollow, darting in and out, their attention captured by the objects that had landed in the middle of their hive. He shifted into forward, hooking the truck around and edging slowly into the mass of swarming bees until, through the window, he could see into the depths of the hollow tree. There was no sign of the stuff he'd tossed in—no sign of the ring, no sunlight glinting off the polished leather of Pomeroy's wallet or off the slick black cover of the little notebook. There was nothing but a million bees and the dark hole that had swallowed what was left of Pomeroy's life.

Oak leaves drifted across the front of the porch where Lorna sat talking to Mr. Ackroyd. Roses bloomed on a trellis behind her shoulder, and she brushed a spray of hair out of her face, letting her hand linger by her temple. Watching her, Klein cut the engine and coasted to a stop across the road, feeling suddenly alone, seeing her there talking to a man he barely knew. The rush of things that he had meant to say to her had vanished, and he realized that in this small way she led a life separate from their marriage, separate from him. He felt suddenly like someone out of her past.

There was no surprise on her face when she recognized his truck, and certainly no joy, just an indifference. He might have been a deliveryman pulling up with a load of bottled water. He pushed open the door and got out, walking across to the steps. Ackroyd stood up and nodded to him, then stepped forward and shook his hand.

"I'll just brew some coffee," he said, and then turned around and went inside without waiting for a response.

"I called Joanne. . . ." Klein said, then faltered. Lorna said nothing. "Look," he continued, folding his arms in front of his chest, "I guess I want to say I'm sorry."

"You guess," Lorna said, still not looking at him.

"No, I don't guess. I *am* sorry."

She nodded, rocking slowly, looking out toward the trees.

Something occurred to Klein just then, in a nasty rush, and he nearly groaned out loud. "Wait a minute!" he yelled through the door, then pulled the screen open and went in.

The old man stood at the kitchen sink, filling a teakettle with water out of the tap. "Don't . . ." Klein started to say. "Do you have any bottled water?"

"Don't worry about the water," the old man said.

"Why?" Klein asked, surprised. Did he know?

"It's spring water. Absolutely pure. Everyone seems to worry about the water out here." He smiled, putting the kettle on the stove and turning on the flame. Then he got a better look at Klein's face and asked, "What is it? What's wrong?"

Klein took a deep breath and started in. This was just the first of it. "There's a man by the name of Adams who's been hanging around the canyon out here. I think he tried to buy you out, or told you that he represented someone who did."

Ackroyd nodded. "He's a persistent man."

"He was," Klein said. "He's found a new line of work, actually. Real estate didn't agree with him."

"Well, that's moderately good news."

Klein reached across and picked up the teakettle, pouring it out into the sink. "He put dead rats into your water tank."

Ackroyd widened his eyes and nodded. "Why on earth would a man do that?"

"It was his idea of a good way to drive you out. You know, make you sick. Make life out here . . . inconvenient, whatever you want to call it."

"And he shot my cat yesterday?"

Klein closed his eyes. The dirty little geek . . . "Yeah," he said. "I don't know that for a fact, but I'd bet he did."

Ackroyd merely nodded, and his silence made Klein feel like a treacherous fool. How the *hell* had he let himself be pushed so far by a creep like Pomeroy? Business is business, he would have said a week ago. Now business looked like something else. "Could you come out onto the porch for a second?" he asked. "I want to tell Lorna about this."

He followed the old man out. Lorna sat as ever. Probably she was thinking that once again he'd walked away just when it was vital that he stay. Had he *always* done that? He pushed the thought aside. "I was just telling Mr. Ackroyd that my business associate tried to poison his water supply."

Lorna reacted now, her eyes narrowing with shocked surprise. She shook her head slowly, as if at the betrayals and at the depths to which Klein had sunk.

"He put two or three dead rats into the tank," Klein said. "I didn't know about it till afterward. If I'd known what he was going to do I would have stopped him, but I didn't know."

"When *did* you know?" Lorna asked.

Klein suddenly remembered unerringly what he had felt when he'd first heard about the hillside slippage years ago, about the accident that had hurt the boy. He remembered the weeks of rationalizing and the knowledge all along that it wasn't any good, that words would never efface what had happened, nor would anything else— gifts, tickets to the baseball game, everything else he'd tried. In the years since, his doing nothing about the rats was the worst thing he'd done.

"You knew yesterday morning," she said, "when you had the fight with him."

"Yeah."

"And you didn't *say* anything? Why? How long were you going to let it go?"

"I wasn't . . . I was afraid, that's all."

She nodded, not asking for details. He couldn't think of anything more to say about it, to excuse it. He was willing to reveal all of it to her, but not in front of the old man, and for a dozen reasons, too. There was no use compromising a man like Ackroyd. From what Klein had heard from Lorna, Ackroyd was some kind of a missionary, a moral streak like a stone spine; there was no telling what he'd think he had to do if he knew about all of it—the fraud, the swindles.

"Well," Ackroyd said. "You've told me about it now, haven't you?"

"Believe me; I'm sorry it wasn't sooner."

"I believe you," Ackroyd said. "I suppose this man hoped to cause some kind of bacterial infection, probably salmonella. That's most likely. It's possible it hasn't had time to incubate yet. The water's cold. I drank tea this morning, so the water was boiled. Probably there's no harm done, except that I'll have to net the rats out and drain the tank."

"I'll pay to have it done," Klein said, hating the sound of the words even as he said them. "I don't mean that I think that makes up for anything, I just . . ."

Ackroyd waved the idea aside. "I know what you mean," Ackroyd said. "I'll take you up on it. I've got enough bottled drinking water to last a month. I'll use it for the coffee." He nodded and turned back through the door.

Klein sat down in the empty chair, already feeling battered. Lorna looked done in, like she hadn't slept worth a damn, and of course she hadn't. Suddenly he wondered how much he *could* tell her. How much could she stand? Maybe she'd just go to pieces on him. "I guess the first thing . . ." he started to say.

"The first thing is what were you doing last night? I can't believe you'd do that right there, in our own house, and when I was *there*, for God's sake. Don't you have *any* shame?" She shook her head slowly at him to illustrate her disbelief. A week ago the gesture would have been infuriating. "When that man called on the phone I thought he was lying, or crazy—anything else but that he was telling the truth."

"That bastard has *never* told the truth about anything," Klein said.

"Until last night, apparently," Lorna said.

Klein was silenced. "Until last night," he said finally.

"Who is she?"

"I don't know."

"You don't *know*?"

"She was the girl of my dreams," Klein said.

"God."

"I don't mean it like that. I mean the dreams I've been having—all of it happened last night, just like I dreamed it. I didn't even know at first if maybe it *was* a dream." He searched for the right words. This was coming out like some kind of idiot's excuse, like he was saying that the devil made him do it.

She was silent, staring across the road, where the wind was blowing through the trees again. The side of the house protected them from most of it, but a stray gust shook the roses, and a rain of white petals fell to the porch, a couple of them landing like big snowflakes on Lorna's sweater.

"Okay, that's partly a lie," Klein said. "I guess I knew it wasn't any kind of dream. I don't know what the hell it was."

Abruptly she started crying. Klein was lost. He wanted to put

his arm around her shoulder but he couldn't. He couldn't touch
her. She wouldn't want him to. Or even if she would, he didn't
know how. He never had touched anyone, not like that. He made
himself lay his palm on her arm, squeezing just a little. Then he
brushed the rose petals from her sleeve. "What can I say?" he
whispered. "I didn't . . . It wasn't . . ." He looked away,
breathing deeply.

"What does that mean?" she asked. "What you said about
your dreams?" She wiped her eyes with the sides of her hands.

"Nothing," he said. Thank God he'd never told her about them
in detail. It would just scare the hell out of her now. "It was just
a figure of speech. I guess what I meant was that the dreams were
guilt. If you really want to know, I met her at . . . through Winters," he lied. "You know him from the Spanglers' party. Big
guy, hugs everyone. He was putting together that charity trip
down to Mexicali."

She nodded, saying nothing.

"Well, she worked for him. Some kind of clerk or something.
She came to lunch a couple of times. I ran into her by accident
out at the mall once. Then she came by the house one day when
you were out at the club, said she just wanted to be friends and
all. I just . . . I don't know. She wore me down, I guess. The fight
we had yesterday and all. I had a couple of glasses of scotch. She
showed up last night, late, said she wanted to talk. . . ."

"And then she forced you to have sex with her."

"Don't *talk* like that. You know what I mean. *No*, she didn't
force me to do anything. We didn't *do* anything. You know what
happened. Everything just went crazy."

"What will the two of you do now?"

"The *two* of us? What do you think, we're a *couple*? She's
gone. It's over. I made that clear to her."

"Who was the man with the shovel?"

He shook his head. "I didn't even know she had a damned
husband. He followed her over or something. What a damned
mess that was."

"And I nearly shot him," Lorna said.

"That's all over and done. You *didn't* shoot him. I don't know
how to say this, how to make it sound right, but whatever happened yesterday or in the past, I want us to forget that. We have
to. We don't have a choice."

"Forget it?"

"What you were saying yesterday, about us being on the same

side and all instead of enemies. I never understood that before. I never thought about it. There was a lot I never thought about."

"Me too, I guess," Lorna said.

Klein wondered if she was talking about herself or about him. He hoped like hell she wasn't going to bring up the drinking. There was too much to talk about without that. And he was in no position to be critical of her, not right now. This was his time to unload, and he'd barely even got started. And now that it was happening, now that he was telling the truth at last, it was all coming out lies. Well, it wasn't the facts that mattered a damn bit. It was what it all meant, and he wasn't lying about that.

There was the smell of coffee just then, and Ackroyd came out through the screen with the pot and cups on a tray. "I've just got a few things to look after," he said, and went straight back inside.

Klein drank his coffee in silence, wishing that Lorna would say something, anything to make it easier on him. He realized suddenly that it was getting on into evening. The sun had disappeared behind the tree line, and the tree shadows were long and dark across the road.

"I guess I'll go after we finish the coffee," she said.

"Sure," he said. "You all right driving back at dusk like this? Visibility's bad."

"Yes."

"Did you mean what you said yesterday, about us being on the same side? Has that changed now?"

She shrugged. "I can't talk about that now. Give me some time to think."

"All right. But I've got something more to tell you, and it's not an easy thing to say. It's going to be part of what you think about, though, so I have to say it now, before you go. Afterward you can get mad or whatever you want, and I'll go or stay or . . ."

"It's that man again," she said to him. There was sudden fear in her voice, and she put her hand to her mouth. He shook his head even though it was true. He was almost happy that she reacted like that. It meant she still had a stake in him and in what he was. "How bad is it?" she asked. "What have you done?"

"I don't know," he said. "I honestly don't know. But I'll tell you what I tried to do."

**7**

BETH WATCHED FROM THE DOORWAY AS PETER ONCE AGAIN RE-
arranged the odds and ends on top of the old bookcases along the
wall. She felt restless and out of place, almost intrusive, and as
he worked, making what must have been minute adjustments in
the positions of things, he'd grown silent and preoccupied, and
the atmosphere in the room was leaden and close. What the room
needed—what Peter needed—was a dose of Bobby's Whoopee
Cushion. Or maybe just a dose of Bobby himself, although by
now she was glad she hadn't brought him along. This was too
morbid, too unsettling.

"What was the name of the Jetsons' dog?" she asked suddenly,
trying to distract him. "It wasn't Conroy, was it?" Her voice
sounded utterly out of place in the room, and the question fell
flat. It even sounded to her like lunacy. She'd meant to force him
to sing the theme song to the old television program, but something in the atmosphere made that kind of clowning around almost
physically impossible.

And anyway, he didn't answer. After several seconds of silence
he looked up at her with a puzzled frown, then went straight back
to work, polishing the glass panes in the bookcase doors now.
Many of them were cracked, and the glass was so dusty and filmy
that the few books within were visible only as a dark blur. As he
wiped them clean, the glass reflected the candlelight, and the
books behind the glass gained dimension, their outlines and age-
dimmed colors growing distinct. Outside, the wind seemed to
heighten, as if it drew energy from the darkness.

Peter moved a glass decanter on the bookcase a half inch to
the right of where it had been sitting, then leaned over to examine
the wood, shifting the decanter slightly again. There were four
cut-crystal glasses next to it. Two of them were broken, but he
arranged the broken glasses as carefully as the others, examining
the wood closely before drawing a book out of the case and laying

it next to the glasses. After peering at all four edges of the book, he picked it up, put it back into the case, and drew out another one, blowing the dust off the top before laying it down.

"It's strange how you can tell just where things ought to go," he said suddenly, the sound of his voice breaking the tension in the room. He struck a match, stepping to one of the tarnished old candleabras and relighting two candles that had gone out.

"*Ought* to go? According to whom?"

"According to all the marks on things, the traces and shadows. You can see the rings where the glasses and the decanter sat. Must have been years in the same place. The finish is discolored underneath. It's the same under the book. It's lighter than the wood that was exposed around it. Out of all the books in the crates, I think I've found the one that must have been left sitting there."

"Good," she said. "It probably *wants* to be there, after all that time."

"That's it exactly." He stood back and looked at the wall, gesturing at one of the chairs in front of the hearth. "Go ahead and sit down," he said. But abruptly he leaned down and looked at the chair legs, then shifted the chair minutely on the rug.

"Just right," she said, testing out the chair cushion. "We'll be living easy when the porridge cools down."

"I want to reproduce a scene," he said, oblivious to the tone of her voice.

"Why does that give me the creeps?" she asked.

He busied himself with the fire, carefully feeding it broken eucalyptus branches.

"Why don't we trade chairs for a while, just to break the spell? You sit in mine and I'll sit in yours. Maybe *I'll* get a chance to see the ghosts then, and you'll have a chance to see it all from my perspective. And while we're at it, I don't mean to complain, but those paintings on the wall are just downright ghastly, aren't they? Whoever painted them never paid any attention to sunlight."

He looked distant, lost in thought, as if he couldn't or wouldn't listen to that kind of talk, and for a moment he sat there in silence, tilting his head slightly as if he were listening.

"Did you know that a few minutes ago you called me . . ." she started to say.

He held his hand up, and she stopped, waiting for him. Then she heard something. From somewhere far away, and yet from no real direction, there came a scattering of sounds—nothing she could identify absolutely, what with the wind and the crackling of the fire. Taken altogether it sounded vaguely like the rustle and shuffle and clink of an occupied room. There was a sound like a cat meowing, and then, unmistakably, a door shutting. Peter narrowed his eyes, waiting, but the sounds diminished and were gone. "I guess it's nothing," he said finally.

"No, it wasn't nothing," she said. "I heard it, too."

"Did you *smell* anything?" His voice was animated, eager.

"The fire, maybe. It's pretty smoky in here. Look, I think I really *did* hear something. What's going on?"

"I don't know. I thought I smelled whiskey, and maybe jasmine, a woman's perfume."

"You're more tuned in," Beth said. Too tuned in, she thought.

"Did you start to say something a moment ago?"

"I was going to say that you called me Esther again."

"When?" He stared at her.

"Just a moment ago, when I was standing in the doorway. I *guess* you were talking to me."

"I remember saying something, but I don't remember what."

"I'm *very* skeptical of this," she said seriously.

"Think of it as a scientific test." He stepped away from the fire and surveyed the room critically.

"Do you want me to write it all down?" she asked. "Maybe by being *really* scientific about it we can keep it under control."

"Like having rules in a boxing match," he said. "Marquis of Queensberry."

"Exactly. We'll force it to behave rationally. That's the thing with ghosts. They're like spoiled children, always demanding to have their way. Sometimes you've got to take a hard line with them."

He grew silent again, distant, clearly unable to keep up any kind of banter. "What do you think of the room?" he asked finally, gesturing at the newly rearranged furniture, apparently satisfied at last.

"Nice," she said. "Good thing the light's dim, I guess."

"I wanted things to be perfect, the way things used to be. I've got this picture in my mind that's almost photographic—sort of developed while I was working, as if the room was waiting all these years to be restored."

"Uncanny," she said flatly.

"There were depressions in the rug from the feet of the chairs

and tables, and the wall was shadowed around where the bookcases used to stand. There was even a sort of afterimage of
shadow on the bookcase shelves so that I could make out where
each of the books had been. Mostly they're old medical books,
but there's a few novels that must have belonged to her."

"Esther, you mean?"

He nodded, lost in thought again.

"I'm not sure you should be so anxious to give these things
what they *want*."

"You sound like Mr. Ackroyd."

"It's because I don't know what we're doing, and I'm telling
you it's starting to scare me. I'll admit it. In the daylight it all
sounded reasonable. Now it doesn't."

He reached across the table and put his hand on her arm. "I
still don't know what happened to Amanda and David," he said,
"but I believe they're here somewhere. I don't think they ever
left at all."

"You've said that. After all that's happened to you, I guess I
can't argue with it. But admit it—it's just a little obsessive, re-
storing the room so fanatically, putting everything in its place like
you were getting ready to perform a spell. It's like sending the
devil an invitation."

"Listen to that wind!" Peter said, sidetracking.

"I don't like the wind," she said. It made a strange humming
sound outside, blowing through chinks and cracks in the old
house, which shook ominously with successive gusts.

He left her statement hanging in the air, unanswered. The
flames in the fireplace burned with a silvery glow, threads of
trailing smoke drawn downward, through the cracks between the
stones of the hearth. It was a miracle that the old chimney was
standing at all.

Suddenly nervous, she stood up and walked to the window,
looking out at the dark woods. She was damned if she was going
to be a prisoner of another woman's chair, no matter how carefully positioned it was. Peter sat in silence, seemingly unaware
that she'd gotten up. She glanced back at him. He was gone again,
lost in the ozone. It was going to be an evening of long silences
despite the very nice afternoon they'd spent together. Actually,
the afternoon had contained some long silences, too, but of a
different variety.

After their doughnut conversation she had known that they
were going to see their various troubles through together. She'd

had to convince him of that—to let her stay with him tonight, as a sort of brake. In the end he'd seen reason. And now here she was, trying to talk him out of whatever harebrained thing he was up to.

The moon hadn't risen yet, and the night outside the windows was a mass of moving shadows that were only barely discernible as trees. The candles cast a flickering glow that seemed almost to reflect off the wall of darkness beyond the glass. Dimly, from somewhere out in the night, came the sound of weeping. She tensed, listening. It trailed away into silence. She heard only the wind and the clicking of leaves and twigs against the wooden siding like tapping fingers. The crackling of the fire sounded unnaturally loud behind her, and seemed to contain within it the noises she'd heard earlier—the clink of glasses, the groaning of springs in a seat cushion, the swish of book pages turning.

She glanced at Peter. He seemed almost to be scowling, his face dark and unhappy.

"Penny for your thoughts," she said, walking to his chair.

He was silent. She could see the fire reflected in his unblinking eyes.

"What's six times six?" She looked straight into his face, waving her hand in front of his eyes, snapping her fingers.

"What?" His voice was flat, trancelike.

"Quick," she said, "what's the capital of Ohio? Say something. *Speak.*"

He stared into the fire.

"Where did King Henry keep his armies?" she asked, right into his face. "Come on, tell me. Don't make me hurt you."

He blinked at her, shook his head, maybe grappling with the ridiculous question.

"In his *sleevies*," she said, then waited.

He looked at her in utter bewilderment, as if she'd gone crazy.

"It's a *joke*. Get it? Armies, sleevies, handsies . . . Heh, heh." She laughed woodenly.

Then, in a voice like an incantation, Peter said, "Moses supposes his noses are roses, but Moses supposes erroneously."

"Thank God," she said, collapsing backward into her chair. A cloud of dust rose around her, and she waved her hand through it, turning her face. "I thought you wigged out on me. Are you okay? You keep zoning out. It's better if you talk."

"What's better if I talk?" He yawned and stretched. "I nearly fell asleep there."

"With your eyes open? What were you staring at?"

He started to say something, then stopped abruptly. His head swiveled toward the window, and a noise escaped his throat—the sound of raw fear. Beth twisted around to look, half standing up out of the chair, her heart accelerating.

A boy stood just outside, staring in, his face the color of gray clay in the dim light. The wind blew through his hair, and one of his hands was pressed against a pane of glass. His dull eyes searched the room for a moment before he turned away, gliding into the darkness beyond the edge of the window frame.

KLEIN TOLD HER ALL OF IT—ABOUT WINTERS AND SLOANE, about Pomeroy and their dealings with the local cabin owners, the fraud, the collusion. Getting out from under it would cost them. If they were lucky they could resell the cabins at some kind of profit, pay off the fronts, pay off Winters and Sloane, put it all behind them. The words rushed out until he had played it all through, even his finding out about Pomeroy's obsession with Beth and his confrontation with Pomeroy in Beth's house yesterday.

She looked at him and shrugged, shaking her head again. "I don't know what to say," she said. "Except that I knew. I knew there was something, and I knew that it was getting to you. That's what I was talking about yesterday afternoon."

He realized suddenly that he'd come to the end of it. He couldn't tell her anything more. He had driven out here determined to unburden himself of the whole story—the blackmail, revelations about his past. But he saw that there was no reason for that now. Pomeroy was dead. And he knew that he couldn't tell her about the blackmail anyway. If holding that back was the same as lying, then he'd have to learn to live with being a liar. Telling her anything about Pomeroy's death, about moving the body, ditching the car and identification papers, would make her an accessory. What could she do, turn him in? Or would she live with the day-to-day, month-to-month fear of his being arrested?

Once again Pomeroy would have insinuated himself into their lives, his ghost muttering threats, making his nasty phone calls from the grave. Bury him, Klein told himself. For Lorna's own protection he had to stop talking now. Confession was over. It was true that a day might come when there was a knock on the door, and men in gray suits stood outside wanting to ask a few questions about a body found in the hills. But if that day *did* come, then at least he could tell Lorna truthfully that he had kept it from her out of love and hope. . . .

She was staring at him, waiting for him to say something.

"That's all," he stammered. "What I want to say is that I know I haven't been paying any attention to us, to you. It's obvious now. But I swear it wasn't obvious a couple of days ago."

She nodded now, instead of shrugging. And it wasn't exaggerated; the nod wasn't meant to be ironic. She understood him. He reached across and squeezed her arm again, and although he had to force himself to do it, he said, "I love you," and then sat back in his chair, the words sounding rusty from disuse.

She smiled just a little, as if at the idea of him trying so damned hard to do something he wasn't very good at. "I was thinking of going to the AA meeting at Saddleback Hospital Tuesday night."

"Why?" he said, suddenly coming to her defense. "There's no way you've got *that* kind of problem. Just because I might have said a couple of stupid things . . . "

"They weren't stupid things. They might have been *mean* things, but they were true."

He started to argue with her, but then stopped abruptly. He was doing it again—pretending that nothing mattered, that it was better to keep your head in the sand. "All right," he said. "There's no harm in checking it out. Maybe I'll tag along."

She set her coffee cup down and stood up, leaning against the porch railing. The moon was just showing above the ridge, and the sky was full of stars. He stood next to her and put his arm around her awkwardly, half expecting her to shrug it off. After a long time she said, "It's beautiful out here when the wind blows," and she leaned her head against his shoulder.

**9**

BETH FOLLOWED PETER THROUGH THE BACK DOOR, DOWN THE wooden stairs, grabbing onto the handrail to steady herself against the wind that swept across the road and rushed through the forest trees. The gray trunks of alders bent before it, and the heavy limbs of oaks and sycamores swung ominously in the darkness. Moonlight shone on the bricks of the walkway, illuminating the leaves that skittered past, the moon itself barely risen above the ridge.

Something moved along the edge of the house, in the dark shadow of the rock retaining wall. Peter stopped abruptly, shouting to warn her, and she grabbed his arm to steady him, looking past him, expecting to see the boy. Instead, a man stood staring straight back at them, through them, his dark coattails flapping in the wind, his hair wild, eyes livid with rage. He held a piece of broken tree limb in his hand, which he threw angrily into the forest, suddenly striding forward as if he meant to run them down. Peter trod backward, pushing Beth behind him, and just then the man vanished. For an instant he was a mere patch of pale radiance like moonlit dust, and then he was gone.

She was aware of the boy crying now, the sound of it close, impossibly loud on the wind. She stood clutching Peter, who breathed heavily, his face a mask of fear. He shut his eyes and said to her, "Did that look like me?"

"What do you mean?" she half shouted, barely able to hear him above the wind. The night was full of noise, the crying and a deep buzzing like bees in a hive.

"He looked like me."

She shook her head and shouted, "*No*, he didn't." The man, ghost, whatever it was, hadn't looked anything like Peter. He was dark, with deep eyes, and heavy browed. . . . "Let's go back in," she shouted, pulling on Peter's arm. But he cocked his head then, listening, as if just now conscious of the crying.

The latticework gate blocking the open cellar swung slowly

open on its hinges, and something darted past, straight into the
cellar. A cat? She'd seen only a gray shape. Peter stepped warily
toward the gate, shining the beam of a flashlight along the retaining wall. They stopped outside, peering in, Peter playing the light
across the stone piers and the broad base of the chimney.

Was the boy under there? She pictured the face at the window,
blank and staring, discolored by the yellow light of the candles.
*It's just a little boy,* she told herself, listening to the crying. It
was farther away now, maybe deeper under the house, maybe
somewhere off within the fringe of the woods.

"All right!" Peter shouted. "Come on out!"

There was no response, no movement in the darkness. He bent
over and shined the flashlight into the recesses of the cellar, but
the beam was weak, and the cellar itself was full of rubble and
stone piers and wooden supports that threw myriad shadows,
making it impossible to see clearly beyond a few feet.

Then something fluttered against the downhill lattice, not ten
feet distant—a pale shape like a drift of suspended muslin buoyed
by the wind. Peter pointed the flashlight at it, and for an instant,
just before the beam illuminated it, Beth saw that it was the figure
of the boy, standing with something in his arms—the gray cat.
Then the light shone on it, revealing a broad drape of dusty cobweb hanging from an overhead beam. The wind pushed it sideways, into an amorphous shape. There was no cat, nothing at all
human about the cobweb.

Peter stared at it for another moment before turning toward her.
He took a step away from the gate. "Why don't you go back
inside?" he said, gesturing with the light toward the candlelit
parlor windows. She could see the old bookcases inside, along
the far wall, the decanter and glasses on top, the framed pictures,
the two empty chairs. From outside it looked almost elegant, pris-
tine, unaffected by the years and neglect. She shook her head.
"Not without you."

The gate started to creak shut, and Peter reached out and
pushed it solidly open, then rolled a rock in front of it, blocking
it there. He suddenly bent down and kissed her, and then, taking
her hand, he ducked into the interior of the cellar.

She could just barely stand beneath the low beams, and she
raked the air in front of her to push away cobwebs. The cellar
stretched away before them, the height of the ceiling diminishing
nearly to nothing at the uphill end. The fireplace chimney sat next
to the gate, its wide base flaring down into the ground almost like

tree roots. The chimney was massive, as if the builder had gotten carried away with the abundance of river rock lining the creek and hadn't known when to stop building. The stones were mixed up with patches of clinker bricks, the joints slopping over with old mortar.

She followed Peter as he moved toward the center of the room, picking his way through the debris that lay in the loose dirt—scraps of lumber and iron pipe, broken clinker brick, and old garden tools. He cast the beam of the flashlight into the far corners and along the wall, stooping beneath sagging floor joists that were black with age and strung with the silky white orbs of spider eggs.

Dead autumn leaves lay heaped in a low hillock against the wooden lattice that fenced the cellar, and Beth could hear the *snick, snick, snick* of something moving through them. They stirred in a mass, like a sleeping person shifting beneath bed covers. When the flashlight shone on them, Peter recoiled, as if he'd seen something there. She heard him whisper.

"What?" she asked.

Silence.

"You said something."

"Nothing." He turned the light away, sweeping it across the base of the chimney before shining it on the leaves again.

"I don't think he's under here," Beth whispered. "What are you looking for?" There was a vague glow to the darkness, a phosphorescent haziness, as if smoky moonlight were filtering through the lattice, filling the room. It came to her that smoke was drifting downward from the fireplace in the room above. It swirled in the eddying winds. The hillock of leaves shuddered again.

"*She's* here," Peter whispered. The crying had diminished now, the wind momentarily hushed.

Beth held her breath, looking at the leaves. She could almost make out a human shape in it now—the curve of a shoulder and hip, a woman lying on her side, covered in a cloak woven of autumn leaves.

"Amanda?" Peter whispered.

Beth put her hand to her mouth. Peter's voice was husky, deeper. He stepped toward the leaves, falling to his knees in the soft dirt and rock, reaching out a trembling hand to caress the assemblage of leaves with the beam of light.

"Peter?" Beth said to him, her voice rising. She pushed his shoulder.

He was oblivious to her. A gust of wind rattled the lattice, as if in answer, the leaves sighing out a sibilant whisper. Peter dropped the flashlight into the dirt. He shook his head slightly, as if denying something. His words sounded like a quiet prayer. The room was aglow now, the dirt and debris of the floor shining silver. Tendrils of smoke gathered on the floor, circulating in the drifting air. Peter bent forward and ran a hand carefully across the top of the leaves, which bunched together, pressing up along the lattice in a dark mass like a half-animated thing trying to rise. A scattering of them pushed through the lattice and whirled away into the moonlit night.

Beth took an involuntary step backward, suppressing the wild urge to run toward the propped-open gate. She searched the ground around her, looking frantically at the collection of junk that lay scattered in the dirt. There must be something, anything. . . . She snatched up a straight stick, the handle of some long-ruined garden tool.

The leaves tilted toward Peter, shuffling together, drawn upright. A voice whispered—"Esther," it said, a man's voice, not Peter's, a voice full of sadness and longing. She turned and looked behind her, lifting the stick, but there was nothing there, nothing but the heaped stone and brick of the chimney, occluded by the smoke that curled languorously before it, rising like a candle flame.

Beth stepped past Peter, striking out with the stick, flailing at the moving leaves, slashing at them as Peter recoiled in evident horror. He snatched frantically at the stick, stumbling to his feet. She evaded his grasp, lunged forward in a crouch and whipped the stick left and right, leaves scattering, flattening against the lattice. The air was full of them, a sudden whirlwind of leaves, the wind moaning, the walls vibrating.

"Stop!" Peter shouted, grabbing at her wrist, his face twisted into such an expression of fear and anger that she hardly knew him. His features flickered in her vision, and she was filled with the strange sensation that Peter was falling away from her, as if into a vast chasm, and that some other thing was rushing forward to occupy the space where he had been. The standing smoke in front of the old chimney pulsed and swirled. Beyond it a shadow grew, filling the smoke with darkness and solidity.

Peter's hand clasped her arm as he reached again for the stick. She jammed her elbow backward, feeling it hit his chest. Jerking away from him and taking the stick in both hands, she waded forward into the leaves, swinging the stick like a baseball bat. It tore through them, the dry leaves spinning behind it, the stick whirring around so fast and hard that she turned with it, unable to stop it from cracking Peter on the forehead as he lunged in to grab at her again.

There was a sharp snap as the stick broke, and a simultaneous rush of wind and sound. She dropped the stick and grabbed Peter's shoulders with both hands as he stumbled forward, a line of blood appearing on his brow over his left eye.

"I'm sorry!" she shouted, trying to dab at the blood with the sleeve of her shirt and at the same time to drag him toward the open gate. He shrugged away from her, staggering against a post that supported the floor. He touched his forehead with his hand, looking blankly at his bloodstained fingertips. There was a sound like static on a television tuned to a dead station, and disembodied voices drifted on the circulating air.

A window appeared in the twilight in front of her eyes, a pale, hovering rectangle that seemed to open onto infinite space. Through it Beth could see a black shadow like something crouched toadlike in the far distance. The sound of the staticky wind rushed in her ears. She could hear a tumult of faint noises above it, within it—the boy's weeping, a woman's voice calling from somewhere far away, the sound of laughter and of glass clinking against glass, the cheerful fluting of "The Merry Old Land of Oz."

The shadow within the rectangle drew nearer, approaching her in little staccato leaps like a jerky black-and-white film. It was the figure of a man, rushing forward now. She stepped backward, throwing up her hands, and felt a rush of cold wind that droned through the cellar like flies in a paper cup. She threw her hands up in front of her face, recoiling from it, turning toward Peter, then shouting out loud in fear and surprise.

Peter was gone.

A man stood in the center of the cellar—the man they'd seen outside. He seemed to look straight through her, as if she weren't there at all, his features growing slowly more animate, like a man just regaining consciousness.

She ran, through the propped-open gate, around the side of the house and out toward the windswept road, where she looked back over her shoulder at the house. Shadows moved within the candlelit parlor, and the wind carried to her ears the myriad sounds of the room coming back to life at long last.

**10**

ACKROYD FOUND IT IMPOSSIBLE TO READ, ESPECIALLY TO READ Chesterton, who demanded more concentration than he possessed tonight. There was too much wind, too much noise and movement. The moonlit road outside was a constant distraction. He shut the book and laid it on the table. Since dark he'd seen no one out and about in the canyon, not even a car. And probably he wouldn't, not on a weekday night and with the Santa Anas blowing. People were locked inside their houses, waiting out the darkness and the weather.

He stood up and walked to the bookcase, sliding back one of the doors and removing a big mahogany box. Inside the box lay a set of painted tin soldiers, the paint half chipped off. He had lost a couple of the soldiers over the years, but that and the chipped paint and the years themselves were simply the price you had to pay for your memories. Esther had never tired of helping him build fortifications out of stacks of books on the parlor carpet—caves and canyons, tall towers with hidden rooms smelling of dusty old paper, regiments of soldiers marching down the long Sunday afternoons to do battle on fields of dark green Chinese wool.

He took out a few of the soldiers now and set them on the dining room table, glancing up at the photo of him and his sister and suddenly feeling a little sheepish, as if she could see him there, still playing with tin soldiers at his age. Moonlight shone on the road outside now, but the road was still empty, and maybe just as well so. There was no percentage in chasing phantoms through the night, trying to recapture something irretrievably lost years and years ago.

He recalled the day she'd gotten back from a summer visit to Michigan. He and Aunt Lydia had met her at Union Station in Los Angeles, and when she'd climbed down off the train with her newly bobbed hair, she was carrying the box. He'd known straightaway that it was for him. He could see it in her eyes, although she'd pretended it was a fruitcake, so full of brandy, she said, that he wouldn't even be allowed to taste it. She had peeked inside, laughing, rolling her eyes as if clobbered by the reek of brandy. Finally he'd snatched it out of her hands, pulling back the lid to reveal the ranks of soldiers within, line after line of them in neat little doweled racks.

He could remember everything about that day—the palm trees against a blue sky, the vast station with its leather seats and chandeliers and painted ceilings, the long platforms, the sound of the train whistle, the reek of smoke, the milling of the crowds. They'd eaten in an elegant restaurant, and his aunt, he remembered, had ordered Belgian hare, and he had done the same, proud to be ordering something so exotic that he had no idea what it was. When it turned out to be rabbit, he couldn't eat it, and so he had sat through the meal in disgrace, his food untouched.

Laying all of the soldiers except one neatly back into the box, he shut the lid, then set the box back onto its shelf. The leftover soldier he put into his pocket where he kept other small mementos, not luck charms, really, just—what?—maybe small fragments of memory. He had a token from the Chicago World's Fair, an abalone button that he'd found among his mother's things, a big blue rhinestone that he'd unearthed digging in the vegetable garden. Sometime last week he lost a polished opal that he'd carried in his pocket for years, and now this soldier would volunteer to take its place.

Yesterday at the veterinarian's office he had decided to give the box of soldiers to Bobby, to Beth's son. The boy had taken it hard—Sheba's being hurt—even though he didn't really know the cat very well. It was tough now just to think about it, the boy sitting beside her in the backseat all the way down to Dr. Stone's office. He'd talked to Sheba continually, trying to convince her to hold on, even told her a quiet story about when he'd hurt himself falling off a fence, but it turned out to be nothing, which was almost always what happened. Well, *something* had convinced the old cat to hold on; why not believe it was a six-year-old's compassion? Probably Bobby wouldn't have eaten the Belgian hare, either, once he knew it was really a rabbit.

It was time to turn out the lamp; there was nothing to be gained by summoning up memories like old ghosts. Inevitably they'd vanish into the darkness. He walked across to the oil lamp next to the reading chair and twisted the wick down, then cupped his

hand over the chimney and blew the flame out. At that moment,
when the room plunged into darkness, he saw a woman on the
road, and he had to grab onto the back of the chair to steady
himself.

He saw then that she had long blond hair. It wasn't Esther.
She swept her hair back with her hand, running up the stairs onto
the porch, pounding on the door even as he stepped across to
open it.

HE WENT OUT INTO THE NIGHT WITHOUT HIS COAT, FOLLOWING
Beth onto the porch and into a blast of wind, dragging the door
shut behind him as she took his elbow and hurried him forward.
She shouted into his ear, the wind snatching her words away. He
caught only bits and pieces of what she was saying—Peter's disappearance, the ghosts, something about the cellar. . . .

The lights of the house shone through the trees, and he could
see moonlit smoke tumbling out of the chimney. His fingers
closed around the tin soldier in his pocket as dust swirled up from
the road, gyrating toward them in a dozen skittering wind devils.
He heard on the wind what sounded like the scratchy notes of
antique music. He recognized the melody. In his memory he could
hear his sister humming it.

Her face came into his mind. He recalled the touch of her hand
on the afternoon of their parents' funeral, when he was five years
old, the timeless week that followed, Esther reading to him for
hours on end—*On the Back of the North Wind, The Princess and
the Goblin, The King of the Golden River*—the two of them in
the back garden through the still and sunny afternoons, their
chairs shaded by tall rows of pole beans, the air heavy with the
scent of orange blossom.

"Hurry," he whispered, but already she was stepping into the
darkened living room. She pulled the door silently shut behind
them. At the opposite end of the room a flickering light shone

past the edge of the nearly closed parlor door. There was a sleepy, languorous atmosphere in the house, something molasses heavy, scented with the smoky menthol smell of burning eucalyptus from the fireplace in the parlor. He couldn't hear the music anymore, and the sound of the wind diminished to a distant rush beyond the sheltering walls of the house. Their footsteps creaked on the floorboards, and he could hear his own breathing and the sound of blood rushing in his ears. He peered past the edge of the parlor door, into the candlelit room. . . .

Esther sat in her customary chair before the fire. Her hair long, grown out. The doctor, Dr. Landry, hadn't liked it bobbed—too frivolous. And she'd taken to dressing in dark colors, usually black, as if she were in mourning for something she'd lost. She was dressed that way now, exactly as he'd seen her when she stood on the road two nights ago, her hair swept by the wind, the dress a dusty black in the light of the moon. Now she was composed, sitting in front of the hearth, a book open in her hands.

Her husband sat in the other chair, a decanter and glass on the table. The boy, Jamie, lounged on the rug behind them, his back to the window, playing an endless game of Puzzle Peg. His hand moved across the board, picking up the blue-painted wooden pegs and dropping them to the carpet, new pegs appearing on the board in an endless succession, the discarded pegs blinking away one by one. There was the sound of book pages turning, of the logs crackling in the hearth, of the *click, click, click* of the wooden pegs. The fire rose and fell in the fireplace as if it were breathing.

He remembered the room from sixty years past, knew now what he had known then, when he was fourteen years old and had visited his sister that last lonely time—that this room was an extension of the man who had built it, a manifestation of his will. The enchantment in its careful design was meant to function as an impenetrable hedge of briar. There was nothing that betrayed the room's connection to the outside world, not a stray slip of paper, not a piece of newsprint, not a hint in the carefully arranged ornaments and books or in the solemn, timeless prints on the wall—nothing suggested that the room was subject to time or change.

He felt something tugging on his sleeve. The sensation registered slowly, calling him back along the years. Beth stood behind him in the dark living room. She gestured at the front door, urging him to follow her. She whispered something, but he only half heard it. He shook his head. He couldn't leave now, not yet. He peered into the still room again, listening to her footfalls across the wooden floor, hearing a door close in another room. Then, when he was alone in the empty darkness, he whispered his sister's name, half expecting that the room and all that was in it would vanish on the instant, like an image in a suddenly broken mirror.

UTTERLY ALONE, BETH WENT OUT THROUGH THE BACK DOOR, remembering that the flashlight was under the house where Peter had dropped it. Maybe it wasn't broken or burned out. He'd put away the tools that used to be scattered around the parlor floor, but she remembered a length of pipe lying in the dirt of the cellar. That would do.

The moon had risen in the starry sky, illuminating the chipped white paint that peeled from the woven lath of the cellar gate. She held on to the rough, weathered frame, looking once again into the dim room beyond, at the sloping dirt of the littered floor, the dark hidden corners. She stepped inside, moving across to the chimney, and ran her hand across the patchwork masonry, the random masses of clinker brick and stone, and the crumbling lines of mortar slopped from the untooled joints. She snapped a long slab of it loose and dropped it into the dirt.

On the ground lay the piece of pipe, a couple of feet long and half-hidden by junk. She grabbed the end, twisting it out from under scrap wood and debris, then knocked it against the chimney stones to shake loose the clinging webs and leaves and dirt. Gripping it solidly, she swung it at a heavy granite boulder, the cornerstone of the chimney. The pipe hit it with a dead ring, rust flakes spraying across the backs of her hands. She hit it again, harder, knocking off a fragment of stone that flew up and stung her cheek, and she dropped the pipe and wiped her cheek with her sleeve.

The wind gusted, swirling through the lattice behind her, raising a cloud of leaves and dust that nearly choked her. She buried her face in the crook of her arm, waiting it out. Abruptly she swung the pipe again, slamming it into a patch of bricks now, the echoing *thump* filling the cellar. Cracks radiated outward from where the pipe crushed into the brick, and mortar and brick chips cascaded to the ground. At the next blow a grapefruit-sized stone broke free and fell out whole. She stepped out of the way, leaned back and chunked the pipe into a patch of cracked bricks, which showered to the floor in a dusty avalanche.

The air swirled with brick grit and windblown leaves and rang with the sound of falling debris and of iron clanging over and over against stone until finally she tossed the pipe aside, unable to swing it any more, and began to pull fragments of brick out with her hands. Abruptly a patch of bricks fell inward, exposing a rectangular hole, nothing but black air behind it. She stopped, suddenly fearful, almost surprised to discover so suddenly that she'd been right: the deep base of the chimney was hollow. Carefully now she dislodged more bricks and stones, wiggling them out of their slots and depressions. Lines of mortar tugged away, and loose bricks simply fell out, tumbling to the floor.

The flashlight . . . She turned and saw it through the hovering dust, lying where Peter had dropped it. She picked it up and pushed the switch, the light feeble and dim until she shined it into the utter darkness of the cavity within the hollow chimney. At first she could see nothing, just a cloud of dust slowly settling. Then she could see that something stood against the outside wall of the chimney, maybe two feet away from her—a couple of narrow shelves suspended from chains and hooks affixed to the mortar. There were objects sitting on the shelves, ill-defined shadows growing slowly visible in the settling dust. . . .

On the top shelf a black beaded purse sat tilted against the stones. There was the likeness of an owl on it in white beads, and the name ''Esther'' beneath the owl's feet. The beadwork was ragged and patchy as if the purse had been carried for years, perhaps by a child. Next to the purse stood a photograph in a frame of hammered copper—the likeness of a man and a woman. She shined the flashlight on it. Even through the dust the man's eyes looked dark and obsessed. The woman held something in her hand, which was curled back across her chest, and she gazed at some distant point, as if her mind were miles away. Next to the photograph lay a silver-handled hairbrush and matching hand mirror, the mirror's dust-hazed glass reflecting the darkness

above. Lying atop the mirror was a gold ring—a wedding band—
and a bracelet that was a spiral of tarnished silver set with dark
stones that might have been jet. Beside the mirror sat a crystal
bulldog with garnets for eyes. Behind it, also tilted against the
stones, was a book with a pale leather binding, on the cover of
which was painted a single blue lupine. A crystal perfume bottle
sat open and alone near the edge of the table, its faceted stopper
lying beside it.

When she saw the dark residue of the evaporated scent in the
bottom of the bottle, it seemed to her that she could smell jasmine
on the cool cellar air. She knew exactly why the bottle had been
left unstoppered. Then into her mind came the image of the
woman in the photograph, walking along the windblown ridges
above the canyon, her dress and hair blowing out behind her. She
clutched a handful of enormous papery white poppies that stood
out against blue sky like clouds.

ONLY VAGUELY CONSCIOUS OF THE SOUND OF THE WIND AND OF
a muffled pounding somewhere far away, he stood in the doorway
watching her for an indeterminate time. She hadn't looked up
when he whispered her name, hadn't glanced away from the fire.
The logs in the fireplace settled, a wash of sparks rising up the
chimney, and the wind keened through the dark night.

And even if she knew him after the long years, what would he
say to her that she didn't already know?

He could see now that she looked like photographs of their
mother—the raven hair, the dark eyes full of a sadness like the
passing of seasons as she stared over the top of her book, mes-
merized by the flames. He hadn't been old enough to see it when
she'd died—neither the resemblance to his mother nor the autumn
shadow in her eyes. He realized now that all his memories of her
were circumscribed by a few brief years of his boyhood like the
handful of trinkets in his pocket. The scattered moments were

reflected in the pages of illustrated books read in a sunlit back garden, in rainwater pattering against parlor windows behind tin soldiers ranked along the wooden sill, in dusty country roads where they would find the first wildflowers of spring. She would let him pick only a few, only the prettiest, because a star would fall out of the sky, she said, and somewhere a person would die, for each flower in the bouquet.

Now, as he watched her sitting before the fire, the sadness in her eyes was as clear to him as the passing years, and he regretted that he'd left the quiet of his house and come out into the night. The wind blows to the south, he thought, and goes round to the north; and on its circuits the wind returns. . . .

He opened his hand and looked at the painted tin soldier that he'd been holding in his palm like an amulet. After a moment he returned it to his pocket.

A SCATTERING OF CHILDREN'S TOYS STOOD ON THE SECOND shelf—marbles and a windup tin duck, a pocketknife, and the carved wooden head of an Indian that sat atop three dusty books, the spines turned away so that she couldn't read the titles. A dozen feathers lay next to the books, their quills tied together with a string. There was another framed photograph, too, this one of a thin ascetic-looking boy with sleepy eyes. He stood holding a gray cat in his arms in a sunlit clearing in the woods.

The hollow within the chimney was a shrine, set up to the memory of the woman and boy, the collection of trinkets reverently arranged, and then the narrow room sealed up like a crypt. She was reminded suddenly of Peter, arranging and rearranging the parlor with a thoroughness that was nearly fanatic, trying to re-create something, to reanimate something that was long ago dead and gone. . . .

She set the flashlight on a shelf of broken brick so that it illuminated the interior of the chimney, then leaned in, reaching through the darkness to pick up the perfume bottle. The scent of jasmine was strong within the enclosure, mingled with the smell of smoke. She cast her eyes downward to the floor below the edge of the shelf. Against the wall lay a tin pail, a rusted trowel, a gallon jug, and a small heap of brick. Sitting atop the brick was a glass tumbler and a tarnished silver flask.

Beside the flask lay a dead man, his face tilted up toward the light.

She jerked her hand back, accidentally sweeping the glass stopper off the shelf with the edge of her palm. Something pushed her, solidly, like hands against her shoulders, and she reeled backward, grabbing onto an edge of broken brick to keep from falling. She heard the stopper clatter against the tin pail, its ringing echo reverberating against the walls of the chimney.

There were sounds of movement in the room above, telegraphed through the stones of the chimney itself, growing in volume until she could hear every small rustle and click, even the breathing of the three occupants, as if the reanimated family had grown even more insistently real. She pressed her hands over her ears, trying to crush out the noise, but that seemed only to magnify it, and her head was filled with the sound of voices raised in anger, a woman's drawn-out scream, the plaintive cries of a lost child wandering through the windy, midnight darkness. . . .

A wild, disconnected terror arose in her mind, like a night fear rising through a dark and incongruous dream. In her panic she turned toward the open gate, suddenly compelled to flee. Beyond the moonlit wall the forest trees bent and waved, ridden by the wind. She heard the sound of a woman's voice, calling from somewhere far away, from the open spaces above the canyon. And then abruptly, as if awakening from a dream, she realized that the voice was her own. She stood looking around her at the dim cellar, breathing in ragged gasps.

Picking up the flashlight, she forced herself to look at the thing on the floor inside the chimney. It sat in a slumped heap, a mummified human dressed in dusty rags, the leather-covered skull bent forward across the collarbone. Its cheekbones showed through rents in the dried skin of its face, the color of dirty ivory in the reflected light, and its hands were curled and brown like monkey paws.

She stared at him, the house quiet now. How long ago had he locked himself away behind the layers of brick and stone? And the flask—poison? Did he drink it and *then* set about bricking himself in, mixing mortar in the pail while the poison worked? When the last brick was set, he must have lain dying in utter and complete solitude and darkness, waiting for the oil lamp to wink out, too weak from the poison to change his mind. It was nearly impossible to imagine the perverse will, the desperate self-loathing that would have been necessary to carry through with such a thing.

The carefully arranged shrine was easier to understand—the choosing of the magic-laden objects, of photographs that captured exactly what it was about the person; the eyes had to be right, the mouth, even the tilt of the head. He had taken the top off the bottle of perfume, filling the narrow tomb with scent, maybe staring at the sad photograph, the beaded purse and the jewelry until darkness hid it from him. . . .

She bent forward, her hand closing over the crystal perfume bottle. Instantly she was slammed backward again, and she kicked through the debris on the floor, tripping and falling into the dirt. A voice shrieked in her ear as wind howled through the lattice, and the floor above her creaked ominously, as the entire room shifted on its stone piers.

At that moment a man's face flickered into existence in the dark window she'd broken into the chimney. The eyes jittered spastically, and the mouth worked as if the face would speak, but couldn't. It was pale white, like smoke. She could see the chimney through it as it drifted toward her, the shelves full of trinkets hovering behind its eyes. Almost without thinking, she hurled the perfume bottle at it, pushing herself to her feet as the bottle flew straight through it and broke on the stones of the outer wall, showering the narrow shelves with glass fragments that rang like crystal bells.

Again the ground heaved as if a wave had run through it, throwing her down again into the chalk-fine dirt and debris. There was a rumbling, like rocks turning over in a flooded river, and the beams and joists that supported the floor groaned and popped above her. Dust fell from the old wood, sifting out from between cracks in the floorboards, and a broad section of brick and rock fell out of the chimney in a dusty heap.

**15**

AMANDA AND DAVID SAT AT THE TABLE AT THE END OF THE
kitchen playing Crazy Eights, the pale cards spinning across varnished wood, their plastic surfaces reflecting a dull light. Peter
walked slowly toward them. Behind him everything was dark,
hidden—something he knew without having to look. The kitchen
lay in shadow, and the cupboards and counter, the stove and refrigerator, were dark rectilinear masses without any real dimension, flat sketches of shadow. Only the distant table was
illuminated with a glow something like the light of fireflies, em-
anating from the atmosphere itself.

Suddenly he stood next to the table, looking down at the litter
of playing cards. On the edge of the table, next to the window,
sat a glass pitcher of green Kool-Aid and ice. Beads of condensation hazed the glass, and someone had drawn a smiling face in
the moisture, long drips of water trailing away from either corner
of the mouth. Beside the pitcher lay a plate heaped with Oreo
cookies.

Amanda poured Kool-Aid into a clear glass tumbler and set it
in front of an empty chair, then gestured at the chair and whisked
up the cards, shuffling them together, clicking the deck against
the top of the table. There was darkness outside the window.
Something that looked like sheet lightning shimmered in the distance. She flicked the cards out onto the table, dealing out three
hands.

Abruptly he was looking down at the table from above, as if
he were floating on the ceiling. He could hear distant thunder
now, although it occurred to him dimly that it could as easily be
the sound of the wind. The light diminished, and the facedown
card that left Amanda's hand moved sluggishly in its course, a
slowly spinning white bee against a red background, the tiny
white diamonds around the bee revolving like a spiral nebula way
off in the twilight.

Slowly he was conscious that it *was* the wind blowing somewhere far away, outside, beyond the dark window. Its sound suggested to him that there was something he knew but couldn't
remember, something desperately important. . . .

He touched his forehead. On his fingers was a red smear of
blood. Abruptly he pictured a man's face in his mind, vaguely
familiar, then the uncanny notion that it was his own face he saw,
reflected in a fog-shrouded mirror. A curtain seemed to have lowered itself between the present moment and the past. Memories
shifted in the darkness beyond it, memories shaped like the shadows of moving trees, or of hillsides, or of clouds in a windswept
sky. Some forgotten thing wandered deep in his mind, lost in the
darkness of unlit corridors. He could hear the echoing sound of
its footsteps growing slowly louder until those footsteps became
a heavy pounding that nearly shook the house.

Then the pounding stopped, the room grew lighter, and the
notion that he was searching for something slid past him and was
gone. The cards accelerated, spinning crazily, dropping to the
tabletop and sliding away across it. David twisted an Oreo apart,
holding the halves up in the center of each palm like stigmata,
one black, one white with frosting. "To undo it, you unscrew it,"
he said, then scraped the frosting off with his front teeth, leaving
a dark sort of two-lane highway across the center of the frosted
half.

Peter picked up his hand. The twelve cards were sticky with
chocolate and Oreo frosting and Kool-Aid. All of the cards were
spades. Only the eight was missing. It dawned on him suddenly
that he couldn't win, not with this hand. She'd dealt him worthless
cards on purpose. "This isn't fair," he said. "I have too many
cards." This was what he was doomed to: playing out a losing
hand.

He sniffed the air, smelling fireplace smoke now—the menthol
smell of burning eucalyptus logs. There was the low sound of
muttering voices, as if from the other room, but when he turned
and looked through the kitchen door into the living room, he
could see almost nothing at all, just hazy gray-tinged darkness
like a densely foggy night. Shapes moved through it like shadows
on a screen. He heard the pounding again, very distant now, but
it meant nothing to him. On the tabletop, moving hands placed
card after card faceup on the discard pile.

"I don't love you anymore," Amanda said to him without
looking away from her cards. "I used to, but now I don't. It

wasn't easy, realizing that. Or maybe admitting it wasn't easy. Maybe I realized it years ago. You know what's funny?"

He stared at her. "What's funny?"

"I can still remember *why* I loved you. None of the memories have changed, you know. I thought maybe they'd rot, like old pieces of fruit, but they didn't. All of them are still there—the trip to Maui, that old apartment in Carlsbad, all those breakfasts at that waffle place downtown—remember that? The walnut-and-cinnamon waffles every Sunday morning? David growing up . . . Remember that school of crazy-looking squid we found? What island was that?"

"Antigua," he said mechanically.

"That's right. I wouldn't change a thing—not any of that. It was all good, and still is. And yet what's funny is all of it's changed in some bigger way. We can still have all those things, we can still keep them, but we can't have any *more* things, not together, we can't. That's what you need to know. It's what you haven't understood. Here, look at this," she said. "I've kept it all."

From somewhere she produced the small handbag he had bought for her years ago, during their trip to the Caribbean. He peered inside as she held the handbag open. Down in the bottom lay a scattering of big jewels, lumps of facet-cut glass in gaudy colors like a kid's pirate treasure. There were tiny shadows moving within the glass, and he was filled with the certainty that if he held them up to the light he'd see things in there—happier times, maybe. Abruptly he remembered a time when he and David had buried a cigar box full of rhinestones and dime-store rings and glass marbles in the back garden, late one rainy Sunday afternoon. How many years ago was that?

"A long time ago," David said, studying his cards. "I forgot all about it. I was just a kid then."

"So did I," Peter said. "I forgot, too." It was still buried out there, had to be, the mahogany cigar box bug-eaten and decomposed. He thought about going home and digging it up, but then it seemed that he already was home, although the direction of the backyard—or the back door, for that matter—was lost to him, hidden somewhere in the recesses of his memory.

Amanda closed the bag and put it away someplace. "I'm keeping these safe," she said. "But that's all. There won't be anything more to add to it. It's finished, like a book."

He couldn't answer her. He realized abruptly that the same

thing was true for him. There were some things that had happened to them both, together, in some other lifetime—bright memories like fallen stars that he had picked up off the sidewalk and kept in his pocket. Already they were artifacts, museum pieces. Now there was nothing left between him and Amanda, no connection— that's what she was saying. Nothing except David.

He looked at his son, astonished at how grown up he looked. It seemed like only yesterday that he was four years old, not even in school yet, and they had all the time in the world. He wondered vaguely about the box of treasure out in the garden, whether digging it up would mean anything to David anymore.

Outside the window nothing had changed. Lightning flickered in the dim distances. The wind murmured beyond the wall. Unable to play his hand, he watched sadly as Amanda and David tossed cards onto the growing pile.

"You should let it go," Amanda said.

He couldn't answer her. It was already gone.

"Hearts," Amanda said, changing the suit by laying down the eight of spades.

He was suddenly aware of a rattling sound, like glass figurines clattering in a china hutch. Something shook the kitchen floor. Amanda and David still played steadily. He was reminded of— what? Somewhere he had to be. Something left undone. The unreality of his surroundings swept through him, and he looked around with growing unease.

The room shook again, the ice cubes clinking together in the pitcher, and suddenly the muttering voices in the other room rose in volume, massing together into a beehive-like humming. The wind rose outside and, with a sudden sound like the hissing of an ocean wave melting into a sandy beach, the condensation on the outside of the pitcher swept in a curtain down the glass and into a pool on the tabletop.

Peter clutched the edges of his chair and held on as the ground heaved and groaned, the windows rattling in their frames. The night through the window was illuminated by a sudden flash of lightning, very close now. . . .

And right then an object fell out of the sky, straight through the roof, clattering onto the center of the table with enough force to dent the wood. Atop the varnished maple, spinning to a slow stop, lay the cut-glass stopper from an old perfume bottle.

# 16

SHE STOOD UP AND WALKED TOWARD THE CHIMNEY AGAIN. THE dead man's face stared out at her now through the enlarged opening. She looked away from it, reaching in to pick up the purse now, knowing exactly what she had to do. Peter had given the dead man what he wanted; she had to take it away again. . . .

The fabric of the purse was rotten with age, the threads disintegrating, the stitches pulling apart. A shower of tiny glass beads fell away, salting the broken mortar and brick and stone. She dropped the purse next to the corpse. "I'm sorry," she whispered, even then hearing the wind rise outside, the old house moaning and shifting. She picked up the glass dog, then turned toward the gate and hurled it into the woods. She reached in after the mirror and hairbrush, breaking the glass against the stones, throwing the brush into a distant dark corner.

Random fears flickered through her mind like a succession of rapid nightmares: Bobby crying, lost and alone in the darkness; the sudden sensation of falling; the sound of water rushing across stones; herself locked in an empty house, the door slamming open in a windy rush of leaves and shadow and a man walking slowly toward her bed, where she lay clutching her blankets, back pressed against the wall—the dead man, his face hovering inches in front of her own. She screamed, breaking the spell, the face dissolving again into the air.

Wind hammered at the house. She heard the groan of old nails prying loose, and a section of lattice tore away from the side of the cellar, whirling into the darkness. Her foot kicked the length of iron pipe, and she stooped to pick it up from where it lay half-buried, thinking suddenly of the strangely dressed boy, his own sad box of trinkets beneath the abandoned house. She whispered another apology, and with both hands slammed the pipe against the bottom shelf, sweeping the books and toys into the rubble. She swung the pipe again, smashing it into the side of the chim-

ney, then leaped out of the way as a crack radiated up through
the mortar, widening into a fissure. A ton of stone and brick
collapsed in a mass, burying the corpse, the jewelry and toys and
photographs, the flask and lantern, obliterating the sorrowful remnants of three weary lives.

Moonlight and night wind flooded in through the suddenly cre-
ated hole in the wall. The ground shook, throwing her sideways.
She grabbed onto a post with both hands, closing her eyes and
mouth against the rising dust. There was a slow cracking sound,
like stressed wood giving way, and one of the long beams sup-
porting the floor lurched downward, broken in the center. The
floorboards above it tore themselves apart, and Beth threw herself
forward, crawling toward the gate as dust whirled up around
her—dust smelling of jasmine and old books, of whiskey and
eucalyptus smoke. She burst out into the night, scrambling over
the rock retaining wall and into the trees.

The sound of a vast rending and cracking filled the night. The
parlor tilted crazily, the floor collapsing in sections, the latticework walls of the cellar snapping outward, the entire room collapsing like a card house, its roof caving in and smashing down
over the ruined furniture and books, a cloud of dust rising into
the night sky like a vast ghost.

THE NOISES IN THE OTHER ROOM WENT WILD, AS IF A THOUSAND
conversations were murmuring at once. Outside, the wind
shrieked, and waves of lightning fell down the sky like rain on
a window. And for one long moment, while thunder rumbled in
the distances, Amanda and David grew insubstantial, like
ghosts, so that Peter saw through them as if they were holes in
a cleverly painted curtain. On the other side lay glimpses of a
room that he recognized—a fireplace, two easy chairs, books,
candles burning. He stood up, knowing abruptly where he was
now, where he *must* be.

Amanda was dealing out another hand of Crazy Eights. He pushed the cards away, standing up and reaching for her wrist. There was no time; they had to leave, to get out. The desperate notion struck him that they might be lodged there forever, dwelling on the past, listening to the click and swish of the playing cards glancing across the tabletop. Still there was nothing but shadow at either end of the kitchen, and the night outside was impenetrably dark.

Something shattered, sounding like glass thrown against a wall. Cracks radiated out from the center of the window, which reflected the room now like a broken mirror. Smoke curled from the cracks, filling the room with the scent of eucalyptus and jasmine and the smell of rock dust and dry wind.

The floor tilted wildly, the table and chairs sliding sideways, playing cards pitching off onto the floor in a rush as the Kool-Aid pitcher shivered into fragments, vanishing into the air. The top of the perfume bottle blinked away like a soap bubble along with the glass tumblers and the plate of cookies. There was the sound of wood cracking, and the broken ends of wooden beams tore through the ceiling, pushed up through the floor, tilted out through the walls.

Peter grabbed David and Amanda both, dragging them behind him through the kitchen and into the foggy darkness just as the entire room collapsed inward behind them, smashing down over the table and chairs. He looked back, saw the scattered cards whirl away on the wind like autumn leaves, the chairs and table following, careening away into the night.

They ran through the darkness of what might have been a vast and empty house. Shadows of furniture loomed on either side, falling away behind. Random sounds rose and fell in volume: distant weeping, recorded Victrola music, the sighing of the wind, the crackling of a fire, murmured conversation, a cat crying, the sound of footfalls echoing down a long, empty corridor. . . .

Then he was aware of the wind blowing, and the shadows of trees on either side, the feel of gravel under his feet and the smell of open places, of sage and dead leaves and rock. They ascended a steepening hillside. The ground itself seemed to tilt, trying to spill them off, and the wind was full of the sound of cracking and rending, as if some vast construction—perhaps the entire world—were tearing itself to pieces.

Ahead of them loomed the mouth of a cave, impenetrably dark, seeming to rush toward them now as they were swept along by the furious wind. There was the sound of cascading water, of windblown vegetation, and abruptly he felt himself falling, the darkness suddenly illuminated by a full moon that cast their three black shadows against the cliff wall unreeling behind them. His own scream echoed in his ears as he plunged headlong toward a rock-strewn pool of water.

WHEN THE FOUNDATION SHOOK FOR THE SECOND TIME, IT THREW Mr. Ackroyd against the doorframe. He caught himself, holding on as the joints in the old house creaked and strained. The parlor floor seemed suddenly to plunge downward at the far corner, with the sound of wood snapping, and the door slammed open against the wall. He could see the candle flames and the fire in the hearth tilt sideways as if borne down by a heavy pressure. Cracks appeared along the corners of the ceiling, and a sheet of plaster cracked loose and fell to the floor, throwing up a cloud of dust.

Esther half stood up, a cry of fear escaping from her throat. She called the boy's name, "Jamie!" out loud, looking around as if suddenly fearful that he was gone, and Dr. Landry's head swiveled toward the door, looking straight at Ackroyd with an expression of stark terror. He rose from the chair, his hand reaching out, palsied and groping as if he were suddenly blind.

The doors in the bookcases flew open, and books spilled out onto the floor. The decanter and glasses fell, the glasses rolling off onto the carpet. The pictures on the wall tilted crazily, and rubble cascaded downward into the fireplace, nearly smothering the fire.

Dr. Landry stood up, futilely grabbing at books, snatching up the fallen glasses, pushing at picture frames. Wind buffeted the house, rattling the windows, drawing a rush of sparks up the chimney. Again the house shook, even more violently. Ackroyd staggered backward into the dark living room, gripping the back of a chair to steady himself. There was the sound of something crashing down outside, as if the chimney itself had collapsed, and suddenly the wind blew through the house in a wild gust. Through the open parlor door he saw the bookcases topple forward and the pictures leap from the walls. He heard his sister's voice calling for her son, and he crawled forward toward the door, trying to reach her, suddenly sorry that he'd hesitated, that he hadn't at least tried to make himself clear to her. . . .

Now it was too late. The walls buckled, and the rug dipped, long cracks opening in the wooden floorboards beneath it. Already the three of them had lost their substance. They seemed to be defined by displaced wind, and by the smoke wreathing out of the rubble-choked hearth—three dark shadows swept away into the night as the old parlor collapsed on its piers, tearing away from the rest of the house so that Ackroyd found himself looking through an open door into the windy night.

He heard the sound of her voice again in the distance, calling plaintively, and he turned and hurried through the still standing living room and kitchen, out the rear door and into the darkness of the woods. He could just make out three shadows, dark swatches of night moving upward along the moonlit trail.

He had to follow, to know what would happen to her. The idea of her forever wandering the hills on windy nights was more than he could bear. . . .

He saw Beth then, standing in the shadows at the edge of the trees. She was safe. He realized with a pang of guilt that he'd forgotten her, so completely had he been caught up in his own drama. He waved at her and turned away now, hurrying up the trail. For a moment he lost sight of them, but then saw their shadows pass in front of the moon-silvered shrubs. He thought he heard voices murmuring, smelled traces of her perfume despite the wind that sheered across the open country. He realized suddenly that he was nearly running, and he slowed down, feeling a twinge of pain in his chest. He pushed on, unwilling to lose sight of them. This was no time for his heart to betray him. Not until he knew their destination. . . .

A black line of trees rose in the night ahead—the alder copse that grew along the top of Falls Canyon. It seemed to him that he saw a shadow pass across the moonlit boughs, merging with the darkness of the hollow that led in among the trees. He didn't slacken his pace, but plunged forward into that darkness, slogging through the ankle-deep creek water. He caught at tree limbs, trying to support himself, to keep from falling. A few yards ahead of him lay the edge of the cliff. He could hear the rush of water falling into the pool in the depths of the canyon.

Carefully he drew closer to the edge, forcing himself to slow down, scrabbling to find a firm footing among the rocks. He peered over into the darkness, seeing the sheer rock walls of the canyon falling away on either side, the dark trees, the narrow trail winding downward on the left hand. The precipice was so steep that he had to edge out even farther, into the wind, until he could look down the vertical cliff-face.

And there, far below, three dark, vaguely human shapes lay sprawled in the shallow pool surrounded by lapping, starlit water. As he watched, the figures very slowly faded, as if they were nothing but moon shadows diminished now by passing clouds, and the reflected stars seemed to rise through them out of the depths of the pond.

SOMEONE SPOKE TO HIM, BUT THE WORDS DISAPPEARED BEFORE he could grasp their meaning. He saw a man standing two feet away, vaguely familiar, his sleeves rolled up, wearing an old hat. A small dog sniffed around his feet, then lay down in the dirt.

"What?"

"Didn't happen to make that grocery run, did you? I'm about out of suds."

Grocery run, suds . . . The words sounded alien to him. . . .

He realized suddenly that he stood on the drive in front of his house. The parlor was wrecked—the roof collapsed, the walls tilted in against each other. Broken glass and rock and roof shingles littered the drive. The retaining wall was half-buried. The wind whispered through the debris, rustling the pages of a book that lay open on the ground.

The dog rolled over onto its back and kicked its feet in the air, sandpapering itself against the ground. "Freeway," Peter said the dog's name out loud. In a rush of knowledge it came to him, as

if the word were an incantation—where he'd been, what must
have happened.

"... goddamn dry rot, probably," Bateman was saying. "That
and the termites. But I never seen a house go down like *that*.
Maybe if you'd a put a couple braces under the floor, you
might've saved her. Now, though ..." He shook his head. "I'd
get me a trash bin."

Peter saw Amanda and David then. They stood very still among
the trees, in the spot where he and Beth had seen the woman
materialize—when? Only yesterday afternoon? They stirred now,
like statues just coming to life, and stepped out into the moonlight, Amanda holding David's hand. She looked at Peter, shaking
her head, her eyes puzzled.

"Well, don't that bake the doggone cake!" Bateman said, just
now seeing them. "Looks like your loved ones come home safe
after all. That's *good*. I *like* to see things work out like that." He
stepped forward and shook Amanda's hand. "I hear you and the
boy been out of town. . . ."

She stepped past him, and Peter grabbed both Amanda and
David and hugged them, holding them for a long, long time. Two
figures appeared in the moonlight, high up on the trail to the ridge.
They were descending into the canyon—Beth, with old Mr. Ackroyd leaning heavily on her arm.

Holding on to Amanda and David as if he might lose them
again, Peter set out up the trail, the dog Freeway running on
ahead, disappearing into the darkness of the overshadowing oaks.

THE WIND BLEW ACROSS THE SANTA ANA MOUNTAINS, ANGLING
through the canyons and gorges, scouring the arid ridges where
the chaparral plants, unnaturally silver in the bright moonlight,
jittered with a sound like dry husks rubbing together. The air
swirled with dead leaves and particles of twigs. Slowly, inces-
santly, the wind reduced the sage and greasewood and sumac to

dry skeletons, tearing away the brown leaves, snapping off small branches and whirling them away into the sky until nothing remained but gnarled trunks and stones.

A dark mass like a bundle of old rags rolled between the barren sticks, animated by the wind and emitting the papery rasping of air forced out of desiccated lungs. It rose slowly, like a gas-filled bag, roughly the shape of a man, his neck broken and his head lolling to the side, his arms hanging dead like the arms of a marionette. Its feet dragged across the top of the chaparral, its face lit by the moon now, eyes dark hollows, lips and ears and cheeks devoured by animals. Its foot caught a bent stick and it jerked to a stop, rocking back and forth momentarily, a dark silhouette against the moonlit sky, and then the wind tore it loose again, half spinning it around, propelling it along the dirt trail, where it scraped through dust and gravel.

It hurried along on the wind now, leaning slightly forward, its open mouth mumbling out a dead language of dry leaves and dirt. The dark canyon spread out beneath it, and in the dim distance shone the lights of scattered houses. At last the trail ended, and a path declined steeply toward the last of these houses. The thing jerked to a stop and hung there as if on a hook, inches above the ground, surveying through empty eye sockets the windy, moon-haunted landscape below before descending the hillside in a rush of wind and shadow.

Klein jerked awake, throwing his arm out to ward off the thing that rushed at him—Pomeroy, Pomeroy's corpse, bloated and animated by the wind. He sat in bed breathing hard, his eyes pressed open, staring in horror at the pole lamp in the corner, its shadow cast by moonlight against the wall behind it. Slowly his breathing calmed and he saw what it was—a dream. Nothing but a shadow on the wall. Lorna lay beside him on the bed, and the sudden knowledge of that was comforting. He lay back down and closed his eyes, grateful that she hadn't waked up.

Years ago he had dreamed night after night about sitting in a dark house that slowly tilted sideways until the chair he sat in began to slide away across the floor. There had been a tearing noise and a sound like muffled screaming, and more than once he had awakened at the moment of falling to discover that it was himself screaming, his face buried in his pillow.

He lay now listening to the silence, the night around him familiar again, empty of ghosts. After a time he turned onto his side and watched Lorna sleep. She was willing to try to make a go of it, and without any halfway measures. When they had gotten home from Mr. Ackroyd's house, she had cooked pork chops and scalloped potatoes.

Unable to sleep, he got up finally and looked out the window into the backyard. There was no wind, and the eastern hills were tinted with dawn light. The trail wound upward toward the ridge, empty of rushing shadows. He picked up his pants and shirt from the chair and located his slip on deck shoes under the edge of the bed. It was too good a morning to sleep in. He'd let Lorna do that. What he would do was clean the pool, then spackle up the poolhouse door and get a coat of paint on it. It was suddenly vital to restore order out of the windblown chaos of the last few days. At nine, whatever he was doing, he'd put it all down and cook her breakfast—pancakes with canned corn in them, coffee and juice, maybe fry up some bacon. That was her favorite.

He stepped out into the morning, smelling the cool, oak-scented air off the hills, filling his lungs with it, letting it chase out the ghosts and the cobwebs. Taking the pool net off its hooks, he went to work, skimming dead leaves from the still surface of the water.

"IT WAS A CASE OF SOMETHING CALLED HYPO-VALIMIC SHOCK," Ackroyd said, coming in from the kitchen with a pitcher of lemonade. "That's what Dr. Stone said. He took one of the pellets out of her spleen. The man's a day-and-night genius. He drives an automobile with a wooden frame that's apparently being eaten by termites. Sounds like organ pipes when it gets up to speed." He set the pitcher down on the table and then picked up two espresso-sized teacups from on top of one of the bookcases, carrying them over to where Bobby and David arranged ranks of tin soldiers on the floor. "These might work as some kind of vehicle," he said.

"Maybe for the general's bathtub," Peter said helpfully.

"The general doesn't take baths," Bobby said. "He takes showers. These are alien spacecraft." He set a plastic alien in each of the cups so that they looked out over the rims.

"I think these kinds of ships are called 'nosers,'" David said. "They set their own course by radio signal, and you put money into them to make them go. I read about them in a book."

"They only accept gold," Bobby said. "This mountain is a gold mine, and the aliens want to rob it in order to have enough money to get home again."

One of the Navajo rugs lay bunched up on the floor, contoured like a wind-eroded mountain. Soldiers aimed rifles over the parapets of gullies and trenches; others lay hidden in the shadows of shallow caves. A company of foot soldiers marched along a high-road that descended toward a village built of playing cards, some of the structures three tiers high. The fireplace bellows lay aimed at the village, two more aliens standing on the wooden handle.

"When we get the soldiers hidden in the village," David said, "the aliens turn on the hurricane mechanism."

The door opened and Beth came in, carrying a basket full of feathery-looking weeds. "Anise, nettle tops, watercress, spearmint, and black walnuts," she announced, holding the basket out. "If we can find a hammer, Peter, maybe you could crack the walnuts."

"Hammer's hanging in the front closet," Mr. Ackroyd said. "I'll mix up a vinaigrette and put the muffins in the oven."

"What are *we* going to eat?" Bobby asked, looking at the stuff in the basket. "How about pizza or something? Peter can drive out and get it."

"Cheeseburgers!" David said.

Peter looked up hopefully, but Beth was already shaking her head.

"I've got sandwich makings," Mr. Ackroyd said from the kitchen. "How about toasted cheese?"

"Sure." Bobby turned back to the aliens, getting them set to work the bellows, and David very carefully stood a soldier inside the second-story doorway of a card house.

Across the road the sun shone through the canopy of alder leaves over the creek, illuminating the willows and wild figs and sparkling on the moving water. A cluster of roses bowed in front of the window, dropping snowy petals onto the front porch in a wind that blew softly from the west now, heralding a change of weather. And away off to the north, above the sunlit ridge, scattered white clouds drifted up the afternoon sky.